Praise for

Monica Burns

"Burns doesn't disappoint!"
— **RTBOOKreviews**

Monica Burns writes with sensitivity and panache.
— **Sabrina Jeffries, NYT bestselling author**

"powerfully done…the scenes between Tobias and Jane mesmerized me. I loved it."
— **Joey W. Hill**

"No one sets fire to the page like Monica Burns."
— **eCataromance**

"Definitely recommended reading."
— **The Romance Studio**

Forever Mine

by

Monica Burns

Copyright © 2014 by Kathi B. Scearce
Cover Design for Reissue: Viviana Izzo, Enchantress Design & Promo
Copyeditor: Rosie Murphy
Line Editor: Ann Conrad

Kathi B. Scearce DBA Monica Burns—Maroli SP Imprints
P.O. Box 75072
North Chesterfield, VA 23236

Publishing History
Print 1.0 edition / 2014
Print 2.0 edition / 2017 New Cover
Print 3.0 edition /2021 New Cover

ISBN: 978-1-948505-05-5

Table of Contents

Author Note

This book is more than a book of my heart. It's part of my soul. Yes, I'm a storyteller and often prone to exaggeration. However, it's not an exaggeration that numerous scenes were a gut-wrenching experience for me to put the words on paper. The journal entries in particular were difficult to write. There are also moments and words I didn't add because they are so deeply and profoundly personal.

I believe, with all my heart, the emotions in this book are my expression of a timeless love I've experienced over dozens of past lives. Am I foolish to believe in past lives? Some will say yes, but I disagree. I've experienced too many moments of familiarity with a place or objects, not to mention my ability to pull small bits of trivia and knowledge out of the ether that research after the fact confirms my original knowledge. Those instances are rare, but it's the depth of knowledge I possess in those instances that is the most disconcerting. The tidbit of knowledge is so obscure I couldn't possibly have learned it in this life unless I researched the information extensively, which I do after moments such as those. It always reconfirms my spiritual beliefs related to past lives, beliefs I've possessed since childhood (not many 12-year-olds devour Edgar Cayce books).

When I speak of past lives, I need to be clear that I'm not talking about idyllic past lives of wealth or social position. The regression sessions I've done have shown me several of my past lives that were on the bottom rungs of the ladder. They were lives filled with the same strife as all humans experience. However, the pain experienced in those lives was made bearable because in many of those lives I loved and was loved in the same way Nicholas and Victoria have.

I believe I've experienced, and will again, a love that crosses the boundaries of time. A love so deep and profound, my soul has no choice but to search for its mate, no matter whether it's across the boundaries of time or in the vast corners of the universe. Love is everything, never stop searching. Never accept anything less than you deserve in life or in love.

Dedication

For My Nichola

Chapter 1

"I don't believe it."

"Which is *precisely* why you owe me fifty pounds, oh, ye of little faith." From her seat on the brown leather couch behind him,, Nora snorted with laughter.

Nick Barrows ignored his sister's gloating comment as he stared in amazement at the two paintings set up on easels beneath the Barrows Art and Antiquities logo. Once authenticated, the landscapes by Constable would be the biggest pieces the shop had ever acquired.

"And you found these in *Nebraska?*"

"I told you unclaimed property auctions were worth the travel expense."

"Are you telling me there weren't any other art dealers there? "

"A few. Like other states, Nebraska puts ads in the papers about their yearly sale, but most of the time the items are jewelry, coins, electronics, and other collectibles. I don't think anyone realized what these were."

"I suppose you're going to want to go back," Nick Barrows looked over his shoulder and grinned before looking back at the paintings.

"Of course, and you know, I think this brilliant acquisition of mine deserves a raise."

"Uncle Charles gave you a raise a year ago," Nick chuckled at his sister's teasing jab. A second later, he realized his mistake and closed his eyes. He was an idiot. Filled with regret, he turned to face his sister. "Damn, I wasn't thinking, Nora."

"It's okay. He would have said the same thing." She shrugged her shoulders, then laughed softly. "Then the next minute he'd be waltzing me around this tiny office of yours."

Nora was right. Uncle Charles would have been overjoyed by her find and its impact on the shop. The old man had loved this place as if it were his child. He'd always said the shop possessed a soul. Nick had never understood his uncle as well as Nora had. The two of them had often talked about ghosts, past lives, and supernatural theories well into the night. It was one of the reasons Nora had taken his death so hard. She'd lost the one companion who 'got her' as she was fond of saying.

"Somehow, I think he'd be more proud than excited," Nick said. "We've come a long way from those two angry American teenagers he brought to England and took into his home."

"I don't know how he managed it. Confirmed bachelors aren't poster children for parenthood." Nora shook her head in disbelief. "And we weren't exactly easy to live with."

"He understood. We were grieving for mom and dad, just like he was." Nick stared down at his shoes for a second before he looked up at his sister. "It always amazed me how he seemed to know exactly what we needed and when."

"I miss him, Nick." Sadness filled his sister's voice.

"I do too."

His gaze swung to the portrait of the Countess of Guildford on the wall across from his desk. His uncle had taken him to the Brentwood Park estate sale years ago, and the moment Nick had seen Lady Guildford's portrait, he'd stopped dead in his tracks. Uncle Charles had simply squeezed his shoulder, then bought the portrait and gave it to Nick with nothing more than a simple statement that the portrait was his to do with as he wished.

How the elderly Englishman had sensed how much he'd wanted the countess' portrait, he would never know. But he'd worked hard to show his uncle how grateful he was for the extraordinary gift. Emotion pushed its way to the surface, and he swiftly buried it. Determined to lighten the atmosphere, he folded his arms across his chest and pinned his gaze on Nora.

"I imagine you're going to be impossible to live with for the next month or two."

"Oh, you can count on that." His sister's forced laughter revealed how close she'd been to tears. "Especially since a certain *someone* said my trip would be a waste of money."

Nora eyed him with a scowl, and he released a rueful sigh. She was going to make him pay dearly for having questioned her unusual gift of finding extraordinary pieces.

"Truce." He held his hands up in a gesture of surrender. "From now on, your word is law when it comes to acquisitions. Satisfied?"

"It's a start." This time, her laughter wasn't filled with tears, and she waved a hand at the portrait hanging on the wall behind the couch. "What about her, are you going to start listening to me about the countess as well?"

A familiar tension slid through his muscles, tightening his chest. His amusement disappeared in an instant. His gaze flitted back to the portrait of Victoria Thornhill, Countess of Guildford before he frowned at Nora.

"That implies I need advice, and I don't. The woman's been dead for more than a hundred years."

"But you have to admit your attachment to her portrait is a little extreme."

"It's not unusual for an antiquities dealer to have art work hanging in their office." His comment made Nora snort.

"Artwork, yes, but not a portrait you've drooled over

ever since we were teenagers."

"You're exaggerating again."

"Am I?" She eyed him intently for a long moment. "Then prove me wrong. Sell it."

"*No.*" Tension charged the air with electricity as he glared at his sister.

"That's what I thought." Her matter-of-fact tone rubbed him the wrong way.

"What the hell is that supposed to mean?"

"If I tell you, you're just going to tell me to fuck off."

She was right. He knew what Nora believed, but he just wasn't buying it. The notion that he'd known the Countess of Guildford in a past life was just as crazy an idea now as it was every time Nora broached the subject with him. Nick saw her sly look, and he clenched his jaw as he refused to take her bait.

Without a word, he turned away from her and picked up several invoices off the top of his desk. The figures were a blur as the image of Lady Guildford filled his head. What if his sister was right? What if he was—*Christ*, if Nora could read his mind right now, she'd hound him until the day he died. Who was he kidding, she'd do that anyway. He blew out a harsh breath of annoyance. At the sound, Nora scrambled to her feet.

"Oh for Pete's sake, Nick. Isn't it time you took a really hard look at yourself and that portrait?"

"Is there a point to this line of conversation?" he asked as nonchalantly as possible, while continuing his pretense of studying the invoices.

"*Yes.* The point is—you're in love with a ghost." Nora had never confronted him so bluntly before. He scowled at her over his shoulder, then returned to his feigned review of the paperwork in his hand.

"Don't look at me like that, Nicholas Barrows. That damn portrait is what's keeping you from leading a normal life. When was the last time you had a date? Even a one-night stand?"

"My sex life isn't any of your *damn* business," he said through clenched teeth. The invoices in his hand crackled in his tight grip.

"Right. Sorry." The tense atmosphere hung between them for several seconds before he released a noise of frustration. Dropping the papers onto his desk, Nick turned around to face her. Leaning back, he rested his hips against his desk, then folded his arms across his chest.

"Look, you and Uncle Charles have always believed that old family legend. I never have." He didn't flinch as his sister glared at him. "That damn necklace is a myth. Even if the earl gave his wife those sapphires, they were either sold or stolen a long time ago. My money's on the sold theory. And I sure as hell don't believe Lady Guildford is coming back from the dead to reclaim the damn thing. It's a story. Nothing more."

"All right, if you don't believe the legend, why do you keep the woman's portrait on the wall?

"*For Christ's sake*. I like the painting. It gives me pleasure. How is that an issue?"

"It's an issue because you're pining after a dead woman."

"God damn it, Nora. It's just a portrait."

"All right, then answer me this. Why is it you only date women with auburn hair and blue eyes like the countess?" The accusation in his sister's voice made Nick rolled his eyes while scrambling for an excuse that would stop her inquisition.

"I *don't* only date women with auburn hair."

"Oh please," Nora snorted. "Shall I list them by name? Vivian, Viola, Veronica, Virginia, and my personal favorite, Vickie. Notice a pattern here? And isn't it ironic their names all start with the same first letter as Lady Guildford's name? *Victoria*."

"Coincidence," he snapped, glaring at his sister.

"The landscape painting? What about that?" Nora eyed him with that unnerving shrewdness that always made him think she could see through him or anyone else she talked to.

"What of it?"

"It's taken you almost twelve years to agree that we put it up for sale. Why don't you ask yourself why you've not been able to part with it or, for that matter, the portrait of the countess?"

"*Fuck,*" he snarled. "You're blowing this out of proportion.

"And the third painting?" Nora narrowed her gaze at him. "The one Uncle Charles kept stored away? The moment you discovered it in his things after the funeral, you took it home."

"Christ almighty, Nora. I deal in art and antiques. What's wrong with me admiring the work of a man who painted two different portraits of the same woman *as well as* a landscape?"

Nick strode toward the window that overlooked the showroom. The second portrait of the countess had been far more intimate than the one he kept in his office. Although discreetly covered with a sheet, it was still a seductive, enticing portrait, one he'd not been willing to share with anyone. Even allowing the framer to see the portrait had filled him with a possessiveness he found confusing. Hands braced against the waist tall window sill, he stared down into the gallery. There were a few customers studying various items, but they were nothing but blurred images in his head.

"Fine." Nora's voice echoed with irritation at her failed attempt to persuade him that he was obsessed with the Countess of Thornhill. Deep inside, he knew it was an accurate assessment on his sister's part, but admitting that to Nora would open up doors he wasn't willing to go through.

Nick fought to focus his gaze on the people in the gallery, but instead, the lovely features of Victoria Brentwood Thornhill, Countess of Guildford, filled his mind as clearly as if she were alive and standing in front of him. Dark auburn hair framed around an oval face. Full lips curved in an inviting, sensual smile. Brilliant sapphire eyes sparkling with mischief.

Nick tightened his grip on the window ledge. Nora was right. He was in love with a ghost, or at least the image of one. A shrink would tell him he was avoiding personal relationships because of some trauma in his past, but it went deeper than that. There was a knowing that filled him every time he looked at the countess' portrait. He couldn't explain it, and he sure as hell wasn't about to tell his sister about it either.

About to turn away from the window overlooking the gallery, Nick's gaze caught sight of a woman standing in front of their collection of English pastoral scenes. When she tilted her head to study one of the canvases, the muted light from the ceiling's track lighting set her auburn hair on fire. In the next moment, the woman turned to face one of the sales clerks, and he inhaled a sharp breath.

Almost immediately, his chest constricted and his heart slammed into his ribs. Only twice before had he ever experienced this sensation, and each of those times it had been when he'd found a portrait of the countess. Transfixed, he stared down at the woman.

"God, Nick, are you okay? You look like you're ready to pass out." Nora joined him at the window. The moment his sister's gaze landed on the woman, she gasped loudly. "*Holy fuck.*"

Without a word, Nick brushed past Nora. As he headed toward the door, her hand caught his arm. He paused to meet her gaze and shook his head in a silent command not to stop him. Reluctance visible on her face, his sister released his arm. Nick wanted to run down the steps to the showroom, but he forced himself to descend the stairs at a slow pace. He was insane to think this was anything more than a coincidence. As he approached the woman, her distinct American accent floated through the air as she spoke to the salesclerk.

"I don't know—thirty-five hundred pounds is a little more than I can really afford."

"Think of it as an investment, miss."

"An investment in the exchange rate, you mean."

The dry note in her voice forced Nick to cough as he stifled a chuckle. She turned at the sound, an impish smile curving her full mouth. But it was her eyes that made him stare at her. They were the same sapphire blue as the countess's. Again, he marveled at the resemblance. Without warning, she queried his opinion.

"What do you think?" she asked.

Nick met the brilliant blue gaze twinkling up at him. If he didn't know better, he would have sworn Lady Guildford had stepped out of the portrait hanging in his office. The woman tipped her head back as she returned his stare with equal intensity. In an absent-minded gesture, her long fingers brushed a stray strand of auburn hair off her cheek. A quickening surged deep inside him, like the sudden stirring of a long-lost memory. The sensation swelled.

Stunned by the force of the emotion, he realized somewhere in his past he'd experienced a moment similar to this one before. The sensation grew in strength. The smile curving her full mouth faded as confusion furrowed her brow. Mentally shaking his head, Nick forced himself to answer her question.

"Like Robert says, art is an investment, but I like to think of it more as an investment of the heart. Ask yourself if you can live without it."

"No, I don't think I can." She turned back to the painting. Under the track lighting, her auburn hair shone like lustrous silk. She sighed. "There's something so familiar about it."

For the first time, he looked at the canvas she was interested in purchasing and went rigid. He'd been so focused on her, he'd not even bothered to look at the painting she was standing in front of. It was Lockwood's oil painting of Goodman Cottage at Brentwood Park. The landscape depicted a pond glistening in the afternoon sun as it played host to a pair of swans. Close to the water's edge, the thatched roof cottage sat nestled in the warm embrace of a small grove of trees. The sparsely covered trees with red, gold, and purple leaves indicated it had been close to the end of fall when the artist had painted his picture.

Nick had found the landscape in his uncle's bedroom after the man's heart attack. A little known artist, John Lockwood, had painted both portraits of the countess, as well as the landscape. The barely legible inscription on the back of the Goodman Cottage canvas, *for my wife, Victoria. Nicholas— Christmas 1897*, indicated the landscape had been a gift from Lord Guildford to his wife.

"Have you ever been to Brentwood Park?" He clenched his teeth. Why the hell had he asked her that?

"Brentwood Park?" She shook her head in puzzlement.

"It's an estate a little southeast of the city. The cottage in the painting still sits on the grounds." He nodded toward the canvas on the wall, but didn't look away from her.

"I've never heard of it. If I have time next week, I might be able to check it out," she murmured as she turned back to the painting and reached out to touch the frame. Uttering a small noise of decision, she turned her head toward the sales clerk. "Well, I guess I can't leave without it."

"Very good, madam. If you will come this way, I shall be happy to arrange the sale."

"Robert, I'll take care of the sale," Nick said quietly as he reached out to grasp her arm and hold her in place.

He never heard the sales clerk's response as electricity shot up his arm. The strength of the sensation barreling through him made him feel like someone was pummeling his entire body until he had no breath left in his lungs. Images flashed through his head like a carousel of pictures careening out of control.

Of all the faces dancing through his brain, she was always

there. She was like the North Star, guiding him to a place he didn't know existed. He couldn't explain it, but it was as if this moment had happened before. As he stared down into her blue eyes, she shook her head slightly, and he was certain she was experiencing the same sensation.

"What's your name?" His voice was hoarse as he struggled not to say something bizarre that would frighten her, or worse, make her dart out of the shop.

"Victoria Ashton," she breathed as she reached up to brush a lock of hair off his forehead. In the next instant, she jerked her hand away, clearly horrified by her action.

"Oh Lord, I'm sorry…that was incredibly rude of me."

"No. It felt right." He didn't have the slightest idea why her touch seemed so natural and perfect, but then nothing about the last couple of minutes made any sense to him.

"I…have we met somewhere before?"

"That's my pickup line, I think," he said with a grin.

"Yeah, I suppose it was."

Her laugh was as full-bodied as he remembered. Remembered? Nick pushed the absurd notion aside as he watched a flush of pink rise in her cheeks. Without thinking, he brushed his fingertips across her face. The moment he touched her, her hand came up to cup his, and she turned her mouth into his palm. The visceral emotion the action stirred in him made him pull in a sharp, deep breath.

"I don't know what the hell is happening," he rasped. "But you'd better tell me to stop now if you don't want me to kiss you."

Her sapphire eyes widened, before she closed the distance between them and there was only a hair's breadth of space between. Her hand reached up to touch his brow, and she smiled.

"I won't stop you," she whispered.

Locked in the grip of something he didn't understand, Nick bent his head toward her. God, all he wanted was to taste her again. He needed to know if she tasted as sweet as he remembered. His mouth never touched hers as the explosion roared through the shop like a freight train.

The force of the blast threw him backward, and he fought to stay on his feet. A screech of metal tugged his gaze upward. Before he could react, the ceiling's track lighting crashed downward, then slammed into Victoria's head and chest. He heard her grunt with pain as the blow sent her staggering backwards. In an involuntary effort to remain standing, she flung her arm outward to grab hold of something to save herself from falling.

Before he could leap forward or shout a warning, she grasped the black wire dangling from the ceiling. Agony contorted her features as electricity flowed through her, then sent her flying backward to hit the wall like a rag doll. The unframed landscape of the cottage fell from the wall to the floor and landed beside her limp hand, the painting brushing against her fingers. Screams of pain and fear from inside and outside of the shop filled the air.

Leaping past the live wire, he crouched down beside Victoria's still form. His hands shook as he gently rolled her onto her back, sliding the painting away from her. She wasn't breathing, and he couldn't find a pulse in her neck or on her wrist. A wave of helplessness rolled over him. It had been like this the last time. He'd not been able to do anything to save her.

A growl of rage erupted from his throat. *No. Not this time.* He'd lost her in the past, and he refused to lose her now. Without thinking, Nick began to administer CPR. Nick didn't know if he was doing it right, but he couldn't just stand by and do nothing. He'd failed the last time. Nick refused to let it end like that again. Quick chest compressions, then two strong puffs of air into her mouth. Repeat.

Somewhere in the distance, he heard an ambulance siren growing louder. Panic set in as his efforts to revive her received no response. In a voice he didn't recognize as his own, he called out her name, then blew two hard breaths into her before increasing the strength of his compressions against her chest.

"*Fight, Victoria, fight*," he commanded in a savage tone. "Do you hear me? I said *fight*."

His command was harsh and inflexible, and he sensed a stranger slipping into his head. Relentlessly, he alternated between breathing into her mouth and returning to the sharp cadence of chest compressions. Deep within his memory, he recalled the pain and agony of a similar experience long ago. The indefinable connection to her that he'd experienced moments ago had become something even more tangible. A gentle hand touched his shoulder.

"Nick, she's gone." His sister's words ripped a roar from his throat.

"*No. You're wrong*," he snarled as he knocked his sister's hand aside.

With renewed force, he pounded on Victoria's chest, then breathed air into her lungs. Logic disappeared to become raw, agonizing desperation. Unfamiliar images from a distant past merged with the present to fill him with dread. The savageness of his anguish choked him and threatened to push him over the edge as he worked to breathe and pound life back into her.

"God damn it, Victoria. Fight, damn you. Come back to me."

The savage command went unanswered, and his anguish was an unbearable vise engulfing his body. A wounded howl of grief ripped out of his throat. She was gone. He'd lost her again. Life had lost its meaning.

Chapter 2

October 1897

The darkness of the dream enveloped Victoria as she spiraled downward to land on her bed with a jerk as pain rippled through her. Thousands of razor sharp needles stabbed at every inch of her. God, it was as if someone had doused her in gasoline then set her on fire.

The dream had become a nightmare of agony, and she ordered herself to wake up. She forced her eyes open to see nothing but a white mist filled with gray shadows. Oh God, she was blind. Panic flooded her veins as she tried to reassure herself it was a nightmare. Her eyes fluttered closed for a fleeting second. When she opened them again, there was nothing except the fog cluttered with dark shapes. Voices echoed nearby, but a loud ringing in her ears made it difficult to make out what they were saying. Yet out of all the indistinguishable voices, there was one she recognized. It was demanding. Arrogant. But she couldn't remember where she'd heard it before.

Victoria tried to turn her head toward the voice, but the movement sent a stabbing pain through her temple. She cried out. A dark shape suddenly blotted out the cloudy landscape of her vision. A warm hand touched her forehead before the shape abruptly disappeared. Slowly, the voices and ringing in her ears ebbed away. Victoria blinked several times in an attempt to clear her vision, then sat up.

The instant she moved, she uttered a cry of misery at the explosion of pain in her head. The heel of her palm pressed against her forehead, she bit back the bile threatening to rise in her throat. After several long moments of anguish, the pain and nausea eased.

This had to be the worst fricking hangover she'd ever had. Not that she'd had that many. She winced. Had she gone to a bar last night? She didn't remember going to one. Hell, she didn't remember much of anything over the last several weeks. The one thing she did remember was her argument with her father a year ago and what had happened a few hours later. She pushed back the tears. Images whirled and flitted through her brain. She was on vacation. She remembered *that* much, at least. But there was one thing she was certain of. This was *not* her hotel room. Her gaze swept over the simplicity of the stark room. Despite the brilliant stream of sunlight flooding through the window, it was cold. She shivered. Someone had set the AC way too low.

If it weren't for the fire in the hearth, the room would be even colder. It didn't make any sense why someone would have a fire with the AC going. Her gaze swept across the room's meager furnishings. Planks of rough-hewn wood served as the floor, while a white plaster covered the walls. It looked like something out of a Jane Austen movie. Oh God, had she decided to do one of those reality vacations? No, she couldn't afford something like that, even if she'd wanted to. What was the last thing she'd been doing? She breathed in a quiet breath as she tried to ignore the hot needles that assaulted the back of her head. Where was she, and exactly how had she gotten to wherever *here* was? She groaned as the headache spread to her temples.

Victoria tossed her blanket off to one side and swung her legs out of bed. Fire streaked across her skin once more, while her chest hurt like someone had kicked her repeatedly. Had she been mugged? Even though she was in pain, self-preservation had her on her feet the minute a woman scurried into the room.

"Good heavens, my lady. You shouldn't be out of bed just yet."

"Who are you?"

Her words sounded hoarse, stiff, and stilted. Laryngitis. Could you get that from a hangover? If you were shouting over loud music all night long? Maybe she'd been mugged and choked. It would explain her voice, the pounding in her head, and the way her body ached. It would also account for not knowing where the hell she was.

"I'm Bessie, my lady. Thomas Goodman's wife. He found you near the pond this morning. You were like death warmed over when my Thomas brought you in."

"Pond?" The hoarseness in her voice had disappeared, but it still sounded funny to her.

"Yes, my lady. Soaked through and through. If my Thomas hadn't found you, I fear the worst might have happened."

Victoria shook her head in denial and winced as she pressed her hand against her forehead. She hadn't been anywhere near a pond. She'd been in an art gallery. The sudden sliver of a memory tantalized her before it evaporated and pain took its place.

"Where am I?"

"Why Brentwood Park, my lady." Bessie patted Victoria's arm in a comforting manner.

"Brentwood Park," she murmured. Where had she heard that name before? Another stab of pain erupted in her head, and she groaned softly. God, jackhammers were going off inside her head. She looked down at the white cotton gown she wore. She never wore nightgowns. Normally, she chose to sleep in the nude, although she would occasionally sleep in a pair of pajamas. Nightgowns? Never. They were little more than straight-jackets, and she never got a good night's sleep with one on. Beside the bed, her hostess poured water from a beige earthen pitcher into a matching bowl. Wringing out a cloth in the basin, the woman turned her head to Victoria and smiled.

"Now then, my lady, let me see if I can clean that cut of yours."

"Cut?" Victoria blinked with confusion.

"I don't believe it will need stitching." Bessie's weathered features wrinkled up into a reassuring look as she dabbed gently at Victoria's forehead. "Lucky is what you were. Another inch lower and you could have lost an eye."

Baffled, Victoria gasped as cold water stung a tender spot just above her right eye. She lightly touched the wound and drew in a breath of surprise as Bessie gently pulled her hand away. When had she cut her head? Questions. Every time she answered one, half a dozen more sprang to life. She pulled away from the woman who was clucking over her like a worrisome mother hen.

"You said I'm at Brentwood Park. Is this a hospital of some kind?"

"Heavens, no, my lady. This is Goodman Cottage. Thomas and I are tenants of his lordship."

"His lordship?"

"Lord Guildford, my lady. Don't you remember?" The woman stared at her with a worried frown.

"I don't know any Lord Guildford." Victoria wanted to shake her head, but was afraid to for fear of pain.

"Oh, dear…you must have hit your head much harder than we thought." Bessie clucked her tongue in sympathy. "Now don't you fret, I've seen this happen before. Your memory will come back right enough when you're ready."

"I haven't lost my memory," Victoria muttered stubbornly.

She remembered her name, her childhood, the night her father had died. She shoved that unpleasant memory into a separate compartment. Right now, she had to focus on figuring out where the hell she was. England. She was in England on vacation by herself. It was impossible to know how long she'd been out, and right now all she wanted was to get back to her hotel. She frowned. Why didn't she hear traffic outside? The quiet reminded her of the woods near Kerrigan Stables, where she rode twice a week. A chill ran down her spine. If it was quiet outside, it meant she was in the country. She'd been in the city. How in the hell had she gotten from London to wherever this was?

"If you don't mind, I'd like my clothes back so I can return to my hotel."

"But, my lady, you just can't—"

"Can't what?" she snapped, more out of fear than anger. "Please bring me my clothes. I want—"

The door swung open with a loud screech. Instantly, she turned toward the sound and inhaled a sharp breath. Everything receded into the background as she met the hard, green-eyed gaze of the man entering the room. Before his arrival, the room had been comfortable in size, but now it closed in on her.

Power. Sheer power was the first thing that came to mind as her gaze ran over him. He was dressed for riding, but he wasn't wearing jeans as one might expect. His apparel seemed more appropriate for a horse show. Fawn-colored breeches hugged sleek, muscular thighs. The snug fitting pants were tucked into a pair of shiny black boots with a dark brown cuff at the top. A starched collar jutted upward to part slightly at his throat, while a narrow, black tie encircled his neck. Dark wavy hair and those piercing green eyes of his completed the image of a man born to command. She swallowed hard. The man didn't just ooze sex appeal, he defined it.

Deliberate and unhurried, he removed his black riding

gloves and slapped them into his hand with a vicious crack. She jumped. Like an animal fascinated with its predator, she met his narrowed gaze warily. His barely restrained anger saturated the room with its raw heat.

Okay, now she was worried. Had she wrecked her rental car and damaged his property? Wait, did she even have a rental car? Damn it, how could she remember things from months ago, while the past couple of days and weeks were hazy at best?

"That will be all for now, Bessie. You may bring the countess her clothes shortly." Despite her apprehension, the deep timbre of his voice turned her inside out. The man could easily give a woman an orgasm with that voice. Wait. Countess? What countess?

"Yes, my lord."

Bessie quickly left the room as the stranger's gaze remained locked with hers. The door closed behind the older woman, and something flashed in the man's eyes as he moved forward. Victoria instinctively jumped backward as he brushed past her. He walked with a distinct limp as he crossed the room to the small window beneath an eave. Had he been in an accident or was the handicap from birth? The vague whisper of a memory teased her as she studied the back of his dark head. She tried to catch the thought, but it winked out of her grasp. Frustrated, she grimaced, then started as the man turned and directed a harsh look in her direction.

"Do you want to tell me where the devil you've been for the last three weeks, Vickie?"

"I'm sorry?" She scowled at him. She'd never liked people calling her by that nickname. For some unknown reason, it had always had a negative connotation to it, and she hated the way it made her feel when someone called her by the name.

"Three weeks, Vickie." The sharp words cracked through the air and made her flinch. "I've had private investigators looking for you for the past three weeks."

"Look, you've obviously got me confused with someone else." Bewildered, she shrugged her shoulders. "I don't know you. My name is Victoria Ashton, and I don't know this Vickie person."

"Memory loss? Your creativity astounds me, my dear." The condescension in his voice made the hair on the back of neck stand upright. Sex appeal or not, the man was an arrogant bastard. Victoria narrowed her eyes at him.

"I didn't say I'd lost my memory. I said, I don't know you." She silently dismissed her inability to remember the past couple of days or weeks. That didn't count. She knew who she was.

His eyes were shards of green ice as he stared at her for a long moment. Then with an indifferent air he took a seat in the room's only chair. Sitting sideways, he draped an arm over the wooden chair's spindled back and crossed his bad leg over one knee. His relaxed posture only enhanced his commanding presence. Sexy or not, she was certain he'd be a dangerous man to cross.

"So you think I've confused you with someone else." He surveyed her from head to toe with an insolent gleam before looking at the ring on his finger. "An odd statement considering I'd be hard pressed not to recognize my wife."

The soft words sent her reeling back two steps. Frantically, she tried to recall what she'd been doing before she woke up in this nightmare. There was no way in hell she could be married. Was there?

She squeezed her eyes shut as if that would help her remember. The image of a large room with paintings flitted through her head. An art gallery. She'd been debating whether or not to buy a landscape. Hadn't she? Images flew through her head so fast she couldn't recognize most of them. An explosion. Had there been an explosion? It would explain the cut on her head if she'd been near glass.

Desperately, she tried to remember more. She'd been

with someone. Who? Acute pain pulsed viciously in her head. Victoria tried to ignore it, but the harder she tried to pull answers from the shadows, the more intense the vicious pounding in her head. She released a soft sound of misery and gave up trying to recall the last couple of days. The moment she did so, the pain eased to a minor throb.

She was barely aware the stranger had moved until his sudden proximity enveloped her in a white-hot, sultry heat. Firm fingers grasped her chin, and he tilted her face toward the sunshine streaming into the room. The pads of his fingers seared her skin, and she drew in a sharp breath. Hell, this man wasn't just hot to look at. With one simple touch, he'd managed to make her legs wobbly as Jell-O. She dragged in another quick breath.

He smelled of horse, leather, and something spicy. He was raw male, and the potency of him made her ache for something she hadn't had in a long time. All the man had to do was kiss her, and she'd be melting in his arms. The thought made her lick her lips nervously. His eyes narrowed and darkened to a shade of evergreen before he jerked away from her and put several feet between them.

"I grow weary of this game you're playing, Vickie."

"I'm *not* your wife," she snapped.

"Then tell me who you are, my dear." The icy contempt in his voice could have frozen the air between them, and for the first time she realized she might be in real trouble.

"I told you, already. My name is Victoria Ashton," she said as calmly as possible. "I don't know you or how I got here. I just want my clothes back so I can get a ride back to London."

For the briefest of moments, she could have sworn she saw doubt in his green eyes before a shutter fell into place, revealing nothing but amused cynicism. The insolence of his smile made her draw in a breath of irritation.

"A convincing tale, madam, but it lacks a certain, shall we

say, finesse," he drawled.

"Are you calling me a liar?" She wanted to kick herself. Of course he was.

"I'm simply stating the obvious. Your acting abilities have improved considerably, but this is a bit much, even for you."

"Look, this is crazy. I was in an art gallery in London. I think there was some kind of explosion. The next thing I knew, I woke up here." Her words instantly made her head hurt, and she winced.

"I'm a patient man, Vickie, but this charade is growing tiresome." Anger tightened his sensual mouth. The fact that she was even thinking about his mouth annoyed her as much as his refusal to call her Victoria.

"So help me God, if you call me Vickie one more time…" She gritted her teeth and suppressed her anger. It wasn't going to help things if she lost her temper. "I'm *not* your wife. My name is Victoria Ashton. I don't know how I got here, and at the moment I don't really care. If you'll just give me my clothes back, I'll get out of your hair."

"*Enough.*" The barely controlled fury in the command made her flinch. "If you continue with this farce, I'll be forced to have you examined by a physician from the county asylum."

"Don't you *dare* threaten me," she said fiercely as she returned his glare.

"It's not a threat, Vickie. You're clearly unwell."

There was something about his icy demeanor that sent a shiver down her spine. He was dead serious. Fear slithered through Victoria. The man was clearly off his rocker. Her clothes were missing, and no one knew where she was. Hell, *she* didn't even know where she was. Out of the corner of her eye, she saw the door and lunged toward it.

With the advantage of surprise, she was slamming the door behind her before the stranger could stop her. Victoria heard him utter a violent curse, but didn't wait to hear more.

A cramped stairwell was only a couple feet away, and she plunged her way down the steep, narrow steps.

As she reached the last step, she stopped and stared. The large room looked like a historical exhibit. The woman who'd cleaned the cut on her head stood bent at a huge open fireplace stirring something in a kettle. Victoria hadn't paid much attention to the woman's apparel earlier, but now she realized Bessie was a walking advertisement for a tourist attraction. The rotund woman wore a brown dress that almost brushed the floor with a white apron tied around her waist. Victoria looked around the room in the hope her clothes might be close by, but they were nowhere in sight.

"God damn it, Vickie. Stop."

The stranger's voice held a dark and dangerous edge to it, and Bessie looked up from her kettle to stare at Victoria in astonishment. Not about to let the woman stop her, Victoria threw open the only door in the room and bolted outside. The cold air and patches of snow on the ground stunned her. It was the middle of May. Did England have snow as late as this? She squinted against the sunshine and paused for a second to adjust to the light. Behind her, the door to the small house swung open.

"Bloody hell, Vickie. Don't be a fool. You're not dressed."

Victoria ignored his harsh words as she fled. Rough stones bit at her bare feet as she sprinted along the dirt path leading away from him. In front of her was a large pond, and at the water's edge, the trail split to follow the shoreline all around the pond. Behind her, she heard her jailor call out a man's name. A responding shout echoed out of the woods surrounding the water. Horrified, she saw men emerge from the forest on each side of the pond.

With a glance over her shoulder, she saw her delusional interrogator gaining on her. For a man with a limp, he moved quickly. Frantic to escape, she realized the water was her only hope. She was a fast swimmer. If she swam to the opposite end of the pond, she might be able to escape. Self-preservation drove her forward, and she ran the last two steps to the water and dived in head first.

Cold fire engulfed her the instant she hit the water. Shock pushed Victoria back up to the surface with a loud gasp. Ice cold, the water sucked the air out of her, forcing her to fight hard to draw air back into her lungs. The fire feeding on her skin was almost as intense as the pain she'd endured when she'd woken up in this terrible dream. She was a strong swimmer, but the frigid water stole every ounce of strength she had. Desperately she fought to breathe as her legs gave way, and she sank beneath the water.

Come back to me.

The whisper echoed in her head, and she recognized it. But from where? Victoria stretched her hand out toward the sound. Strong fingers gripped her hand and pulled her back from the brink. Air filled her lungs as she sputtered and coughed violently. A moment later, a steely grasp encircled her waist to pull her upright.

Panic sailed through her again as she looked into a pair of green eyes, blazing with anger and something else. Although she was exhausted and horribly cold, she found the strength to struggle against his grasp.

"*Damn it to hell, Vicki.* No one's going to hurt you. Stop fighting me," he growled as he swung her up into his arms and carried her out of the water.

The sincerity in his voice pierced the fear twisting through her as his heat pushed its way into the icy cold layer of her skin. When they reached the shore, he set her down. Deprived of his warmth, a shudder whipped through her followed by another until she was shaking like a piece of paper dancing in the wind. A second later, his riding coat covered her shoulders.

"Come, Bessie will get you out of this wet garment," he

said.

Before she could protest, he swung her up into his arms again and started back toward the cottage. She didn't want to go back, but she was so damn cold. Worse, she didn't know where to run to. Despite his warmth, she continued to shiver. The sound of his boots crunching against a small patch of snow on the trail made her wince.

"Why is there…snow on…the ground?" she asked through her chattering teeth.

"It's not unusual for snow to fall in October, you know that."

"*October.*" Victoria looked up at him in horror. Her teeth still clicking rapidly, she shook her head. "It can't…be…October. It's…May."

"I can assure you, my dear, it *is* October."

"The…date?"

"I believe it's the thirtieth."

"October…thir…thirtieth." Something deep inside prompted her to ask what she didn't want an answer to. "The…year?"

"The year is eighteen ninety-seven, my dear," he said quietly as he came to a halt.

"Not…possible," she chattered as shock rippled through her. Victoria's stomach began to churn savagely, and she pushed at his shoulder. "Please…I'm…throw up."

Without hesitating, he lowered her until her feet rested on his boots in an apparent attempt to keep her bare feet off the ground. Bile rose in her throat, and she violently twisted free of his grasp, then stumbled into the snow-patched grass lining the path. A moment later, she threw up as if she'd been out drinking all night.

Cool hands gently pulled her hair away from her face, holding it out of the way as she threw up whatever was in her stomach. As her heaves abated, he offered her a linen handkerchief lightly scented with the crisp odor of mint.

Victoria wiped her mouth with the white square and closed her eyes.

"It's a bad dream. Just a *really* bad dream," she mumbled to herself. Screw Einstein's theory of relativity. It wasn't possible to travel through time. "Wake up, Victoria. It's just a nightmare."

Victoria slowly glanced around her and sucked in a quiet breath of despair. She was still here. Silently, she stared at the cottage in front of her. It looked so familiar, but she couldn't remember where she'd seen it. Snow dusted the roof and brightly colored leaves clung with desperation to tree branches hanging over the small house. She drew in a sharp breath. The art gallery. She'd been about to buy a painting of this cottage.

A shudder hammered through her, and she pulled the stranger's riding jacket close around her. He uttered something harsh under his breath, then swooped her up into his arms again. In silence, he carried her toward the cottage. Scared, exhausted, and confused, she didn't have the energy to protest. She closed her eyes again as she struggled to accept her situation.

"You recognize the cottage." The quiet statement made her glance up at him, and she nodded.

"I saw it in a painting," she answered hoarsely. "At the art gallery in London."

"And yet you still maintain you don't know me." There was a hard note of skepticism in his voice. "Perhaps your head injury is more serious than Bessie suspected."

"What? Oh, yes, my head." She probed the swelling cut at her temple. She instantly regretted it as her head throbbed with pain again.

"I believe the first order of business is to get you into dry clothes. At the moment, your appearance is in a sad state of disrepair, and I have no wish to see my wife bounding about the countryside in a nightdress."

"I'm *not* your wife." With her chattering teeth, it was

impossible to sound convincing.

"I believe we should have Dr. Bertram call on us. I'm sure he would find this unusual story of yours quite interesting."

The threat of a doctor made Victoria flinch, and she looked away from him. Whether this was a dream or reality, she needed to bite her tongue. Mental health had only just come out of the dark ages in her own time. If she really was in the past, the last thing she wanted was a ticket to an insane asylum.

"I don't need a doctor." Her quiet response appeared to satisfy him. Several seconds later, he carried her into the cottage where Bessie greeted her like a mother hen would a lost chick.

"Bessie, I believe it's time the countess was dressed properly," he said as he kept his gaze on Victoria. "I'll wait for her here."

"Aye, my lord."

"My coat, madam, if you please. It's a bit chilly today," he said in a clipped tone of voice. A shudder rippled through Victoria at his words. It was more out of regret than her frozen state. He'd been cold because of her.

"I'm sorry. I was scared."

She still was, but she wasn't about to admit it to him. With a grimace, Victoria removed his coat and handed it back to him. Surprise flashed across his face before he masked the emotion with indifference. He bowed slightly.

"I'll leave you in Bessie's capable hands. When you're dressed, I'll take you home."

"But…I don't even know who you are." Her cheeks grew warm with embarrassment at the look of disbelief he directed at her.

"So you've said," he said dryly as he arched his brow in icy disdain. "Very well. I'm Nicholas Thornhill, Earl of Guildford. And you, madam wife, are Victoria Brentwood

Thornhill, Countess of Guildford."

With that introduction, he turned and limped away to stand in front of the fireplace with his hands outstretched to warm them. Something about his posture made Victoria long to run to him and reassure him that everything would be all right. Victoria blinked at the crazy thought. She had enough to worry about. A shiver skimmed down her back.

"Come along, my lady. We'll get you warm and dry in a moment." Half-hearing Bessie's chatter, Victoria allowed the woman to lead her up the stairs to the room she'd fled a short time ago. After a few minutes in front of the fire, Victoria was feeling less frozen.

"Here you are, my lady." Bessie held up a royal blue dress. "I'm afraid the gown's ruined, my lady. Thomas found you lying by the pond."

Huge patches of caked mud declared the silk gown had seen better days. As she stared at the dress, her shivering returned. Ice sluiced over her skin as if she were drowning in the pond again. A shadowy image flashed in front of her, and she jerked in surprise. More images streaked through her head in a wild whirlwind of incomprehensible events. A singular, horrifying sound accompanied the pictures swirling in her mind. It was the distinct sound of a shovel hitting the ground with a sickening thud before earth scraped across the metal. Fear lodged in her throat as she saw part of a blue gown disappear beneath clumps of soil. It was the same gown Bessie was holding. Victoria's stomach lurched violently.

"My lady, are you all right?" Bessie exclaimed. "You're white as a sheet."

"I'm fine," she focused her gaze on the older woman as the images faded into oblivion.

"Now don't you worry about how it looks, my lady. As soon as you get back to the manor, you'll have dozens of gowns to choose from," the woman murmured soothingly. The motherly clucks of dismay returned, as Bessie helped

Victoria change out of her wet nightgown. In need of more information about the countess to help her navigate the minefield she was in, Victoria cleared her throat.

"Bessie, do you know anything about the…my disappearance?"

"Well, as I heard it, you left Guildford House for a fancy ball, but never arrived. His lordship searched high and low for you, he did. But you'd just upped and disappeared." As the woman rattled on with her tale, Victoria dried off in front of the fire. "Of course, Lord Darby didn't help matters none when you went missing. Thomas' brother, George, works for the man. George says Lord Darby was running about all crazed like. He said Lord Darby accused his lordship of doing you in. And right there in front of the Prince of Wales himself, no less."

When Victoria was dry, the servant woman threw a white, lacy undergarment over her head. Engrossed in the tale, Victoria didn't protest as Bessie helped put a corset on. It was more like a bustier, and she was surprised it fit her full-figured curves so well. As Bessie reached for the muddied gown, the woman shook her head.

"Bless me if it wasn't a scandal. There was talk of a magistrate and all sorts of doings. Right glad I am that you're back, my lady. Lord Guildford is a good man. He don't deserve to be treated like a criminal. He'd never hurt anyone."

Victoria didn't respond as she tried to process everything Bessie had shared. A murder accusation. No wonder the man was furious. The real question to ask was since *she* wasn't Lady Guildford, exactly where was the earl's wife? The memory of the dark images she'd seen made Victoria shiver. What if…no, she wasn't going down that road. Wherever Lady Guildford was, Victoria didn't enjoy the thought that the woman was in a shallow grave somewhere. Deep in the back of her mind, a voice argued with her, but she ignored it.

As Bessie slipped the gown's soft, blue silk over her head,

Victoria prepared herself for more unpleasant imagery. When nothing happened, she exhaled a sigh of relief and stood still as Bessie buttoned the dress the earl's wife had worn. What was her connection to the earl or his wife? With everyone mistaking her for the countess, did she actually look like the woman? What if she didn't look like herself? A shaft of panic shot through her.

"Bessie, do you have a mirror?" she rasped.

"But of course, my lady. It's just a hand mirror, but it should do well enough. Let me fetch it."

Bessie hurried from the room, leaving Victoria to stare down at the mud on her dress. No, the countess' dress. Where had the woman been to get so dirty? Dark images fluttered through her mind again, and Victoria pushed them out of her head. A moment later, Bessie returned and handed her a mirror. With a trembling hand, she lifted the hand-held mirror. Relief streamed through her as she recognized the reflection.

"Thank God." A split second later she inhaled a sharp breath of fear. Her voice was different. Oh God, what she'd thought was laryngitis wasn't that at all. A crisp, aristocratic accent had replaced her American one.

Chapter 3

Present Day

Nick paced the floor of the hospital waiting room. It had been almost an hour since he'd been ordered out of the trauma room filled with doctors bent over Victoria. Where his CPR skills had failed, the paramedics had succeeded, but she'd failed to regain consciousness. God, if he lost her again. Again?

Why in the hell would he think he'd gone through this before? He shoved a hand through his hair and stopped his pacing. What the fuck was happening to him? He was beginning to think he'd lost his mind. He'd just met the woman, and yet deep down in his soul, he knew his life would never be the same if she didn't survive. The sound of feminine heels clicking against the floor made him turn around. As Nora entered the small visitors' lounge, Nick closed the distance between them and gave her a hug.

"You okay?" he said huskily as he stepped back and inspected her face for any injuries.

"Just shaken up a bit. I was still upstairs when the explosion hit."

"*Christ*, the shop—"

"It's fine, just minor damage. I left Robert in charge," Nora said in her practical manner that was at odds with her personal beliefs. "He's arranging for security and repairs."

"What the fuck happened? A gas leak?" Nick eyed his sister with disbelief.

"No. A bomb." Anger darkened Nora's features. "Some environmental extremists targeted the ad agency across the street for a recent campaign the agency did for an oil company."

"Christ almighty," he said with a shake of his head.

"I hope they catch the bastards and put their balls and heads on the Tower's spikes," Nora snapped viciously, then eyed him with a look of worry. "Have you seen a doctor about this cut?"

"Cut?" He reached up to touch his face, and Nora immediately smacked his hand aside.

"Don't be an idiot. You need to have a doctor look at this. It might need sutures." Nora's gaze swept over him, then gasped in horror. "*Oh my God, your leg.*"

"My leg?" Nick looked downward to see his pants leg was split open and a long, deep gash that ran the length of his calf.

"Aren't you in pain?" Nora asked, her face pasty white.

"No," he said as he realized that wasn't quite true. His leg had been aching from all the pacing he'd done. "It must be deep enough to have cut off the nerve endings. And stop looking at the damn thing before you pass out.

"You need to get that leg looked at, *now*," his sister said firmly despite the sick look on her face.

"I'm not doing anything until I know Victoria's all right."

"Victoria?" His sister arched her eyebrow at him in a silent demand for an explanation.

"She told me her name right before the explosion." He heard the defensive note in his voice. "She's been in the trauma center for more than an hour. *Fuck*, if you'd seen the way she looked in the ambulance..."

Nick's throat tightened and closed as fear threatened to suffocate him. His fingers gripped the back of his neck. He would never forget the light fixture as it crashed downward and slammed into Victoria, or the look of agony on her face when she grabbed the live wire. Tension hardened his muscles as he remembered the way her entire body had jumped on the gurney when they'd shocked her heart.

"The ambulance? They don't let people ride in the back."

"I didn't give them a choice," he muttered with a grimace. "I told them I was her fiancé, and I was going with them."

"Good lord, Nick. What were you thinking?"

"I don't *know* what I was thinking. It's like someone else has been in my head from the moment I first saw her. The only thing I'm certain of is that I can't lose her again."

"*Again?*" Nora stared at him like he'd lost his marbles, which was precisely how he felt at the moment as he met his sister's gaze of astonishment. "How can you lose someone you don't even know, Nick? You're confusing her with that damn portrait."

"Now *you're* the skeptic? And yeah, I've been questioning my sanity," he said between clenched teeth. "But *tell* me Nora, what are the odds of a woman who's a dead ringer for the Countess of Guildford, with the same first name of said Countess, coming into our shop out of all the hundreds of galleries in the city to buy the Goodman Cottage painting."

"Lockwood's painting?" Nora gasped. He waited for her to say something, but she simply stared at him in shocked disbelief.

"What? No words of wisdom or insight as to the fact that there *are* no coincidences in life?"

He knew she didn't deserve the sarcasm, but he was fresh out of polite sentiment at the moment. Fresh out of patience with all this past lives talk of hers. He'd been listening to it for so long he was starting to believe it himself. What the devil made him think he knew Victoria? His imagination was running amok because of guilt. Guilt that he was okay, and that Victoria had nearly died and still might. He ignored the voice protesting vehemently in the back of his head.

"What would you like for me to say?" Nora asked quietly. His jaw tightened as he noted the pained look of disappointment in his sister's brown eyes.

"You didn't deserve that. I'm an ass," he said as she dismissed his words with a wave of her hand.

"Do you want to tell me what happened?" she asked.

"Not particularly."

As much as he hated to admit it, he didn't know how to talk about it. He didn't have the words to explain how one brief touch had bonded him to a woman who was a total stranger. How the fuck was he supposed to explain something like that? Especially when he didn't understand it himself.

Nora sank down into a nearby chair as he returned to pacing the floor. Silence drifted between them for several long moments until another sound echoed in the hallway. Turning toward the door, Nick recognized the man entering the lounge as the trauma room physician.

"Mr. Barrows?" The doctor crossed the floor to close the distance between them and shook Nick's hand. "I'm Doctor Bertram. We've stabilized Miss Ashton. She suffered second-degree burns on her hands where the electrical current entered and exited her body. They're not life threatening, but you'll need to avoid touching her hands when you see her. We'll continue to monitor her for any other physical reactions to the electrical shock."

"What else," Nick demanded as he saw something flicker in the man's eyes.

"Unfortunately, Miss Ashton has slipped into a coma."

"A coma?" Fear knotted his gut at the doctor's resigned expression.

"It happens sometimes in cases such as this. She was resuscitated three times before we managed to stabilize her heart rate."

"When will she wake up?"

"There's been a great deal of stress to your fiancée's system. She's lucky to be alive, and a coma is often the body's way of healing itself."

"You didn't answer my question. When will Victoria wake up?" He watched the man closely. Searching for something, anything that would tell him Victoria was going to be all right.

"I can't answer that, Mr. Barrows." The regret on the doctor's face sent an icy chill through Nick. Barely meeting his gaze, the doctor cleared his throat. "Her brain activity readings are unlike anything I've seen before. I'm not able to determine the level of brain damage."

"What do you mean, brain damage?" Nick snarled as his insides tightened with dread.

"Her brainwaves appear to be continuously fluctuating between an active and almost vegetative state." A perplexed frown wrinkled the doctor's brow. "I'm at a loss to explain it. I've called in our best neurologist to see if she has any answers."

"So, Victoria could easily wake up at any moment."

"Possibly, but I've no idea how extensive the brain damage—"

"I want to see her." Nick's demand made the other man nod.

"Of course, but first we need to sew up that gash on your leg and cheek. The cut on your face isn't too bad…" Dr. Bertram frowned. "But that leg definitely needs attention now. I'm surprised one of the nurses didn't shuttle you off to one of the trauma bays."

"It can wait."

"No, Mr. Barrows, it can't. When we've fixed your wounds, I'll make sure you see your fiancée."

"Fine." Reluctantly, Nick agreed to the doctor's inflexible command with a sharp nod. "And I'll need something to sleep on. I intend to stay with her."

"Is that wise, Nick?" His sister's brow was creased with worry. "What good does it do if you stay with her?"

"I want to be there when she wakes up."

"Mr. Barrows, even if she does wake up, it could be days, weeks, even longer before she does so." The doctor's protest only reinforced the conviction taking root inside him and growing stronger by the second.

"Have you ever had a medical case surprise you, Dr. Bertram?"

"On occasion, but your fiancée—"

"My fiancée is going to surprise you. Victoria is going to surprise everyone, except me. Now get me sewn up so I can see her."

Chapter 4

October 1897

Nicholas ushered Vickie out of Goodman Cottage. His wife looked presentable despite the mud-stained gown she wore. He also noted there was a significant amount of blood on the shoulder of her dress. More than one might expect from the size of the cut on her forehead. That fact didn't just puzzle him, he found it disturbing.

Usually it was easy to see through Vickie's deceptions, and it irritated him that he'd failed to catch her in an outright lie yet. But that was about to change. Nicholas walked to where Zeus was tethered and quickly mounted the stallion. Pawing the ground, the restless animal danced about as Vickie drew near. Without any visible effort, he brought the animal under control.

"You'll have to ride pillion, madam."

He smiled coldly at her as he offered his hand to her. If there was one thing Vickie was afraid of, it was horses. She never rode, and even riding behind him would probably terrify the hell out of her.

"Don't you have another horse?"

"Another horse?" Nicholas murmured with satisfaction as he waited for Vickie to demand he return home and send a carriage for her.

"Yes. One for me to ride." Her response was so unexpected all he could do was stare at her in amazement. It wasn't a pleasant sensation to be at a loss for words where Vickie was concerned.

"Why the devil would I bring a horse for you when you don't ride?" he snapped as he gestured for her to step forward.

"Because I've been riding since I was a kid," she said with obvious exasperation.

Without blinking an eye, she boldly and fearlessly walked up to Zeus. The stallion turned his head in her direction, and she stroked the bridge of his nose as if it were something she'd done a thousand times before. Stunned, Nicholas remained silent as his wife hitched up her skirts, accepted his hand, and jumped up behind him. The instant his hand touched hers, a bolt of electricity vibrated through him. It was the same sensation he'd experienced every time he'd touched her today.

She wiggled into a comfortable position behind him, then wrapped her arms about his waist. The heat of her pressing into his back made him go rigid. *Christ Jesus*, what the hell was wrong with him reacting to her like this. This was Vickie. A woman who enjoyed humiliating him whenever the opportunity presented itself.

With a nudge of his heel, he urged Zeus forward, guiding them into the trees behind the cottage. The trail they followed opened up onto a large green expanse of pasture land sprinkled with patches of melting snow. As they rode out into the sunshine, Vickie rested her forehead on his shoulder. Was she going to be sick again? God help him, she could be pregnant with Darby's bastard. He wanted to kill her in that brief second. He grimaced. Ironic, given so many people thought he'd already done so.

"Are you feeling ill again?" he asked coldly.

"No," she said. "Your shoulder just makes a good sunshade. I wish I had my sunglasses."

Tension crept into his muscles at the response. It was a

minor complaint, but nowhere in her voice or words was there a hint of the spoiled, petulant woman he was married to. Whatever game she was playing, she was doing so with a skill that surpassed anything Vickie had displayed before. As Zeus reached the top of the knoll overlooking Brentwood Park, she raised her head and gasped.

"Is that Brentwood Park?"

"Yes. It was part of your dowry." He failed to keep the bitterness out of his voice. Damnation, he knew better than to let her see she could evoke a response in him.

"*That* was a wedding present?" she muttered with disbelief.

Once again, her reaction baffled him. A dowry wasn't a wedding present. It was a business transaction. But the incredulous note in her voice actually sounded genuine. He suppressed a snort of disgust. Vickie had never been sincere about anything in her entire life. Her first and only concern was for herself.

"Which of your friends shall we notify first about your safe return?" he asked coldly.

"Do we have to tell anyone?" Her trepidation ignited a bitter rage inside him.

"Madam, in the past three weeks, I've been questioned by the police, accused of murder, and subjected to veiled insults from most of the Marlborough Set," he snarled. "Considering the rumors surrounding your disappearance, I intend to let *everyone* know you're alive and well."

"*Oh Lord*, I'm sorry," she gasped. "I didn't realize—of course we'll have to tell people your wife has…that I've returned."

"I'll send a notice to the *Times* and *Daily Telegraph* today," he bit out fiercely.

"I really am sorry, but the thought of questions…I've never really liked being the center of attention." Her soft comment made him snort with a hefty dose of cynical amusement.

"I don't recall you ever being reticent for talking about yourself, my dear."

"Well, *that* must have been boring."

The dry note of humor in her words shot a bolt of tension through his body. God help him, he could almost believe she wasn't Vickie. Bitterness quickly crushed his doubts.

"Your exploits have been never boring, my dear. Decadent and depraved perhaps, but never boring."

Her gasp illustrated the brutality of his statement, and his immediate regret angered him. Damn it. Once again, she'd succeeded in making him feel like a bastard. It was a sensation his wife had never aroused in him before, and he didn't like it. Silence surrounded them as Zeus carried them with ease across the pastures until they reached the manor's front door. Tall and cadaverous looking, his butler, Jamieson, hurried down the wide, marble steps to greet them.

"Welcome home, my lord. May we express our delight at her ladyship's safe return?"

Nicholas smiled grimly at the man. Behind him, Vickie sighed softly. Was there a hint of regret in that sound? No, he knew his wife too well. With a limber movement, he swung his good leg over Zeus's neck and slid to the ground.

"Thank you, Jamieson. Her ladyship and I appreciate your good wishes."

Nicholas turned and grasped Vickie by the waist, then lowered her to the ground. The intensity of the heat flooding through him as her body slid down his chest sucked a sharp breath from him. What the fuck was wrong with him? Not even before their wedding had he experienced this visceral type of sensation where his wife was concerned.

It was such an intense physical connection with her that it stunned him. Staring into the brilliance of her sapphire eyes, he saw a glimmer of fear. Nicholas frowned at her, and she immediately turned her head away from him. Why would she fear him? He mentally shook his head. He was letting her odd behavior get the better of him. Disgusted with his reaction to her, he put some distance between them and turned to his butler.

"Jamieson, the countess has suffered a head injury and is having difficulty with her memory. Please inform the staff she may require assistance remembering where things are." Not waiting for the butler to reply, he turned back to her. "If you require anything, ask for Mrs. Beechum."

"Thank you." Her quiet, pleasant reply aroused the devil in him.

"Perhaps I should mention that we have guests coming for the weekend."

"*Guests*?" The alarm in her voice amused him. He'd rarely seen Vickie unnerved by anything, but her apprehension was clearly visible.

"Friends of mine. Naturally, if the idea of entertaining is an overwhelming one, I'll be happy to express your regrets."

Nicholas couldn't resist taunting her. The moment Vickie learned Eleanor was in the house, she'd reveal herself, and this ridiculous game she was playing would end. With restrained amusement, he watched uncertainty flit over her features before she narrowed her gaze at him.

"Why do I get the feeling you're hoping I'll make a scene?"

"Hoping? My dear, I've come to *expect* tantrums where you're concerned," he said with a scornful smile.

The Countess of Guildford was in for an unpleasant surprise. A twinge of guilt pricked his conscience at the confused look of alarm sweeping over her features. He crushed the emotion. Vickie had never displayed a care for anyone's feelings, and he was not about to have her make a mockery of him with this pretense of hers.

"Your wife must be a real bitch to make you hate her so

much."

The quiet words make him jerk with surprise as he tried to convince himself the sympathy on her lovely face was a farce. Speechless, he managed to maintain a stoic expression as she turned and followed Jamieson into the house. He'd fully expected a tirade, not this dignified condemnation of his mockery.

With a shake of his head, he watched her disappear into the manor. Damn if the woman wasn't acting strangely. If he didn't know better, he'd say she was telling the truth. But then Vickie only told the truth when it suited her. He'd learned that particular lesson all too well the day of their wedding. The memory wasn't a pleasant one.

His gaze narrowed and focused on the façade of the manor. The return of Brentwood Park to his family's holdings was a small consolation given the state of his marriage. Nicholas made his way into the house, then walked through the library to the hallway leading to his study.

Closing the door behind him, he limped to his desk and sank down into his chair. His leg was throbbing. His boots were damp on the outside, and although the insides were relatively dry, the leather still held the icy temperature of the pond. Vickie would be fortunate if she escaped a bout of pneumonia from her panicked plunge into the pond. Jaw tight with tension, he tried to comprehend what would make Vickie do something so foolish. Her flight had been one of abject terror. Nicholas immediately snorted with disbelief. It had been a brilliant performance by his wife. Nothing more. The throbbing of his leg broke into his train of thought. He grunted at his stupidity for not going upstairs to change first. The cold penetrated its way down to the bone that had never healed properly. Forcing himself to ignore the pain, Nicholas reached for pen and paper.

He quickly wrote an announcement for the Times and Daily Telegraph. As Vickie's parents had died of influenza several months after their wedding, her closest living relative was an aunt, and Nicholas made sure to write the woman as well. With each note he penned, one weight after another lifted from his shoulders. The last letter was to Scotland Yard, and as he signed his name, he breathed a sigh of relief.

Although the police might pay them a visit, he was hopeful they would simply wait until they returned to town in a few weeks. He'd deliberately omitted any reference to Vickie's claim of amnesia. He wasn't about to be humiliated by announcing a condition his wife was using to make him the laughingstock of the Marlborough Set.

When they finally returned to London, she would have returned to her usual self, and they would continue as they had for the past two years. Two strangers living under the same roof. Nicholas stood up and pulled the bell cord, then returned to his desk to address the notes. He'd just completed sealing the envelopes with a wax seal of the Guildford crest when a knock on the study door announced Jamison's entrance.

"Jamieson, have one of the stable hands deliver these letters as soon as possible. I'd send them by telegraph, but I'd preferred they be delivered in person, to ensure they're not lost in the shuffle. It's imperative these reach the appropriate individuals as quickly as possible."

"Yes, my Lord." Jamison hesitated for a moment, and Nicholas eyed the man with curiosity.

"Yes?"

"It's… I simply want to say that the staff and I are relieved and happy that your lordship's recent troubles have been resolved."

"By that you mean the hangman's noose is no longer a threat," Nicholas said quietly. He couldn't deny the relief he'd not dared to feel until this instant. It was a heady sensation, and he struggled not to believe it was a dream.

"Yes, my lord."

"Thank you, Jamison, and express my thanks to the staff as well." The butler nodded.

"I'll see that these letters are sent immediately, my lord."

Jamieson accepted the letters as the faint clattering sound of carriage wheels on gravel filtered into the study. Jamieson turned quickly with the obvious intent to head toward the front door, but Nicholas forestalled him.

"I'll greet my guests, Jamison. Those letters are too important to delay sending. Have Albertson and Baker come assist with the baggage."

"Yes, my lord."

Nicholas followed the man out of the office and walked to the front door. As he descended the steps to the driveway he saw his friend, Sebastian Reddington, Viscount Starling, assisting his wife Anna out of a black carriage Nicholas had arranged to have waiting for his friends at the train station. Sebastian greeted him with a rueful twist of his lips.

"Well, Nicholas, I believe you've won our small wager. You told me we wouldn't make it before three, and you were correct," Sebastian said with amused resignation. Laughter parted Anna's lips as she touched her husband's cheek in a tender gesture.

"You must forgive him, Nicholas. I'm to blame. Sebastian tried to depart earlier, but you both know I'm habitually late, no matter how hard I try to be on time." The Viscountess Starling moved forward to kiss Nicholas's cheek with affection.

"I'm sure he finds it easy to forgive you most anything, Anna."

"Almost, but not quite," she said with an impish smile directed at her husband. "I can recall several moments when I feared he would not be so charitable."

Nicholas suppressed a twinge of envy as he watched Sebastian capture his wife's hand and raise it to his lips in a loving gesture. Her hand still enclosed in her husband's, Anna turned back to him.

"The others will be along later. Eleanor had a social engagement she couldn't put off. Charles stayed behind to serve as her escort. John had an unexpected business meeting until one this afternoon. So I imagine everyone will be here by five, well in time for supper."

"It's just as well. I have something I wish to discuss with you both without the others present," he said. Nicholas gestured toward the house.

With Anna in the lead, the trio climbed the manor's marble steps and entered the massive foyer. As he did almost every time he crossed the threshold of the manor, Nicholas looked upward. The unusual skylight with its stained glass replica of the Guildford coat of arms illuminated the main foyer. Four generations ago, a Guildford had wagered and lost the manor to one of Vickie's ancestors in a card game. Although the house had been renamed, the skylight with the Guildford crest had escaped demolition.

` A wide staircase swept up to the second floor in a smooth circle, enhanced by a warm oak banister. Family portraits lined the walls going up the stairs, while a salon and library faced each other across the large foyer. With a small sweep of his hand, he invited his friends to enter the salon. Nicholas closed the double doors behind Anna and Sebastian, then crossed the carpet to the sideboard. As his friends seated themselves near the fire, he poured some Madeira and offered it to the couple before taking up a position at the fireplace in the hope the crackling fire would warm his leg and ease its throbbing.

"What is it you wish to discuss with us, Nicholas?" Sebastian asked with curiosity.

"Vickie has returned." The words resounded like a gunshot in his ears, and Nicholas heard Anna gasp.

"*Good God,*" Sebastian exclaimed. "Did she say where she's been?"

"Actually, she claims she's not Vickie. There's a rather nasty bruise and cut on her forehead, and she says she has no memory of where she's been." Nicholas took a sip of wine, then examined the shape of his glass as if it would provide him with an explanation for his wife's strange behavior.

"But if that's true, how did she know to come here?" Curiosity filled Anna's soft question.

"Precisely." The muscles in Nicholas's cheek twitched as he fought to hide his anger.

"Forgive me, Nicholas, but does she have the capacity for creating such a complex alibi?" Sebastian offered a look of apology to Nicholas.

"I confess it's one of her more elaborate stories. But I don't think she had any help."

Nicholas felt the same frustration Sebastian did. He knew his friend was thinking about Vickie's connection to Jack Reardon and the man's radical politics. The man's recent propaganda had been enough to have alarmed Sir Kenelm, the Home Secretary. Up until Vickie's disappearance, he and Sebastian had been quietly monitoring Reardon's movements at Sir Kenelm's request.

"The fact that Lord Darby is in Reardon's pocket isn't a good thing," Anna said with a look of concern on her face. "If she is involved, it will make things extremely difficult for you, Nicholas."

"Christ, Anna."

Sebastian groaned as Nicholas stared at his friends in amazement. What the hell had the man been thinking to share information with his wife? Anna was trustworthy, but one innocent slip of the tongue to another woman, and the entire Set would know they were watching Reardon, which meant the man would know too.

"I figured it out on my own, Nicholas," Anna said with a shrug. "Sebastian didn't tell me anything. I simply told him what I'd deduced or…imagined."

"In another time, you'd be burned for witchcraft, my love." Sebastian glared at his wife, who smiled serenely back at him, which made his friend's frown grow more stern. "As it is, your…insights, while valuable to me, are not easily explained to others."

Although Nicholas had known about Anna's intuitive ability for some time, this was only the second time he'd witnessed it firsthand. Anna's unique skill gave Sebastian an advantage that no one else possessed, but it was one that was tricky to manage. Nicholas studied the woman for a moment as he considered her observation. Anna was right. If Vickie was involved in any of Reardon's plans, as her husband it would put him in a damned awkward position. He quickly rejected the idea and shrugged as he shook his head.

"Vickie might be rather blind to government politics as opposed to society ones, but anarchy? No, she's vain, thoughtless, and spoiled, but nothing more. I'm certain her only connection to Reardon is Darby."

"You said she has a bruise on her forehead. The fact that she's been missing for so long might mean she was attacked and left to die somewhere. Possibly even held prisoner and escaped."

Sebastian's theory made sense, but he knew his wife well. If anything, Vickie had fallen and was using her injury in one of her manipulative games. What he wanted to know was where she'd been hiding for three weeks. He shook his head as he rejected his friend's hypothesis.

"No, I think Vickie simply wants to play an elaborate game to garner sympathy for herself."

"And what if she's telling the truth?" Anna's quietly spoken question caught him by surprise.

Nicholas frowned as he recalled Vickie's panicked flight from the cottage and her lack of fear with Zeus. The woman he'd married would never have run from him, let alone come close to drowning in an effort to escape. Nor would Vickie have so fearlessly stroked Zeus' head before mounting the stallion. Even despite this unusual behavior, he found it impossible to believe her lies.

"My wife has a talent for lying, and like all her fabrications, this game will end sooner or later," he said with a firm shake of his head.

"Perhaps you should reexamine what you do know." Anna smoothed her skirts in a brisk manner. "The first question to ask is *why* she disappeared. Sebastian said you hired a private investigator when she went missing. Did they offer up any idea as to why she vanished?"

"No. She left Guildford House at dusk, and her maid said Vickie requested a hack as she was having dinner with friends before the Grenville ball."

"How odd." Anna mused in puzzlement.

"What? The hack?" Humiliation made his gut twist as if a knife had stabbed him. "Vickie is fairly discreet when it comes to her romantic liaisons. She'd never do anything to jeopardize her position in society."

"Oh…I didn't…I am sorry, Nicholas." Anna's face took on a pained expression, and Sebastian leaned forward in his chair to squeeze his wife's hand.

Nicholas watched the loving exchange with envy. Such intimacy was out of his reach. Like him, Vickie had no desire for children, but he'd hoped for a marriage of mutual respect and affection. He had no one to blame but himself. His jaw clenched as he swallowed the bitter pill of what lust for a woman and his need for Brentwood Park had brought him.

"As I said, Vickie knows how to be discreet, while still finding a way to make me look a fool. Although, her association with Darby would have gone unnoticed if the damned fool hadn't caused a scene in the Marlborough Club. The Prince was far from pleased with the man's belligerent behavior."

"So you really have no idea why she vanished?" Anna

probed.

"None. I've had plenty of time to consider the possibilities, but nothing seems to fit."

"Well, either she's attempting to play you for a fool or she truly has lost her memory." Anna arched her eyebrows at him. "You could always remind her that as your wife there are certain…duties she must perform. It might help you solve your dilemma."

"The devil take it, Anna," his friend growled softly.

Meeting her husband's disapproving frown with a matter-of-fact expression, Anna didn't flinch beneath the viscount's dark scowl. Her gaze turned back to Nicholas, and he chuckled at her pragmatic expression. He could just imagine what Vickie's response would be to his sudden demand she let him into her bed.

"It's quite all right, Sebastian," he said with a dismissive wave of his hand. "It's no secret my marriage is far from idyllic, and Anna's suggestion is one I've already considered."

The idea of demanding his conjugal rights had been simmering in the back of his mind since Vickie had first started this game. There was little love lost between them, but something deep inside made him reluctant to outline his expectations to her.

Vickie would reject him outright, but if the woman upstairs was telling him the truth, she would reject him as well. It was far from the ideal tactic to use in getting to the heart of the matter. Without warning, his body grew hot at the memory of his wife pressed close to his back as they returned to Brentwood Park.

Desire for his wife. It was a foreign sensation. Lust had always driven him where Vickie was concerned, but today had been different. His reaction to her had been more than just a raw, primal instinct. There had been a connection to her that he couldn't describe. It was a link he didn't know how to break, and the thought scared the hell out of him.

Chapter 5

Victoria sneezed from the heavy, exotic scent that filled the opulent bedroom Jamieson had shown her to. She scrunched up her face in distaste at the personal domain of her double. The Countess of Guildford's room was dark, almost sinister. Maroon drapes blocked out the sunlight, which did nothing to dispel the dark intimidation of the room.

With a grimace, she stood at the foot of the bed, noting how the huge, dark wardrobe and dressing table only added to the room's oppressive atmosphere. One item of furniture served as a misfit in the dark, exotically forbidding room. Delicate and fragile looking, a secretaire stood near the window, a thin ray of light streaking across the desktop. Drawn to the dainty piece of furniture, she circled the desk. Ivory parchment lay on the wood surface as if someone was preparing to write a letter.

Brushing her fingers across the soft sheen of wood, she saw the ink well and the fountain pen with its fine-tipped nib at the top of the secretaire. Curiosity prompted her to pick up the writing instrument. The moment her fingers wrapped around the elegant pen, the dark images she'd seen before swept through her head.

This time she heard voices. Men arguing. The sound of a shovel slicing into dirt was followed by earth sliding off the spade onto a body. Fear made her recoil from the desk as she dropped the pen onto the wood surface.

Blindly, she stumbled her way out of the room. The door

closed behind her with a thud, and she pressed one hand on the wall to steady herself. Her heart pounded loudly in her ears, and she swallowed hard as fear held her muscles tight with tension. She was in the past, and suddenly she'd developed psychic abilities. If she didn't know better, she'd say she was insane. The way things were going, she was closely considering the possibility.

Victoria glanced back at the countess' bedroom door. There was no way in hell she was going back into that room, let alone sleep there. Not even Lord Guildford could make her do that. She'd sleep in the stables first. The sudden jingling of keys made her turn toward the sound. Small in stature, a woman approached, her face pinched with an emotion Victoria recognized as fear.

"Welcome home, my lady." The woman's voice quavered, and she kept her eyes downcast as she halted in front of Victoria. "Did you not find your room in satisfactory condition?"

"Are you Mrs. Beechum?"

"Yes, my lady." The woman eyed her with a timid air of caution. "You don't remember me, my lady?"

"I'm afraid not, Mrs. Beechum, and I have a small problem." Victoria said as she nibbled on her bottom lip for a moment. "I'm afraid I don't like my bedroom."

"My lady?" Mrs. Beechum stared at Victoria in amazement.

"It's a mausoleum in there. I'm not sure how the count…I slept there. It's far too dark and depressing. I was wondering if there was a different bedroom I could use. Something cheerful and bright."

"Of course…my lady. If you like…I can show you the Queen's room." Clearly still bewildered, the housekeeper nodded.

"Any room will be preferable to this one, Mrs. Beechum," Victoria said with a nod toward the countess' bedroom door.

"Yes, my lady."

The housekeeper gave her a strange look before turning around and leading her away from the countess' room. They passed the main staircase and walked the length of the manor to stop at a door almost at the end of the corridor. With her head bowed, the petite woman opened the door and stepped aside so Victoria could enter the room.

Victoria drew in a sharp breath of pleasure as she moved deeper into the room. The sun-filled bedroom was larger than any she'd ever seen. Curtains of the palest yellow tint covered the ceiling-high windows. A lounge sofa at one of the room's windows was angled for maximum usage of light when reading. The bedspread was a lemon-striped pattern that complemented the sofa's pale green upholstery.

Slender bedposts at each corner of the bed stretched upward, their dark wood draped with a delicate white fabric. The fragile looking material drifted downward from the elegant canopy above. To the left of the bed, there were two doors. One in each corner of the room. On the wall opposite the bed was a chifforobe and dressing table.

"The bath is in here, my lady."

The housekeeper crossed the room to the far corner and opened the door. Warily, Victoria followed the woman to peek into the room. A moment later, she breathed a silent sigh of relief. Tap water and a flush toilet. Although the plumbing looked like antiques, at least she wouldn't have to forego *all* modern conveniences. She moved back into the bedroom, and for the first time since her nightmare had begun, a sense of peace enveloped her. There was something familiar and comforting about the room. She looked over her shoulder at the housekeeper and smiled.

"It's perfect, Mrs. Beechum."

"Very well, my lady," the housekeeper murmured, still looking confused.

"I'd like to take a bath, are there towels?"

"They're in the cabinet behind the door, my lady. I'll have Molly run your bath for you."

"That's not necessary, but would it be possible for you to provide me with something different to wear?" Victoria looked down with distaste at the large mud stains covering her dress.

"Of course, my lady. I can have your dresses moved right away."

"Thank you."

"I'm afraid Mrs. Stonner is no longer with us, my lady. Would you like Molly to assist you until you have time to secure the services of another lady's maid?"

For a moment, Victoria almost rejected the offer. She'd been dressing herself since she was a child. The last thing she need was a maid. The memory of Bessie tying up her corset in the back made her rethink her position. Dressing might be more of a problem than she realized.

"I'm sure Molly will be a big help." Victoria nodded. "Thank you."

Victoria eyed the woman with amused empathy as she waited for the housekeeper to lose her dazed expression. The poor woman looked almost as bewildered as Victoria felt. Mrs. Beechum straightened her shoulders as if aware she'd been staring and sent Victoria a timid smile.

"Then if you'll excuse me, my lady, I'll see to everything," Mrs. Beechum said as she bustled out of the room.

When the woman closed the door behind her, Victoria went to the bathroom to run a hot bath. While water slowly filled the claw-foot bathtub, she took a moment to wander about the bedroom, enjoying the sensation of warm wood beneath her fingertips as she caressed pieces of furniture here and there. From the moment she'd entered the room, she'd sensed something special about it. She knew it was impossible, but it was as if she'd been here before. It was a sense of familiarity she couldn't dismiss.

A beautifully made secretaire stood between one of the windows and the fireplace. It was exquisite. Everything she saw was beautiful, the room, the house, the earl. The man was more than beautiful. He was as hot as they came. She froze. That kind of thinking could get her into trouble. The man was married. Married to her, a sly voice in the back of her mind murmured. Her gaze drifted to the large fireplace with its intricate mantle carvings. Moving closer, she ran her hand over the beautiful detail of roses and thorns sculpted into the wood. The carvings wove their way up the sides of the fireplace until they met in the center of the mantle in a bouquet of roses. She'd never seen anything so lovely.

Turning away from the fireplace, she remembered her bath and hurried back to shut off the spigot. She dipped her hand into the water and sighed with pleasure. Perfect. Eager to wash off the dried grime of her earlier ordeal, Victoria reached behind her to undo her dress. It was a struggle to undo the small buttons, and she'd managed to undo the dress almost to the waist when she heard the bedroom door crash open. Startled by the noise, she whirled around to see the earl standing in the bathroom doorway.

"What the hell do you think you're doing?" he snarled. His anger was almost as furious as it had been at the cottage, but this time she wasn't afraid of him.

"Getting ready to take a bath?" she said sarcastically.

"This game of yours has gone far enough, madam. I demand to know why you aren't in your usual bedchamber."

"It's a mausoleum, and I asked Mrs. Beechum for a different room.

"And you selected this room out of all the other bedrooms in the house." The icy pond she'd plunged into earlier could not have felt colder on her skin as the earl pinned his harsh gaze on her. Victoria shook her head in confusion.

"I liked the room. It's warm and cozy. I feel safe here."

"You expect me to believe you had no other reason for selecting this particular room?" Despite his outrage, she saw puzzlement darken his gaze.

"What other reason would I have?"

At her reply, he limped forward and caught her by the arm, then half dragged her out of the bathroom. With a vicious jerk, he opened the door she'd not opened and pointed to the opposite end of the short corridor.

"This hallway, madam, leads to my bedchamber."

His words were ice chips scattering through the air. She shrugged, and one of the sleeves of her gown slipped off her shoulder. Frustrated, she tugged it back into place.

"You're upset because I picked a room that happens to be next to *yours*?"

Arms folded across his chest, the earl remained silent, his expression indicating he expected some sort of explanation from her. Completely at a loss as to what he wanted her to say, Victoria shrugged again. This time she was forced to pull both sleeves back up to her shoulders. She returned his glare, irritated they were arguing about what room she should be sleeping in when she could be soaking in a hot bath.

"What?" she snapped.

Victoria rolled her eyes at him as she waited for the man to explain why he was so upset that she was in the room next to his. Dark eyebrows arched in a disdainful sneer, Nicholas pointedly slashed his gaze toward her bed, then turned back to her and glared at her in derision.

"I have no intention of sleeping in your bed after all the lies between us, madam." His cold declaration made Victoria's mouth fall open before she narrowed her eyes at him.

"Of all the arrogant, egotistical…I didn't have any idea this room was next to yours. Not that I care, because I have *no* intention of sleeping with you either," she snapped as her own anger flared. The man was crazy if he thought she was interested in sleeping with him. In the back of her mind, she heard a cackling laugh. She ignored it.

"Now *this* is the Vickie I'm accustomed to seeing."

Smug satisfaction crossed his face as he mocked her. Infuriated by his condescending tone, Victoria fought back the urge to respond with a scathing retort. If she got angry, she might say something that would get her locked up in that asylum. She whirled around to stalk back to the bathroom, stumbling over the hem of her gown as she did so.

"*Damn it,*" she muttered as she regained her balance. She'd almost reached the bathroom when firm hands caught her arms, and she was tugged backward into a hard chest. Heat swept across her skin like wildfire, then sank through her pores into her blood until it spread through every inch of her. Swallowing the knot about to close her throat, she tried to shake off his grip.

"Let me go," she said, her words clipped as she tugged against his grasp.

"Why, Vickie?" he murmured. The warmth of his breath singed her earlobe. "Perhaps I should take advantage of our close proximity to each other. After all, you *are* my wife."

The caustic remark made her go still. Did he really expect her…with a violent twist of her body, she freed herself from his grasp, tugging the straps of her sleeves back up to her shoulders. Her gaze met his, and heat skimmed over her skin once more as she stared up at him. God help her, the only smoldering looks she'd ever seen were in the movies, but this one outdid all of those. It took her thoughts in a dangerous direction. She gulped, then drew in a deep breath.

"You can wish all you want, but it's not happening, because I'm *not* your wife," she said as a huff of frustration blew past her lips. "And *stop* calling me Vickie."

"What exactly do you propose I call you?" he asked with more than a hint of sarcasm. She ignored his mockery.

"Victoria. It's my name."

"You hate being called Victoria. You think it makes you sound like a dowager countess," he said coolly, but with a distinct note of confusion in his voice.

"What your wife prefers, and what *I* prefer, are two different things. I've *never* liked being called Vickie."

She lifted her chin in defiance, determined to make him use her proper name. She'd hated being called Vickie all her life. It had always made her feel as if she'd done something wrong. Speculation darkened the green eyes studying her before he nodded abruptly.

"Very well. Victoria."

"Thank you," she said. Surprise crossed his face, and she released a soft sniff of disbelief. "Let me guess, your wife never says thank you."

"I don't believe it's in your vocabulary…Victoria," he said with a small smile that hinted he was baffled by her behavior.

The moment he spoke her name, her skin tingled as if she'd just been shocked. There was a seductive quality to the deep timbre of his voice that made her heart race and released butterflies in her stomach. Even his green-eyed gaze made her heart jump in her chest. God help her if he decided to unleash the full force of his good looks and charm on her.

"If thank you isn't in your wife's vocabulary, and I refuse to let you call me Vickie, how much of a leap is it to accept that I'm Victoria Ashton, not your countess?"

"An impossible one." The impassive, unyielding mask had returned to his face. "I admit your performance is quite remarkable, but I doubt I'll ever be convinced your anyone other than my wife."

"What would it take to convince you?"

The quiet sincerity and frustration in her voice seemed to touch a nerve in him. A strange look crossed his face, and he closed the distance between them. Victoria struggled to keep her pulse under control as his quizzical gaze warmed her skin.

With a swift movement, he captured her chin in his strong fingers, his thumb tracing the fullness of her bottom lip. The unexpected caress made her quiver as her heart pounded a fierce rhythm inside her.

"I wonder," he murmured, almost as though speaking his thoughts aloud. Mesmerized by his hooded gaze, anticipation sent a delicious warmth racing through her body. She licked her lips and drew in a quick breath as the earl's head descended toward her mouth.

The instant his lips met hers, a wave of desire swept her out into the depths of a sea she'd never swum in before. Fire blazed its way through her limbs, and she trembled with an unexpected need.

Base instinct took control as she returned his kiss, her tongue teasing his lips apart until it danced with his. The growl reverberating in his chest sent a frisson tingling through her as she pressed her body into his. God, her knees were actually rubbery from his kiss. None of the other men she'd dated had ever made her feel wobbly like this.

Warm hands pushed the sleeves of her gown downward until she heard a soft ripping sound. The sleeves fell away from her arms, and the gown's bodice fell to her waist. A low moan rose in her throat as his hand caressed the top of one shoulder before he wrapped his arms around her to pull her tight against him. Their kiss deepened as his tongue mated with hers in a furious dance of desire.

Victoria murmured a protest as his lips slid away from hers to glide down the side of her neck to her shoulder. Lost in the fire of his touch, she didn't realize he'd undone the laces of her corset until his mouth caught the tip of her breast in his mouth. She shuddered as he sucked on her nipple, then gently bit down on it before swirling his tongue around the hard peak until her skin was hot.

An ache latched itself to her insides, and she realized she was wet between her thighs. The heat melting through her tugged another moan from her, and her hands slid through the black thickness of his hair. Oh God, she wanted him. She wanted him now. On the floor, on the bed, she didn't care, as long as he eased the intense longing clutching the lower half of her body.

He'd not changed out of his riding clothes, and her hand slid downward across his chest to his erection. It was hard and thick beneath his breeches. A dark rumble sounded in his throat as she stroked him through the fawn-colored material. Trembling with a frightening need for him, Victoria uttered a soft cry as a shudder rippled through her, and she recognized it for the small climax it was.

If the man could make her have an orgasm with only a kiss, heaven help her when he actually entered her. Lost in the heated pleasure of the moment, she vaguely heard the knock at the door. The knock sounded again, and with a sharp movement, Nicholas released her. Quickly stepping away from her, he tugged her corset and dress up before he issued an authoritative command to enter. As a young woman entered the room, Nicholas was already heading toward the connecting door between their room.

"Molly, see to it that the countess is downstairs in the salon within the hour," he ordered brusquely over his shoulder, then disappeared from the room.

Denied what her body craved, Victoria experienced a powerful wave of disappointment. She immediately drew in a swift breath as she realized what had almost happened. Simply because everyone thought they were married didn't make it right. The real countess could return at any moment. Sharp and abrupt, a dark certainty swept through her. The Countess of Guildford wasn't coming back because the woman was dead. Victoria didn't know how she knew it, but her body reacted to the knowledge with a violent wave of nausea.

Ice coated her skin, and she fell forward into a dark pit. The hard ground rose to meet her as she stared up into a dark abyss. Tiny pinpricks of light pierced the darkness, and she realized they were stars. Dark forms suddenly blocked out the star-filled sky. The insidious sound of a shovel slicing into dirt with a sharp scraping sound echoed loudly in her ears before dirt landed on top of her.

Fear slithered through her veins as her body remained stiff and unmoving no matter how hard she tried to take control of her limbs. More dirt splattered across her face. Desperately, she struggled to breathe as the earth clogged her nose and mouth. Fire filled her lungs, while the rest of her body was cold as ice.

She wanted to sob from the pain, but couldn't. Suddenly, the pain disappeared as a white mist surrounded her. A peaceful quiet filled the fog and soothed her. Voices echoed from a distance, and a whisper she'd heard once before filled her ears.

"Fight, Victoria. Come back to me. Come back to me now."

She knew she should recognize the man's voice, but she couldn't remember how or why. She took a step toward the roughly spoken sound, when the mist blew away as swiftly as it had come. Victoria took a breath and shuddered as fresh air filled her lungs. Strong arms held her steady, and she blinked several times until her gaze focused on the Nicholas's worried expression. She was at Brentwood Park.

"Nicholas?" she murmured.

"It's all right," he said in a gentle voice. "You fainted and managed to give Molly quite a scare."

"Fainted?"

Victoria shook her head slightly, thinking it might throw off the dizziness still making her feel off balance. His fingers lightly brushed her forehead, and a sensation pierced her disoriented state. The rock hard strength of Nicholas's arms around her. It was a strong and protective embrace, and she'd never felt so safe.

"My lord, shall I call for the physician?"

The young woman who'd entered the room earlier stepped into view, and the fearful apprehension on the maid's face made Victoria shake her head quickly.

"*No.* No, doctors."

"You're clearly unwell, Victoria." A dark frown creased his forehead, giving him the appearance of a dark angel, but she wasn't frightened. It was the look of a man intent on protecting her.

"I fainted. I'm sure it's from hunger. I don't remember the last time I ate." Victoria stared up at him with a silent plea not to call a physician. He studied her for a long moment before he nodded.

"No doctors," he said. "But if this happens again, I *will* call Dr. Bertram."

"Thank you." Her response caused his eyebrows to arch.

"Three times in one day," he said quietly. His puzzlement said he was struggling with his conviction as to her identity. "Molly, help the countess with her bath and arrange for a meal to be brought up. As for you madam wife, you're to spend the rest of the evening in bed."

"But—"

"No arguments, Victoria."

The inflexible set to his features made her frown, but she remained silent. When she was capable of standing on her own, he released her from his embrace. The moment her body was deprived of his heat, she wanted to throw herself back into his arms again. She swallowed hard as he retreated for a second time to the corridor connecting their rooms. Once again his departure left her feeling bereft, but this time she didn't want to try and determine the depth of the sensation.

Chapter 6

Present Day

The hospital room was quiet except for the steady beep of a heart monitor as Nick stared at the woman in the bed. Nothing made sense to him anymore. One minute he'd been arguing with Nora about a portrait he'd been unable to part with since he was a teenager, and in the next he'd seen that portrait come to life in the gallery. Out of the corner of his eye, he caught the movement of the door opening. He'd expected the nurse and was surprised to see his sister walk into the room. With a quick glance at his watch, he realized it was eight in the morning.

"Hi," Nora said softly. "How is she?"

"The same."

"I brought you a change of clothes since you were so damn determined to spend the night." Nora held up an overnight bag, and he nodded.

"Thanks," he said quietly.

"You look like crap. When was the last time you had something to eat?"

"I'm not hungry," Nick muttered as he shoved his hand through his hair.

"Did you get any sleep?"

"Enough." He didn't bother to point out it had been impossible to sleep.

"Damn it, Nick, you can't stay glued to this woman's side day and night. It's crazy." Nora glared at him with sisterly concern.

"I'm not leaving her."

"Well, for God's sakes, take the time to visit the cafeteria. If you insist on staying here, you at least need to eat."

"When I get hungry, I'll go down and get a sandwich. Will that satisfy you?"

"For now, but I'm more concerned as to why you feel the need to stay with her twenty-four seven."

Nick heard the troubled note in his sister's voice, but ignored it. He shifted his gaze to the hospital bed, and the woman attached to an IV and two different monitors. He'd never been a believer in fate, but the last twenty-four hours were making him wonder about a lot of things. The one thing he knew without doubt or reservation was that it was impossible to leave Victoria's side. *She's everything to me. My life. My world. Without her, life has no meaning.*

The sound of Nora's gasp made him jerk his gaze back to his sister, and the look on her face made him realize he'd spoken his thoughts out loud. He stood up with an abrupt motion, rubbing the back of his neck as he tried to think of a way to explain his strange behavior to Nora. Even for all his sister's beliefs in the occult, he wasn't sure he could explain everything he was feeling. He walked to the side of Victoria's bed and lightly caressed her wrist just above the gauze that protected the burn on her hand.

"I think it's time we had a heart to heart," his sister said firmly.

"I don't need you trying to get into my head, Nora." He shot a warning look over his shoulder at her. "Nothing's going to change the way I feel."

"And what about Victoria?" Nora bobbed her head in the direction of Victoria's still form. "What are you going to do if she wakes up and doesn't feel the same way?"

"She will," he uttered the words with a fierce conviction he didn't understand but believed with a certainty that stunned him.

He looked down at Victoria and her pale features. Gently, he brushed a strand of auburn hair off her cheek. She looked as though she were sleeping and would wake up at any moment. It was precisely why he *wasn't* going to leave her. He wanted to be here when she woke up, and no matter what Dr. Bertram or any of the other doctors said, Victoria *was* going to wake up.

"What makes you so sure she's going to feel the same way you do?"

"If I knew that, don't you think I'd tell you?" He closed his eyes for a moment, then faced his sister. "Nora, with the exception of that portrait in my office, you *know* I'm the most practical, logical man you'd ever hope to meet."

"Are you telling me that's changed?"

"I don't know." Nick shoved his hands into his pants pockets and shrugged. "The only thing I'm sure of is that I've spent most of the night trying to figure out what the hell is happening to me."

"Could you be feeling guilty?" Nora asked softly.

"Guilt?" He frowned. "You mean because I wasn't hurt and Victoria was?"

"Yes." His sister nodded and watched him with that assessing gaze of hers.

"No," he said with a soft grunt. "I've already considered that. This isn't guilt."

Nick moved to stare out the hospital window, his brain vaguely noting how the morning sun illuminated the hospital garden below. Memories of yesterday afternoon flooded his head. The first moment when he'd seen Victoria in the shop. The explosive sound of the blast. The sight of Victoria's agony as electricity lashed through her body. The way she'd collapsed like a rag doll against the wall. But it was the *knowing* he'd lost her somewhere in the distant past that confused him the most. He was finding it almost impossible to reconcile what happened yesterday with the logical order of his daily life.

A low moan from the hospital bed jerked Nick's attention away from the window as the monitor started beeping madly. In three strides, he was at Victoria's side. Gently, he wrapped his hand around her wrist and brushed his fingers gently across her forehead.

"Victoria. Can you hear me? Victoria."

"No. Not. Vickie." Her words were barely distinguishable, and Nick leaned closer in hopes she would say something else.

"*Fight, Victoria. Come back to me,*" he rasped urgently. "Come back to me now, my sweet witch."

The door to the hospital room burst open as two nurses charged into the room. As they checked Victoria's still motionless body and reviewed the monitors, the equipment alarms shut off abruptly. Once more, the steady beep the monitors had maintained throughout the night filled the room. Victoria didn't make another sound, and Nick lowered his head to kiss her forehead.

One of the nurses gently pushed him out of the way so she could examine Victoria's responses. When she'd finished, the nurse looked at her colleague and shook her head. Fear sliced through him. What if he was wrong? What if Victoria never woke up from this coma? He pummeled the defeatist thought into submission. He wasn't wrong. She would wake up. A few moments later, the nurses left the room, and Nick moved back to Victoria's side.

Silently, he urged her to hear him. Urged her to come back to him. Nick grew still as he remembered what he'd murmured to her. *Sweet witch?* It was too specific an endearment for him to simply brush aside, and it only increased his confusion as to what was happening to him.

"*Sweet witch?* Not sweetheart? Where in the hell did you

come up with that one?" Nora asked with bemused curiosity.

"I don't know," he bit out in a tight voice as he looked over his shoulder at her. "It just came out."

"Right," she said softly with a look of skepticism.

"Let it be, Nora." He turned his head to stare down at Victoria again, his hands gripping the metal side bar of the bed. "I'm dealing with enough right now as it is."

"I have no doubt of that." Sympathy filled Nora's voice as she moved forward and rubbed her hand on his back before she went up on tiptoe and kissed his cheek. "I need to get to the shop and deal with the cleanup and the insurance people."

Nick nodded his head as she walked toward the door. Not once had his sister even suggested he should be at the shop and not the hospital. Somehow, like his uncle, she understood he needed to be here.

"Anna, thank you."

"What did you call me?" Nora asked as she whirled around to face him. There was an odd expression on her face, and he shook his head.

"What?"

"You called me, Anna."

"No, I didn't," he said with a frown as he struggled to grasp the fact that Nora might be correct. He was so damned tired he couldn't remember much of anything at the moment. He pinched the bridge of his nose with his fingers. "If I did, I'm sorry. I'm tired. One of the nurses must be called Anna."

"I'll see you later," his sister murmured. "If you're going to insist on staying here, open up that recliner and try to get some sleep."

Nick met his sister's penetrating look. She smiled slightly then walked out of the room, leaving him to contemplate the fact that he'd used an unusual endearment with Victoria, and in all likelihood he'd called his sister by another name. He slowly returned to the recliner, trying desperately to understand what was happening to him. As he sank down into the vinyl-covered chair and closed his eyes, Nick knew he was stumbling across a landscape he'd always brushed aside as being unrealistic. Now, he was no longer certain of anything, except the fact that the only thing in his life that mattered was Victoria.

Chapter 7

October 1897

"Fuck," Nicholas muttered as he limped through the connecting corridor that ran between his room and Vickie—no, Victoria's. She'd been vehemently insistent that he call her Victoria. He liked the sound of it. Instantly, his brain shouted at him for being a fool to be taken in by the woman's performance.

An almost flawless one. His wife had always excelled at small dramas, but this…this was something so beyond the bounds of anything she'd ever done. Nicholas threw open his bedroom door, then slammed it behind him.

Frustrated, he rubbed the back of his neck as he glared at the closed door. The vulnerability she'd displayed only a moment ago had shaken him more than he cared to admit. He'd told her she'd fainted, but that was a half-truth. Her shallow breathing had become almost non-existent as he'd taken Victoria's limp form from Molly's shaky grasp. Not even his light pats to her cheeks had stirred her out of her almost death-like state.

Perhaps the most disturbing thing of all was the way her face had contorted with pain as she'd regained consciousness and taken that deep breath of air into her lungs. At that moment, he'd come close to believing she really wasn't his wife, and the fear she might die in his arms had filled him with emotions he didn't understand.

Nicholas didn't know what was worse, thinking Victoria was on the verge of dying or the fact that he'd been ready to bed her before he'd left her room the first time. He'd not been that hard for a woman in a long time. Not even when courting his wife had he been consumed with so much lust. And she had wanted him as much as he'd desired her. Vickie would never have caressed his cock the way Victoria had. If Molly hadn't knocked on the door when she had, he didn't think he could have stopped himself from bedding her.

"Damn her."

Nicholas limped his way to the window overlooking Brentwood Park's ornamental gardens. Vickie's behavior had always been easy to predict. However, this new personality of hers was one he'd never seen before. Victoria. The name suited her changed behavior. Was it possible she was telling him the truth?

"You're a bloody fool, Guildford." He snorted with disgust. "This is your wife. The woman who's done nothing but humiliate you since the day you married her."

Humiliation. His hand gripped the window's drapery in a tight fist. He'd suffered more than his fair share of degradation over the past three weeks. First, there had been the frantic search when Vickie failed to arrive at Grenville's ball. Then the suspicious looks, the police investigation, and the rumors. Not willing to rely solely on the police, he'd hired his own investigators.

It wasn't until Darby had drunkenly confronted Nicholas at the club and accused him of murder that things had taken a turn for the worse. The moment Scotland Yard had knocked on his door, he'd not only been humiliated further—he'd begun to worry what would happen if Vickie didn't return. The snap of the wooden curtain rod penetrated his thoughts as the dark green drapes collapsed on his head, forcing him to fight his way out from under the heavy expanse of material.

"Damn it to hell."

"My lord, I'm aware you're not fond of frivolity, but the curtains protect the carpets from the sunlight," his valet said in a wry tone as he entered Nicholas's bed chamber.

Small in stature, Gerald Roberts moved quickly to Nicholas's side to help him escape the weight of the drapery. The manservant efficiently folded the drapes up into a tidy bundle and set them on the bed before picking up the broken curtain rod and leaning the pieces against the wall.

"I'll have Mrs. Beechum arrange for repairs to be made tomorrow."

"Thank you," Nicholas grunted. Roberts had been with him for years and their relationship was more of a friendship than employer and servant. He owed his life to the valet.

"I understand her ladyship has returned." The valet moved to the wardrobe to pull out Nicholas's evening clothes. "I'm certain you're relieved she's returned safe and sound."

"Relieved that I'll keep my neck is what you really mean." He eyed the older man with a sardonic twist of his lips as he watched the valet prepare the shaving cream to remove Nicholas's afternoon shadow. The valet nodded toward a nearby chair.

"That too." Roberts chuckled as Nicholas limped forward and sank into the chair. The valet frowned at him. "Your leg is bothering you more than usual, my lord."

"It's nothing," he said with a wave of his hand.

"You forget how well I know you, my lord." Roberts covered Nicholas's face with one of the hot wet towels he'd brought with him to the room. "I've heard you exercised it quite a bit at Goodman Cottage this morning."

Nicholas tugged the towel off his face and glared up at the valet. Clearly unrepentant for his observation or the fact that he'd been listening to gossip about what had happened at the cottage, Roberts met Nicholas's gaze with a look of chastisement. With a noise of disgust, Nicholas covered his face again with the warm towel.

"I might have strained the leg a bit more than usual," he mumbled through the towel.

"I'll prepare some liniment for you to use before you retire, my lord."

Nicholas grunted his appreciation while experiencing a sense of guilt. He would have gladly sacrificed his leg ten years ago if it would have changed things. Roberts pulled the towel off Nicholas's face and lathered his skin with shaving cream.

"Her ladyship's return has caused quite a stir in the household." Roberts set the shaving cream aside to sharpen a razor blade on a leather strap. "Mrs. Beechum was amazed at Lady Guildford's pleasant manner and other remarkable changes."

"Am I to interpret that to mean Mrs. Beechum's astonishment at her ladyship's request to occupy the room next door?" Nicholas narrowed his gaze at the manservant.

"I believe it was her ladyship's apparent distaste for the room she normally occupies that surprised Mrs. Beechum more, my lord. Even Jamieson expressed a modicum of surprise at her ladyship's polite manner."

"*Good God,*" Nicholas exclaimed softly. "Jamieson? The man is unflappable."

"Indeed, my lord. Apparently, he was quite startled by the sight of her ladyship dismounting from Zeus, and her lack of fear."

"Jamieson's correct. Her ladyship showed no sign of the terror she normally exhibits around horses."

Nicholas frowned as he remembered Victoria had shown no fear of Zeus and even *asked* for a horse to ride. The only thing that seemed to terrify her was the day's date. When he'd told her the year, the color had drained from her face until she was paler than when he'd pulled her from the icy pond. Seconds later, he'd set her down and watched as she retched in the snow. While it was possible she was carrying Darby's child, instinct told him she wasn't. What troubled him more was the terror and hopelessness reflected in her blue eyes when she'd clearly recognized the cottage.

"Perhaps it has something to do with her head injury," Roberts said as he worked swiftly to shave Nicholas's face.

"Possibly," he murmured. From the look of her injury, she'd clearly taken a severe blow to the head. Was it possible her wound accounted for her new behavior? "However, I'll be interested to hear your impressions once you're reacquainted with the mistress of the manor, Roberts."

"I shall be happy to give a full report when I do, my lord."

"And do you expect to find the lady as changed as the rest of my staff do?"

"While I confess to curiosity about her ladyship's behavior, I believe we both know my presence has always made the lady in question most uncomfortable."

"You mean rude," Nicholas snapped. "My wife has always been a self-centered woman who's cared little for anyone except her own comforts."

"Which will make it all the more interesting when I come face-to-face with her ladyship."

Roberts smiled as he lightly scraped shaving cream off the side of Nicholas's face with the straight razor. There was a mischievous sparkle in the older man's eye, and Nicholas snorted with soft amusement. If there was any sure way to prove Victoria's story was false, it was simply to put her in the same room with Roberts. Vickie had always been visibly uncomfortable in the presence of his valet.

Nicholas's gaze fell on the disfiguring scars covering one side of Robert's face. Scars the man had earned saving Nicholas from the fire at his paper mill in Lydney shortly after he became the earl. He frowned as he remembered how shortly after their wedding Vickie had insisted he dismiss Roberts simply because she couldn't bear to look at the man.

It was something he'd never do. Roberts had saved his life, and for that the man would always have Nicholas's loyalty and affection.

More than an hour later, Nicholas headed downstairs. As he passed Victoria's bedroom, his stride slowed a fraction as he envisioned her in bed with her auburn hair spread out on her pillow. Infuriated with the direction of his thoughts, he uttered a small oath of self-loathing and pushed the image from his mind.

This weekend was supposed to have been nothing more than a quiet visit to the country with Anna and Sebastian for company. He'd simply wanted a reprieve from the gossip and unexpected visits from Scotland Yard. That plan had crumbled into disarray the moment Eleanor overheard him discussing the weekend with Anna. The duchess had seized the moment to enlarge the party, and before he'd realized what was happening, Eleanor had arranged everything.

He was fortunate the gossip columns hadn't learned of the house party. They would have had him swinging from the garrote for entertaining while his wife was missing. At least that problem had resolved itself, despite Victoria's unusual return and preposterous tale. Now the only problem to solve was Eleanor Legette, Duchess du Chatelaine.

The woman had been pursuing him for months. He should have discouraged her from the start, but she'd proven amusing company. Still, he had no excuse for allowing her to invite herself, the Palmertons, and Charles to Brentwood Park this weekend. He wasn't an imbecile. He should have ended the weekend before it even began.

Even if he'd *wanted* to make the woman his mistress, he wouldn't. His wife might not honor her vows, but his honor meant a great deal to him. Liaisons presented a number of dangers. The most treacherous of which was the possibility of a bastard. The thought of siring an heir to his title was horrifying enough. In that respect, Vicki's liaisons saved him from sharing her bed.

As he reached the foot of the stairs, he heard laughter echoing out of the salon. Nicholas entered the room to see Catherine Dewhurst, Viscountess Palmerton sitting on the loveseat with Anna, while Charles Barrows, Sebastian, and Catherine's husband, John, were pouring drinks at the liquor cabinet. Eleanor's absence wasn't surprising as the woman was always late.

"Nicholas, you're here," Anna exclaimed as she smiled at him. "We were just discussing Vickie's return."

"Victoria." The automatic response earned him a raised eyebrow from Anna, but his best friend's wife didn't question him.

"Anna and Sebastian told us that Vickie showed up out of the blue this morning," Charles said with amazement.

"One of the farm tenants found Victoria unconscious outside their cottage." Nicholas nodded as he crossed the floor to the liquor cart and poured himself a brandy.

"Damned peculiar," Charles said as he shook his head in disbelief.

"Since when did you decide to call her Victoria?" Sebastian asked quietly as he took a drink of brandy.

"When she asked me too." Nicholas shrugged. Exactly what had prompted him to do as she asked?

"Why on earth would she ask you to call her, Victoria?" Charles snorted disparagingly.

"She says she's hated the name Vickie since she was a child." Nicholas frowned and shook his head.

"It's just damned peculiar, that's all," Charles muttered.

Sebastian nodded his head as he took a drink of brandy.

"I'm afraid I agree with Charles," Sebastian murmured quietly. "Tread lightly Nicholas. Whatever she's up to, I have no doubt it will not be in your favor."

"I'm sure you're right, but I took Anna's advice, and—"

"Nicholas, you wound me to the quick, *mon cher*. Do you not value my counsel as well?"

Eleanor's small cry of disappointment forced its way into the conversation, and Nicholas turned to face the petite woman standing in the salon doorway. The woman's petulant look annoyed him, but it was his comparison of the hard calculation in Eleanor's blue gaze to a warm sapphire one that irritated him more. He didn't like making comparisons where Victoria was concerned.

"Anna offered her advice before you arrived. It was sound counsel from a trusted and loyal friend." Nicholas almost regretted his chilly reply as Eleanor flinched as if he'd hit her. A split second later, she'd regained her composure.

"Forgive me *mon cher*, of course, you should value the advice of your friends. I was simply expressing the hope that you hold my friendship in similar regard." She crossed the room and laid a hand on his arm.

Not about to give the woman any hope, he offered her a brief smile then turned to pour her a glass of Madeira. As if aware he was in a dark mood, Eleanor crossed the floor to take a seat opposite Anna and Catherine. As she accepted her glass, the duchess glanced around the room.

"You really should do something different with this room, Nicholas," she said with open disdain. "The décor is…"

The color suddenly drained from Eleanor's face and shock flashed across her pale features, followed by a look of such intense fear that it contorted her lovely face into something ugly. Instantly, Nicholas leaned toward her in concern. Just as quickly as the horror had appeared on Eleanor's face, a mask of polite interest covered her features.

Curious as to the reason for Eleanor's reaction, Nicholas turned his head to see Victoria standing in the salon doorway. The desire he'd experienced earlier returned with the strength of a raging storm. He wasn't sure what made him angrier, her defiance of his order to stay in bed or his inability to control the need burning its way through his limbs. Nicholas quickly moved toward her, ignoring the twinge of pain that shot through his leg.

"I told you to stay in bed," he whispered roughly. She looked up at him and smiled. The warmth in her eyes made a knot form in his throat.

"I wasn't sleepy. Besides, as I recall, you expect me to make a scene. I'd hate to disappoint you." The amusement in her quiet retort made him want to throttle her and laugh at the same time. The realization startled him. Nicholas grasped her arm and pulled her deeper into the room.

"I believe you've met everyone here, except for Eleanor." He guided Victoria forward to where Eleanor sat. "Victoria, may I present Eleanor Legette, Duchess du Chatelaine. Eleanor, my wife, the Countess of Guildford."

"Hello," Victoria said as she extended her hand to Eleanor. With an imperious nod of her head, the duchess ignored Victoria's outstretched hand.

"Lady Guildford." It was an obvious effort on Eleanor's part to gain the upper hand in terms of pecking order. "Forgive me, Nicholas, but wasn't your wife thought to be dead."

"I'm sure he wishes I was at the moment," Victoria murmured, and he glared in her direction.

Her mischievous smile caught him off guard, and he realized she was completely unperturbed by Eleanor's haughty manner. The woman he'd married would never have allowed Eleanor's behavior to go unremarked upon. What kind of game was she playing? The sound of violent coughing made Nicholas look in Anna's direction. The sight of his friend struggling not to laugh made him realize she'd overheard Victoria's blithe comment. He glared at first Anna and then Victoria, only to have both women return his glare with unrepentant looks before he turned back to Eleanor.

"As you can see for yourself, Victoria is alive and well."

"So it would seem," the duchess snapped, but the fear he'd seen earlier flickered in her cold blue eyes once more.

"Nicholas has told us you've lost your memory," Anna said as she stood up to face Victoria. "I take it you don't recognize me?"

"No, I'm afraid I don't." Victoria shook her head.

"I'm Anna Reddington, the Viscountess Starling," she said as she offered her hand to Victoria.

As the two women shook hands, Anna paled and a brief flash of shock swept over her face. Unless one knew Anna well, it was impossible to detect that shaking Victoria's hand had upset her. But he'd known Sebastian's wife for a long time, and Anna was struggling to control her surprise. Anna's gaze moved from Victoria's face to her husband's. Silent exchanges weren't unusual between the couple, but this was different.

It was almost as if Anna were signaling her husband for help. Out of the corner of his eye, he saw Sebastian moving quickly to his wife's side. Despite her disconcerted state, Anna smiled at Victoria. Her hand reached up to touch her husband's hand as it settled on her shoulder.

"And this handsome devil is my husband, Sebastian."

"Hello," Victoria offered her hand to Sebastian who bowed and kissed the back of her hand. Clearly surprised, a warm flush of color rose in her cheeks as she quickly pulled her hand free of Sebastian's. If he didn't know better, he would have thought Victoria was unaccustomed to the polite gesture of greeting.

"It must be extremely unsettling for you not having any memory of the past," Anna said with a soft note of curiosity in her voice.

"Frightening is a better word." Victoria's expression grew somber as she bit her lip in a display of distress. Suddenly her face lightened, and a smile curved her lips. "Although I think my reputation for having a very unpleasant personality is much more intimidating."

Anna laughed at Victoria's confession, and Nicholas saw Sebastian raise his eyebrows before a smile curved his lips. *Damnation*, the woman was determined to charm everyone she met. God help him if she decided to entice him into her seductive spider web. A part of him acknowledged that he'd already had one foot in that web. With a small sweep of her hand, Anna took charge of making the rest of the introductions.

"How terrible for you," Catherine exclaimed as she shook Victoria's hand. "Do you mean to say you don't remember where you've been these past three weeks?"

"Actually I don't remember anything before waking up in the cottage."

"I'd venture to say that bruise you have has a great deal to do with your memory loss," the Viscount Palmerton stated pragmatically as he nodded toward Victoria's head. John frowned as he studied her head. "Quite a nasty bump you have there."

Victoria reached up to touch the large bruise and cut on her forehead, and Nicholas quickly caught her hand to stop her from touching the wound. She jerked her gaze toward him and smiled as if understanding he was preventing her from doing further damage to her injury. Something tightened in his gut as he wondered if her changed behavior was related to the blow she'd taken to her head.

All her lies in the past made him unwilling to believe anything she'd said. Instead, he'd simply judged her and condemned her in one fell swoop. What if he was wrong? Nicholas almost snorted at the direction of his thoughts. His wife was simply a skilled actress, and he refused to be taken in by her exceptional performance.

Still, it was impossible not to admire the way she calmly fielded the multitude of questions from his friends. Unexpected concern flooded him as one of Charles' questions made her flinch. The sudden urge to protect her made him clear his throat and waved his hand in a peremptory fashion.

"I think we should forego any further inquiries for the moment so as not to overtire Victoria."

"Really, Nicholas, you're treating your wife as if she were a fragile piece of china, which we all know she isn't. I'm sure Lady Guildford is far more resilient than you think, *mon cher.*"

Eleanor's voice rang out in the room as the cacophony of questioning voices ebbed away. The mockery in the duchess' voice set Nicholas on edge. Whether or not Victoria was telling the truth, she did not deserve to be insulted in her own home. Before he could say a word, a hand touched his arm. Startled, he looked down to see Victoria shake her head.

"I've never been much for titles, Eleanor, so please call me Victoria." There was no rancor or sarcasm in her smile as she met the duchess' imperious gaze. "And you're right. I *am* far more resilient than Nicholas will admit. But, I'm grateful for his concern. I'm surprised he's able to tolerate me at all, considering my terrible reputation."

Hate and fear filled the venomous look Eleanor cast in Victoria's direction. He was just about to put himself between the two women when Jamieson appeared in the salon doorway and announced dinner. Everyone looked to Victoria, but she simply stared back in confusion. Anna smiled.

"It's customary for the hostess to direct which gentleman escorts which lady into dinner, my dear."

"Oh." Victoria's blank look made Nicholas take pity on her.

"Charles, will you take Eleanor into supper? Sebastian, if you'll escort Catherine, John can escort Victoria, and I'll accompany Anna," he said. His direction did not make Eleanor happy, but at the moment he didn't give a damn. With Anna on his arm, they walked toward the doorway.

"I like her, Nicholas," his friend murmured. That Anna would say such a thing amazed him. There had never been any love lost between the Vickie and his friends.

"It's an act."

"If you mean her skill at hiding how terrified she is, then yes, it's an extraordinary performance."

"The only fear my wife has ever shown has been where horses are concerned."

"You misjudge her, Nicholas," Anna said firmly. "She is who she says she is."

"What the devil is that supposed to mean?"

"You know precisely what it means." Anna met his gaze and eyed him as sternly as a nanny might a child in her charge. "I know Sebastian has told you about…my ability to determine the worth of a person with just a handshake."

"Are you trying to tell me—"

"I'm telling you that the woman I shook hands with is *not* Vickie."

The emphatic note in Anna's voice made Nicholas's jaw go rigid. Although he'd always been skeptical of his friend's intuitive manner, he couldn't remember a time when she'd been wrong. A voice in the back of his head reminded him that there was always a first time.

Throughout the evening meal, Eleanor's flirtations slowly became tedious. Even more annoying was the amusement on Victoria's face whenever he glanced in her direction. He was certain she knew Eleanor's behavior annoyed him, and he didn't enjoy the fact that she was aware of his discomfort.

"If you continue to frown like that Nicholas, your forehead is apt to stay wrinkled." Seated to his right at the dinner table, Anna's light-hearted words made him smile.

"I didn't realize I was frowning."

"Obviously. It must be a very serious matter you're considering."

"Not so serious that I should neglect my duties as host."

"Then tell us what excitement you have planned for us tomorrow?" Still smiling, Anna took a helping of fresh vegetables from the platter a servant held in front of her. Seated on the opposite side of the table, Viscountess Palmerton set her wine glass down.

"Yes, Nicholas, are we to ride in the morning as we usually do? You always have the best mounts of anyone we know."

"Yes," he said with a nod in Catherine's direction. "I bought several new horses at Tattersall's last month. I've been told they've settled in quite nicely."

"And will you join us, Lady Guildford?" Smiling like a well-fed cat, Eleanor looked in Victoria's direction. His wife's loathing of horses was a fairly well-known fact among the Set, and Eleanor's question caught the attention of everyone at the table. Silence filled the air until Nicholas smiled and lifted his wineglass in a mocking toast to his wife.

"Victoria is *not* an avid rider, are you my dear?" A streak of devilish satisfaction flashed through him as he met Victoria's eyes over the rim of his glass. "However, should my wife decide to join us, I'll have one of the *older*, more reliable, horses saddled for her."

Victoria's intense glare of irritation made his mouth twitch with amusement. She might have managed to act her way through that ride on Zeus, but anything beyond that wasn't possible. Deep in the back of his head, he heard mocking laughter and forced himself to ignore it. Victoria's gaze never left his, and he waited patiently to see how she'd extricate herself from the morning ride so that he'd be able to expose her charade.

"The answer to your question, Eleanor, is yes. I'll be

riding tomorrow." Victoria's quiet response made Nicholas stiffen as he slowly set his glass back on the table. What the devil did the woman think she was doing?

"I was under the impression that you do not ride, Lady Guildford," Eleanor said with a disagreeable frown.

"Then you've been misinformed." Victoria smiled defiantly.

Silence reigned for several awkward seconds before the conversation resumed. When they'd finished dinner, they returned to the salon. For Nicholas, the evening dragged on interminably, with Eleanor continuing with her attempts to provoke Victoria. To his continuous amazement, Victoria seemed oblivious to the duchess' barbs as she quietly listened to Anna and Catherine's conversation.

Victoria was the first to excuse herself for the evening, which he found extraordinary. His wife never retired early, particularly if there was another woman in the room whom she viewed as competition. Nicholas frowned as he caught a glimpse of the weariness she was hiding from the others. She had the look of someone exhausted from shock. Perhaps he'd been harder on her today than he should have been. He stopped her as she headed toward the door. She winced as she met his gaze.

"Is your head still bothering you?" he murmured.

"A little, but I'll manage." The weak smile touching her lips aroused his protective instincts. It was a strange sensation to have where his wife was concerned, and he wasn't sure he liked the feeling.

"Do you wish me to escort you upstairs?"

"No," she said with a soft laugh. "I'm not the helpless female your duchess is."

"She's *not* my duchess." He eyed her coldly, and she blinked at him in obvious surprise at his brusque response.

"Well, you'd better tell *her* that," Victoria said without malice or sarcasm as she chuckled. "The woman is definitely on the prowl, and whether you like it or not, you're her next meal."

With a mischievous smile, she walked around him and left the room. As he stared after her, he heard Eleanor's plaintive call for him to join her at the card table. Slowly he turned and rejoined his friends with Victoria's words ringing in his ears. She seemed completely unconcerned that he might be engaged in a liaison with Eleanor. The realization confused him. And he didn't like being confused about anything.

Chapter 8

One by one, his guests retired for the night until he and Eleanor were the only ones left in the salon. Their card game was almost finished, and he was eager to be done with her company. She laid a card down in the middle of the table, and Nicholas took the winning trick with a careless gesture. He didn't bother to gather the cards to shuffle them, and Eleanor rose gracefully from her chair to stand at his side.

"You look so troubled, *mon cher*, tell me what's wrong." Her fingers lightly stroked his forehead. Nicholas caught her narrow wrist and pushed her hand away. Rising to his feet, he crossed the floor to the liquor cart to pour a small amount of brandy into his snifter.

"While I appreciate your concern, Eleanor, I don't need the kind of comfort I think you are suggesting."

"Surely you can't mean that," she said in a voice that held the assurance of a woman determined to find her way into a man's bed.

"I do, Eleanor, and I'm not interested in furthering our friendship beyond its current boundaries."

"But we would be so good together, Nicholas," she exclaimed softly. "You know we would."

"No, I don't think we would suit each other at all," he mused as he studied his brandy for a second before taking a drink of the smooth liquor.

"How can I make you believe me, Nicholas? I could

make you happy."

The pleading expression softening her features emphasized the heartfelt emotion threading through her words. Caught off-guard, he stared at her for a long moment. Was it possible Eleanor truly cared for him? If so, then he'd done her a disservice by not having this conversation with her sooner.

"I have no interest in taking a mistress, Eleanor. I'm a married—"

"How do you *know* she's your wife?" Eleanor interrupted angrily. The question sent a chill through Nicholas as he met her gaze.

"Exactly *what* are you implying, Eleanor?"

"She does not act like the Vickie everyone knows," she said with a defiant tilt of her chin. "We all saw it. What if she's an imposter?"

An icy chill slid through Nicholas at the harsh words. Eleanor was right. So certain his wife's behavior was an elaborate charade, he'd failed to realize others might come to a different conclusion. The repercussion of others thinking his wife was an imposter could be devastating. The memory of Victoria adamantly stating she wasn't his wife made his gut twist violently.

Was it possible he'd erred in his judgment? If he had, then he'd forced Victoria into playing the role of his wife. Her innocence would be difficult to prove after his announcement of her return. Worse, if she was an imposter, where was Vickie? Angry at the ludicrous direction of his thoughts, he sucked in a breath and released it, then glared at the duchess.

"For the past three weeks, the rumors of foul play surrounding my wife's disappearance have hung like Damocles' sword over my head, Eleanor," he said through clenched teeth. "I do *not* appreciate the suggestion that I've replaced my wife with an imposter."

"Dear God, Nicholas," Eleanor exclaimed as she hurried

forward to touch his arm. "I would never suggest something so reprehensible. But Vickie was gone for such a long time. It would be easy for an imposter to take advantage of you and take her place."

"Now you're questioning my ability to recognize my own wife," he snapped.

"No, of course, not." Eleanor shook her head in dismay. "Nicholas, you mis—"

"My wife has suffered an injury to her head, Eleanor. It has clearly affected her behavior," he said coldly. "I've no doubt she'll be back to her usual antics soon enough."

"Vickie's behavior need not destroy what we have, Nicholas. I know—"

"We have nothing but friendship between us, Eleanor. If you thought otherwise, I'm sorry."

"Oh please, Nicholas," she whispered as both her hands clutched at his arms as though he were a lifeline. "Please don't push me out of your life. I cannot bear the thought of it."

The desperate note in her voice made him frown as he looked into her terror-glazed eyes. Nicholas frowned as he studied her with curiosity. As if aware she had somehow given something away, she took a quick step back and looked away.

"If you do not mind, Nicholas, I should like to leave first thing in the morning." The strain in her voice vibrated with something more than rejection, but he was at a loss to decipher what it was. She moved toward the salon door, then paused and turned her head toward him. "Would you be so kind as to explain to the others that I remembered a previous engagement?"

"Of course," he said quietly. "I'll arrange for someone to take you to the station at first light to catch the early morning train."

"Thank you," Eleanor said in a tight voice as she continued toward the doorway. One hand gripping the frame of the salon door as if her life depended on it, she glanced back over her shoulder at him. There was a look on her face that made him realize she was hoping he would stop her from leaving. When he didn't move, she uttered a soft sob and fled the room.

Guilt washed over him. It was clear he'd sent Eleanor mixed signals, and he'd hurt her in the process. Damnation, he was an insensitive bastard. Nicholas tossed the last of his cognac down his throat. He should have made it clear to Eleanor from the beginning that friendship was all there could ever be between them.

Disgusted with his behavior, Nicholas limped out of the salon and made his way up the stairs. The ache in his leg seemed to have worsened as the evening wore on. He could only assume it was a forecast for a cold winter. In his bedchamber, a small blaze crackled in the fireplace, while an oil lamp at his bedside illuminated his room with its soft glow. Nicholas undressed, then shrugged his night robe onto his shoulders and cinched the garment's belt. Wearily, he sank into the fireside chair.

The past three weeks had taken their toll, and he was afraid it was about to get worse. Eleanor's suggestion that Victoria was an imposter made him realize just how precarious his position was where she was concerned. Victoria's return and odd behavior would no doubt be just as problematic as her disappearance had been.

Nicholas rubbed his forehead before gingerly stretching out his painful leg. Even the brandy he'd imbibed had failed to take the edge off the throbbing tenderness that had reverberated through the limb all evening. Without warning, the ten-year-old memory of the paper mill fire pushed its way into his thoughts.

He drew in a sharp breath as the vivid recollection thrust him back to those last terrible moments in the mill. Flames crackled and popped like a live thing intent on devouring everything in its path. He'd managed to help several people toward the exit when Nicholas saw him. Eyes wide in his face, the boy stared at him across a wide barrier of fire.

The lad couldn't have been older than twelve, and he was frozen with fear. The roar of the fire echoed in Nicholas's ears as he jumped across fallen equipment and wood to find a way through the wall of flames separating him from the boy. Behind him he heard Roberts' shout, but he ignored the man's warning.

Frantically, Nicholas jerked off his coat and covered his head as he prepared to leap through the growing flames to reach the boy. A loud crack echoed from above, and a split second later one of the roof's triangular trusses knocked him to the ground and pinned his leg to the floor. A howl of pain ripped its way out of his throat. Trapped beneath the flaming piece of wood, Nicholas forced himself to sit up, but nausea made him fall backward as he saw bone jutting out of his lower leg in two places. Flames licked at his skin, and he desperately fought to remain conscious. Dazed, he looked for the boy. The lad was staring at him in horror.

"Jump, boy. *Now.*"

Nicholas urged the boy to run through the flames toward him with a wave of his hand. Their gazes locked, and the boy took a step forward when a loud crack split the air. Nicholas's gaze jerk upward as the boy screamed in terror. In a split second, a large support beam silenced the boy's shrill cry.

Another shout erupted from Nicholas's throat, this time it was a roar of rage. The next few moments were still a blur, but he remembered Roberts shouting his name. A moment later, the man had freed Nicholas's leg from the narrowly constructed wood beam and dragged him out of the building. The quiet sound of his door opening jerked him out of the waking nightmare. He turned his head to see his valet entering the room.

"Roberts, I thought, I told you I wouldn't need you this evening."

"You did, my lord," the older man said with a fatherly smile as he displayed the small tin in his hands. "But, I've brought the salve for your leg as promised, my lord."

"Thank you, I won't deny that I need it." Nicholas winced as he straightened in his chair and glanced at his valet.

The man had been no more fortunate than he had been that night at the paper mill. A sheet of flames had laid waste to the left side of the man's face as he'd helped pull Nicholas to safety. They were both lucky to be alive, but it had been Roberts who'd ensured their survival. It was a debt he could never repay.

"No doubt all the extra exercise hasn't helped, my lord."

"Why do I have the feeling you're chastising me?"

"I would not presume to do such a thing, my lord."

"Of course, you wouldn't," Nicholas said dryly as he eyed his valet with a hint of amusement.

"Would you like me to apply the ointment, my lord?"

"No, I can do it myself." Nicholas rejected the offer with a small wave of his hand. "Go on to bed, Roberts."

"Are you certain, my lord?"

"Yes, I'll sit by the fire for a little while. Between the salve and the fire's heat, the leg will be much better in the morning."

"Very well, my lord. Good night." With a nod, the valet left the room.

Nicholas shifted slightly in his seat and drew in a hiss of air as the movement sent pain shooting up his leg. Tugging his robe away from his leg, he stared down at the scarred tissue on his calf. With a grunt of discomfort, he shifted his leg and liberally applied the special salve Roberts had concocted for him years ago. In moments, the liniment eased his pain as it melted down into the muscles beneath the ugly scars that ran from his ankle almost to his knee. Using the towel Roberts had set out on the side table, he cleaned his hands then leaned back in his chair and stretched his leg out to capture the added heat of the fire. Nicholas closed his eyes again in an effort to quiet his racing thoughts. Slowly, the throbbing in his leg subsided and his thoughts slowed and he dozed off.

A scream echoed loudly in his dream, and Nicholas jerked upright in his chair. The fire in the hearth in front of him had burnt down to embers, and he berated himself for having fallen asleep in the chair. The night's stillness embraced him, and he rose to his feet. Cautiously applying weight to his leg, he was relieved to find the salve and fire's warmth had eased much of his pain. The silence was suddenly shattered by a scream from Victoria's room. Fully awake now, he quickly limped his way through the connecting doors and into his wife's bedchamber.

The small fire in the fireplace created dancing shadows on the bedchamber walls. In the dim lighting, Nicholas saw Victoria writhing beneath her sheets. Fear punctuated her soft moans, and he moved quickly to her bedside. Suddenly, she flung her arms outward and violently clawed at something only she could see.

"*No. Stop.*" The raw panic in her voice ended on a sob of horror. Despite all that had passed between them in the past, Nicholas didn't enjoy seeing her suffer. He slowly sat down on the edge of the mattress and tried to soothe her.

"Shhh, Victoria. Everything is all right. I'll not let anyone harm you. You're safe here. You're safe with me."

Gently, he brushed his fingers across her brow in a soft caress. She jerked against his touch and whimpered with fear. An urgent need to protect her from the demons haunting her sleep made him stretch his body out beside her. Warning shots fired in the back of his brain as he brushed his mouth against her silky hair.

"You're safe, Victoria," he murmured. "There's nothing to be afraid of. I'm here now."

Nicholas continued to whisper soothing words of reassurance, and relief swept through him as her nightmare ebbed away. Gently, he wiped away the tears on her cheek and stroked her forehead until she was sleeping quietly in his arms. When had he ever seen his wife so vulnerable? He hadn't.

Victoria shifted unexpectedly, and her soft form suddenly snuggled into his side like a sleek kitten. One cheek burrowing into his shoulder, her arm slid around his waist as though clutching a pillow. Startled, he realized his wife was naked beneath the soft muslin sheets. The Vickie he knew found the habit of sleeping in the nude common and revolting.

Despite his shock, his body instantly responded to the soft body pressing into his. The tangy scent of lemons in her hair filled his nose. In the two years they'd been married, he'd not bedded a woman, including his wife. Now, here she was naked and pressed into him as if she belonged in his arms. His mouth grew dry as he remembered the way she'd responded to him earlier in the day.

Soft and pliant in his arms, she'd been eager for his touch. She'd not uttered a single protest, but had responded to him with an abandon that had incited him to explore as much of her as he could. The image of his tongue flicking and swirling around the tip of her breast tugged a small groan from him as he experienced the intense craving to repeat the action. Heightening that longing was the memory of how she'd caressed him through his trousers. In a split second, his cock was hard with need.

Without thinking, his fingers traced a path from her shoulder down to the full curve of the breast that was pressed into his chest. Almost as if she understood in her sleep what he wanted, her body shifted in his arms and exposed a lovely breast. His fingers trailed across her skin to the nipple that grew stiff as he caressed her.

Victoria murmured something unintelligible and rolled onto her back. The sheet fell down to her waist, and his throat closed as he experienced a rush of desire he'd not experienced in a very long time. Another soft sound passed Victoria's lips as her eyes fluttered open. Sleepily, she stared up at him, then reached out to touch his cheek.

"Nicholas?" she whispered.

"You had a nightmare," he choked out as a burning need hardened every one of his muscles. God help him, but she was lovelier than he'd ever seen her.

"I did?" she frowned before a sleepy smile curved her lips. "You came to make sure I was safe."

"Yes," he rasped as he lowered his head and brushed his lips against hers.

A soft sigh escaped her, and she arched her body up against his as she sought to deepen their kiss. Her hands pushed their way past his robe to run over his chest. The touch set off a chain reaction of lust and desire that made him tug the sheet away from her body.

His mouth left hers and he worked his way downward until he could suckle her breast with unrestrained pleasure. She whimpered as he tugged at a rigid nipple with his teeth, then turned his attention to her other breast. With each flick of his tongue, she pushed her body upward against his in a wanton display of desire.

Lost in the sweet, fresh scent of her, Nicholas's brain stopped functioning as she pushed his robe off his shoulders. The garment fell away until her smooth, silky skin pressed into his. The moment her hand slid between them and grasped his erection, he shuddered and released a low groan. His hips rocked against her hand, and she applied just the right amount of pressure on his cock that blinded him to everything but the pleasure she was giving him.

Slowly, he slid his hand up a lush rounded thigh, and her

legs parted slightly to give him access to what he was seeking. The moment his thumb rubbed the plump piece of flesh just above the rim of her core, a soft cry parted her lips, and her hips jerked up off the bed.

"Nicholas, please…." The desperate plea in her voice was accompanied by her hand tightening around his erection and pumping him in an almost painful, but immensely pleasurable fashion. God help him, he wasn't going to last much longer. His body slid over hers until his cock was brushing against her sex.

"For the love of God, Nicholas, please. I need you inside me."

Her quiet appeal was like being doused in ice water. What the fuck was he doing? He knew better than to make love to his wife or any other woman. If he was responsible for…he didn't finish the thought. A dark growl of self-disgust erupted from his throat as he jerked away from her. In the dark, his hands scratched desperately across the sheets to find his robe. The garment in hand, he stumbled out of bed to cover himself in jerky movements. His groin shouted its objection, but he ignored the painful ache.

"Nicholas," the embarrassment in her voice made him stiffens. "I'm sorry… I…we're not even married."

"A topic of some debate," he bit out as he glanced over his shoulder at her, willing his cock to stop protesting the denial of release.

"I…I was sleepy…"

"I took advantage of you."

"No, you didn't," she said quietly, and he knew she was now fully awake. "It was my fault, but it just felt so…right."

Her words slammed into him like a sledgehammer. It was the truth, and he didn't understand how or why such a sensation was possible. He'd gotten lost in her curves, her smooth skin, and soft lips. Everything about her was intoxicating, and he didn't understand how he could have lost control like that with her. Vickie had stirred his lust, but this had been different.

This had been a hunger not only to possess, but to be complete. Nicholas quickly suppressed a snarl of self-loathing. He was imagining things. Tonight was simply a reminder he'd been celibate for a long time, and what he needed was a good fuck. The relief he needed could only be achieved with his own hand.

"Go back to sleep, Victoria," he bit out harshly as he headed toward the short hallway connecting their rooms.

Not waiting for a response, he closed her door behind him and returned to his room. With a vicious swing of his arm, he slammed his bedroom door shut. Nicholas pressed his back into the wood door as if his soul would perish if he moved. His gaze focused on the brass doorknob just below his hip. With just one twist, the door would open, and he could go back to claim what Victoria had so willingly offered to him. Eyes closed, he dragged in a deep breath. The scent of her was still on him. It was like an intoxicating drug that tested every last ounce of willpower he possessed not to go back to her. Christ Jesus, he needed to forget what had happened

Unable to help himself, he remembered the soft, lush feel of her body. The dangerous thought came at a price as his cock hardened and demanded its release. In his mind, he envisioned the look of passion he'd seen on Victoria's face as he pumped his flesh with hard, fast strokes. The memory of her needy cries made his blood flow hot and with a restrained cry of release he spilled his seed.

Slowly he pushed himself away from the door and crossed the room to pick up the towel Roberts had left him earlier. God help him, but he'd almost lost all reason a few moments ago. He'd never been so out of control in his life. What happened in Victoria's bedroom moments ago was something that threatened to consume him even now.

Nicholas moved to his bed and slid beneath the cold

covers. For a long time, he stared up at the ceiling, trying to make sense of the current state of affairs. His eyelids drooped, and the last thing he saw before sleep claimed him was a seductive sapphire gaze and a body made for lovemaking.

Chapter 9

The thud of the door closing behind Nicholas echoed softly through the air, and Victoria closed her eyes in humiliation. Dear God, what had she been thinking to offer herself to him like that? Victoria sat up in bed and wrapped her arms around her knees. She was an idiot. The man was married. No. He's a widower. The emphatic thought made her groan.

How could she possibly know her look-alike was dead? A familiar pounding took root in her head. Victoria rubbed her temple, her fingers grazing over her wound. The cut stung at her touch, and she winced. Before she'd gone to bed, she'd examined her head. Just as Charles Barrows had pointed out before dinner, in addition to a cut, there was a small knot and a sizable bruise on her head. The cut wasn't deep, but it hurt like hell at the moment. Had she hit her head on something?

The pain intensified, and she sat as still as possible, hoping if she remained still the headache go away. As the throbbing eased slightly, she exhaled a slow breath. Whatever had happened, she was fairly certain she'd been knocked unconscious. Her headaches and injury were firm evidence of that. The question still to be answered was what had happened to the countess? Had the woman hit her head on something and died, then by some bizarre twist of fate, Victoria had taken her place? Did that mean she was dead in the future? The horrifying thought intensified her headache, and Victoria gasped at the stabbing rhythm shooting through her temple.

The vicious pounding drowned out everything else, and she wrapped her hands around the back of her neck then pressed her forehead into her knees. Nothing. She had to think of absolutely nothing. As she cleared her mind of all questions, the pain diminished to a dull throb. Obviously, asking questions meant severe headaches. Maybe she was just supposed to accept her fate. That wasn't an appealing thought at all. She'd been quite happy in her own time period. Victoria snorted softly. She was kidding herself. Her trip to England was the first vacation she'd had in forever and look how good that was turning out. She grimaced in frustration. The worst of it was that she knew the only thing she had to go home to was a dead-end job, an empty house, and the regret.

Regret. Funny how one couldn't escape one's mistakes even in the past. A tear slid down her cheek as she remembered the way she'd stormed out of the house more than a year ago. Her dad and she were always at loggerheads. But she'd loved him dearly. They were just too much alike...*had been* too much alike. When she'd lost him, she'd been completely alone. If she'd only been able to tell him she was sorry. Slowly, Victoria laid back into the mattress and pulled the covers over her. Curled up in a ball, she realized she had nothing in the future to go home to, and she had nothing or anyone in the past either. She'd never felt so alone in her entire life.

Laughter floated out the front door of Brentwood Park Manor. Victoria, who was the first one outside, turned and saw Nicholas and his guests descending the marble steps.

"Good morning," Anna called out cheerfully as she crossed the pebbled driveway toward her. "You're an early bird."

"I'm looking forward to our ride this morning." Victoria smiled at the other woman. There was something warm and considerate about Anna, and she found herself thinking that at any other point in time they could be friends. As the viscountess stopped next to her, she tipped her head to one side.

"Did you sleep well?" Anna asked with a slight frown.

"Yes." The moment the lie passed her lips, Victoria saw a dubious expression cross Anna's features.

"As bad as that?" the other woman said sympathetically.

"Yes," she admitted with a sigh. Anna reached out and squeezed her arm in a reassuring manner.

"There's nothing to fear. You're among friends."

"Am I?" she murmured.

Victoria's gaze drifted to Nicholas's tall form. He was having a discussion with one of the groomsmen, and her heart skipped a beat as she remembered how close she'd come to having sex with the man. If her headaches didn't kill her, failing to hide her attraction for him would do the trick.

"Don't let Nicholas intimidate you. He's very good at that," Anna said firmly as she glanced over Victoria's shoulder. "Aren't you Nicholas?"

"Good at what?" There was the hint of a smile in his voice, but when Victoria looked at him, his expression was unreadable.

"Intimidation." Anna laughed.

"I never intimidate. I simply have expectations that people should meet." The teasing smile he unleashed on Anna made Victoria suck in a quick breath. God help her if he ever looked at her like that.

"Is Eleanor not riding with us this morning?" Anna looked around at the small group on the driveway.

"I am afraid Eleanor remembered a previous engagement. She returned to London early this morning and begged everyone's forgiveness for her hasty departure."

Victoria's eyes widened, and she looked at Anna. The other woman turned her head away and coughed. Even on short acquaintance, she'd learned how to tell when Anna was laughing. Nicholas narrowed his gaze at the two of them, but said nothing as his hand cupped Victoria's elbow and drew her away from Anna.

Electricity streaked through her, making it difficult to breathe until Nicholas released her as they stopped in front of a placid-looking mare. The animal nuzzled his shoulder as though expecting a treat. In response, Nicholas retrieved a piece of apple from his coat pocket and offered it to the horse. Enjoying his interaction with the solid-looking bay, Victoria rubbed the mare's nose.

"What's her name?"

"Desert Wind," he answered with a small twist of his lips as though enjoying a private joke. "You're not nervous about riding, are you? The mare won't give you any trouble, but if you wish to beg off—"

"No, I'm good," she said tightly. "Does she like to run?"

When he didn't answer, Victoria turned her head and saw him studying her in puzzlement. It dissolved into amusement as he looked at her, and his smile sent her senses reeling. The tremor passing through her made her quickly stiffen her shoulders to hide the shudder.

"Run?" A wicked chuckle escaped his lips. "On occasion."

Nicholas didn't elaborate before he walked away to look after his guests. Victoria bit her lip pensively. Something was wrong. The man was far too pleased with himself. Convinced it had to do with the horse he'd selected for her, Victoria glanced over her shoulder. With a silent gesture, she beckoned to one of the stable hands. The boy sprang forward quickly.

"Yes, my lady." He removed his cap from his head in a gesture of respect and bowed slightly. Victoria stroked the mare's velvety nose as she smiled at him.

"What's your name?"

"Mickey, my lady."

"Do you think you could find me a horse that's a bit more spirited, Mickey?"

"I'm not sure that's wise, my lady. His lordship gave orders you were to ride Desert Wind here. She's an easy goer."

"I see." Victoria's jaw tightened with irritation. She understood Nicholas's refusal to believe her story, but she didn't like being patronized either with his choice of mounts. "I'm sure his lordship means well, but I can easily handle a more spirited animal."

"Well, there's Mischief, my lady. I was keeping him around the corner in case one of the gents was dissatisfied with their choice of mounts," the boy said thoughtfully. "But I have to warn you, he can be a handful."

"He sounds perfect," she said with a smile. Mickey grinned.

"Let me put your saddle on him, it won't take but a moment."

"I'll come with you."

With the small mare in tow, Victoria followed the young stable hand around the corner of the manor's front portico, which jutted outward from the two wings of the house. It created a shield from the other guests and prevented Nicholas from realizing what she was doing. Tied to a hitching post, a magnificent roan stallion tossed his head in a spirited manner.

"He's beautiful," she breathed.

"Aye, that he is, my lady."

Pleased with her reaction, the boy grinned and quickly set about changing saddles. Mickey had tightened the girth strap on Mischief just as she heard the others calling her name. Hands locked together, Mickey formed a single step for her to use in mounting the stallion. As she settled into the odd saddle, Victoria tried to figure out where her legs and feet should be placed.

"Are you sure you shouldn't ride Desert Wind, your ladyship?"

Concern crossing his features, the young stable hand frowned. Victoria shook her head as she figured out that her right leg needed to overlap the saddle horn. She quickly slipped her feet into the stirrups, then adjusted her riding habit.

"Don't worry, Mickey. I'll be fine. It's been a while since I rode side saddle," she fibbed.

She heard Nicholas shout her name, and with a soft laugh she winked at Mickey, then urged Mischief forward with a slight nudge of her heel. Silence greeted Victoria as she rode out from around the portico. Except for Anna, everyone stared at her with a dumbstruck expression. Victoria's stomach lurched slightly as she wondered whether it had been a mistake to do something so unlike the woman she had no choice but to impersonate. Nicholas was the first to overcome his surprise.

"*Mickey.*"

The roar of anger in that one word made Victoria flinch. She glanced over her shoulder to see the stable hand come running from around the portico. Fear on his face, the stable hand took his cap off and bobbed his head.

"Yes, my lord."

"*What the hell is the countess doing on that animal?*" Fury blistered through the quietly spoken question. Mickey paled in the face of Nicholas's wrath, and Victoria maneuvered her horse so it stood between the boy and Nicholas.

"Mickey was following *my* orders. Even if he'd refused to do as I asked, I would have changed the saddles without his help."

"Get off that horse, Victoria. He's too high strung for you to handle." The harsh command made her roll her eyes at him.

"More temperamental than Desert Wind, you mean."

"This has gone far enough, madam. I chose the mare because she won't bolt or throw you," he bit out in a low voice. For an odd reason, the thought that he'd been concerned for her well-being warmed her inside.

"I appreciate that, but I'm more than capable of managing Mischief."

"*Damn it to hell.* Get off that horse right now, Victoria."

"No." At her firm rebellion, he narrowed his gaze at her.

"I'll not tell you again, Victoria. Get off that damn horse, *now.*" Despite the low, menacing note in his voice, Victoria met his furious gaze without flinching and smiled.

"Or what?" she inquired sweetly.

"Or I'll remove you myself," he growled with a ferocity that made her realize being the focus of his anger wasn't a good thing. Nicholas urged his stallion forward and leaned down to capture Mischief's bridle. Glaring at him, she sent Mischief prancing sideways with a slight touch of the reins before Nicholas could grab the bridle.

"I think that might be more difficult that you think, my lord," she said defiantly before she maneuvered Mischief away from him until Anna's horse stood between her and Nicholas's stallion. At the scowl on Nicholas's face, Anna smiled mischievously at him and then Victoria.

"It appears everyone has a mount, shall we be off?" Anna said as she prodded her horse forward and away from the manor. She clearly knew where she was going, and Victoria drew alongside her. The other woman looked over her shoulder, then back to Victoria. "He's angry because he's quite bewildered by you."

"I doubt he's as confused as I am," Victoria said as she kept her gaze focused on the gently rolling landscape they were riding toward.

"It must be terribly hard to feel as though you're all alone in the world." The soft words made her jerk her head in

Anna's direction.

"I'm not sure what you mean," she said as she looked away from the other woman's assessing gaze.

"Victoria, I have a…special ability," Anna said softly and looked over her shoulder as if to ensure no one else could hear her. "When you shook hands with me yesterday, I knew you weren't Vickie. I also know how frightened you are, and you shouldn't be."

The woman's words thundered through Victoria's head. Anna knew she wasn't the countess. Fear scraped across her nerve endings. She'd denied being the countess from the time she'd woken up in Goodman Cottage, but no one had believed her. Now Anna had just said she wasn't the countess. Did the woman intend to expose her as an imposter?

"Victoria, please, you're in no danger," Anna said fervently.

Despite Anna's attempt to reassure her, Victoria's heartbeat thundered in her ears. If Anna knew the truth, how long would it take others to realize she wasn't the countess? The moment people learned she wasn't the countess, they'd start asking questions. Questions she couldn't answer. And unanswered questions meant suspicion and a lot worse.

Nausea twisted her stomach as she stared blindly at the landscape in front of her. If only she could wake up from this nightmare. She just wanted to go home. Without a second thought, Victoria urged Mischief forward into a canter and then a hard gallop. The stiff wind lashed at her cheeks, but all she could think about was freedom. Ahead of her, she saw a low brick wall. Just before the stone barrier, the stallion gathered himself, easily clearing the hurdle.

Her inexperience riding sidesaddle unbalanced her for a moment as the horse landed on the opposite side. It took only a brief second to adjust her seat as the stallion pounded toward a tall hedge. Leaning forward, her cheek close to the animal's neck, Victoria felt Mischief's powerful muscles flex beneath her. The animal leaped up into the air and soared across the shrubbery as if he had wings.

Open pastureland stretched out in front of them, and Mischief's stride never hesitated at any of the barriers they approached. With effortless ease, he rose up and over every hurdle in his path. She had no idea where she was going. All she could think about was escape. Behind her, she heard a shout. She glanced over her shoulder and saw Nicholas gaining ground on her. He'd make her go back. There would be questions, and she wouldn't know how to answer them.

Frantically, she urged the big horse to increase his pace. They sailed over fence after fence when, out of the corner of her eye, she saw Nicholas coming alongside her. Hooves thundering against the ground beneath them, the two stallions raced neck and neck toward a wall of gray stones. A second later, both horses sailed over the wall with Nicholas landing close beside her.

Before she could bat his hand away, he had hold of Mischief's cheekpiece, bringing the stallion to a slow halt. The moment the horses were standing still, Nicholas grabbed her by the waist and lifted her off Mischief. Physically spent from the hard ride, Victoria didn't protest as he dropped her unceremoniously in his lap. She knew he was angry, but being in his arms felt as if she'd come home. It was an odd sensation, and Victoria brushed it aside.

"I ought to thrash you for such a fool stunt," he bit out as he grabbed Mischief's reins.

"What fool stunt?" Victoria shook her head, knowing exactly what he meant.

"Your insistence on riding the damn horse." His mouth thinned with anger. "If Mischief had thrown you at that fast pace, you could have been killed."

"It wasn't a stunt. I told you I know how to ride," she said with an exasperated sigh.

"You might think you know how to ride a horse, but you

chose to ride a horse that would test even my skill."

Despite his censure, she heard a distinct note of puzzlement in his voice. The pounding of hoof beats made Victoria turn her head toward the sound. Sebastian and Charles were the first to reach them, and the two men appeared deeply concerned.

"Is she all right?" Sebastian asked.

"I'm fine." Victoria glared at Anna's husband.

"From her waspish tone, I think we can safely assume she suffered no injuries."

The wry note in Nicholas's voice made Victoria look up at him. Amusement curved his lips slightly as he arched his eyebrows at her. Something flickered in his green-eyed gaze that made her heart beat faster. God, if the man turned up the charm dial, last night would be a simple heat wave compared to the inferno she was certain he would unleash inside her. More hoof beats echoed in her ear, and the rest of the party surrounded them. Out of the corner of her eye, she saw Mickey, his face pale and drawn, bringing Desert Wind to a halt a few feet away. Immediately the air was buzzing with a cacophony of questions and comments.

"How is she?" the Viscount Palmerton asked with concern as he looked at Nicholas. Irritated that the man hadn't simply asked her, Victoria started to answer the question but was forestalled from doing so by other voices.

"I say, you were quite lucky, Victoria," Charles Barrows exclaimed.

"Oh, my dear, we were so worried. Are you all right?" Catherine gasped with concern. Eyes wide with horror, the viscountess leaned forward in her saddle. "How on earth did you manage to keep your seat on a runaway horse?"

"Mischief didn't—"

"Thank god, you're all right, Victoria," Anna interrupted her with a warning look in her direction. "I thought the worst when Mischief shied, then bolted away. Nicholas, you should take Victoria back to the house immediately. She's clearly exhausted from such a terrifying ride."

When she opened her mouth to protest, Anna's look made Victoria realize it was best to remain quiet to avoid any further suspicion. It was also true she was weary from the ride. The roan stallion had tested her skill and strength, and her arms ached from controlling the horse. Not to mention the fact that she had the beginnings of another headache. She glanced up at Nicholas, who eyed her with curiosity, and Victoria looked away.

"I think I would like to lie down for a while," she murmured. "I'm sure Mischief will be quite sedate on the way back."

The air was abruptly filled with objections, except for the man holding her in his arms. When she tilted her head to look up at Nicholas, he eyed her with an autocratic expression of disapproval.

"You will *not* ride Mischief again," he said loud enough for everyone to hear before he bent his head and lowered his voice. "*Ever.* Is that clear?"

The determination in his gaze dared Victoria to argue with him, but she was too tired to object. She nodded and remained silent as he lifted his head to look at his guests.

"I'll return Victoria to the house, while the rest of you finish your ride." Although his words were met with protests from the others, Victoria was relieved when he waved them into silence. "I insist. Victoria and I will take our time returning, and by the time you return to the manor, breakfast will be ready and waiting."

The riding party continued to protest, but Nicholas refused to be swayed. With great reluctance, the small group of riders cantered away while Mickey remained on the horse Nicholas had originally selected for her.

"My lord, I should have—"

"All that matters, Mickey, is that her ladyship wasn't

harmed. However, in the future, the countess is not to ride Mischief again. Do I make myself clear?" At his quiet, yet firm words, the stable hand nodded his head vigorously.

"Yes, my lord," he said with a look of relief on his face. Mickey looked at her, "I am sorry, my lady."

"You have nothing to apologize for, Mickey." She smiled at the boy and was relieved to see him grin back.

"Take Mischief back to the house," Nicholas ordered quietly as he handed the stallion's reins to the boy. Mickey accepted the horse's leather leads, then urged Desert Wind into a canter with Mischief trailing behind him. As the boy rode away, Nicholas nudged Zeus forward in a slow walk along the stone fence. Silence hung between them for several minutes before Nicholas spoke.

"You were frightened," he observed quietly.

"No, I wasn't," she said emphatically. "I know how to ride, and Mischief didn't bolt."

"I'm not talking about the horse. You were trying to run away, and I'd like to know why." The soft words stole Victoria's breath away. How could he know? When she didn't answer, he blew out a noise of aggravation. "Tell me why you were running away, Victoria."

"Because I don't belong here." She didn't look up at him and kept her gaze fixed on where the stone fence ended at a smooth dirt roadway. "I'm not your wife."

"Ah, that again." His resigned tone of voice made Victoria stiffen with irritation.

"Yes, *that* again. I don't know why it's so difficult for you to believe me.

"It's not so much a matter of believing you, Victoria. It's a matter of proof." For a moment, she didn't speak as she absorbed his words. Was it possible he had doubts?

"Isn't the fact that I rode Mischief the type of proof you need?" she asked in a hopeful voice. "I'm not an idiot. You made it clear last night you expected me to fail Riding 101, but

I passed with flying colors."

"Riding one 'o' one?"

"It's an expression, it means a beginner class," she snapped with frustration. "Admit it. You didn't expect me to ride this morning, and you sure as hell didn't expect me to ride Mischief."

"You're correct. I didn't expect you to ride this morning." The rueful reply made Victoria grit her teeth as he caught her chin in his fingers and made her look at him. "But you've not yet told me why you were running away."

Chapter 10

"I wasn't running away."

"You're not a very good liar," he murmured at the lack of conviction in her voice.

Nicholas went rigid with amazement. He'd actually been able to tell she was lying. Vickie had always been so adept at lying it was difficult to know when she was or wasn't telling the truth. Her habitual deceit had forced him to operate on the premise that she *always* lied. But this was the first time in recent memory, if ever, that he'd been able to discern that his wife was telling the truth.

"And you're an obstinate bastard." The sarcastic reply made him chuckle.

"I'm not as obstinate as you think, madam wife, and your language has become…quite colorful during your absence." He suppressed another laugh.

"You have *no* idea how colorful my language can be," she muttered in a bristly manner.

"Tell me where you were running to, Victoria."

He tried to keep his voice gentle, despite his determination to have the truth from her. The irony of the thought made his mouth twist slightly with frustration. His fingers captured her chin and forced her to look at him. The helplessness reflected in her sapphire gaze aroused a sudden urge to protect her. The sensation made him bite down on the inside of his cheek. The woman was weaving her magic over him, and he needed to remember who he was talking to. A voice in the back of his mind whispered something he wasn't ready to accept, and he crushed the sound.

"Answer me, Victoria," he said quietly.

"I don't know." With a tug, she pulled free of his grasp and turned her head away.

"Shall we take a different tack?" he said with a sigh. "If I hadn't stopped you, where would you have gone?"

"London, I suppose. I don't really know."

"Are you afraid of me, Victoria?"

"Have I acted like I'm afraid of you?" she said with light-hearted sarcasm.

"With the exception of jumping into an icy pond, I'd say no."

The moment he spoke, her tension vibrated its way into him. Anna was correct. Victoria was frightened. She was so frightened she'd been willing to risk drowning in her effort to escape. What could have her so terrified? Had she discovered something about Reardon and was frightened the man would hurt her. He'd never let that happen.

It was his duty to protect his wife, but his reaction to the idea of someone harming Victoria filled him with an inexplicable rage. The intensity of his anger was startling enough, but it was the fear accompanying his fury that alarmed him. It suggested his feelings for his wife were changing. Silence stretched out between them with the only other sounds being the clattering of pebbles beneath Zeus' hooves and the occasional chirping of a bird. After several minutes, he bent his head toward her.

"You must trust me, Victoria," he growled with frustration. The fear in her eyes made him long to comfort and reassure her all would be well. They were emotions he didn't want to feel, but he was incapable of pushing them aside. Nicholas brushed his fingers across her cheek. "I can't help you, if you won't trust me."

"You *can't* help me," she whispered in a despondent tone.

"Why don't you let me be the judge of that?" A tremor rippled through her, and he gently nudged her chin upward with his knuckle. "What if I agree to hear your story with my solemn oath that there will be no repercussions?"

"I don't understand." She studied him with a wary look.

Nicholas bit down on the inside of his cheek. Was he actually considering the possibility that she was telling the truth? His jaw grew tight with tension. No, he was simply trying to understand who or what she was running from. Now, *he* was the one who was lying. He wanted her to trust him completely, just as much as he wanted to trust her. Nicholas swallowed the knot lodged in his throat at the revealing thought.

"Whatever you tell me will be in complete confidence. I swear not to use it against you."

"How do I know I can trust you?"

"My word is my bond, Victoria. I will *not* break it." Jaw clenched with angry indignation, Nicholas drew himself up straight, and Victoria had the grace to look remorseful.

"No matter how outlandish my story?" she asked hesitantly.

The cautious look on her face emphasized her fear. Impulsively, he stroked her cheek again. As his thumb rubbed against her lower lip, he realized how natural it felt to caress her this way. He jerked his hand away from her as a jolt of electricity surged through him. What the hell was wrong with him? He cleared his throat.

"No matter how ridiculous or outrageous your story sounds, I will not break my word." He met her gaze and waited for her response. With a slow nod, she inhaled a deep breath as she stared at him.

"I'm from the future."

The cadence of Zeus' hooves on the driveway didn't

change as Nicholas frowned. What the devil was the woman talking about? He shook his head in puzzlement. He'd bluffed yesterday when he'd threatened to take her to the asylum, but now he wondered if he'd erred in not having Bertram at least have a look at her head. Irritation settled on her face.

"Aren't you going to say something?" she snapped.

"I'm uncertain what it is I'm supposed to say," he said with a bewilderment he'd not experienced since the day he and his sister, Abigail, had discovered the truth about their brother Edmund.

"Oh, that's reassuring," she said sarcastically.

"I'm trying to understand, Victoria, but you must admit it sounds like a ludicrous, far-fetched fabrication that—"

"*Don't*," she interrupted him. "I'm *not* crazy. And you promised you wouldn't use any of this against me. I'm not going to let you put me in a straight-jacket."

"I wasn't about to suggest that at all," he said as he suddenly envisioned her in an entirely different kind of restraint.

The image of her pinned beneath him as he thrust into her until she exploded over his cock knotted his muscles with intense desire. The strength of his need for her tightened his gut as he grew hard. He quickly shifted his body in an effort to avoid his erection from pushing into her hip. A knot threatened to remain lodged in his throat as he realized how much he wanted to bed her.

She was wreaking havoc on his senses in a way Vickie never had before, and he didn't like it. Desperately, he fought to remain focused on their discussion and not the things he wanted to do with her body.

"Then what *were* you going to say?" She looked up at him as she waited on his answer.

"I was going to say it's a story not even Vickie could invent." He knew how preposterous Victoria's explanation was, but he was certain she was telling the truth as she believed it to be. What he didn't understand was how she was nothing like Vickie. Her speech, mannerisms, and even the way she responded to his touch. She was as different from the woman he'd married as was possibly imaginable.

"Oh." The subdued response made him chuckle, and she scowled at him before her expression lightened.

"Well, at least you've come to the realization that I'm not your wife." The satisfaction in her voice triggered a stab of regret in him.

"No, I've not reached that conclusion at all."

"You just *said* that Vickie couldn't invent a story like this."

"Victoria, you sustained a nasty blow to your head." His hands tightened on Zeus' reins as he sensed her disappointment and frustration. "Injuries such as yours can manifest any number of fantasies, including one that makes you believe you're from the future."

"It's not an illusion. I'm not from your time. I don't belong here."

The mutinous tilt of her lips barely covered her fear and aroused something strong and visceral inside of him. He longed to make her feel safe. He wanted to hold her in his arms and press his body into her sweet curves like he had last night. His heart thundered almost painfully in his chest at the memory of how close he'd come to burying himself inside her hot core.

Christ Jesus, without protection he might have fathered a child. He struggled to breathe. Nicholas fixed his gaze on the road and shook his head as if that would rid himself of the sensations gnawing at him.

"Tell me what this future of yours looks like."

"Well, in my time, you're dead and buried, obviously." It was a blatant retaliation for what he was certain she perceived as his attempt to appease her like a child.

"That is a decidedly unpleasant picture," he murmured

as he fought not to laugh. "But if that's true, then it makes you *much* older than me."

"You can be a real jerk, you know that."

This time he couldn't restrain his laughter. He didn't know what a jerk was, but he was certain it wasn't a compliment. The scowl on her face only emphasized the fact. Suddenly, her irritation evaporated, and laughter lit up her features.

A vise tightened with unexpected speed around his chest at the sight. He'd never seen his wife laugh at herself or laugh with such unrestrained amusement. Victoria's laugh was far from the artificial sound of amusement Vickie had, and he realized he liked the change in her laughter. Alarm bells went off in the back of his head.

The witch was turning his world upside down, and that was something Vickie had never done. His wife had evoked lust and desire in him when they first met, but those feelings had died on their wedding day. But the one emotion he'd never experienced with Vickie was this constant sense of being off balance. He found it difficult to think clearly when she was near. Worse than that, he wanted her in his bed. In an effort to regain control of himself, he cleared his throat.

"You were telling me about this future of yours."

"I'm not sure how much I should tell you." Victoria's laughter disappeared as uncertainty clouded her expression. "I don't want to do anything that might change the future. Although I suppose if I tell you just the basics that would be okay."

"I doubt anything you say will alter the course of history, Victoria," he said in a reassuring manner.

"Well, I'm not much of a historian, but I know you don't have cell phones, doors that open by themselves, or television." She winced suddenly, as if in pain. He eyed her carefully and instinctively knew her discomfort was not contrived. As much as he was interested to know about doors that opened by themselves, he was certain Victoria had over stretched herself.

"I think we'll continue this discussion at a later time. You're clearly not feeling well."

"It's just a headache."

"You've had several headaches since you returned to Brentwood Park." With a squeeze of his legs against Zeus' sides, he urged the horse into a slow trot. "You've pushed yourself too hard by refusing to rest, and you had a restless sleep last night."

"Yes," she whispered as she darted a glance up at him then quickly looked away.

Nicholas's gut twisted as he realized she was remembering what had happened between them last night. Somehow, he needed to make her understand he'd not meant to let things go as far as they had. In the back of his mind, he admitted he wanted to repeat the events of last night and see them through to their completion. His cock stirred in his breeches again. Determined not to allow his body to respond to her, Nicholas drew in a deep breath and cleared his throat.

"Victoria, about last night—"

"There's no need to explain."

"You're wrong, Victoria. I took advantage of the situation." Nicholas wanted to shake her for refusing to let him apologize.

"Well, the next time you start something like that, finish it," she said as she scowled at him.

"I will," he snapped.

Nicholas stiffened as the full impact of their exchange rang in his head like a church bell. *Fuck*, had he just admitted regret for failing to do as she'd just insinuated? Eyes widening with horror, Victoria jerked her gaze away from him. Was she appalled by his response or her obvious frustration that he'd left her unfulfilled last night? The silence between them thickened with a tension that was almost painful.

"Let's just forget it happened. Okay?" she whispered with a hint of what he was certain was humiliation.

"As you wish," he replied at a loss for words that would ease the mortification he knew she was feeling.

He wasn't sure what bothered him the most. The idea that her desire excited him or the realization that last night had impacted him more than he cared to admit. The manor appeared in front of them, and relief swelled through him. Several minutes from now, he'd be able to put some physical distance between them. Last night had left him aching for something he didn't understand and holding her in his arms like this was becoming damned uncomfortable.

"You don't like your wife very much, do you?" It wasn't an accusation so much as a simple observation.

"I've not been given enough reason to do so," he snapped as he remembered the scene he'd stumbled upon in Lord Brentwood's library the day of their wedding.

"What did she do to hurt you?"

"Humiliation is a better word. I found a footman and Vickie a few short hours after we were married in a…compromising position."

Nicholas's body hardened as he remembered the raw pain of humiliation he'd endured those few minutes as he'd stared at Vickie bent over a library table, while a footman fucked her from behind. His teeth clenched, he forced himself to push the loathsome image from his mind. She drew in a sharp breath as she met his gaze.

"You were in love with her."

"No," he shook his head.

"If you didn't love her, why did you marry her?"

Unprepared for the question, Nicholas stiffened against her. Why in the hell was he responding to her questions as if she wasn't his wife? Unconsciously, his fingers tightened on Zeus' reins until the stallion tossed his head in protest. Nicholas quickly eased up on his taut grip of the horse's reins.

He didn't like the fact that he had to remind himself that she was his wife. Changed perhaps, but she was still the Countess of Guildford. A sound of regret escaped Victoria.

"I'm sorry," she said in a repentant tone. "That was rude of me."

"We had an arranged marriage," he said in a dispassionate voice, surprised at how easily she apologized when she was in the wrong. "Your father wanted a title for you, and I…I wanted Brentwood Park."

"Brentwood Park must mean a great deal to you if you were willing to marry a woman you don't love."

"Marriage is a business arrangement. Love seldom comes into it," he said firmly as mocking laughter sounded in the back of his mind. That he'd confused love for lust only made his marriage to Vickie that much more of a disappointment.

"I won't marry someone I don't love," she said in a resolute voice.

"You're already married, madam wife." At his dry response, she rolled her eyes at him.

"You'll eventually have to admit that I'm not your wife."

"If I did, we'd both be in a great deal of trouble."

He frowned. If Victoria's story was true, then where was Vickie? Was it possible Vickie might be dead? He suppressed a snort at the ridiculous notion. Such a thing was impossible when he was actually holding his wife in his arms at this very moment. He no longer believed she was Vickie playing an elaborate game, but he didn't believe she was from the future either. There had to be a medical explanation for Victoria's behavioral changes. He'd have to find a way to convince Victoria to be seen by Dr. Bertram.

"I ran away because Anna knows I'm an imposter." The unexpected confession took him by surprise, and he experienced an unexpected rush of pleasure that she'd trusted him enough to tell him why she'd run away.

"Anna will not betray your confidence. She and Sebastian

are my closest friends. They'd never do anything to harm me," he said in a reassuring tone of voice. "You can trust them just like you can me."

"So what you're really saying is that I have to continue pretending to be your wife until the real countess returns." Fear echoed in her voice, and he pulled her tighter into his chest.

"Victoria, has it occurred to you that the life you say you have in the future might be your mind's way of helping you deal with the trauma you suffered? We have no idea what happened to you, and it's possible you're blocking out the incident." His question made her jerk her gaze up to him, and she shook her head.

"It's not," she said with a quiet conviction that had him questioning his own certainty.

"Tell me what you remember before Thomas Goodman found you."

"I was in an art gallery. The picture of the cottage was there. I think I was going to buy it…" She gasped and pressed her hand up against her head. It was obvious she was in pain, but her gaze never left his. "I remember a man. He was in the gallery too. He was with me, but something happened. If I could just remember…"

A sharp cry escaped her before she lost consciousness and fell backward over his arm. Nicholas uttered a soft oath and quickly shifted her body until her cheek was against his shoulder. Her face was ashen, and her breathing was slow and ragged, just as it had been yesterday.

"Bloody hell," he said fiercely and jabbed his heel into Zeus' side to send the horse into a full gallop.

As the stallion thundered toward the manor, Nicholas glanced down at Victoria's pale features. She looked like someone on the brink of death, and the thought put the fear of God in him as he pulled Zeus to a sliding halt in front of the manor. He allowed Victoria to slump against the horse's neck as he quickly dismounted. As his feet hit the ground, he winced as the force of the impact shot a pain up his leg.

"My lord," Mickey called out behind him.

Gently, he pulled Victoria off the stallion and glanced over his shoulder at the young stable hand running toward him. With Victoria cradled carefully in his arms, he limped toward the front steps of the manor.

"Take care of Zeus, Mickey."

"Is her ladyship—"

"*Do it*, Mickey," he growled as he climbed the marble steps and crossed the manor's threshold into the foyer.

"We were beginning to wonder where—dear Lord, what's happen?" Anna's cheerful greeting became one of horror.

"She fainted," he growled as he carried Victoria toward the stairs. The rest of his guests hurried out of the dining room and into the hall at Anna's exclamation of fear. Sebastian strode past his wife and hurried toward Nicholas.

"Nicholas, spare your leg. Let me take her upstairs," his friend said with a dark frown of concern.

"No," he rasped harshly. "She's my wife. Send someone for Dr. Bertram."

"Right away," Sebastian said as he turned away to complete his task.

Nicholas nodded before he continued toward the staircase. Pain shot up his leg into his hip as he climbed the steps with Victoria in his arms. Last night he'd witnessed vulnerability in his wife, and for the second time in two days, she was exhibiting a death-like state that emphasized she was far more fragile than he thought. A visceral fear struck at his heart as he carried Victoria down the hall to her room. Behind him, he heard Roberts clucking like a mother hen as he followed Nicholas into Victoria's bedroom.

"If you continue abusing your leg like this, my lord, you're going to be laid up," Roberts said sternly.

"I'll be fine," he replied in a terse voice as he bent over Victoria and debated whether or not he should undress her. A knock on the bed-chamber door made him look over his shoulder, and Molly entered the room.

"You should let Roberts see to your leg, my lord. I'll tend to her ladyship," Molly said in a quiet voice. About to chastise the maid, he turned around too quickly, and his leg gave way beneath him. He barely escaped a fall as his hands grabbed the edge of the mattress for support.

"*God damn it,*" he bit out fiercely as nerve endings fired off pain signals in his head. Roberts was at his side in an instant, but Nicholas waved him off with a sharp gesture as he balanced his full weight on his good leg. "Bring me a chair, Roberts."

"Molly is quite capable of ensuring her ladyship—"

"Bring me a God damn chair."

Nicholas turned his head back to Victoria, lying so still on the mattress. Why the devil didn't she wake up? She'd not been unconscious this long yesterday. He leaned forward to ensure she was still breathing. Relief surged through him as the soft breeze of her breath brushed his face. Her cheeks were still pale, but he was certain there was a hint of color beneath her skin. At least that's what he wanted to believe.

Roberts placed a chair beside Victoria's bed, and Nicholas sank down with relief. He leaned forward and took her hand in his. Despite the pallor of her complexion, her hand was warm. As he studied her features, he contemplated their discussion on the way back to the manor. Clearly her mind was confusing reality with fantasy. A sudden, intense fear made him go rigid as he considered the possibility she might not wake up.

The thought filled him with a foreboding unlike anything he'd ever experienced before. He tried to dismiss the emotion, but it remained. How was it possible that in less than twenty-four hours, Victoria had managed to make him feel things he'd never felt for Vickie? Not once in his marriage had he ever experienced such a sense of fear and helplessness where his wife was concerned.

"Nicholas…Nicholas." Anna sounded as if she were far away. He slowly looked up at his friend to meet her sympathetic gaze. "You need to let Roberts tend to your leg."

"My leg is fine," he lied. Until now, he'd managed to ignore the fiery pain shooting up his leg and into his side. "I'm not leaving her until she wakes up."

"Will you trust me when I say she'll be fine?" Anna studied him intently.

Behind her, Sebastian nodded in silent confirmation of his wife's words. Nicholas wanted to vehemently reject Anna's request, but her certainty made him nod his acquiescence.

"I'm to be told the moment she wakes up. Is that understood?"

Anna silently acknowledged his order. Nicholas looked back at Victoria. He didn't want to feel anything for this woman, but he did. The realization scared the hell out of him. Slowly, he made his way to the door connecting his room with Victoria's. He looked back over his shoulder one last time at Victoria's still form in the bed before he limped his way out of the room.

Chapter 11

Present Day

The wild shrill of alarms jerked Nick out of sleep. In an instant, he was on his feet and beside Victoria's hospital bed. In the hallway, he heard the frantic squeak of shoes against tile as medical personnel raced toward the room.

"Victoria, can you hear me? It's Nicholas. You need to wake up, sweet witch."

The endearment had become a regular refrain in his efforts to awaken her over the past four days. Victoria's eyes moved beneath her eyelids, and hope welled up inside him. Two nurses rushed into the room, followed by Dr. Bertram. As usual, he was shoved to the sidelines as the nurses checked her IV and monitors. Nick stood at the foot of the bed while Bertram leaned over her as if he was listening to her speak. His heart slammed into his chest at the sight.

"Let me talk to her, Bertram."

Nick met the doctor's gaze of frustration. They both knew the only real responses they'd gotten from Victoria were when he was talking to her. Bertram looked at the nurse on the opposite side of the bed and nodded sharply. The moment the woman stepped back, Nick took her place. Leaning over Victoria, his fingers caressed her brow in gentle strokes.

"Victoria. I'm not going to leave you. Come back to me."

At his words, her lips moved.

"I can't…find you." It was the merest hint of a whisper, and he sucked in a breath at the note of confusion he heard in her words.

"I'm right here, sweet witch. I'm right here." Nick's heart pounded frantically in his chest. "Victoria, wake up. Come back to me."

Despite his urgent plea, the alarms immediately stopped shrieking, and Victoria went still again. With a loud noise of defeat and anguished desperation, Nick whirled around and strode out of the room. He crossed the wide corridor and furiously slammed the flat surface of his fist against the concrete wall.

"*Fuck.*"

Hands braced against the wall, he bent his head and closed his eyes. Each time Victoria seemed on the verge of waking up, she slipped back into her coma. As a hand touched his back in a compassionate gesture, Nick straightened upright and turned toward the doctor. Pressing his back against the wall, he met Bertram's sympathetic look with a sense of helplessness.

"I realize how frustrated and worried you are, Barrows. But every time she has one of these episodes, it's a good thing. It means she's still in there, fighting to come back. You need to be patient."

"It's hard to be patient when there's the possibility she might not have the strength to come back," he snarled.

The words struck at something deep inside him that made him want to lash out at the world. He'd just found her again, and the thought of losing her filled him with the depth of a torment he'd never dreamed possible. Nick tipped his head backward to rest it against the wall. For the first time, he was experiencing doubt Victoria would come out of her coma.

The realization was like a knife cutting deep into his soul. How could he be in love with a woman he'd spoken only a few words to? He wanted to reject the idea, and yet he knew it was true. The pain engulfing him every time Victoria slipped away from him was so intense he had no choice but to believe he loved her.

"For someone who insisted Miss Ashton was going to surprise everyone, but you—I'm amazed at your sudden about face."

"You heard what the neurologist said yesterday," Nick snarled.

"What I heard Dr. Mitchel say was that she didn't know how to explain what was happening to Miss Ashton." Bertram met his gaze with empathy. "Just because a medical condition can't be explained doesn't mean the situation is hopeless. I've seen cases where I thought all hope was lost, but the power of love created miracles where modern medicine failed."

"And what makes you think this is going to be one of those cases?" Nick bit out in a hoarse whisper.

"Because, you've made a believer out of me, Barrows. I think it's time you start believing again as well."

With an abrupt nod, Bertram headed down the hall to the nurses' station. Nick stared after the man before he slowly pushed himself away from the wall and returned to Victoria's room with its quietly beeping equipment. Drawn to her side, Nick stared down at Victoria as his fingers stroked her hair and then her cheek.

"Come back to me, sweet witch. Don't leave me again," he whispered. The soft plea came straight from his heart, and he could only pray she would hear him.

Chapter 12

October 1897

The mist was so thick it reminded her of fat, fluffy cotton balls. She stretched out her hand to test her theory. The only thing that brushed across her fingers was a warm breeze. Somewhere close by she sensed there were other people, but it was impossible to see them.

"Hello?"

A faint noise drifted through the dense fog. It reminded her of a small bird chirping. She took a hesitant step toward the sound and then another. Each step she took was an effort in sheer willpower. It was as if there were weights on her feet preventing her from doing anything more than slowly taking one step at a time. Quiet murmurs floated in the air nearby, and she turned her head, trying to see who was talking. Through the mist, a powerful, deep voice scraped across her senses. She took a slow step toward the voice.

"Hello, is anyone there?"

The bird began to chirp rapidly in the way a small chick might when frantically searching for its mother. The man's commanding voice echoed in her ears again, but this time it was behind her.

"Stand still, will you," she muttered with irritation. "I can't find you in this fog if you keep moving around,"

She took one step and then another. Each step seemed

to take forever, and she was exhausted after only three steps. She stopped, waiting for the man to speak again.

"Victoria, wake up. Come back to me." The man's voice was barely a whisper, and it had changed direction again.

She turned toward the sound and took another step forward. A split second later, she plummeted downward and jerked as her body hit a soft mattress. Victoria blinked several times, and the hazy mist evaporated to reveal the organza canopy of her bed at Brentwood Park. Disappointment made her heart sink. She was still in the past. Disoriented, she cried out in fear as someone touched her wrist.

"Don't be alarmed, my lady. I'm simply taking your pulse."

She turned her head toward the voice, and she saw a young man sitting on the edge of her bed staring intently at a pocket watch. The sharp, stabbing pains in her head had ceased, and just as she had at the cottage, she felt as though she had a bad hangover. Wetting her parched lips with her tongue, she tried to sit up.

"Oh, no you don't," Anna said firmly from her position opposite the doctor. Gently, the woman pushed her back into her pillows. "You're going to stay right where you are until Doctor Bertram says it's all right for you to get up."

"Could I have something to drink?" she whispered hoarsely.

A moment later, Anna held a glass of water to Victoria's lips. The cool liquid soothed her throat, and she drank until the inside of her mouth no longer felt like cotton candy. Outside, the afternoon sky filtered its last light of the day into the room's floor to ceiling windows. Noting how the sun had dipped low in the sky, she frowned.

"Have I been asleep all day?" she rasped.

"*All day*?" Anna exclaimed in a soft voice. "You've been unconscious since Nicholas brought you back to the house yesterday morning."

A snap pierced the air as the young doctor closed his timepiece. Shoving it into his waistcoat pocket, he leaned forward to peer into Victoria's eyes. Next, he pressed the sides of her throat then examined the cut on her forehead. Sitting back, he crossed his arms and smiled at her.

"I understand from Lord Guildford that you've had several of these troubling headaches." The doctor eyed her carefully, and she nodded.

"Yes," she murmured.

"I'm not surprised that you're having headaches given that nasty bump you have there." Dr. Bertram nodded toward her forehead. "Do you always faint with these headaches?"

"No, only sometimes." Suddenly aware that she needed to guard her words, she didn't volunteer any unnecessary information.

"His lordship also tells me you remember nothing prior to your return to Brentwood Park," Dr. Bertram said in a matter-of-fact tone. "Although that's not uncommon with a head trauma, I have limited experience with the disorder, but I'd like to call in a consultant as a precaution."

"*No.*" Panic sent Victoria's heart slamming into her chest as she looked away from the doctor. Fingers digging into the sheets, she shook her head. "My memory will come back when everyone stops all this poking and prodding."

Before the doctor could reply, Nicholas walked through the connecting door of their chambers. As her gaze met his, she could have sworn she saw an expression of relief sweep across his face before he scowled at the doctor.

"I seem to recall telling you that I was to be informed the moment my wife was awake, Bertram," Nicholas said in a menacing voice.

"And *I recall* telling you to stay off that leg," Bertram snapped rudely. The two men glared at each other for a long moment before Nicholas accepted the rebuke with an abrupt nod

"Since I'm already here, I'll have a few moments alone with my wife, if you please."

At the arrogant statement, Dr. Bertram narrowed his eyes at Nicholas before he jerked his head in agreement. Extending his arm toward the door, the doctor invited Anna to join him.

"Shall we give them a few minutes, Lady Starling?"

"Of course. We'll return when you send for us," Anna said as she gave Victoria's hand a quick squeeze then looked at Nicholas. "You're not to upset her, Nicholas, do you understand me?"

Annoyance crossed his face as he met Anna's gaze, then nodded. As the doctor and Anna left the room, Nicholas crossed the room to her bed, and she frowned. His limp was more pronounced than she'd noticed before.

"You're in pain," she said quietly.

"It's been worse," he said in a noncommittal manner. "How are you feeling? Is the headache gone?"

"Yes, but I feel like I just ran a marathon."

Victoria closed her eyes for a brief moment, then jumped as the mattress sagged beneath Nicholas's weight. Instantly, Victoria's senses went on high alert, and she swallowed the knot that had formed in her throat as she met his astute gaze. He frowned slightly, as if disturbed by something, then cleared his throat.

"Everyone's been worried about you."

Something in his voice made Victoria believe he'd been concerned for her as well. Pleasure rushed through her at the thought before she quickly reminded herself that nothing had changed. She was still in the past, and she was posing as the man's wife. A woman who just happened to be a dead countess.

"Thank you," she murmured as she pushed aside the thought of Nicholas's wife.

"Do you remember what happened?" His question made her flinch, but she nodded.

"I had another headache."

"When you fainted in here the other day, did you have a headache then as well?"

"Yes," she said with a shrug. "Whenever I try to remember how I got here, the headaches start. The harder I try to remember, the worst they get."

"Then perhaps it would be advisable not to try to remember," Nicholas said as he studied her intently.

The assessment in his green eyes set her on edge, and she tried not to blink beneath his penetrating look. What in God's name was it about this man that had her on the verge of screaming with frustration or aching to be in his arms again? Unsettled by his gaze, she looked down to where her fingers were stroking the bedspread's silken material.

"Dr. Bertram is of the opinion that the injury to your head is the reason for your amnesia."

"Is that what you're calling my delusionary behavior now? Amnesia?" she asked in a defensive tone. "Is that why the doctor wants to bring in an expert to poke at me? Someone to see whether or not I'm crazy?"

"I gave my word not to betray your confidence, Victoria." The air between them was brittle with tension as she saw anger darken his face.

"I'm sorry," she murmured. Nicholas accepted her apology with a brusque nod. His sharp gaze still fixed on her face, he arched his eyebrows. She immediately tensed as she recognized the suspicion in his eyes.

"I've been wondering why you came to Brentwood Park, Victoria."

"What?" Victoria tilted her head at him in puzzlement.

"Why would you come back here? You've never cared for Brentwood Park." Nicholas's gaze was hard as he studied her carefully. "Why not go to London? Why here?"

"How many times do I have to tell you I don't *know* how I got here?" Victoria scowled at him. The man was as hardheaded as they came.

Nicholas glared back at her, then reached into his coat and withdrew a letter. He stared at it for a brief second, then handed it to her. Puzzled, she accepted the letter and looked at him in bewilderment.

"What's this for?"

"It's addressed to you." His voice was flat and emotionless. Victoria was certain that wasn't a good sign. She glanced down at the front of the envelope, then jerked her gaze back to him.

"I can't open this. It's addressed to the Countess of Guildford." She handed the letter back to him, but he refused to take it. An unreadable expression on his face, Nicholas folded his arms across his chest.

"I agreed to listen to your story, Victoria, with the understanding I would not divulge what you shared with me. I did *not* agree to believe." Uncomfortable beneath his cold, hard gaze, Victoria struggled not to flinch.

"As far as I'm concerned, nothing's changed. You are still my wife. Now *open* the letter."

This time Victoria did flinch at the harsh command. She flipped the letter over, broke the wax seal, and pulled the letter out of its envelope.

My dearest darling, Vickie,

I cannot express my relief and joy that you are safe, my heart of hearts. I have thought the worst since that terrible night. I have missed you unbearably, my darling, and I cannot wait to hold you in my arms again. Come to me as quickly as you can, my beloved.

Yours forever,
Terrence, Viscount Darby

"Oh, my God. She's cheating on you." At her revelation,

she saw humiliation flash in Nicholas's green eyes before his features became hard as granite and just as unreadable.

"So you are, madam wife."

"*No. I'm not.* Because, I'm not your wife. I'll be damned if you're going to punish me because your wife is sleeping around."

"You're actually going to deny having an affair with Darby?" Bitterness made every one of his words brittle.

"You're damn straight, I'm denying it," she snapped as she flung the letter into his lap. "The more I learn about your wife, the less I like her. I seem to recall telling you that your wife must be a real bitch for you to hate her so much. Well, this letter explains a lot, doesn't it?"

The muscles in his cheeks remained taut and inflexible as she glared at him. No wonder he was so ticked off. His wife wasn't just cheating on him. The woman was doing it for the entire world to see. Nicholas remained silent, his penetrating gaze never straying from her face. She was certain he was trying to figure out a reason not to believe her, and Victoria shook her head in a pessimistic manner.

"You don't hold the market on truth and honor, Nicholas," she said with a sigh. "I'm not a liar, and I think your wife is a fool."

The moment she uttered the words, her mouth went dry with embarrassment. Oh God, what the hell was she thinking? She might think the countess was crazy for playing outside the sandbox, but she damn well needed to keep her mouth shut. Just the thought of his kiss and those few blissful moments in the dark, here in her bed, told her she was in over her head.

Her gaze flitted to the firm line of his mouth, and a knot formed in her throat, making it hard to breathe. She needed to stop thinking about how much she'd enjoyed being in his arms. Nicholas frowned as if aware she was nervous, and he tilted his head slightly as he studied her. She could almost see the wheels spinning in his head, and she prepared herself for him to dismiss her with icy disdain. Suddenly his hands were on either side of her as he leaned forward until the heat of his body pressed erotically into hers.

"Why is it you sound so damned convincing," he murmured as his gaze bored into hers. "I know I shouldn't believe you, and yet those soft, pink lips of yours bewitch me with your truths."

Dark and seductive, his voice sent a frisson dancing across her skin. Instinctively, she pushed her body deeper into the pillows to put distance between them. Her reaction made him study her like a hawk. Victoria's heart pounded in her chest as she stared up at him. A strange, undefinable emotion swirled in the moss-colored depths of his gaze.

Despite the way he unnerved her, it was impossible to avoid noting how wonderful he smelled. It was a spicy, potently male scent. Deep inside her, a voice cried out for her to press her fingers against his beautiful mouth. The thought made Victoria suck in a quick, sharp breath of air. Nicholas's eyes darkened with an emotion she didn't even want to consider defining.

Slowly, he lowered his head until his mouth lightly touched hers. Fire streaked across her skin, its warmth sinking into her pores until it heated her blood like molten lava. She sighed, then parted her mouth to lace his lips with the tip of her tongue. A dark sound rumbled in his chest as his tongue swept its way into her mouth and imitated an act her body suddenly craved as if she were starving.

Pleasure swept its way through her. The fiery sensation of it settled into every inch of her body. He said she'd bewitched him, but she was the one under his spell. His lips teased and seduced hers until her body screamed for more.

She wanted him to touch her. Needed him. She arched her hips upward in a silent plea for his touch, and a dark growl vibrated on her lips as he tugged the covers off her. His tongue swirled around hers, teasing and taunting her with each tantalizing stoke. The hot taste of him made her nipples grow hard until they ached with a pleasurable, tantalizing sensitivity. Eager to assuage the need for his touch, she caught his hand and pressed it to her breasts. A growl rumbled out of him as he rubbed his thumb over the rigid peak. The sensation of soft linen between her skin and his hand made her moan softly as his mouth worked its way across her cheek to her neck where he gently nipped at her skin.

Need spun through her, and as he lifted his head to stare down at her, she saw desire darkening his face. A knot of anticipation tightened in her lower body as his hand left her breast and slid downward to her stomach where the heel of his hand pressed into the sensitive spot at the apex of her thighs. The simple pressure made her suck in a sharp breath, and a small smile curved his lips.

"I want to watch you as I make you shatter from my touch, Victoria." His words whispered across her senses as his hand pulled the hem of her nightgown upward to expose her completely.

She tried to gulp back a gasp of surprise, but failed. Satisfaction swept across his face as he met her gaze for an instant. Slowly, he lowered his head and kissed the inside of her leg, and she released a small cry of delight. With a gentle, but consistent pressure, he nipped at her thigh then used his tongue to circle the small area then nip at her again. Every time he lifted his mouth, she thought he'd tend to a different spot, but he didn't. He seemed to enjoy teasing her with his mouth.

The throbbing ache between her thighs had become almost excruciating, and a sob escaped her as she pleaded with him. The moment she begged, his hand shifted from her thigh and his thumb rubbed against the tender nub of flesh between her slick folds. She jerked from the delicious sensation, and with a moan she shifted her hips to push upward. As he applied a persistent pressure to the plump flesh, he slid a finger inside her.

Instantly her body convulsed as one sensation after another made her buck against his intimate caress. Slowly and deliberately, he pressed a second finger into her and then a third. As his fingers pressed deep inside her then retreated, his thumb continued its pleasurable assault on the sensitive nub of flesh inside her folds. She moaned as the raging sensations clutched every inch of her body.

"Look at me, Victoria," he ordered as his fingers continued to stroke her. A feverish heat spread its way through her as she stared into Nicholas's smoldering gaze. Engulfed in a fiery heat, a small shudder rippled through her, and she moaned as her eyelids fluttered shut.

"Look at me." The command forced her to look up at him. "Now, come."

She gasped as his fingers applied a sudden, hard pressure on a sensitive spot inside her. Instantly, her body responded as the most exquisite sensation shook her body. Her back arching upward, her fingers clutched at the sheets, and her hips writhed against his hand as she sobbed at the shattering release her orgasm gave her. Slowly, the tremors rocking her body eased, and she opened her eyes to stare up at him.

The desire she saw in his jade green gaze sent a tremor racing through her. God, this man was potent enough to make her forget who she was and where she came from. A knot formed in her throat at the revealing thought. She quickly swallowed the lump in order to keep breathing. Regret crossed his face, followed by a look of what she could only describe as disgust.

"*Christ Jesus*, what am I doing?" he muttered as he jerked away from her. The harsh rejection sent mortification speeding through her. Cheeks hot with embarrassment, she quickly adjusted her nightgown and scrambled to the other side of the mattress to stand on the chilly floor.

"What the hell do you think you're doing?"

"Getting out of bed," she snapped. Victoria heard the

humiliation behind her anger. She could only pray he didn't. The last thing she wanted was pity after the way he'd just made her explode in a million pieces. In a sharp, jerky movement, she leaned forward and snatched her robe off the covers at the foot of the bed.

"Damn it, Victoria," he growled as he stood up and scowled at her from across the bed. "It's too soon for you to be up."

"But *not* too soon for sex," she said in a resentful tone. She shrugged into her robe, pulling the sash tightly around her waist.

"That was a mistake. I wasn't think—"

"Stop while you're ahead, Lord Guildford." Her voice sharp with humiliation, she eyed him with disdain. "I don't appreciate being manipulated." *No matter how fantastic the sex was.*

"I wasn't manipulating you," he said in a stiff, angry voice. Frustration darkened his face with a frown. "You made me lose my head."

"Oh, so now it's *my* fault." She glared at him, wishing she could humiliate him the same way he was humiliating her.

"*God damn it*, that's not what I meant," he said in a voice that echoed with a low rumble of thunder.

"Then exactly what *did* you mean?"

"You are a conundrum, Victoria. A riddle I don't have an answer for." He rubbed the back of his neck in an obvious state of irritable confusion. "This new personality of yours makes it difficult to despise you."

"Well, *that's* comforting," she murmured sarcastically. His mouth thinned to a narrow line of proud anger.

"I am not trying to insult you, Victoria. I'm trying to explain my position where you're concerned. The changes in you contradict everything I've come to expect from you. It is difficult for me to take you at your word."

"And what about what just happened?" She bobbed her

head toward the bed as heat burned her cheeks again.

She understood his confusion, but she was just as confused by the power of her attraction to him. What she really wanted to know was if he felt that same gravitational pull. Deep inside, she prayed that's what his caresses were all about. She didn't think she could bear knowing it was nothing more than a physical desire for him..

"I regret taking advantage of you." His features were like a stone statue, hard and unmoving. She looked away from him for a moment, then returned her gaze to his face.

"I don't recall protesting," she in a soft voice. A tic twitched in Nicholas's cheek as he studied her. Hunger darkened his green eyes, and her heart skipped a beat. He studied her for a long moment before he cleared his throat.

"I'll send Dr. Bertram back in to ensure you're well enough to be out of bed."

Before he could move, a sharp rap on the bedroom door made both of them start. Nicholas commanded the person to enter. Dr. Bertram and Anna entered the room, followed by Molly and a man she'd not seen before. The entire left side of the man's face was covered with scars from what she was certain had been a terrible fire. Her heart went out to him at the pain he must have suffered. Dr. Bertram looked at first Victoria and then Nicholas.

"Forgive the intrusion, my lord," Dr. Bertram said in a crisp voice. "I just received word that Mrs. Gower in the village is about to give birth, and I must leave. I've taken the liberty of asking Roberts to assist you back to your room, my lord. You're to rest that leg until tomorrow morning or suffer the consequences."

"You said you were okay." Victoria looked at Nicholas with worry.

"It's simply an old wound," he said with nonchalance. "Bertram here is as much of a worry wart as Roberts."

"If you're ready, sir." The disfigured man approached

Nicholas's side. As the short man briefly glanced her way, Victoria smiled at him.

"Good luck getting him to listen to you," she said dryly. "God knows he won't listen to me."

"Your frustration, my lady, is one I'm well acquainted with," Roberts said with a slight smile.

Amusement sparkled in the man's eyes, and she smiled as Nicholas directed a warning look in first her direction and then in Roberts's. Ignoring their comments, Nicholas gingerly limped toward the door connecting his room with hers. As she watched him leave, Victoria found herself wishing they were alone again with her in his arms. And as much as she understood the danger of such an act, she knew it was an inevitable outcome. Nicholas believed she was his wife, and she knew she wouldn't have the will power to turn him away if he came to her.

Chapter 13

You should be in bed, my lady," Dr. Bertram said sternly as Nicholas left the room. Victoria met his disgruntled gaze and smiled.

"I'm feeling fine," she said.

"Why do I have the feeling you're going to be as troublesome a patient as your husband, Lady Guildford?" the doctor said with amused resignation. Victoria laughed.

"I doubt anyone could be as difficult a patient as Nicholas," she said mischievously. "Will it make you feel better if I promise to get back into bed the minute I start to feel bad?"

"Very well." The doctor nodded brusquely. "But you're not to overtire yourself. Now, I must be off or Mrs. Gower might decide to have her baby without me."

The doctor smiled as he picked up the black satchel sitting on her night stand before heading toward the door. Just as he was about to exit the room, he looked over his shoulder at Molly.

"Molly, make sure her ladyship eats something for dinner.

"Yes, sir," the maid said with a quick nod. "I will, Dr. Bertram.

"That's a good girl." The doctor nodded his farewell to first Victoria, then Anna. "My ladies. Good evening."

"My lady, could I not persuade you to return to bed?"

The maid looked at Victoria beseechingly as she reluctantly straightened the bed covers.

"I have to agree with Dr. Bertram." Anna's statement made Victoria turn her head toward the woman standing near the window.

"I'll be fine," she said with a shake of her head before turning back to the maid smoothing out the bedspread. She laughed. "There's no need to straighten the bed if I need to get back in it, Molly. Leave it. You can bring me dinner in a little while since everyone's insisting on treating me like I'm on my death bed."

Dismissed, the young maid nodded and left the room, the door closing with a quiet thud behind her. Victoria turned back to Anna and experienced a sudden wave of dizziness. The other woman uttered a small noise of concerned annoyance and hurried to Victoria's side.

"You really should be in bed," Anna chastised.

"I've been asleep for more than a day. I think it's time I got *out* of bed."

Anna sniffed her dissension as she escorted Victoria to the chaise lounge near the window. The moment she sat down, déjà vu made her go rigid. Victoria had been here before, in this moment. She was meant to be here. Victoria closed her eyes for a moment as an overwhelming sense of peace swept through her.

It made her believe she could be incredibly happy at Brentwood Park. Suddenly, the future seemed very far away, and the thought that she would never go back wasn't as scary as it had been, up until this moment. The sensation ebbed away as her gaze met Anna's. The other woman looked ill at ease despite the smile curving her mouth. Anna slowly sank down into the chair next to the chaise lounge, her mauve-colored gown rustling with a whisper of silk.

"I must apologize for yesterday morning. I should not have been so blunt," Anna murmured. "If I had waited for a more opportune time to speak to you about…I shouldn't have frightened you like that. Please forgive me."

Victoria bit down on her lip, uncertain whether Anna was truly remorseful or not. It was slowly sinking in that announcing she wasn't Nicholas's wife could have dangerous consequences. She could end up in a psych ward or worse, arrested for impersonating the countess. Even scarier was the thought she could be tried for murder if someone found the countess' dead body. She shuddered. Anna reached out and clasped Victoria's hand in hers.

"I realize we've barely met, Victoria, but you can trust me. I would never do anything to harm you or Nicholas." There was a note of sincerity in Anna's voice, and Victoria remembered Nicholas stating she could trust the woman. If she trusted Nicholas, she had to believe he was right about Anna.

"You said you have a special ability…that you knew, I wasn't Vickie." She studied Anna as a pensive look crossed the woman's face, as if she were afraid to explain.

"I see things…know things."

"Like a medium? A psychic?" Victoria eyed the other woman with understanding, and Anna relaxed as she met Victoria's curious gaze.

"I don't call myself those things, but if you mean that I can see bits and pieces of the future or sense things, then yes."

"And that's how you knew I wasn't the countess."

"With you, it was more of a warmth I felt. Vickie and I have never been friends, but the moment I touched your hand, I knew we'd been friends many times before." Anna smoothed several wrinkles in the skirt of her silk gown. "And it's the only logical answer for everything else I've seen in my visions. I only hope I'm wrong about a great deal of what I've seen."

"Nicholas isn't…?" Victoria's heart skipped a beat in fear at the concern in Anna's voice.

"No, he's not in any danger." A smile curved Anna's mouth. It was almost as if she approved of Victoria's concern. "In fact, I believe he shall most likely live to a ripe old age."

The woman's words eased the overwhelming concern that had sailed through her. Victoria turned her head to look out the window. As she studied the scenery, she emitted a quiet sigh.

"I've been trying to tell Nicholas since I woke up in the cottage that I wasn't his wife, but he doesn't believe me. And when I told…" Victoria halted her explanation as she realized how crazy she would sound. Maybe she was, or maybe Nicholas was right and it was all an illusion.

"You told him you were from the future, and he didn't believe you."

Fear slithered down Victoria's spine as she stared at the woman in horror. Nicholas had lied to her. He'd told Anna what he'd promised not to share with anyone. Nausea swirled in the pit of her stomach. In a quick movement, Anna caught Victoria's hands and squeezed them tightly to gain her attention again.

"Nicholas has told me nothing, Victoria. He told me nothing," Anna said fervently. "It was a knowing when we shook hands. You must believe me."

"All right," she said as she saw the other woman's pleading look. Anna breathed a sigh of relief.

"Nicholas means the world to Sebastian and me. His happiness is quite important to us, and he's been very unhappy since he married Vickie."

"I'm not surprised." Victoria snorted with disgust as she remembered the letter she'd read. "The countess has to be the biggest bitch known to man."

"Um…yes," Anna choked out as color filled her cheeks.

"Sorry." Victoria winced. She'd never felt so gauche in her life. "Nicholas says my language has become…colorful."

"Colorful, indeed." Ann laughed. "However, I do agree

with your lusty sentiment."

"Not even my *colorful* language has been enough to convince him I'm not the countess."

"Convincing Nicholas you're not Vickie is the least of your problems. I have reason to believe you're in grave danger."

The words sent a chill down Victoria's spine. The visions of being buried alive filled Victoria's head. What she'd experienced had convinced her the countess was dead. Her stomach lurched as she met Anna's gaze. With a gasp, the woman's eyes widened.

"*You know.* You know Vickie's dead."

"No, I don't know," Victoria lied.

"Yes, you do. I can see it on your face," Anna rebuked her sternly. "You think she was murdered, just like I do."

"They buried her." She didn't realize she'd spoken until Anna gasped with horror.

"Dear Lord."

"I don't mean they buried her alive. I think she was already dead." Victoria stumbled over her words, all too aware of how guilty she looked. "I wasn't there. At least I don't think I was."

"It's all right," Anna said reassuringly. "Tell me what else you know."

"I keep having this…vision of dirt hitting my clothes…my face." Victoria shuddered, and she blinked away her sudden bout of tears. Anna patted her hand in a gesture of comfort.

"They're visions, Victoria. Visions can't hurt you, but they *can* help save you. What else do you remember?"

"The dress I was wearing when they found me. I think it was Vickie's dress. It was covered in mud. When I touched it, I saw…" Victoria's voice trailed off at the horrible memory.

"Was it a blue dress?"

"Yes." An icy finger scraped down Victoria's back. "How

did you know that?"

"And there were two men with shovels?"

"Yes," she whispered, suddenly fearful at how much Anna knew.

"Victoria, you must trust me. What I'm sharing with you is something only one other person knows, and Sebastian will never betray me."

"You've not told Nicholas?"

"Nicholas is a dear friend, but he's never been able to fully comprehend the extent of my abilities." Anna sighed with resignation. "If he did, it would make things much easier."

"Easier?" At her question, a pained look engulfed Anna's pretty features.

"My gift often shows me things I'd rather not see," the other woman said with sadness. "Vickie's murderers will no doubt see you as a threat. It won't matter whether they believe Vickie miraculously escaped her grave or that you're an imposter. The moment they hear Vickie's returned your life will be in danger."

Suddenly, things had gone from bad to worse in a matter of seconds. She had no idea how she'd gotten here or how to get home. She was having visions that terrified her and headaches that left her unconscious. Now Anna was pointing out the fact that there were people who would no doubt want her dead. Until now, she'd thought going to London might be her best chance to return to her own time.

"Well, that blows a trip to London out of the water," she muttered with sarcasm, determined to hide her fear from Anna even if she couldn't from herself.

"For now perhaps, but you *will go* to London. I've seen you there. Besides, Nicholas's responsibilities in Parliament will require him to go eventually, and you must never be too far apart from him." There was an urgency in Anna's voice that made Victoria frown.

"Why?"

"The future is easily changed by the choices we make. But there are times when I know how important it is to follow my instincts. My instinct tells me to stress how important it is for you to remain as close to Nicholas as possible."

The conviction in Anna's voice drove home an emotion Victoria had been feeling almost since the moment she'd met Nicholas. He would protect her. The strength of that belief was the reason she wasn't so frightened by the prospect of someone trying to kill her. She knew he'd do everything in his power to save her. It was an odd sensation to have about a man she barely knew, but then everything about her reaction to him was confusing. Still, the thought of going to London, even with Nicholas to protect her, had become a frightening prospect.

"Tell me what you're thinking." Anna's request interrupted her thoughts. Victoria shrugged slightly as she stood up to go to the window overlooking the expansive green pastures of the estate.

"Going to London is too dangerous for me. Regardless of what Nicholas believes, others are going to wonder how I can be so different from Vickie. I think it's going to be a really big problem for him."

"You mean the possibility that others will see you as an imposter?"

"Yes," Victoria said as she looked away from Anna and acknowledged the enormity of what she was saying. "If people suspect I'm not the countess, there are going to be questions. Questions that will put Nicholas in a great deal of jeopardy."

"Just Nicholas?"

A small smile curved Anna's mouth. Startled by the fact that she'd given no thought to her own safety, Victoria glanced at the other woman. Anna studied her with an assessment that made Victoria's cheeks burn. She shrugged, while struggling to understand why she'd only been concerned for Nicholas's safety and not her own.

"Slip of the tongue. But I know I have to stay here at Brentwood Park until I find a way back home."

"And what if Nicholas is correct? What if your memories of the future are simply your mind's way of protecting you from whatever horror happened to you before Nicholas found you at the cottage?"

"But you said…you believed I was from the future."

"I'm not infallible, Victoria. I've misinterpreted things before," Anna said softly. "It's possible what I sense as truth is the truth you believe."

"So you think I should consider my visions of the future as nothing more than my brain protecting me." Victoria said with a sense of frustration and confusion.

"I'm simply saying that anything is possible," Anna said with a small sound of regret. "I only wish I could help you more, but we're leaving in the morning."

"*Leaving?*" The thought of losing an ally she'd just made chilled Victoria.

"I fear we must. Everyone only planned for two nights. Tonight will be three. But everyone wanted to stay until we knew how you were feeling. Nicholas has been through so much, and he needs our support." With a fluid movement, Anna rose from her chair and joined Victoria at the window. Capturing Victoria's hands in hers, she smiled. "Nicholas might not understand, but he will protect you. *And* when he persuades you to come to London, you're to let me know the moment you arrive. Promise me that?"

"Persuade? The man isn't above throwing me over his shoulder and putting me in the carriage himself." Victoria snorted with amused disgust.

"Protest all you like, but I already know you'll come to London before the end of winter. Of that, I'm certain," Anna said with an ironic grin. "Now promise me."

"I promise," Victoria said with a smile, then impulsively gave the woman a hug. "And don't take any bets on those visions of yours coming true. Like you said, it's all about the choices we make."

"This is one time I am praying my gift is simply a figment of my imagination," Anna murmured with an odd expression on her lovely face before she smiled. "Now then, let me leave you to rest, and I'll make certain that Mrs. Babcocke puts some hearty soup on the tray Molly brings you."

With a final squeeze of Victoria's hands, Anna moved elegantly across the floor and left the room. Alone with her thoughts, Victoria turned to look out the window. The dying sun painted an angry display of purple, red, and orange across the early evening sky. It seemed like a silent omen and reminded her of Anna's ominous warning. Suddenly uneasy, Victoria turned away from the window. In a single heartbeat, trepidation held her rigid as she stared at the man standing in her room.

Chapter 14

The man stood in the shadows and watched Victoria in silence. A shrill siren went off in her head as she remembered Anna's words of warning. She'd been so certain Brentwood Park was safe, but now she wondered if she'd been wrong. The man suddenly stepped into the thin stream of fading sunlight and smiled at her.

It was a friendly smile that compelled her to respond in kind. As he moved toward her, his gait was ungainly, but it was his open and trusting expression Victoria found so appealing. When he stopped a few feet away, he swayed back and forth like a school child.

"What's my name?" he asked.

"I don't know," Victoria said with a shake of her head and a small laugh at his swaggering demand. "Why don't you tell me?"

"I'm Edmund." Beautiful gray eyes narrowed at her as the man studied her with a healthy dose of suspicion. "Mrs. Bee says you don't remember things."

"No, I don't," she said with a nod as she assumed he was referring to Mrs. Beechum. "I don't remember anything about Brentwood Park."

"Do you still remember my name?"

"Yes, you just told me your name is Edmund." She smiled at him and his obvious effort to test her memory. "I'm Victoria."

"Yep, that's me. I'm Edmund," he said proudly as he stuck his hands in his pocket and rocked on his heels for a moment, then stopped. Head tipped to one side, he frowned at her. "I thought your name was Vickie."

"I never liked that name. I like Victoria better." Her explanation made him nod his head.

"Victoria. It's pretty. Nicholas doesn't like you very much." The unexpected observation made Victoria laugh, and he eyed her with puzzlement.

"No, he doesn't like me very much at all, does he?" she said, still laughing. Her laughter caused a grin to light up Edmund's face.

"You make Nicholas angry."

"Yes, that's true too," Victoria said. Edmund's smile died as he stared at the floor.

"You don't like me. You said mean things," he mumbled, and she frowned. Another reason to despise the countess. The woman seemed to have made it her sole mission in life to hurt others. Victoria suppressed a sigh.

"I'm sorry if the coun…if I was mean to you before. Would you like us to be friends now?"

"Okay." Happy with her response, he stepped forward to grab her hand and pumped it with great exuberance. "I'm Edmund."

"Would you like to sit down, Edmund?" Gently extracting her hand from his, Victoria gestured toward the chaise lounge. With a bob of his head, he hurried to the backless sofa and flopped down onto the padded seat. Hands under his thighs, he tipped his head to one side and frowned.

"Do you have any cake?"

"No, I'm afraid I don't." She shook her head. "Would you like me to have some brought up for you?"

"Oh no," he exclaimed in a hushed voice. "If you ask for cake, they'll know where I am."

"Who will know where you are?"

"Nurse and Mrs. Beechum."

"Are you hiding from them?"

"Yes, I like to do that sometimes, but Nurse gets mad."

Curious as to who Edmund was and why he was at Brentwood Park, Victoria wondered what she could ask to learn more about him. Suddenly, Edmund scampered to his feet and walked to the oak secretaire. Lifting the desk lid, he pulled out a piece of paper and put it to his nose.

"This used to be my mother's room," he said as he sniffed the paper. "It smells nice in here."

"Who was your mother, Edmund?" Puzzled, she watched him play at the desk.

"She was pretty and always smelled nice. She died you know."

Startled by his blunt comment, she stared at him as he sat down at the fragile-looking desk. Grabbing a pen, he dipped it into the ink well and began to draw on the sheet.

"I'm sorry your mother is gone, Edmund. I'm sure you miss her."

"No, I have Nicholas." The man shrugged as he continued drawing.

"Nicholas?"

"Um hum…we're brothers. We'll always be together. Nicholas said so."

Startled, she stared at him in silence. In an abrupt movement, Edmund raised his head. Springing to his feet, he looked frantically around the room. The instant his gaze settled on the bed, he leaped forward and slid his large frame under the furniture.

"They're coming," he mumbled from his hiding place.

Before she could ask who he meant, she heard hushed, frantic whispers outside her room. At the soft knock on her door, Victoria called out for her visitor to enter. Mrs. Beechum was the first person through the doorway, followed by a younger woman with an expression as severe as her hairstyle.

"I apologize for disturbing you, my lady," Mrs. Beechum stammered, "But have you had any visitors recently."

"Actually, I've had several visitors this afternoon. Is there someone in particular you're looking for?" Victoria said with a smile and a wink. The housekeeper's eyes widened with surprise as she nodded.

"We're looking for Master Edmund."

"And is Master Edmund fond of cake?"

"That he is, my lady. If you could point me in his direction, I'll see to it that he gets a piece with his dinner." The housekeeper's smile was bright with obvious affection for Nicholas's brother. Considering the woman's proposal, Victoria shook her head.

"Lady Starling was supposed to send up some dinner for me. Would you please ask Mrs. Babcocke to prepare a plate for Master Edmund as well and add cake to our trays? We'll eat in here."

"Of course, my lady, I'll do that right away." Mrs. Beechum smiled brightly at Victoria's words. "May I introduce Nurse Parkerton? She's responsible for Master Edmund."

The woman dropped a quick curtsey. Her expression looked pinched, which did little to enhance her already plain looks. When the nurse spoke, it was in a high, nasal tone.

"I don't wish Master Edmund to trouble you, my lady. I'll be happy to take him back to his rooms."

"It's quite all right. I don't mind his company at all."

"We'll leave you then, my lady." Mrs. Beechum curtseyed. "Dinner will be brought up shortly, and I'll have Molly come light your lamps for you as well." When the nurse appeared ready to argue, the housekeeper gently pulled the woman out of the room. As the door closed behind them, Victoria moved back to the bed. Crouching down, she pulled the bedspread up to peek under the bed and smile at Edmund.

"It's safe for you to come out now. Dinner will be here soon, and afterward we'll have cake. Would you like that?"

"Yes, please."

For a man his size, Edmund nimbly crawled out from under the bed frame. As he got to his feet, he looked down at her and grinned. He looked quite pleased with himself, and she couldn't help smiling back. Despite his obvious handicap, he was still a charmer. Victoria moved to the chair next to the chaise lounge where he stood waiting for her to sit down.

"What's your favorite kind of cake, Edmund?"

"Apple cake," he exclaimed. "Mrs. Babcocke makes it when the apples fall off the trees. Nicholas helps me pick them sometimes, but he won't let me climb the trees. He says I might fall and hurt myself."

"That makes him a good brother. I wouldn't like to see you hurt either."

"You were mean before you came back."

"I'm sorry," she said. Victoria wanted to find the countess and rip the woman a new one for being such a bitch.

"You're nice now, you're getting me cake."

She laughed. His face reminded her of Nicholas's in its shape, but there the similarities ended. Edmund's mouth did not have a stern line to its form, and his body was lanky and thinner than his brother's. For the next half-hour, Edmund entertained her with stories of his life at Brentwood Park until Molly arrived with their dinner. As Victoria prepared a plate for Edmund, she instructed him to sit on the lounge sofa. Flinging himself onto the striped daybed, he laughed with glee.

"My mother used to tell me about this chair," he said with a trace of bewildered sadness. "She said she used to take naps on it."

"Well, now you can eat here. How about that?"

Pulling a small table from beside her bed over to the couch, Victoria smiled at him. She wasn't sure why he'd talk as if he'd not been in his mother's room as a child, but she put it down to his inability to process information well.

"I like you now." Edmund bit into a piece of roasted

chicken. "You didn't like to talk to me before, except when you told me your secret."

"Secret?" Victoria stiffened at his odd statement.

"I found your book, and you were very angry with me." Edmund glanced around the room as if afraid someone might be listening. "You told me never to tell about the book."

"Do you know what's in the book, Edmund?"

He gave her a funny look before he looked around the room again. There was a distinct expression of fear on his face as he leaned toward her. When he seemed certain that they were alone, he nodded his head.

"Names. Lots of them. Ben's name was in it too." Edmund's expression was worried as he stared at his plate. She smiled.

"It's all right, Edmund. Thank you for telling me about the book. I had forgotten what was in it."

Satisfied with her explanation, Edmund turned his attention to the potatoes on his plate. Victoria resumed eating as well, trying to make heads or tails out of what Edmund had shared with her. Why in the hell would the Countess have a book with lots of names, and who the hell was Ben? Was it a diary, maybe? No, it had lots of names according to Edmund. A ledger of some kind… A little black book. The woman had a fricking little black book. No wonder the woman wanted to hide it.

"I didn't tell anyone, not even Nicholas." The pleading note in Edmund's voice jerked Victoria out of her contemplation. She smiled reassuringly at the man and reached out to squeeze his hand.

"I believe you, Edmund. You kept your promise, and I'm sure that was hard to do. I know I would have a hard time keeping a secret."

"Really?" Eyes round with surprise, Edmund looked at her with an odd expression.

"Really," she said with a nod. "Let's celebrate how good

you are at keeping secrets.”

Victoria picked a plate with chocolate cake on it and handed it to the man. He eagerly accepted the treat and took a large bite out of the desert. His eyes closed in obvious pleasure and Victoria laughed.

“I thought apple cake was your favorite.”

“Chocolate cake.” He swallowed the bite in his mouth. “Is my second favorite.”

Edmund washed his cake down with a huge gulp of milk. The result was a milk mustache on his upper lip. With a laugh, Victoria reached for a napkin to help him clean his face. A sharp rap on the door connecting her room with Nicholas’s made her call out for the visitor to enter as Edmund scrunched up his face so she could wipe the chocolate off his cheeks. As she worked, she glanced over her shoulder and saw the man the doctor had referred to as Roberts staring at them in astonishment. The man quickly cleared his throat as he met her gaze.

“My lady, his lordship would like a word with you. I’ll stay here with Master Edmund until you return,” he said politely. Uncertainty made Victoria grimace as she turned back to Edmund.

“I’ll be back in a minute, okay?” She waited for Edmund’s nod of understanding, then with a smile at Roberts, she walked down the short corridor to Nicholas’s room.

The difference between her room and Nicholas’s was dramatic. It exuded the same strength, power, and commanding nature of its owner. Sage curtains bordered tall windows, while green wallpaper covered the walls. Equine paintings were displayed in various spots, and a wardrobe stood open on the far left wall. A large bed, situated between the windows, faced the dark cherry fireplace, which had a table and chair set in front of the hearth. Nicholas sat in the chair, his leg stretched out in an obvious attempt to let the fire’s heat warm the appendage.

"I understand my brother is dining in your room." The book he held made a loud crack as he snapped it shut, and Victoria jumped slightly at the sound.

"Yes. Is that a problem?" she said with a frown as she remembered the nurse's expression when Victoria had insisted on letting Edmund join her for dinner. Had the woman thrown a fit about Edmund eating dinner with her? "If I screwed up his schedule, I'm sorry."

"In the future, you're not to invite my brother to have dinner with you again," Nicholas replied coldly as he stood up. Although he was at least four feet away, his anger vibrated in the space between them.

"I don't understand." She stared at him in confusion.

"Edmund is different from ordinary people. He has special needs."

"Of course he's different," she said with frustration. "But he still has feelings. He's sweet and extremely well-mannered."

"Nonetheless, you'll refrain from associating with him."

"Why?" she snapped.

"Because the last time you were with him, you told him everyone would be better off if he were dead," Nicholas snarled.

Flinching at the sharp words, Victoria stared at him in horror. Until now, she'd thought the countess was simply a spoiled brat, but this went beyond that. The woman had been cruel and vicious to say such a thing to someone who clearly didn't have a full grasp of the world he lived in. If she wasn't so certain the woman was already dead, Victoria would have hunted the woman down and taken her out. Not only had the countess made Nicholas's life a miserable hell, to treat Edward so callously was unconscionable.

Even worse was the knowledge that there was nothing Victoria could say that would undo what Nicholas's wife had done. When she said nothing, Nicholas closed the distance between them until he was less than an arm's length away.

"What? No pretty denials? No pleas of, I don't remember?" he said bitterly.

"What your wife said to Edmund was horrible. Cruel." She steadily met his stony gaze. "But it wasn't me, and I'm running out of apologies for the awful things your wife did. Personally, I'm glad she's not here, because if she were, someone would have to hold me back to keep me from wringing her God damn neck."

Shock reflected on his face, Nicholas narrowed his green eyes at her. It was a look of shrewd assessment, but Victoria refused to cower beneath his appraisal. Instead, she lifted her chin in defiance. His wife might have been the Wicked Witch of the West, but she wasn't, and she was through being the whipping boy for the woman's malicious behavior. In silence, Nicholas turned around and walked back to his chair. Sinking down into the wingback seat, he picked up his book, then opened it to where he'd been when she first entered the room.

"You're to stay away from Edmund." His voice was devoid of anger, but it was a command, nonetheless. His gaze dropped to his book in a clear sign she'd been dismissed. She tried to drum up anger at his arbitrary order, but couldn't. He believed she was the countess, and she was stuck with the woman's bad reputation. Could she blame him for not trusting her? Without a word, she turned and walked out of his bedroom. As she entered her room, she saw Roberts and Edmund sitting on the lounge sofa chatting away like old friends. When the valet saw her, the man rose to his feet. Edmund followed the manservant's example, and as Victoria drew near, he smiled at her.

"Did you get into trouble with Nicholas?"

"No." Victoria smiled brightly. "But I think it's time for you to go to your room."

"Can't I stay here with you?" Edmund stepped forward and caught Victoria's hand.

"No, I'm afraid Nicholas wants you to go to bed."

"Then can you come see my tree tomorrow?"

"I don't know, Edmund," she said with hesitation as she remembered Nicholas's warning.

"Please, Victoria. I want to show you my apple tree. It's all mine."

The pleading look on Edmund's face made her heart ache, and she knew she couldn't refuse him. No matter what Nicholas said, she couldn't disappoint the man-child staring at her. In some small way, she felt obligated to make up for all the pain the countess had caused. Nicholas would be furious with her, but she didn't care. She felt drawn to Edmund. The delight on Edmund's face said she'd made the right choice, and she smiled. As she turned to Roberts, she saw a look of respect cross his disfigured features.

"We've not been properly introduced, have we? I'm…" she hesitated and frowned as she extended her hand.

"You're the Countess of Guildford, my lady, and I'm Roberts." His expression kind, the valet's eyes twinkled at her.

"Thank you, Roberts. Would you mind taking Edmund back to his room? As for tomorrow, I'll meet Edmund in the garden after breakfast. Will that be all right?"

"I'll see to both of those tasks, my lady. Master Edmund will enjoy the fresh air."

"Thank you." Turning back to Edmund, she smiled. "I'll see you tomorrow, all right?"

"All right, Victoria, and I'll show you my favorite apple tree. You won't forget?"

"No. I won't forget."

Impulsively, Edmund grabbed and crushed her in a tight hug. Surprised, she froze for a moment, before returning his embrace with a laugh. As he released her, Roberts gently ushered Nicholas's brother out of her bedroom.

Chapter 15

Victoria sighed at how tepid the bath water had become. It meant she would have to get out of the water and dress. She needed to get downstairs to say goodbye to Anna and everyone else, but the scented bathwater Molly had run for her was heavenly.

She debated turning the hot water on for the third time, but decided against it. Instead, she pushed herself up out of the water and stepped out of the tub. She turned toward the free-standing towel rack to reach for her towel, but it was missing.

"Is this what you're looking for?"

The deep timbre of Nicholas's voice made Victoria whirl around clumsily, causing her to pitch forward. A split-second later, muscular arms saved her from hitting the floor. Heat suffused her skin as he held her tight against him. One large hand pressed into her back as the other cupped one cheek of her buttocks.

Her heart hammering a wild rhythm in her chest, she saw desire flash across his face as his hand left her bottom to stroke her shoulder, then trail his fingers down her arm. The moment his hand brushed against her breast, Victoria regained partial control of her sense. With a shudder, she pushed him away and freed herself from his grasp. She tugged the towel out of his hand, then spun away from him to wrap the linen around her before facing him again.

"What are you doing in here?" she rasped as a small smile curved his lips.

He didn't answer. Instead, his gaze drifted downward and back up to her face. The look said he'd burned an imprint of her body in his head. God, when he looked at her like that, she wanted to drag him to her bed. She gulped as her eyes locked with his. Nicholas's smile widened as if he knew he had only to crook his finger at her, and she would obey his command without protest. Tension careened through her as she remembered what he'd done with his fingers the last time they were alone together.

"I should have someone paint you like this." There was a seductive quality to his voice that shot a pleasurable heat through her body. "No, not a towel. A sheet draped around you as if you'd just emerged from my bed."

"*I need to dress,*" she said breathlessly.

"Perhaps I should stay and help."

The sinfully mouth-watering suggestion made her heart skip a beat. God help her. All she had to do was take two steps forward, and she'd be in his arms. Her throat threatened to close at the thought. The room was steamy with a tangible moist heat layering her skin. If the man didn't leave soon, odds were he'd have her any way he wanted. Something she was certain Nicholas wouldn't mind one bit.

The thought made her mouth water, and she drew in a quick breath. Making love with this man wouldn't be a quick wham bam thank you ma'am. It would be a long, drawn out pleasure fest, and he didn't have that kind of time. The minute everyone downstairs put two and two together, their surprise at her riding skills would be small in comparison to the idea that Nicholas had made love to a woman everyone knew he despised.

"No," she said between clenched teeth. "I can manage on my own."

"I've played ladies' maid before."

The amused irony in his voice was like a splash of cold water in her face. A dark and vicious jealousy curled its way through her limbs. The idea of him with another woman made her stomach roil, and she struggled to comprehend why she suddenly felt as though her heart was breaking.

"Your friends will be waiting," she choked out. "They might think I've changed, but if we… they know how much you despise your wife…it would be awkward."

Victoria shivered as Nicholas closed the distance between them. She tried to convince herself it was the chill in the air, but she knew better. His hand captured her chin, and he studied her carefully. The air left her lungs as she tried to meet his gaze fearlessly.

"A logical argument, my sweet witch," he murmured. "But what would you say if we had no guests?"

"I don't understand," she lied in a hoarse whisper.

"Don't you?" He wrapped a lock of her hair around his finger. "Then let me clarify. Would you let me into your bed if we were free of any obligations?"

There was an odd gleam in his eyes that made her heart pound harder. Beneath his probing gaze, she lost the ability to speak. Nicholas lowered his head and brushed his mouth over hers. Tantalizing and hot, his kiss held the promise of sinful pleasure. Victoria trembled. God, she wanted him. She'd never wanted a man so much in her life. Suddenly, his heat was gone as he stepped away from her. His features unreadable, he studied her for a long moment before he turned away and walked toward the door.

"Dress quickly. Our guests are leaving after breakfast."

"Yes," she whispered. "I would say yes."

She suppressed a groan of horror as she realized what she'd just done. God help her, she'd just told the man she'd sleep with him. Had she lost her mind? No, that had happened the moment she'd opened her eyes in this reality. She blinked, and for a split second she was certain he'd heard her as he paused for a brief instant in the doorway. It was a small hesitation and as he disappeared through the doorway, she realized he hadn't heard her after all. Victoria sagged as a mixture of relief and disappointment clutched at her.

The gentle thud of the bedroom door closing filtered its way into the bathroom. With a small groan, she wrapped her arms around her waist. God, what the hell was she thinking? She'd actually invited the man into her bed. He was a married man. No, he was a widower. She was certain of that, which meant *she* was the real countess. No, they weren't married. Victoria winced.

Did Occam's Razor apply to her situation? Could Nicholas and Anna be right that her brain had created visions of the future to protect her from remembering some horrible trauma? She snorted. No, this time and place wasn't her reality. If she could find out how she'd gotten here, maybe she could find a way back to her own time. The familiar stabs of pain in her temple made her focus on her present reality. She wasn't ready for another headache.

If she couldn't go home, she needed to figure out how to reconcile her attraction to Nicholas, and his belief she was something she wasn't. Because she was certain the time was coming when there would be no going back where he was concerned. Victoria pulled in a deep breath at the realization. Anna. She had to talk to Anna before she left.

The quiet murmur of conversation filled the air as Victoria made her way through the open corridor that led to the dining room. As she entered the room, all the gentlemen stood up, while Anna and Lady Palmerton smiled their delight at seeing her.

"Victoria, we're so happy to see you're feeling better,

aren't we, John?" Catherine looked at Lord Palmerton who nodded his agreement as he sat down.

"Indeed, all of us are greatly relieved that you're up and about."

Victoria said thank you as everyone continued to express their happiness that she was well again. A footman held her chair for her as she sat down opposite Nicholas. She avoided looking down the table length for several minutes before she darted a look in his direction. To her surprise, he was studying her with a puzzled frown on his face. Their gazes locked for a moment until she quickly glanced away. Breakfast was almost finished before Victoria found an opportunity to discreetly ask Anna if she could speak with her. The other woman immediately rose from her seat.

"Good heavens, I almost forgot that I promised to write down my recipe for treating migraines," Anna exclaimed. "Come, Victoria, I'm sure there's paper and pen in the library."

In seconds, Anna had secured their escape. Arms entwined, they left the dining room. When they were in the library and safely out of earshot, Anna caught Victoria's hands in hers.

"What's happened?" The concern in her new friend's voice made Victoria shake her head.

"It's…nothing's happened…it's just that Nicholas and I…we…oh Lord, I can't believe I'm even discussing this." Victoria stared helplessly at Anna. A knowing smile curved the other woman's lips, and Anna's brown eyes sparkled with something that Victoria thought might be satisfaction.

"He tried to seduce you." Anna's amused observation made Victoria nod her head.

"You might say that. He stole my towel while I was in the tub." Victoria muttered with exasperation, unwilling to share just how far things had gone between her and Nicholas.

"Oh, dear." Anna laughed softly.

"It's not funny," Victoria snapped. *"I'm not the countess."*

"Victoria, have you told Nicholas you're not his wife?" Anna's unhurried tone emphasized her patient expression.

"Yes, you know I have," Victoria said in frustration.

"And we both agree that, while we have no proof to the contrary, the other interested party is no longer with us, correct?"

"Yes."

"And you agree that the truth you believe to be true might actually be a protective measure your mind has created to help you handle a horrible trauma you've endured."

"Yes," Victoria said reluctantly.

"Then you've been as honest and open with Nicholas as you can be. Any speculations you have are just that, speculations," Anna said with an empathetic expression on her face. "I see no reason why the two of you should not enjoy the pleasure of each other's company."

Despite her reservations, Victoria struggled with the happiness her new friend's words brought her. She was already in deep enough as it was. What would happen to her when she returned to her own time? Especially if her heart became involved. She almost snorted at the thought. *If?* She was hanging off the edge of that cliff already. She shook her head, and Anna caught her hand.

"You're precisely what Nicholas needs, Victoria. He's been miserable since he married Vickie. He needs someone to love him."

"I can't—"

"Victoria, has it ever occurred to you that you're here for a reason?"

"A reason?"

"If someone were murdered, their death would obviously require suspects. Individuals who are innocent might be—"

"Nicholas," Victoria gasped in a low whisper. "You think I'm here to save Nicholas."

"I don't believe in coincidences, Victoria. Everything happens for a reason. I believe in destiny." Anna smiled gently. "The things I've seen tell me that you're exactly where you're supposed to be. Remember that whenever you think you shouldn't do something."

"All right, I'll remember," Victoria said with a growing sense of peace. Anna patted her hand.

"Good. Now then, we've been gone far too long. Sebastian has business in London and is already champing at the bit to leave. He'll not be pleased with me if we miss our train. Let me write my recipe for migraines. If you don't return with a piece of paper in your hand, there will be raised eyebrows."

Anna quickly found paper and pen, then proceeded to jot down a list of ingredients. When she'd finished, she handed the recipe to Victoria and urged her back toward the dining room.

A short time later Victoria stood beside Nicholas and watched the last of his friends leave for the train station. She wasn't sure what she'd expected to feel at everyone's departure, but her contentment took her by surprise. It seemed right to be standing next to Nicholas as the carriages rolled away from the manor.

An awkward silence settled between them, and Victoria glanced up at his profile. A sudden urge to touch his cheek made her fingers tingle. The strength of the impulse alarmed her, and she quickly turned to go back into the house with Nicholas following her.

"I like your friends," she said as they paused in the foyer.

"They appear quite taken with you as well." Puzzlement echoed in his quiet observation.

"And you disapprove." The sarcasm in her voice made him arch his eyebrows.

"On the contrary, I've simply never been as easily persuaded as my friends."

"God, you're stubborn." She released a sigh of aggravation.

"You are my wife, Victoria. You'll not convince me otherwise. But I'm convinced your injury has changed your personality in remarkable ways. In ways that are compelling enough for me to believe you're not amusing yourself at my expense or that of others."

"So what tipped the scale in my favor," she said in a wry tone.

Nicholas's green eyes darkened as his gaze swept over her. She had no doubt he was remembering what she looked like naked. A small smile tilted his mouth, and his wicked expression made her body react like a piece of metal to a magnet. The spot between her legs suddenly ached for his touch again, while her breathing became shallow and ragged. He stepped into her personal space, and her heart pounded like a runaway freight train in her chest.

"I think you already know what's influenced my opinion of you. Vickie never responded to my touch the way you do. Nor has she ever put me first in anything she's said or done." He reached out and pressed his thumb against her bottom lip, and she forgot to breathe. "It wasn't a lack of desire that kept you from surrendering to me this morning. You didn't want my friends to think me a fool. That's what tipped the scales in your favor, Victoria. You expressed concern for someone other than yourself. It's a trait that Vickie has no concept of, nor would she understand."

"Oh," she whispered, unable to think of any other coherent response. A small smile touched his lips.

"I think that's the first time since you've returned that you've had little to say during a conversation."

"It's rather difficult to respond to such an eloquent apology."

"Apology?" He frowned in dissension before his lips curved upward again. "Yes, I suppose it was, wasn't it?"

The wicked amusement in his green eyes caused her cheeks to grow hot with embarrassment, and a tremor rocked her body as she tried to avert her gaze, but failed. The man aroused feelings inside her that frightened her. He was a lethal assault on her faculties, and his mere presence guaranteed a complete seduction of her senses. Worse, the man only had to utter a few words, and he easily manipulated her emotions. There were no half measures with him. It would be far too easy to fall in love with the Earl of Guildford, and that was a terrible idea.

"I think I'll take a walk in the gardens," she choked out as she remembered her promise to join Edmund after breakfast. Eager to escape, she turned away only to have electricity spike through her as he caught her arm.

"I have a few items of business to attend to, but I'll join you when I'm done."

At the moment, the last thing she wanted was to spend more time in his company. The dynamics had shifted between them, and she was all too aware that she was only one kiss away from spending the night in his arms. Not that she objected to the idea. In fact, her body was more than willing. But she didn't belong here. She didn't want to return to her time period only to find herself in love with a dead man. With a small gulp, she nodded her understanding. Amusement danced in his eyes as he slowly released her. Clueless as to how to reach the garden, she hesitated. A soft chuckle rumbled out of him.

"You can reach the gardens through the library," he said as he pointed to the room off to his left. "Should I have Molly fetch you a coat? It's unusually warm today, but—"

"No, I'll be fine," she said before she bolted off in the direction he'd indicated.

His soft laughter followed her to a set of French doors leading into the gardens. By the time she was out in the sunshine, her heart rate has slowed significantly.

The air had none of the chill it had when she'd first arrived here in the past, and the patches of snow had completely melted under the warmth of the sun. It was easy to understand why Nicholas had wanted Brentwood Park. She couldn't remember ever having seen anything so breathtakingly beautiful.

In the distance, she saw a long building that she was certain were stables. Any other time she would have thought about changing her clothes and going for a ride. Instead, she followed a cobblestone path on her left that broke away from the brick walkway that led to a gazebo almost completely hidden from view by tall hedges. In the distance, she heard Edmund's voice, and she followed the sound. As she drew closer, she smiled at Edmund's excited chatter.

"I wish she'd hurry up, Roberts. I want to show her my apple tree."

Victoria did not hear the manservant's soft-spoken response. The stone pathway she was on bore to the right, and she walked through an archway of hedges to a lovely columned portico. Halfway down the long, open air walkway, Edmund paced back and forth, while Roberts sat quietly on a nearby bench.

"Good morning," she called out.

"*Victoria, you came.*" Edmund ran toward her and wrapped her in a bear hug.

"Well, I would have been here sooner, but I forgot to ask where we were going to meet." Laughing at his enthusiastic greeting, she smiled at Roberts as he rose to his feet.

"Forgive me, my lady. I should have sent word to you." Roberts apologized with a wince.

"Oh, it's not your fault, Roberts. I should have asked where to meet you," she said with a smile.

"Would you like me to stay with you and Master Edmund?"

"No, I think we'll be fine." Victoria shook her head and

looked up at Edmund, who was fidgeting at her side. "Is that all right with you, Edmund?"

"Yep, I want to show you my apple tree."

"All right." Victoria gave Roberts an amused look, and the man grinned.

"If you'll excuse me, my lady. Now that you're here with Master Edmund, I will see to my normal duties."

"Of course, thank you so much, Roberts."

"Come on, Victoria, I want to show you my apple tree." Edmund, not waiting to see Roberts leave, grabbed her hand as he pulled her away from Nicholas's valet.

With a parting smile in the valet's direction, she allowed Edmund to drag her along the columned walkway out into a lovely garden. Beyond that was a small orchard. Edmund led her to a sturdy tree at the front of a group of trees, which still had a few reddish apples dangling from its limbs. All the other trees had been harvested, which meant Edmund's tree had received special care.

"Isn't it a beautiful tree, Victoria?" he said as he hugged the tree trunk

"Yes," she said with a sense of wonder. His passionate love for the tree made her see it through his eyes. "It's very beautiful."

"Do you want to try one of the apples? There aren't many left. Nicholas said we had to pick a lot of them to keep them from getting rotten."

"I'd love to try one." Victoria laughed.

Edmund grinned at her, then proceeded to inspect the tree's lower branches. After several moments of debating his selection, he reached up and snapped off an apple. With a small bow, he handed it to her. She bit into the fruit, and a trickle of juice escaped the side of her mouth, which she quickly wiped away with her finger. Tart and crisp, the apple tasted like the Jonathans she often bought back home.

"Um." She sighed with pleasure. "Your apple tree isn't

just beautiful, Edmund. Its apples are delicious too."

"Come on, there's lots more to see too." He clapped his hands in delight.

For the next two hours, Edmund took great pleasure in showing her everything in the gardens. They walked through paths laced with autumn flowers and the subtle remains of summer flowers. One of her favorite spots was the hedge maze. When Edmund completed his duties as tour guide, he sat down on a bench in the Italian gardens. Joining him on the wooden seat, she lifted her face to the warm sunshine.

"Thank you Edmund," she said. "I've enjoyed our morning together."

"Nicholas said you're going to have lunch with us today."

"Lunch?" Victoria stared at him in surprise. Surely Edmund was confused.

"Uh, huh."

She winced at his reply. Nicholas had made it quite clear last night that she wasn't to have anything to do with his brother. She understood why. If Edmund were her brother, she wouldn't want the countess anywhere near him either. Not only would Nicholas be angry that she was with Edmund, he'd be furious she'd thwarted his orders.

She needed to get Edmund back into the house before Nicholas realized she was with his brother or there would be hell to pay. At that moment, Edmund leapt to his feet and waved with excitement. She turned her head to see Nicholas walking toward them. Victoria cringed as she realized Judgment Day was at hand.

Chapter 16

The first thing Nicholas noticed as he walked toward Edmund and Victoria was his brother's carefree manner. It had been months since he'd seen his brother in such high spirits. Vickie's cruelty had done a great deal of harm, but even from a distance, he could tell his brother was happy.

It was obvious the two of them enjoyed each other's company. Victoria looked relaxed and content, the sun highlighting the burnished tones of her auburn hair. She had released her shoulder length tresses from its knot, and her hair hung in charming disarray about her unblemished features.

Despite his efforts to bury himself in business matters for the past two hours, his thoughts had relentlessly returned to Victoria. She continued to surprise him. Last night, after Roberts had seen Edmund back to his room, the valet had shared his opinion of Victoria. The interaction that the older man had witnessed between his wife and Edmund had amazed the valet.

Even more astonishing had been the fact that Victoria hadn't been the slightest bit uncomfortable at Roberts' appearance. That alone would have exposed Victoria as a fraud, but she'd even introduced herself to his valet. But the most surprising thing of all had been Roberts' quiet, yet enthusiastic, support of Victoria spending time with Edmund. He trusted his valet, and it was why he'd agreed to let Roberts leave his brother in Victoria's care. It was also the reason he'd decided to arrange a picnic for the three of them.

Now, as he watched her interaction with Edmund, he wondered how he'd ever thought she was playacting. Nicholas was baffled by what had happened to his wife in the three weeks she'd been gone, but he couldn't argue he liked the change in her. He could only hope nothing changed. Nicholas had no wish for things to revert back to the way they were.

Nicholas liked his newly changed wife very much. In particular, he enjoyed the way she responded to his touch. There was fire beneath Victoria's surface that he had every intention of exploring. When he'd heard her say yes to him earlier this morning, it had taken an enormous amount of effort not to turn around. If he'd acted on impulse, he would have carried her to her bed and buried himself inside her.

It would've been a dangerous thing to do without a French letter to prevent impregnating her. Despite the danger, he knew it would be impossible to stay away from her bed. An image of her emerging from her bath filled his head and shot a lightning bolt of desire through his blood. Water glistening on her skin, she'd been softly rounded with full, lush breasts She had the body of Botticelli's Venus. Just the thought of her pulled his muscles tight with a need he'd never experienced with any woman before, not even Vickie. Edmund's shout of greeting jerked him out of his thoughts as he drew near his brother and wife.

Edmund ran to meet him, and Nicholas grinned as his brother hugged him. Over his brother's shoulder, Nicholas studied the look on his wife's face. She quickly hid her trepidation behind a bright smile, but he could read the agitation in Victoria's brilliant sapphire gaze. Her deliberate disregard for his authority troubled her after all. He bit back a smile as he knew he would not be able to resist teasing her.

"*Nicholas.* I showed Victoria all over the gardens," Edmund said with excitement. "She even ate an apple off my tree. You really liked the apple, didn't you, Victoria?"

"I think it must have been one of the best apples I've ever eaten," she said with a smile, but Nicholas could tell she was worried about his reaction to her flouting his orders. He smiled at his brother.

"Edmund, the gig should be ready by now, why don't you run ahead to make sure our lunch is packed and ready to go."

Edmund nodded and loped off toward the stables. Nicholas watched his brother's lanky figure disappear through the hedges that separated the garden from the stable yard. Beside him, he could feel the tension flowing through Victoria's body. Head bent, he clasped his hands behind his back and studied the ground for a moment. When he returned his gaze to her face, mischief crashed through him at the worried look on her lovely features. Clearing his throat, he tried to school his features into what he hoped was a severe look.

"Well, madam wife, what do you have to say for yourself?" He gave her credit for not giving ground as she faced him.

"If you're expecting an apology, dream on."

The defiant toss of her head sent her hair flying, and he suddenly wanted to let her silk tresses slide over his hands as he nibbled at her luscious mouth. He immediately suppressed his reaction to her, then arched his eyebrows.

"You deliberately disobeyed me, Victoria."

"Well, since I'm not your wife, I don't *have* to obey you." Her irreverent response aroused a devil in him.

"Does that mean you're now retracting your earlier agreement?"

"What agreement?" She nervously bit down on her lower lip, and he immediately wanted to taste her mouth again.

"Your acceptance of my offer." Nicholas deliberately kept his voice low as he bent his head toward her. A delicate blush crested over her cheeks.

"I don't—"

"You said yes, Victoria. You said you'd welcome me into your bed." He traced a line from the base of her throat down to the green silk of her bodice. She shuddered at his touch. Nicholas leaned into her, his mouth nipping at her earlobe.

"I'm not sure what pleases me the most, that you said yes or how much I'm going to enjoy having you cream my cock like you did my fingers."

"Oh, God," she whispered as she drew in a sharp breath.

"Afraid?" he murmured.

"Not one bit." Although her breathing was still ragged, she shook her head vehemently and glared up at him.

"Impudent minx." He laughed, enjoying her startled expression. "It appears I was wrong about you and my brother. Edmund clearly enjoys your company."

"He's quite sweet," she said cheerfully, her apprehension gone.

"Well, if I know my brother, he'll be waiting impatiently for us at the stables. Shall we?"

He offered his arm to her and covered her hand where it rested in the crook of his arm. The pleasure it gave him to have her at his side was something he found himself savoring. He couldn't ever remember feeling like this with Vickie. He tilted his head slightly and breathed in the sweet aroma of Victoria's hair. The now familiar scent of lemon and honey filled his nostrils. When he glanced downward, he caught her looking up at him with curiosity. He smiled as a rose flush invaded her cheeks at having been caught staring. How often had he seen Vickie blush? He couldn't recall a single instance.

"So tell me, what wonders did Edmund show you in the gardens?"

"Practically everything I'm sure." Her infectious grin lit up her face. It was clear she'd enjoyed her morning. Deep inside, he realized he wanted to make her this happy every day.

The thought surprised him, but it felt right, just as so much else felt right where Victoria was concerned.

"What was your favorite part of the morning?"

"The hedge maze," she answered with a laugh.

"The maze?" Surprised, he chuckled. "I was a boy the last time I visited the maze."

"You should try it more often, especially with Edmund. He loves to leave you behind so you have to beg him to come find you."

"And did you throw yourself on his mercy and plead with him?" His soft inquiry caused fire to flash in her sapphire gaze.

"Pleading with Edmund is easy compared to others."

"So if you were forced to plead with me, it would be more difficult?" He laughed as she grimaced. "You don't like to be teased?"

"I have to admit, where you're concerned, I'd rather be on the giving end than the receiving one."

When they reached the stables, they found Edmund waiting restlessly next to a small one-horse cart. When they reached the side of the gig, Nicholas released her arm to help her up into the cart. Grinning at his brother's eager manner, he told Edmund to get in the cart while he double-checked the harness. Satisfied with the animal's tack, he climbed into the two-wheeled vehicle.

"Would you like to drive today, Edmund?" he asked as he saw the gleam of excitement in his brother's eyes.

"Yes, please." Edmund waited with restrained impatience as Nicholas seated himself next to Victoria.

"Go easy on Maribelle. She knows the way," he said as he gestured for his brother to take up the reins and buggy whip.

"Yes, Nicholas." Edmund's face took on an air of intense concentration as he lightly tapped the hindquarters of the horse to propel the cart into motion.

The dog cart rolled out of the stable yard and onto one

of the dirt roads that wound their way across the estate. With his brother at the helm, Nicholas sat back to enjoy the ride. With one arm stretched out behind Victoria, he tried to recall the last time he'd been so relaxed. He looked down at her and smiled as he caught her watching him. She quickly averted her gaze and shivered.

"You're cold," he stated as he shifted his position and reached for a jacket lying on the seat opposite them.

"I'm fine," she said as she rejected his offer of the garment. "It's not cold at all."

"This is an unusual day. You should ask Molly to have your winter clothes brought down from storage until you're able to visit your dressmaker in London."

"London?" There was a note of fear in Victoria's voice, and he studied her face intently. She quickly looked away. Narrowing his gaze, he tilted his head to look at her profile.

"I would think you'd want new gowns for the season."

"No, I'm good," she muttered with a shake of her head. "I don't want to go to London, anyway."

"I thought we'd spend Christmas at Guildford House as I have to be in town for the opening of Parliament in January."

"Oh," she said softly. Concentration darkened her features as if she was trying to solve a difficult puzzle. With a small shake of her head, she met his gaze. "Well, thank you, but I'll stay here."

"Would you care to explain that statement?" he drawled, intent on making her reveal why she'd suddenly changed her mind about going to town.

"There's nothing to explain. I just have no intention of going to London." She shrugged.

"I see, and yet you've talked about going to London since your return."

"Well, I've changed my mind." Victoria looked at him with a mutinous expression on her face. "I'm not going to London."

"On the contrary, Victoria. When I leave for London, you *will* accompany me."

"I'd like to see you make me," she muttered beneath her breath as she slid away from him and pushed herself into the corner of the dog cart.

Although her mouth was thinned with rebellious anger, he saw a flash of fear in her eyes. Frustrated, he exhaled a harsh breath of aggravation. The woman was enough to drive him mad in more ways than one. Nicholas sighed with exasperation, remembering the afternoon was supposed to be one of pleasure, and here he was fighting with her. He didn't want that. He'd looked forward to their picnic all morning, and he wasn't about to let a minor disagreement ruin their time together. With a grunt, he shook his head.

"This entire conversation began with you shivering," he observed. He lifted the coat on the seat across from them. "Do you still maintain you're not cold?"

"I'm fine." Victoria defiantly rejected the garment as she leaned forward to look over Edmund's shoulder.

"Where are we going?"

"I thought we'd have our picnic near the lake at Goodman Cottage. It happens to be one of Edmund's favorite spots."

"I see," she murmured. Sapphire eyes darkened with disillusionment, and he frowned.

"You disapprove?"

"No." She shrugged and looked away. "I just thought the picnic was more of a social outing as opposed to a fact-finding mission."

The rueful note in Victoria's voice said his choice in destination had conveyed an entirely different meaning to her than he'd intended. She clearly thought he was interested in probing her thoughts about her return. A visceral sensation gnawed at him. He needed to make her understand he had no ulterior motive for returning to the cottage. Grasping her chin, he forced her to look at him.

"This is not a fact-finding mission, as you call it, Victoria."

The uneasy look clouding her eyes emphasized he wasn't the only one who was afraid to trust. Nicholas steadily held her gaze to give her time to consider his words. Slowly, her uncertainty disappeared as she nodded her acceptance of his explanation.

"Nicholas, do we go left or right at the fork?" Edmund asked.

"Go to the right. We'll come out in front of the old oak tree just down from the cottage."

"Can we eat as soon as we get there?" Edmund asked. "I can smell the potpies Mrs. Babcocke fixed, and my tummy is growling like those tigers you told me about."

"As soon as we set up, we can eat," Nicholas said with a laugh.

Moments later, Edmund guided the small cart into a glen near the cottage. He took great care pulling Maribelle to a halt, and with great attentiveness, he wrapped the reins around a small metal latch on the rim of the gig.

"How's that?" Turning toward his brother, Edmund grinned. "I get better every time, don't I, Nicholas."

The strength of his love for Edmund made Nicholas's throat close. For all his challenges, his brother had the heart of a lion and worked hard to succeed at whatever task placed before him. Bringing him back to England had been not only the right thing to do, but the best thing he'd ever done.

"Well done, Edmund," he said, before moving to the back of the cart and unlatching the door.

He stepped out of the gig, then turned to help Victoria out of the cart. As she climbed down and stood close to him, he lifted her hand to his lips. His action sent a fiery color into her cheeks and behind her, Edmund giggled with unrestrained glee from his seat in the cart. Nicholas released Victoria's hand, and assuming a look of mock severity, he shook his finger at Edmund.

"For someone who was complaining about stomach pains a few minutes ago, you seem to be moving quite slowly."

Edmund laughed at Nicholas's teasing and leaped down to the ground. Accustomed to their picnic outings, Edmund opened a compartment over the wheel mount of the gig and removed several large blankets without instruction. Unlatching the large picnic basket from the opposite side of the cart, Nicholas offered his free hand to Victoria.

Charging ahead of them, Edmund spread the blankets out on the ground in a sunny spot near an immense oak tree. A short distance away, the pond glistened and danced in the sunlight. With Edmund's help, Nicholas spread the picnic out on the blanket. There was a sense of camaraderie in their actions that comforted him. His only wish was that they could have done this as children.

Mrs. Babcocke had prepared several meat pies and added fresh vegetables and fruit to the basket. Pulling the items out of the wicker container, he watched Victoria help Edmund prepare his plate. The sight was just as amazing as it was pleasing. In companionable silence, the three of them relaxed in the sunshine, enjoying their meal. Edmund finished first, and with an inquisitive look at Nicholas, he sat up on his knees in expectation.

"Can I go now, Nicholas?"

"Are you sure you're done eating?"

"Yes," Edmund nodded his head. "I want to go look for turtles."

"Very well." Nicholas smiled before he eyed his brother sternly. "And don't go wading into the water. It's already icy cold."

"All right," Edmund said before dashing off at a full run, his long legs carrying him away at a rapid rate. Watching him bolt away, Nicholas reclined back on one elbow.

"I almost envy him," he mused aloud.

"He does have an appreciation for life that the rest of us often overlook." At her observation, Nicholas shook his head as he met Victoria's dark blue gaze.

"What I meant was, I envy his freedom."

"His freedom?" Puzzlement creased her brow. He smiled at the puckish look.

"Yes. His freedom and innocence." He looked out over the body of water, remembering the first time he had met Edmund. "Edmund will always be a child, no matter how long he lives."

"How old is he?" Victoria asked in a curious tone.

"He just turned thirty-one."

"You're a good brother," she said with a note of approval in her voice. "It's obvious you love him very much."

"I always wonder if it's enough to make up for the past." Nicholas stared out at the pond, but only saw the small, seedy office of a solicitor who'd explained why he billed Nicholas a large monthly sum for services rendered.

"The past?" Victoria's soft voice made him turn his head toward her before he looked away again.

"It's a long story." He picked up a piece of apple and studied it for a moment, then popped it into his mouth. As she leaned toward him, the lemon and honey scent of her drifted beneath his nose.

"I'm a good listener," she entreated. "And we're not going anywhere."

Seated with her legs curled up beneath her, she leveled a patient look in his direction. He held her vivid gaze for a long moment, then turned his head back to study the pond. When he spoke, it amazed him how easy it was to tell her the story.

"In the beginning, my parents failed to realize there was something different about Edmund. I remember my mother saying once he had been a very easy baby to care for. When he turned three, my father called in an expert from Vienna."

He paused for a moment, checking to ensure that his brother was still close by. Catching sight of Edmund's tall form some distance away, Nicholas allowed himself to breathe a little easier as he continued his story.

"At that point, the doctor told my parents Edmund would be dead before the age of twenty, and that it was doubtful he would mature mentally beyond the age of four or five."

Lowering his head, he studied the blanket's weave for a moment, then raised his head to look at Edmund throwing stones into the pond. His brother was the reason the Guildford line would die with him. He darted a quick look in Victoria's direction. She was studying him with a pensive shimmer in her eyes.

"The diagnosis devastated my parents," he said as he looked away from her to stare up at the clear sky.

"I can't imagine how heartbroken they must've been."

"Actually, I think my father was more ashamed than anything else," Nicholas bit out. "Or he wouldn't have done what he did next."

The old bitterness latched onto his insides as he watched Edmund bending over to study something on the edge of the pond. How could his father not have loved Edmund? Nicholas drew in a deep breath, then released it. He was no better than his father. Otherwise, he wouldn't hesitate to try for an heir. Abigail had reminded him time and time again that she had three children who showed no signs of Edmund's handicap. His sister's reassurances had not changed his mind. Nicholas looked at Victoria, who was patiently waiting for him to continue his story.

"The bastard hid Edmund away, then told everyone he was dead."

"Oh, my God." Victoria gasped. The appalled expression on her face resembled his reaction the moment he discovered the truth.

"I have vague memories of Edmund, but I was only five when my parents took him to the continent. They arranged for Edmund's care in a small villa in Italy, then returned and announced Edmund was dead."

"Does he know any of this?" Victoria asked in horror.

"No." Nicholas shook his head. "My mother left a letter for me with the solicitor who arranged for Edmund's needs and kept the family secret safe."

"But he remembers your mother," Victoria said softly. "He talked about her last night."

"That's because my mother went to Italy for three months every year to stay with him." Nicholas winced. He'd always wondered where his mouther had gone on her trips. She'd always been so happy before she left and sad when she returned. "While returning to England, her ship went down in a storm. Edmund was sixteen. I'm just grateful she spent the last three months of her life with him."

"I'm so sorry, Nicholas." Sympathy echoed in Victoria's voice as she laid her hand over his. The sincerity of her compassion sent a powerful emotion pounding through his body.

"My father died seven years later, and it was then I learned Edmund was still alive and living in Italy, where my father had hidden him away from the world."

"And you went and got him," Victoria said softly.

"Yes. My sister, Abigail, and I traveled to Italy to bring him home." He nodded as his gaze settled on his brother again. "The first time we met Edmund, he recognized us immediately. My mother had given him miniatures of both Abigail and me. I cannot describe what it was like to have Edmund greet me as if he'd known me all my life, and yet he was a complete stranger to me."

"What did you tell everyone when you brought him home?"

"I told the staff very little and said nothing to anyone else except my closest friends." Nicholas rolled his shoulders in an impatient shrug. "Everyone believed he was dead, and I left it that way. I wasn't about to let people make him into a figure of fun."

"Did Vickie resent Edmund being here?"

"No. She viewed him as more of an inconvenience." Nicholas shook his head. "The fact that she didn't want children was one of the few things we *did* agree upon. She had no use for children, whereas the risk of siring a child with the same difficulties as my brother is too great."

"You can't mean that," Victoria gasped softly. "The chance of any children you might have been like Edmund is very low."

"Whether they are or not, I have no intention of testing those odds," Nicholas said in a tightly fierce voice. "The repercussions are too great."

Before Victoria could offer any other reason why he shouldn't be so adamant on the subject, Nicholas's attention was diverted by Edmund, who was hollering at them from the other side of the pond. Ignoring the minor ache in his leg, Nicholas scrambled to his feet, then bent to help Victoria up off the ground. Her hand on his arm, she pointed to where Edmund was jumping up and down on the opposite side of the large pond. Together they returned his wave, and Nicholas looked down at her with a smile.

"Would you care to take a walk? Obviously he's eager to show us his discovery."

"Of course." Victoria laughed up at him.

Instead of offering his arm, Nicholas clasped her hand in his, and drew her along the shoreline to where Edmund was waiting. As they moved along the path that bordered the pond, the thatched roof of Goodman Cottage came into view. Edmund ran to greet them and grabbed Victoria's hand to pull her toward a young man sitting in front of an easel. His brother shushed them with a finger against his lips as they drew near. Nicholas grinned at the way Edmund and Victoria communicated in makeshift sign language.

Sapphire eyes sparkling with pleasure, she looked at Nicholas and smiled with amusement at Edmund's excitement. He chuckled and watched as she moved to stand behind the artist. As she stepped forward to study the canvas, the pleasure vanished from her features. In an instant, she became deathly white, an shock twisted her mouth open in a mute cry of fear. A sharp blade of panic speared into Nicholas's gut as he raced forward to catch Victoria in his arms as she fainted.

Chapter 17

Present Day

Nick emerged from the bathroom in Victoria's hospital room, towel drying his hair. His gaze flitted toward Victoria, hoping to see her looking back at him, but nothing had changed. It had been four and a half days now, with no sign of Victoria coming out of the coma.

Barefoot and without a shirt, he returned to the bathroom to hang up the towel, then tugged on a T-shirt that he tucked into his jeans.

He was sitting on the recliner bed that he'd just returned to its upright position when Nora knocked on the door and smiled at him as she walked into the room.

"Any change?" She looked toward Victoria and answered her own question. He continued to tie his tennis shoes as he shook his head. Nora sank down on a nearby chair and dropped her bag onto the tile floor.

"How are things progressing with the shop repairs?" he asked.

"We should be open by Saturday. The guys I hired have done a wonderful job putting everything back together."

"Did the insurance guy give you any more hassle about the security system?"

"No, we're good to go with that. I managed to get the security people to give us an upgrade for just a little more than what we would have paid for the original system." Nora grinned at him, clearly pleased with herself. In the face of her optimism, he couldn't help but chuckle.

"Should I be worried about my job?"

"Lord, no." Nora shook her head vehemently. "I don't mind doing it short-term. Some of it's fun. But long-term, that's your bailiwick, not mine."

With a nod of understanding, Nick's gaze shifted to the woman lying in the bed nearby. He wasn't sure how much longer he could expect Nora to shoulder all the responsibility for running the shop. He knew she didn't mind, but at the moment she was doing everything without any help from him. Nick grimaced. He wasn't ready to leave Victoria for more than a few minutes at a time. But the longer she remained in this damn coma, the harder it was for him to justify staying with her twenty-four seven. Nora squirmed in her seat, and he recognized the signs of his sister's need to broach a topic. A topic he knew he wasn't going to like.

"What?" he said with resignation. He fully expected Nora to urge him to start spending the night in his own townhouse, and he circumvented the argument. "I'm not ready to leave her yet."

"I know," his sister said. "I'm not about to argue with a man in love."

Nick shoved his hand through his damp hair as he looked at the floor. He'd already come to the same conclusion, he just wasn't ready to verbalize it yet. The idea flew in the face of every logical, pragmatic thought he'd ever claimed as true, but he knew his sister had been right all along. Nora directed a reproachful look in his direction. From the moment he'd first seen her, his heart had recognized the truth. His brain just hadn't been willing to consider the idea until yesterday. When he'd stood in the hallway agonizing over the fact that Victoria might never wake up, he'd finally admitted to himself that he was in love with her. It made no sense at all to him, but he'd drive himself crazy if he didn't just accept it.

"So you're ready to admit that you're in love with Victoria?" Nora asked.

"As bizarre as it is, yes. I'm in love with her."

"It's not all that uncommon, you know," Nora said with a shrug. "Love at first sight is usually just two souls who've been together before. Soul mates, essentially."

Nick closed his eyes. It had been hard enough to admit he was in love with the woman he'd spoken to for all of five minutes. He wasn't ready for any more revelations.

"Okay, okay, I can see by your expression I just lost you," Nora said with a deep sigh. "All I ask is that you hear me out. I've got some things I want—need to share with you."

Nora met his gaze steadily, and he clenched his jaw. Occasionally, his sister had the ability to unnerve him with the looks she'd send in his direction. But for the first time, Nick experienced something different in her probing gaze. In the back of his mind, the image of another place and time brushed across his senses. The moment was unclear, but he was certain the two of them discussed Victoria and her importance to him before. The sensation filled him with bewilderment.

"Don't you find it odd you and Victoria have the same first names as Lord and Lady Guildford?"

"No," he muttered. Nick had no interest in heading down the path his sister was trying to take him. He didn't like the way his world had been turned upside down. What he needed was time to take in what was happening. He'd only just admitted yesterday that he was in love with a woman he didn't know, and that was confusing enough. Nick wasn't sure he could handle anything else at the moment.

"Hear me out." His sister's fierce look was a silent demand he listen to her. "We both know the legend."

"There's a reason it's called a legend," he growled. "It's just a tale Uncle Charles liked telling us as kids."

"And yet, here we are in a hospital room with a woman

who's a dead ringer for Lady Guildford."

"Coincidence." The moment he opened his mouth, he regretted it.

"Right," Nora snorted with sisterly derision. "And your behavior since the moment you saw her has been perfectly normal?"

Her sarcasm made Nick wince. He wanted to dismiss what she was saying, but couldn't. His behavior wasn't any less bizarre than the direction he knew Nora was heading. Unable to come up with a logical retort, he grunted.

"Hasn't it ever struck you as odd how the countess promised her husband she'd visit Brentwood Park again in the future?"

"If she were going to come back and haunt the place, someone would have seen her ghost by now."

"No, the legend is very specific. It doesn't say she'll haunt the estate. It says she'll visit Brentwood Park in the *future*."

"For God's sake, Nora. You're talking semantics." he snapped.

"Okay, I'll let that simmer a bit," she said with a shrug as she eyed him carefully. "But there's a part of the legend Uncle Charles never told anyone else. We both know about the sapphire necklace—"

"The Barrows' and Lord Guildford's descendants have been looking for those sapphires for years. Even if someone found them now, I'm so far removed from the family tree their discovery wouldn't benefit me at all."

"I agree you won't inherit anything at all, but there are two other things hidden with the necklace." Nora inhaled a deep breath. "Uncle Charles said there was a locket and a couple of journals hidden with the necklace."

"Journals?" Nick frowned in surprise. A locket didn't surprise him, but a diary was altogether different. "What sort of journals?"

"Supposedly, the earl wrote daily notes to his dead wife.

If the legend is true, then Lord Guildford's journals will confirm his belief that his wife was from the future." Nora met his gaze steadily, and Nick stared at his sister for a long moment. A snort of disbelief escaped him and rejected his sister's suggestion with a shake of his head.

"Well, if the necklace, locket, and journals haven't been found by now, they're not likely to be found at all."

"Maybe, but the legend is pretty specific. It says *the countess*," his sister nodded at the woman in the nearby bed. "Is the one who finds the items in her future?"

"Nora," he said her name with a note of warning in his voice. "If you're suggesting what I think you're suggesting."

"Look, it all fits." Nora pursed her lips and stared up at the ceiling before she began to tick items off on her fingers. "One. There's the painting of the countess you've been unable to part with since you were what, thirteen years old? Two. The painting Victoria intended to buy just before the explosion. Ironic that it was a present from the earl to his countess. Three. You're a descendent of Nicholas Thornhill. Four. You both have the same names as the earl and the countess. Five. Victoria's physical likeness to the woman in a portrait you can't bear to part with is extraordinary, and then there's you."

"Me?" Nick wanted to discount everything his sister was saying as extraordinary coincidence, but knew he couldn't.

"Yes, *you're* the fifth item on the list."

In silence, he watched her retrieve four books from the bag on the floor. Something told him that whatever his sister was about to tell him would not sit well with him. Nora's look of awe scared the hell out of him, because he instinctively knew the books she held would send his logical world tumbling into a black void.

"Have you ever seen a portrait of the earl?"

Nick hesitated, trying to recall if he had. There had to be a portrait of the man somewhere at Brentwood Park, but he couldn't remember ever having seen it. He shook his head.

"There are a lot of family paintings at the mansion," he said. "I could have seen it, but I don't recall."

"Actually, there isn't," Nora said with a frown. "It went missing about fifty years ago, and no one's ever been able to figure out where it went."

"And this has to do with me, how?"

"About two years ago, Uncle Charles and I were talking about your fascination with the countess' portrait, and he showed these to me." Nora tapped the books in her lap as she blinked back tears. She dragged in a breath, held it for a moment, then released it. "Uncle Charles made me promise not to show you the books until the time was right. I'd say the past couple of days meet that criteria. I waited because I wanted to be sure you were in love with her."

"What does my being in love with Victoria have to do with these books?" Nick crossed his arms over his chest.

"This book here wouldn't be much to shout about, except for the fact that it's a history of several families in Guildford, where Brentwood Park is." She raised her eyebrows at him before continuing. "What's peculiar is the picture Uncle Charles found of the Earl of Guildford in the book."

Nora opened the largest of the books and flipped to a page that was marked with a paper bookmark. She remained silent as she handed the book to him. Even though he was sitting, the earth shifted beneath him. In the back of his mind, Nick wondered if the chair he sat in might collapse into the yawning hole he felt opening up before him.

Unable to speak, he stared at the caption beneath the picture. It read Nicholas Thornhill, Earl of Guildford. It was like looking in a mirror. He knew family members could bear striking resemblances to ancestors. But this picture made him look like he was a carbon copy of the Earl.

"Coincidence. That's all it is. I'm the man's descendant for crying out loud," he rasped.

"It gets better. Take a look at this. I nearly choked the first time I saw it." Nora offered him a smaller book. Nick accepted the book and glanced down at the title. *The Red Badge of Courage.*

"Where did you find this? I went looking for it a year ago on my bookshelf and couldn't find it," he said. He opened up the book and saw his signature, then flipped through the pages. The book was still in excellent condition, but it looked like it had aged fifty years in the past twelve months.

"Take a close look at the copyright page." Nora's voice was strained as she met his gaze, and he frowned. Exasperated at her mysterious manner, he turned the page and stared down at the copyright.

"Published eighteen ninety-five, Heinemann Publishing." He stared at it for a moment before looking up at his sister in annoyance. "You're not making any sense, Nora."

"Look again, Nick. It's a first edition."

The quiet words made him jerk his gaze back to the copyright page. Only the first publication date was printed on the page. There was no reference to other editions of the book. He also knew damn well his copy of the book wasn't a first edition.

"Now look at the signature again." At Nora's instruction, Nick flipped to the inside front cover of the book and studied the name staring back at him. Nicholas Thornhill.

"So the earl of Guildford and I have the same taste in books."

"Compare that signature to this," Nora said softly.

She pulled out an invoice from the book bag that had been folded several times until the signature was the only handwriting visible on the paper. Without fanfare, she laid the document with his signature directly beneath the signature in the book.

"Tell me that's not your handwriting."

His sister's voice was emphatic as she tapped the inside of the book cover. He glanced down at the two signatures and shook his head. There had to be a logical explanation.

"Don't you dare tell me that isn't your handwriting, Nicholas Barrows," his sister snapped in a harsh whisper as she darted a look at Victoria lying in her bed.

"I'll concede they're similar, but identical…" Nick shook his head as he desperately back-pedaled from the idea.

"Don't be an ass. It's your handwriting, and you know it," Nora said with disgust. "Your problem is that you don't believe it's possible that you could have written it more than a hundred years ago."

"I'm certain there's some reason that can explain the similarities." Denial surged through him as he sprang to his feet and handed the book back to her.

"Do you really believe that?" Nora scowled at him in exasperation. "If you do, then maybe you can tell me why you had the reaction you did to Victoria when she entered the shop, the portrait you can't let go of, the fact you're a dead ringer for the earl, or signatures that are identical?"

"What you're suggesting is that I'm Nicholas Thornhill," he snarled softly.

"Nicholas Thornhill, *reincarnated*," she emphasized.

"*Fuck*. I can't believe you just said that."

"And I can't believe you're not willing to even consider the possibility since you've confessed to being in love with Victoria. It's not like it's that much more of a leap."

Nick glared at her. The fact that her argument was starting to make sense made his gut clench. All around him he could see the walls of his structured, logical, cataloged world collapsing in on him. Reincarnation had never been something he believed in, but everything Nora was throwing at him was forcing him to reconsider his belief structures. He released a harsh breath of angry denial. He *wasn't* Nicholas Thornhill. He was Nick Barrows.

All the coincidences Nora had spouted off could easily be explained away. He was certain of it. As if reading his mind, his sister pinned him with that unique piercing gaze of hers. Again, he experienced a sense of having argued with her before about Victoria. Somewhere from the dark recesses of his mind, a voice murmured the name Anna. Yes, she was just like Anna. His thoughts swerved and came to a dead halt. The other night he'd called his sister, Anna. Who the fuck was Anna? He shook his head. He was definitely losing it.

"I know you think I'm crazy, Nick, but I want you to look at one more thing." Nora eyed him sternly and nodded at the seat beside her. Reluctantly, Nick returned to his chair. "The staff found Victoria's purse in the rubble and gave it to me for safe keeping. I wanted to make sure it was hers—"

"God damn it, Nora," he growled. "You went through her purse?"

"I don't recall her producing an insurance card for her medical expenses, did you?" Nora rolled her eyes at him as he twisted his mouth in an acknowledgement that she'd done the right thing. "While I was looking through her purse, I came across this journal she was writing about her trip."

"Christ—"

"I didn't read the damn thing," she said as she stared at him. "But there was something about her handwriting that struck me as odd."

"Odd how."

"This spiral notebook belongs to Victoria," Nora said as she handed it to him in an open position. She opened another weathered hand bound journal and laid it over half of the spiral notebook so it was possible to see samples of handwriting from both books. "This is one of two journals the Countess of Guildford wrote in for the ten months prior to her death."

"And?"

"Look at the writing, Nick."

He stared down at the writing, seeing but refusing to believe. Nora drew in a sharp hiss of air.

"For crying out loud, Nick, the countess' handwriting is identical to the writing in your Victoria's vacation journal."

"Damn it, Anna, that's fucking insane," he said softly through clenched teeth. "They aren't the same."

"If it's so insane, why did you just call me Anna?" Nora smiled with satisfaction. "Ironic too that the countess' journal mentions her friend, Anna. Ready to believe now?"

Nick sprang to his feet to pace the floor. Fuck, she really believed he and Victoria were the Earl and Countess of Guildford reincarnated. Unbelievable. No, it was insane, and yet a part of him was urging him to believe. He came to an abrupt halt and rubbed his hand through his hair.

"I'm feeling like I need to be in a psych ward," he said with a sense of bewilderment.

"Nick, it's going to be okay." His sister quickly got to her feet and crossed the floor to touch his arm. "Sometimes we just need to take a leap of faith."

Nora placed the weathered journal in his hand.

"You should read her journals, Nick. It's… I don't know how to describe it," Nora said softly. "Once you've read the countess' journals and you tell me you still think all of this is just a coincidence, I'll never mention any of this again."

Nick didn't say a word. He simply wrapped his fingers around the books' binding. His gaze met Nora's, and he shook his head. She offered him a smile of encouragement and squeezed his arm.

"If you need anything, call." Nora kissed his cheek, then walked out of the room.

Chapter 18

November 1897

S he'll be fine, Edmund. She simply fainted."

Victoria blinked as her gaze focused on Nicholas's concerned features, while Edmund hung back a small distance with a frown of worry on his sweet face.

A few feet away, the artist studied her with obvious concern. Cradled in Nicholas's strong embrace, she raised her hand to her brow and probed gently at her head. The pain had diminished to nothing more than a minor headache.

"How do you feel?" His touch gentle, Nicholas brushed a lock of hair off her cheek.

"A bit woozy. Did I faint again?"

"Yes, but only for a minute," he murmured as he glanced at the canvas on the easel.

Her gaze followed Nicholas's. The painting. It was almost finished, but it was the one from the London art gallery. She was certain of it. A shiver raced through her as a detailed image of the gallery filled her head. She tried to remember more, but it only intensified the terrible pressure in her head. She pressed the heel of her palm into her brow, attempting to stop the pain.

"Is the lady all right, sir?" The artist asked.

"Yes, I'm feeling much better," Victoria answered the question before Nicholas could.

"Better or not, when we return to the house you're to take a nap."

"You like to boss people around a lot, don't you?" she said with annoyance. A half-smile curved his mouth, but he refused to take her bait.

"Edmund, stay with Victoria. I'll bring the cart around."

"No." She shook her head. "I'm not an invalid. I can walk."

"I think it best—"

"I *said* I can walk," she snapped as she felt her strength returning.

Nicholas eyed her sternly, but when she scowled at him, he reluctantly nodded. With Edmund's help, Nicholas helped Victoria to her feet. He wrapped his arm about her waist, and the simple gesture reinforced her belief that he would always protect her. Edmund's gray eyes filled with worry, he moved to support her elbow opposite Nicholas. As they walked away, Victoria took one last look at the painting. It was hers. She knew it as sure as she was breathing. It meant she wasn't going insane.

Victoria jerked upright in bed with a cry of fear. Trembling, she stared at her surroundings and recognized her bedroom at Brentwood Park. She bowed her head as the remnants of the now familiar nightmare filled her head. The awful sound of a shovel scraping dirt, the earth splattering across her and the countess' blue dress, and the inability to breathe.

She swung her legs off the mattress and sat still for a moment. When they'd returned to the house, Nicholas had followed through with his insistence she take a nap by escorting her to her bedroom. Although she'd protested, she admitted his command had been a sound one. Other than the receding fear from her nightmare, she was feeling a lot better.

Victoria went to the window to stare out at the landscape. Brentwood Park was one of the most beautiful places she'd ever seen. It would be easy to spend the rest of her life here. The thought startled her as she suddenly realized her priority of going home had changed dramatically. The idea of remaining in the past was a troublesome one. She would have to continue living a lie.

She wasn't the real Countess of Guildford, and if anyone discovered Vickie was dead, the real nightmare would begin. Victoria drew in a quick breath then released it. The most problematic issue of staying here was Nicholas. Not only did the man send her senses into overdrive, but she liked him. His actions indicated he was a good man. Even when it was clear he believed she was the wife he despised, he'd taken care of her. Then there was Edmund. Nicholas loved his brother. The fact that he'd brought Edmund back from Italy to live with him said Nicholas was a man of integrity.

The loyalty of his staff and friends indicated he was also kindhearted and a man of honor. He was a man her father would've liked. The memory of her father sent a wave of grief cresting through her. His absence was simply a reminder that there was no reason to go back to her time period. Her mother had died when she was a baby, and she had no siblings. She had friends, but their lives would easily go on without her. She leaned her head against the window frame and focused her gaze on the pastures surrounding the manor.

The sun was slowly sinking toward the horizon, and she knew it wouldn't be long before Molly came to help her dress for dinner. On a distant knoll, Victoria saw two riders who were resting their horses. They were small shapes against the horizon, but a small voice in the back of her mind said they didn't belong there.

Victoria looked over her shoulder at the door of Nicholas's room. Maybe it would be a good idea to tell him about the riders. She turned back to the window, and an uneasy feeling washed over her the moment she saw the riders were gone. It was nothing, she reassured herself. If she kept expecting the worst or *seeing* things, Nicholas would have no other choice but to commit her to an asylum.

With a frown, she turned away from the window. Her gaze fell on the secretaire, and she remembered how she'd been keeping a diary of her trip to England. It might be helpful if she kept a journal of events that happened here. It might even help her figure out how she'd gotten here. Victoria sat down at the desk and opened the lid. Inside the desk were several thin journals. Most of them were filled with comments about dresses, social events, gossip, and household matters.

Victoria quickly sorted through the thin volumes until she found an empty journal. She opened it to the first page and picked up the fountain pen. As Victoria wrote, the tension inside her slowly ebbed away. There was something cathartic about putting her thoughts on paper. A long while later, Victoria realized she'd filled more than a quarter of one of the slim volumes with her thoughts.

A quiet knock sounded on her door, and she hastily pushed her journal into the dark recesses of the secretaire. The last thing she wanted was for someone to read the diary. She'd be deemed certifiable. As she closed the desk's lid, she called out for the visitor to enter. She turned her head to see Nicholas walk into the room. Startled by his appearance, she quickly stood up, and her stomach lurched at the charm in his smile.

"You're feeling better." It was just as much a statement as a question.

"Yes, thank you." She nodded. "Is Edmund all right. I could tell he was upset."

"He's been worried, but understands you simply fainted and needed rest." Nicholas paused for a brief second before clearing his throat. "He's not the only one who's been concerned."

"Oh." An awkward silence fell between them before she smiled. "As you can see, I'm feeling much better now."

Victoria cringed inside as her attempt to appear unaffected by his presence fell short. Almost as if he knew he'd made her uncomfortable, his mouth quirked in a small smile before his expression sobered.

"You recognized the painting earlier."

"Yes." She winced as her headache abruptly returned. It had only troubled her briefly while she was writing in her journal, but now the pain had grown sharp again. "It's my painting."

"Your painting?"

"Yes," Victoria said as her headache grew worse. "It's the one I bought in the art gallery."

"There must be another explanation, Victoria. The painting wasn't even dry." Disbelief filled his voice.

"I'm telling you, it's the painting I bought in the art gallery," she snapped, then moaned softly.

"You have another headache." At his question, she nodded. A frown darkened his face. "These spells seem to occur only when you're thinking about the past and the time you were missing. For the time being, I believe we'll forego any further discussion on this matter."

"Fine," she said with frustration at his inability to believe her. Nicholas must have realized she was annoyed as he smiled.

"I came to ask if you would like to join Edmund and me for supper." His gaze locked with hers, and her pulse immediately took off like a rabbit racing for safety.

"That would be nice," she said as she relaxed slightly. "I'm sure it will reassure Edmund that I'm quite well when he sees me."

"Affirmation he has refused to accept from me," Nicholas said in an ironic tone of voice. "Come."

"But aren't you… we…changing for supper?"

"It's unnecessary this evening since it will only be the three of us."

"All right," she said as he moved to hold the door open for her. Just as she was about to pass through the door, Nicholas bent his head toward her, his warm breath singeing her ear.

"And you look delectable no matter what you wear…or don't wear."

The suggestive words made her cheeks burn, and she jerked her head up to look at him. Amusement and a wickedly seductive flame flashed in his eyes as he stared down at her. With her heart racing, Victoria stepped out into the hallway and walked toward the stairs. Self-preservation urged her to run away as fast as she could, but she stubbornly refused to let him know how much his words had made her senses reel.

Nicholas easily caught up with her, but didn't speak as they made their way down the main stairs and to the dining room. The moment Edmund saw her, he was on his feet and hurrying toward her. He stopped in front of her and studied her carefully.

"Are you all right, Victoria?" The concern in his voice touched her heart.

"Yes. I'm fine. In fact, we could take a walk in the gardens tomorrow if you like?"

"You won't feel bad then?" Edmund asked, and as she shook her head, he grinned. "All right. That would be fun."

Edmund stepped forward and gave her a gentle hug, as if he were worried he might hurt her. Victoria returned the hug, then encouraged him to take his seat at the table. Uncertain where to sit so Nicholas's effect on her senses was limited, Victoria chose the chair opposite Edmund. Although she'd be much closer to Nicholas physically, at least she could avoid eye contact during the meal. Before she could pull out her chair, Nicholas was there first. The moment she was seated, his fingertips grazed the back of her neck. She stiffened, but didn't look at him. Lord, the man was making it difficult to think clearly. In an effort to slow her racing pulse, she smiled at Edmund.

"Did you… did you enjoy our picnic this afternoon?" she asked Edmund, eager to put some distance between her and the feelings Nicholas aroused in her.

"Yep," he replied before his expression fell. "But I didn't like the man who painted. He made you sad."

"I wasn't upset with the artist, Edmund." Victoria shook her head. "His painting brought back—bad memories."

"Oh," Edmund said in puzzlement before his face suddenly brightened with understanding. Beside his brother, Nicholas snapped his napkin open and laid it in his lap.

"Speaking of that artist, I met with him while you were sleeping." Nicholas's tapered fingers drummed lightly against the linen tablecloth. Startled, she jerked her head toward him.

"Why?" she asked with a puzzled frown.

"I wanted to review more of his work. He's quite talented, and I've asked him to paint your portrait."

"*What?*" she gaped at him.

"It's time your portrait hung in the salon."

"But I don't—"

"The subject is not up for debate. I'll not be swayed in this, Victoria." The arrogant statement made her glare at him.

"You know, you get your way far too often." Uncertain whether to feel annoyed or amused at his smug look, Victoria shook her head in disgust. He merely smiled.

"Why wouldn't I?" he responded. Victoria rolled her eyes at him before she looked down at her plate.

Throughout the meal, Victoria gave thanks for Edmund's presence. She doubted she would have been able to match wits with Nicholas without his brother present. When supper was over, Edmund bid the two of them good night and left the dining room. Alone with Nicholas, she met his searching gaze for a moment before placing her napkin next to her plate.

"How do you usually spend your evenings when you're not entertaining guests?" she asked, hoping to avoid any flirtations that could easily get out of hand.

"Sometimes my estate clerk has papers for me to review or I'll read a book."

"Then you won't mind if I get a book from your library?"

"I didn't say I *always* do those things." He smiled at her with a hint of amusement. "I just elaborated on how I usually spend my evenings alone. But I'm not alone, am I? Perhaps you would like to play cribbage."

"I'm not very good at it." She shook her head at the suggestion before making one of her own. "You have a chess set?"

"God in heaven, woman." He threw back his head with a shout of laughter. "What makes you think you can play chess?"

"If you'll recall, you didn't think I could ride either." Bristling, she glowered at him.

"Very well, but be forewarned, I'll not grant you any quarter."

"Then put your money where your mouth is," she snapped. "If you win, I'll agree not to make a fuss about this damn portrait you're so determined to have done."

"No, I think I'll have your agreement to two portraits, then I'll accept your wager."

"*Two?* You said one just a few moments ago."

"Now, I wish to have two. One for the library and a second one for my personal enjoyment." He leaned back in his chair and took a sip of wine from his glass, studying her over the rim.

"What's this second portrait supposed to be like?" Whatever he was up to, she knew her pride wouldn't allow her to avoid his trap. Besides, she was good at chess, which meant she had the element of surprise on her side. Nicholas smiled and set his glass down on the table.

"I told you this morning that I wanted a portrait of you wrapped in a sheet, as if you'd just woken up in my bed. This new portrait would be for *my* viewing pleasure only, of course." The seductive quality of his voice sent a shiver down Victoria's spine as she stared at him, speechless, while a smile touched his mouth.

"Well? Are you afraid you'll lose?" The cocky note in his voice made Victoria glare at him.

"You're on," she snapped. "If I win, I don't have to do either of the portraits. If I lose, then I agree to do both of them without any argument. Now where's the damn board."

"In the library," he murmured with satisfaction. The confidence in his smile only irritated her more, as she walked with him to the drawing room. She gritted her teeth with determination.

More than an hour later, the two of them studied the chessboard in silence. The board held just a few key pieces, and Victoria tried to stifle her sense of triumph as she reached out and moved her queen into position. One more move and his king would be hers for the taking. She held her breath as she waited for Nicholas to take his turn. With a decisive moment, he slid his bishop across the board, and she smiled with elation.

"Checkmate." Nicholas's soft words destroyed her euphoria. Stunned, Victoria stared at the board in disbelief. How in the hell had he managed to outwit her? She'd used the same game strategy that had never failed to win her a game until now.

"An exceptional game, sweet witch." Nicholas sat back in his chair, a relaxed, yet slightly confused, expression on his handsome face.

"But I still lost," she said, scowling at the board and then at him.

"Yes," he said amusement. "Which means you'll sit for two portraits with *no* arguments."

"Fine," she snapped. "And you don't have to look so damned pleased with yourself."

"If it's any consolation, you had me concerned until your last five moves."

In a small way, his words made her loss easier to bear. But she wasn't happy about losing, especially when it came to the second portrait she'd agreed to sit for. The thought of being painted with nothing but a sheet wrapped around her was embarrassing, particularly when Nicholas had said it was for him.

"Where did you learn to play chess so well?" Nicholas studied her with curiosity, as if he'd just realized something unexpected.

"My father."

"Brentwood played chess?" The incredulous note in Nicholas's voice made her frown with frustration.

"No," she emphasized in a quiet, firm voice. "My father, Thomas Ashton."

"Victoria—"

"Don't. Just don't," she said with a resigned sigh. "I am *not* going to argue with you about it again. Either you believe me or you don't."

Without waiting for a response, she got up from her chair and walked towards the door. As she passed him, Nicholas's caught her by the arm to stop her and stood up to face her. Hands clasped behind his back, he eyed her with sympathy.

"Consider my position, Victoria. My wife vanishes for three weeks. When she returns, the cut and bruising on her head indicates she's suffered a head injury. Not only that, but she insists she is not my wife, and that she's from another time and place. What am I to make of all that? What would you believe?"

The moment he put the question to her, Victoria winced. It was a fair one to ask. What *would* she do in his place? As much as she wanted to think she would believe his story, she knew it would be difficult for her to do. A strong hand captured her chin, and she met his puzzled gaze.

"It will be all right, Victoria, but despite the miraculous changes in you, I cannot believe your story. It's too incredible to believe. I think your mind has created a false reality to protect you from whatever happened to you while you were gone. Your headaches and fainting spells only reinforce my conviction."

With a nod of understanding, she pulled free of his grasp and walked away from him. As she reached the doorway of the salon, she turned her head toward him.

"I understand your skepticism, Nicholas, but ask yourself this. How could a woman who's terrified of horses and can't ride, skillfully ride one of your stallions? How did the same woman almost beat you at chess? How is it all the other things I've said and done not made you realize I am who I say I am? Do you really think all of that can be attributed to a bump on the head?"

She met his green-eyed gaze steadily, and Nicholas could have sworn he saw disappointment flicking in sapphire depths. An almost inaudible sigh drifted past her lips before she turned away and went up the stairs. Why was it so important to her that he believe she was from the future? The answer ringing in her head frightened her. Quickly, she blocked it out of her thoughts. She knew who she was, and she refused to forget it.

Chapter 19

Nicholas stared at the empty doorway Victoria had passed through. With a quiet oath, he slammed his fist into the padded back of his chair. God help him, he wanted to believe her.

Every time he turned around, Victoria was saying or doing something that would be impossible for Vickie to do. The riding he could have put down to sheer stubbornness on Vickie's part, but tonight—their chess game had defied all logic. Vickie could no more tell a knight from a bishop to save her life, yet Victoria had come close to winning their game, and he rarely lost.

No, it was much easier to believe Victoria's head injury was responsible for the remarkable changes in her behavior. If he stopped believing that, it meant he had to address a much darker possibility where his wife was concerned. With a low growl of frustration, Nicholas made his way up to his room. Roberts greeted him as he entered his bed chamber.

"I trust your evening was a pleasant one, my lord."

"It was," he nodded as he remembered how much he'd enjoyed supper with Victoria and his brother at the table. The game of chess afterward had been even more pleasant. No, it had been much more than pleasant. He'd experienced a quiet contentment in Victoria's company. "More evenings like this would be quite pleasurable, Roberts."

Roberts assisted in removing his coat, then hung the

garment in the wardrobe. When Nicholas was ready, the valet held up Nicholas's robe. As he shrugged into the night coat, Roberts cleared his throat.

"May I presume to inquire whether you agree with my assessment about Master Edmund and her ladyship, my lord?"

Roberts' voice pierced Nicholas's thoughts, and he turned his head to meet the older man's curious gaze. With a slow nod of his head, Nicholas looked away. His gaze focused on the fire as he tightened the cloth belt around his waist.

"As always, Roberts, your judgment is impeccable. Seeing Victoria with Edmund today has changed my opinion. I no longer have any objection to my wife spending time with my brother."

Nicholas closed his eyes for a brief second, then moved to the chair in front of the fire. The book he'd been reading for the past few nights mocked him from its place on the table. He was certain reading would be much more difficult tonight than usual.

"Is there anything else I may get for you, my lord?"

"No, thank you, Roberts."

"Good night then, my lord."

"Good night," he murmured as Roberts closed the door behind him.

Nicholas stretched his leg out toward the fire. The pain was moderate this evening, and he knew the warmth of the fire would be enough to soothe his leg. Quickly finding his place in his book, Nicholas forced himself to block out all thoughts of Victoria. More than an hour later, he closed the book with a vicious snap and dropped it carelessly onto the small, half-moon table next to his chair. Reading had proven useless in taking his mind off his wife. Thoughts of Victoria kept interrupting his ability to concentrate.

Bed. Surely, he'd find freedom from his thoughts of her in sleep. Nicholas was halfway to his bed when a soft knock echoed through his chamber. A second later, Victoria stepped through the door.

Instantly, his body tensed and hardened at the sight of her. Her robe clung to her curves, and he wondered if her nightgown was equally snug. On the heels of that thought came the memory that she seemed to prefer sleeping in the nude. Was the only thing against her skin that bloody robe? His mouth went dry at the thought. Nicholas cleared his throat, clasped his hands behind his back, and strove to control the rising tide of desire flooding his body. Concern quickly stemmed the tide as he saw how pale she was. Victoria met his gaze, then bowed her head as if ashamed.

"I…I had another nightmare…they don't normally bother me, but I was afraid to go back to sleep." Color invaded her pale cheeks as she looked at him and averted her gaze once more. "Could I stay with you for a little while? I feel safe with you. It would just be for a little bit."

"Of course," he said softly.

The fear on her face made Nicholas quickly close the distance between them to take her hand. Shock rippled through him at how icy it was in his. Gently, he guided her to the fireside chair. When she was seated, he stoked the flames in the hearth to raise the temperature in the room. Satisfied with the level of heat coming from the fire, Nicholas turned back to her and debated whether to ask her about the dream. He quickly dismissed the idea. She was clearly frightened, and he had no desire to exacerbate her fear. A lustrous lock of her beautiful auburn hair brushed her cheek, and Victoria raised a trembling hand to tuck it behind her ear. Her despondency as she stared into the flames aroused a primal need to protect her from anything that might harm her or make her unhappy. The intensity of the feeling shocked him. A tear rolled down Victoria's cheek, and she quickly wiped it away.

"I think I might be crazy after all," she said in a raw, hoarse voice.

Nicholas uttered a soft oath under his breath and step

forward to scoop her up out of the chair and into his arms. With her cradled against him, he sank down into the chair, ignoring the twinge of pain in his leg. She didn't make a sound as he bent his head to brush another tear off her cheek with his fingers.

"You're not going insane, Victoria," he muttered fiercely. "You've suffered a rather nasty blow to the head. You need to give it, and your mind, time to heal."

She didn't answer, but simply nestled her head against his shoulder. An odd sense of completeness sailed through him as he held her in his arms. There was no rhyme or reason for the emotions this woman aroused in him. She was definitely not the woman he'd married, and it was impossible not to feel the connection he had with her. It was as if they were bound together with invisible strands of thread that would never break, no matter how far the distance between them. If he were a man who believed in destiny, he would say it was almost a spiritual connection. Victoria stirred against him and sat upright.

"I feel better now and should go," she said in a soft voice. "You need—"

"Stay," he rasped. Nicholas wasn't sure which of them was surprised the most by his request. Sapphire eyes wide with astonishment, her breathing suddenly became rapid, and her lovely pink lips parted as if silently begging him to kiss her. His fingertips brushed against the small hollow of her throat.

"What strange magic are you weaving throughout my house, sweet witch?" he whispered. "Is there no one who hasn't succumbed to your charms?"

"Jamieson?" she laughed. The quiet sound held an uneven rhythm of agitation, and he smiled.

"Oh, I think with a bit more effort, my butler will be at your feet like the rest of the staff."

"And you? Will you be at my feet too?" Mischief sparkled in her gaze, but it was the desire he saw shimmering there that hardened his cock. With a slow shake of his head, he leaned forward and kissed the base of her throat. He knew it was madness, but she was too intoxicating to his senses to resist tasting her.

"I think I shall make *you* submit to me, sweet witch," he murmured as he nibbled at the spot where her shoulder met her neck. The small breath she inhaled sent his blood pounding through his body.

"And if I refuse?" The breathy challenge in her voice made him chuckle against the side of her neck as his teeth nipped at her skin. A moan slipped past her lips at his action, and it excited him. Nicholas inhaled the citrus scent of her. It was a fresh, tart scent that was headier than the finest cognac. His fingers traced the edge of her robe where the material met just above her breasts. He slowly parted the garment and sucked in a harsh breath of desire. He'd been right. She was naked beneath the garment. The shudder that rocked through her hammered its way into him. Slowly, his hand exposed one beautiful breast. He cupped her and rubbed her stiff nipple with his thumb.

"Oh, God, Nicholas. Suck on me." Her plea heated his blood even more.

Needing no further encouragement, he captured the tip of her in his mouth. A low, throaty moan poured out of her. The sound made his cock ache as it expanded and hardened even more. *Christ Almighty*, he wanted to thrust into her with hard strokes until he heard her cry out his name, then shatter in his arms.

In a surprising move, she slipped out of his arms to kneel at his feet. Her robe was parted to the waist, and he stared at her full breasts. Eager to touch her again, he leaned forward and lightly rubbed his thumb over a rigid nipple. She trembled at his touch, and he experienced triumph at the desire he saw darkening her blue eyes. God, he loved how she responded to him. She came up on her knees and kissed him. Soft and teasing, her lips had the sweet flavor of honey.

One hand wrapped around the nape of her neck, his tongue swept into her mouth to taste more of her sweetness. Hard and fast, his tongue stroked and teased hers as his need for a more intimate act consumed him. She broke free of the kiss and pushed him back into his chair. A split second later, her mouth blazed a trail of heat across his chest. Nicholas's head fell backward as he allowed himself to enjoy the pleasure of her touch. She tugged gently at the belt of his robe and pushed the garment open. A soft gasp floated upward, and he realized she'd seen his leg. His head jerked forward as he looked down at her. To his amazement, she wasn't looking at his leg, she was studying his cock.

"You're beautiful," she whispered almost reverently.

The unexpected complement startled him, but it also sent a rush of pleasure barreling through him. Nicholas reached out to cup her cheek in his hand, but his fingertips barely brushed her skin before she lowered her head. A warm breeze caressed his erection just before her tongue swirled around the tip of him.

"*Sweet Jesus*," he exclaimed hoarsely.

"Should I stop?" There was a hint of amusement in her voice as she raised her head. In the firelight, her eyes sparkled with a desire he knew matched his own. Unable to choke out an answer, he shook his head, then groaned as she lowered her head again to take him into her mouth.

The hot, moist heat surrounding his cock made it stretch to a point that bordered on the edge of painful. Slowly, she drew him deeper into her mouth, while her tongue stroked and swirled around his length. The sudden touch of her cupping his balls in her hand before her fingers gently played with his sacs made Nicholas jerk in surprise. His hands gripped the arms of the chair as he reveled in the way she was fucking him with her mouth, while massaging his balls. A moment later, she squeezed his balls gently, and he nearly jumped out of his chair.

"*God almighty,*" he rasped. At his low cry, she began to slide him in and out of her mouth at a faster pace. The pleasure thundering through his body beat a primitive rhythm of lust into every inch of him. His cock pulsed with a fiery need, and when she released him, he almost howled with frustration. Still blind with pleasure, he could barely open his eyes as his body shouted impatiently for the release she'd denied him. Through half-hooded gaze, his muscles tensed as he watched her rise to her feet. Her robe slid off her shoulders and fell to the floor.

He'd thought her beautiful when he'd seen her emerge from her bath. Now, standing in front of him, with the firelight giving definition to her curves, he realized how exquisite she truly was. He went rigid as she closed her eyes and trailed her hands over her waist. Slowly, her hands slid upward and over her full, sweetly rounded breasts. Lips parted in a silent moan, her tongue flicked out to wet her lips as her fingers played with her nipples. It was the most erotic thing he'd ever witnessed in his life, and a growl of intense hunger rumbled in his chest.

Coherent thought escaped him as she took a step forward. Roughly, he grabbed her waist and dragged her toward him. She came willingly, and a second later she sank down over him. Hot and slick, she sheathed him in the incendiary heat of her core. Unable to contain it, a low groan rolled out of him. The instant her body clinched tightly around him, he dragged in a sharp breath of pleasure. Slowly, then faster and faster, she moved her body up and down his cock, until she was riding him in furious strokes. His hands gripping her hips, he thrust up into her with each of her downward strokes.

Pleasure, lust, and need charged through his limbs as his hands cupped her breasts, and he rolled his thumbs over her nipples before tweaking them. The fiery sweetness of her as she rode his cock only increased his craving for her that much more. This one moment in time with her wouldn't be enough. It would take a thousand nights like this one to even assuage his desire for her. A low moan escaped her, and her head fell forward as she sought his mouth in a hot kiss. As their tongues mated in a passionate dance, she rode him even harder. Suddenly she jerked against him.

Her body squeezed his cock like a silky hot vise. Hard and fast, her core convulsed and tightened around him with one spasm after another. His hands urged her to keep pumping him as her body shuddered against his. On the edge of an explosive release, a warning bell went off in the back of his mind as he realized he wasn't wearing a French letter. Primal need and lust drowned out the alarm as with a loud cry he thrust upward and throbbed hard inside her. She arched backward, and he braced her with his arms as he savored her final contractions around his cock. Slowly, she fell forward to rest her forehead against his.

"Oh, my God," she whispered. "That was amazing."

Slowly, the realization of what he'd done penetrated his consciousness. Stunned, he froze against her. How could he have been such an imbecile? He should have ended this before it had started. No, he should have simply carried her to his bed and used the protection Roberts always made available in the table drawer next to his bed.

"Nicholas? What's wrong?"

He abruptly lifted her off him and closed his robe as Victoria picked up her robe and clutched it to her body. The look of confused embarrassment on her face made him capture her hand in his and carry it to his lips. It hadn't been his intent to make her feel uncomfortable about what had happened between them. What had just happened had been much more than pleasurable for him, but he refused to explore the depth of its meaning.

"I'm merely annoyed with myself that I failed to use a French letter."

"A what?" Genuine bewilderment furrowed her brow as she stared at him in complete confusion.

"Protection to ensure I don't make you with child."

"Oh, a condom," she said as understanding and guilt furrowed her brow. "I can't believe I didn't think about that either."

"I should have," he bit out with fierce self-remorse.

"So does that mean you regret…regret what happened?"

"No, I have no regrets at all," he murmured as he pulled her into his arms. "I found it even more pleasurable than I'd imagined."

"Imagined?" She breathed as color flooded her cheeks.

"From the moment you returned, I've struggled *not* to think about all the things I could do to your body. Things that would make you weep with need and beg for more."

"Oh, Lord," she whispered. Her throat bobbed as she swallowed hard, and desire flared in her eyes as her tongue flicked out to wet her lips. "Then maybe we should get started."

"Indeed," he said as his body responded to her unconscious action. With a quick move, he swung her up into the air, and she yelped with surprise as he carried her toward the bed.

"Nicholas, your leg. You shouldn't be carrying me. You'll hurt yourself." Her protest made him smiled down at her.

"I'll be hurting elsewhere in a moment if I don't get you into bed right now." He chuckled as he laid her on the mattress. One hand clutching his robe, she tugged him downward.

"Then touch me, Nicholas. Make me burn like you did a few moments ago. I want you touching me, sucking on me…I want you to fuck me until neither one of us can move."

"*Christ Jesus*," he rasped at the lust echoing through her words.

Nicholas's mouth went dry as he stared down at her, and

the desire on her face. God help him, the woman was determined to undo him completely. He'd accepted how colorful her language had become since her return, but the manner in which she'd just asked for his cock made him hard as iron. As if she knew what she was doing to him, Victoria slowly parted her robe and ran her fingers over her breasts, down to her stomach to the apex of her thighs where her fingers dipped into folds he knew would be hot and slick. She arched upward as she played with herself.

Stunned, Nicholas stared at her in fascination. His erection was now painfully hard. Violently, he shrugged his robe off his shoulders and jerked the drawer of the nightstand open with a vicious tug. Seconds later he was on the bed with her, his cock sheathed with a protective covering. His mouth found one hard nipple, and he pulled on it with his teeth. The mewl parting her lips made him wonder how long he could hold out before plunging into her. A sudden resolve surged through him. She'd teased him with that erotic performance a moment ago, and he intended to make her pay a pleasurable penalty in return.

Chapter 20

Pure, intense pleasure spread its way through Victoria's veins until it pulsed its way into every fiber of her being. God, the man used his mouth like a violinist did a bow. He tugged a response out of her that was so strong it frightened her.

Blinded by the smoldering heat of his mouth as he sucked on her nipple, she gasped with delight as he gently bit down on the hard peak. Beneath her skin, one nerve ending after another fired off signals of a deep, passionate hunger.

It rapidly became a fierce need as the fire in her stomach settled in the spot between her legs while threatening to consume the rest of her body. The male scent of sandalwood and another spice filled her senses as she breathed him in. She'd never realized how good a man could smell. As his mouth moved downward, she gasped as his tongue stroked the inside of her thigh. Anticipation spread through her as she expected him to explore her sex with his tongue when he abruptly came up on his knees. Her body instantly protested.

"Oh, God, Nicholas. Don't stop. Please."

"You forget how a short time ago you teased me a great deal before giving me what my cock wanted," he growled as his beautiful mouth curled in a wicked smile. "Can you blame me for extracting a similar punishment?"

His hand caught her ankle in a firm grip, then raised her leg to kiss the side of her foot. The sensual touch made her inhale a sharp breath of pleasure. Slowly, his mouth caressed its way up her leg alternating between small bites into her flesh followed by his tongue soothing the tingling spot. With every touch of his mouth on her skin, it increased the ache between her legs. The pressing need for relief made her slip her hand between her legs. A firm hand quickly stopped her from even trying to achieve satisfaction.

"Not yet, sweet witch. I've not had my fill of you yet," he said as he bit down a little harder on the inside of her thigh.

She cried out in delight at the erotic sensation spiraling through her. His mouth continued on its path toward the apex of her thighs. In one smooth move, his hands slid under her to cup her bottom, then lifted her upward. As he kept her slightly elevated, he lowered his head to seek out the nub just inside her folds. Her entire body shuddered as a small orgasm whipped through her. Dear God, the man seemed to know exactly what she needed at that precise moment.

Another tremor rocked through her as his teeth scraped across the plump piece of flesh of her sex before his tongue probed deeper. An unrestrained cry of bliss escaped her at the roughness of his tongue against her tender, sensitized flesh. No man had ever aroused this much passion and need in her before. With each stroke of his tongue, she thought she'd go mad with desire. Soft as silk, his hair caressed her skin as she spiked her fingers through it. Eyes shut, her hips jerked as his tongue continued to swirl inside her.

Small ripples of sensation cascaded through her body, and she recognized the exquisite onset of an orgasm. A moan rose up from deep inside her as her blood ran hot and thick through her veins. Long and hard, a shudder shook her body as her orgasm built inside her. The vibrations pulsing through her reached a keen threshold until she screamed his name and bucked against him. Strong hands bit into the flesh of her hips to hold her in place as he continued to suck, lave, and nibble on her folds until the stimulation was an exquisite torture.

With a sob of ecstasy, her body came apart until she was consumed with tingling pleasure. Wave after wave of white-hot tremors washed over her until she was drowning in a flood of fiery sensation. Dragging in deep ragged breaths, she trembled as her body slowly calmed to a low, sensitive hum of pleasure. Spent, she lay still on the bed as Nicholas pushed himself up to hover over her. Her eyes fluttered open, and the passion blazing in his eyes made her heart clench in her chest. This man wasn't just devastating to her senses. He could easily carry away her heart. The realization made her mouth go dry. A low growl rumbled in his chest, and it sent a frisson across her skin.

"You realize I'm not through with you, don't you, sweet witch?"

Even if she'd had the energy to answer him, she wouldn't have been able to respond. With a quick move, he easily flipped her over onto her stomach. His hard body pressed into her back as his mouth nibbled on her shoulder.

"You smell of lemons and honey," he whispered as he kissed the nape of her neck. His hand slid across her spine in a lazy move. Lord, now she understood the fascination some women had with a British accent. "And your skin is smooth as satin."

"Do you have any idea how sexy your voice is?" She closed her eyes with a sigh and surrendered herself to the pleasure of his touch.

"Is it?" He chuckled. "Would you still think so if I said I intended to spend the rest of the night fucking you until neither one of us can move?"

"Oh, God," she breathed as she looked over her shoulder at him. "Yes, I find your voice even sexier when you talk like that."

"You, sweet witch, are a wanton hussy." Something odd flashed in his gaze, but it was gone in a brief instant.

His palm caressed her buttocks, and he laughed as she

arched her body upward into his touch. From her bottom, his fingers continued their downward path to slide along the back of her lush thigh. A breath of delight escaped her as Nicholas continued his leisurely path of exploration down to the back of her knee, where she jumped slightly as his thumb traced a circular path against her skin. His quiet laughter said he was well aware that he'd found one of her ticklish spots.

Despite his discovery, he trailed his fingers back to her backside. Suddenly his teeth bit into the plump flesh of her bottom. Startled, she cried out in surprise, and her body tried to shift away from him. He instantly pressed his chest into her leg, making it impossible to escape the second nip at her flesh.

Unable to escape, she inhaled a quick, sharp breath as his hand stroked the back of her thigh, then abruptly pushed her leg to one side to slide three fingers into her. In a split second, the air left her lungs and fire skimmed its way through her blood. Her body clenched around his fingers, and she gasped at how quickly he'd brought her to the brink again.

Each sinfully wicked stroke of pleasure made her gasp at the blissful sensation, and in seconds her body was crying out with a longing to be possessed by him. The ragged heat of his breath singed her back, and she could feel his hard erection against her leg.

"Nicholas, please," she rasped. "I need to feel your cock inside me, now. I need you to fuck me."

"*Sweet Jesus*, your tongue would tempt the devil himself," Nicholas growled as he pulled her bottom higher, then slid into her with a hard thrust.

The size of him filled and stretched her until the acute, intense pleasure of it made her want to sob with delight. The strength of the pleasurable sensations rose inside her much faster this time. The hard thrusts of his body into hers drove her desire to a fervent pitch of bliss. Suddenly, a blast of heat coursed through her until it was a raging fire that exploded and spiraled through her veins.

It streaked through her, igniting an acute sensation inside her unlike anything she'd ever felt before. The intensity of it was mind-numbing as pleasure burned its way across her skin, and she soared upward to a pinnacle of ecstasy. She hung on the edge of a precipice, before a cry of sheer rapture poured out of her and she shuddered hard against him.

Heart pounding, her breathing was little more than frantic pants as she was pulled into a whirlpool of delight. Just as the ripples of sensation eased, the blistering pace of possession pulled her to the next level of pleasure. Stroke after stroke, Nicholas brought her to the edge of the abyss then pulled her over only to take her back to the edge again.

Suddenly, her body clutched hard around him as wild, uncontrollable spasms of heat cascaded through her and she was engulfed in one blissful tremor after another. She sobbed his name as another shudder rippled through her, and Nicholas roared a guttural cry of release as his body plunged into her one last time.

Even despite the wild, unrestrained tremors holding her hostage, she felt him throbbing inside her. They remained locked together for a long moment, frozen in the aftermath of their passion. Slowly sliding forward, she sank into the mattress, delighted to feel him follow her downward. The warm pressure of him on top of her filled her with not only contentment, but a feeling that all would be well as long as she was in his arms. A happy sigh drifted past her lips as Nicholas kissed the back of her shoulder, then rolled off her onto his back. Victoria reached out to stroke the top of his chest.

"Thank you," she whispered. Nicholas turned his head toward her with a startled look on his face. His hand brushed a strand of hair off her brow.

"For what, sweet witch?

"Because that was even more amazing than the first time," she whispered as she moved closer and kissed him. The heat of their kiss slowly spiraled into a fiery passion until

Nicholas pulled away from her with a groan.

"God in heaven, woman. You'll be the death of me." He tugged her into his side and wrapped his arms around her. Snuggling into him, she laughed.

"I take it *now* would not be the time for me to indulge in dirty talk," she whispered.

"No," he growled with a soft trace of amusement. "I only have so many French letters available until Roberts can order more, and I need sleep."

She smiled, then yawned as she buried her cheek into the curve of his shoulder. With Nicholas she was safe, no one would harm her. It was the last thought she had before she drifted off to sleep.

A warm heat surrounded Victoria as her eyelids fluttered open. There was a blue sliver of light pushing through the thin opening in the drapes. It was a soft, lapis lazuli that signaled the night wasn't quite willing to give way to the dawn. The weight of Nicholas's strong, muscular arm was wrapped around her waist, holding her close. Sleepily, she blinked several times to wake up completely. She'd spent the entire night locked in his arms. Victoria released a soft sigh of contentment.

Fully awake, she turned her head to see Nicholas studying her intently. She smiled and reached out to touch his mouth with her fingertips. The man's lips had teased and tempted her last night in ways no other man had. He'd aroused a part of her that was completely unrestrained when she was in his arms. The man set her on fire with his words and caresses. When he didn't respond to her touch, she frowned. Something was wrong.

"Is your leg bothering you?" she asked with concern.

"No," he said in the soft voice. Suspicion narrowing his gaze, he frowned. "Where did you learn to do the things we did last night, Victoria?"

"I don't understand what you're asking." Puzzlement furrowed her forehead.

"Where did you learn to suck on a man's cock or use language designed to stimulate a man's desire?"

The question made her stare at him in amazement. Out of all the things for him to ask, this was the last thing she would have expected. The man sure as hell hadn't complained about her enthusiasm last night. She scowled at him.

"Well, it's not like I'm inexperienced," she said defensively. "I've had a couple of serious relationships."

"Then you *have* slept with other men." The harshly spoken statement made her draw away from him in anger.

"Are you telling me that Vickie is the *only* woman you've ever slept with?"

"My liaisons are of no importance."

He casually dismissed her sarcastic reply, and she stared at him in astonishment. Had the man just said a double standard was okay? In the back of her mind, she understood it was how things worked in his time, but she sure as hell didn't have to go along with it.

"Let me get this straight, your affairs aren't important, but mine are?" She glared at him.

"You've asked me to believe you're not my wife, but your behavior is no different from Vickie's when it comes to other men."

"My behavior is a hell of a lot different than your wife's," she snapped. "When I'm in a relationship with the guy, I don't cheat on them."

"But you don't deny having been with other men." The terseness of his declaration infuriated her.

"No, I don't. Because all the men I've been with were *long* before I ever met you." Indignant, she threw the covers off her legs. "And since we're discussing *my* liaisons, exactly how many women have *you* slept with?"

"That's irrelevant to this conversation." The disdainful note in his voice made her pick up her pillow and swat him hard with it. The pillow muffled his oath of objection.

"*No*," she exclaimed furiously as she scrambled out of bed. "As far as I'm concerned, it's *very* relevant to the discussion."

"Where the devil are you going?"

"Back to my room."

The sheets fell down to Nicholas's his waist as he sat up. Instantly her mouth went dry at the sight of his well-toned chest and arms. God, he was magnificent. She winced at how easily just looking at him could distract her thoughts. Desire flashed in Nicholas's eyes as he studied her, and Victoria quickly shrugged her robe over her shoulders to cover herself.

Part of her wanted to fling herself into his arms, but she refused to give in to temptation. There were lines that had to be drawn somewhere. She hadn't asked to be in this time, but she was damn well going to live here on her terms if at all possible. With sharp, jerky movements, she cinched the sash of her robe and glared at him. She didn't know what infuriated her the most, the fact he'd compared her to Vickie or his judgmental inquisition about her past. Victoria decided it was the comparison to his wife that bothered her. She was nothing like his wife.

"You're not leaving until we settle this matter," he growled.

"Watch me." She sniffed with derision.

With the speed of a panther, he was out of the bed and blocking her way out of the room. Instantly, her body was like a needle pointing to the North Pole at the sight of his naked, muscular form. Every cell in her body was on alert. Her gaze flitted over him and drank in the beauty of him.

As she looked at his bad leg, she drew in a sharp breath

at the badly scarred limb. She'd seen it up close last night, but things had gotten out of hand before she could ask him what terrible thing had happened to him. And now certainly wasn't the time. She flinched and shook her head as he stepped toward her.

"There's nothing to settle, Nicholas. My past isn't yours to judge. And it sure as hell doesn't even come close to Vickie's behavior," she said bitterly. "I say we just forget last night happened."

"*God damn it*, Victoria, that's not what I want, and I—"

"What *you want* is irrelevant," She flung his words back at him.

"Damn it Victoria, I'm willing to forgive you."

Dumbfounded, she stared up at him slack jawed. He was willing to forgive her? For what? The only thing she'd done wrong was land up in a time period that wasn't her own with a man who believed she was his wife. A man who had rocked her world last night in bed and was now willing to be magnanimous and forgive her for her past. Her thoughts tumbled one over the other as she eyed him with bitter anger.

"*You forgive me?*" she sputtered as her outrage kicked up another notch. "What the hell for? I've not done anything wrong."

"You're not listening to me," Nicholas said in a resentful tone. "I don't care who the men were, I'm willing to put all of this behind us."

"You are *definitely* not helping your case here," she said in a caustic voice. "I don't recall asking for your forgiveness, and I'm sure as hell not about to apologize for anything either. I suppose I should appreciate the irony of the whole thing. You admit how different I am from Vickie, and yet you still think I'm just as much of a slut as she is."

"I didn't say that," he snarled as he grabbed her arms and shook her slightly.

"No, you didn't have to," she said as a sliver of pain and

disappointment pierced her heart. "But the fact that you have this need to forgive me says everything."

Victoria jerked free of his grasp and headed toward the door that led to the corridor between their rooms. Nicholas's hand curled around her arm, and he firmly halted her departure. She stared up at his handsome face, and her heart was suddenly weighted down by the confusion she saw there.

"Victoria," he paused. "God help me, when you look at me like that, it's as if nothing in our past matters."

"But it does matter to you, doesn't it, Nicholas?" She rolled her shoulders and released a resigned sigh. "I understand why it matters to you, but in my mind my past shouldn't even be a part of what we shared last night."

With a quick tug, she pulled free of his grasp and left him where he stood and walked out of the room.

Chapter 21

Rain hit Nicholas's office window with increased force as the wind blew harder. There was a cold bite to the wind that combined with the rain made his leg ache. He reached out to wipe the condensation off the glass pane to improve his view of the wet landscape.

The gray weather suited his morose mood. This morning he'd managed to bungle his way through his argument with Victoria like a clumsy oaf.

Last night had been incredible. The way she'd responded to him had fired his blood. No woman had ever aroused him to the point he'd completely lost all control of his faculties. Not using protection when he'd made love to her told him just how bewitched he was where Victoria was concerned. He could only pray he'd not sired a child. And the way she'd sucked on his cock. She'd seemed to understand exactly what he needed and when.

The way her tongue had stroked every inch of him made him believe she'd cared as much about his pleasure as she did hers. But it was her naughty manner he loved the most. With just a few words, she had managed to fill him with a powerful need to possess her.

Then in the morning's cold light, he'd realized just how experienced his wife was and why. The knowledge had stirred feelings deep inside him that were alarming. The thought of her with another man twisted his gut with anger. It was a territorial emotion that made him want to eviscerate any man who had even dared to look at her, let alone touch her.

It had blinded him. The need to guard what he'd claimed as his was an unfamiliar sensation. It had driven him to question her about her past. He should have realized before he spoke how Victoria would react. Since her return, she had acquired a number of different habits and social behaviors that could have predicted her reaction to his queries. She was right in thinking that the past shouldn't matter. But it did matter to him. Just not in the way she thought.

What the hell was happening to him? He'd told Victoria last night that she had bewitched his entire household staff. What he hadn't told her was that she was bewitching him too. Now he had to consider how to set things right with her. Victoria hadn't been just angry with him. There had been a disappointment and a sense of defeat about her. He had injured her greatly by implying she was just like Vickie. He knew better, but his poorly made argument had only erected a brick wall between them. A wall he wasn't sure how to bring down. A knock on his office door made him turn around as Derek Elrod, his estate manager, entered the office.

"Good morning, Elrod." Nicholas walked to his desk and sat down. He gestured to his estate manager to take the seat opposite him.

"What do you have for me this morning?"

"Just a few things, my lord."

Seated behind the large desk, Nicholas watched his estate manager sit down across from him and open a leather folder. Elrod retrieved several documents and passed them across the desk. Accepting the paperwork, Nicholas quickly flipped through the documents. He set aside three documents he wanted to review in detail at a later time, while asking questions as he perused the remaining paperwork. When he'd finished signing the documents that required his signature, he handed them back to the estate manager.

"I'll review these other documents and have them back to you by the end of the week." Nicholas nodded to the papers he'd set aside. "Is there anything else?"

"A few items came in the post this morning. They were included in the paperwork you just reviewed. However, there is an odd piece of mail I wanted to bring to your attention."

The strange note in Elrod's voice told Nicholas that this particular piece of mail had caused the estate manager concern. He arched his eyebrow as the man reached into his coat pocket and withdrew a slim piece of parchment. With a worried frown, Elrod leaned forward and handed him the note.

"I apologize for opening it, my lord. But it wasn't marked any different from the usual mail," he said quietly. As he accepted the note, Nicholas grew uneasy at the worried look on Elrod's face. Slowly Nicholas unfolded the letter.

Lord Guildford,

Has your wife truly returned, or is it all an elaborate hoax? How convenient and amusing that she has lost her memory. It allows one to fill another's shoes so easily, does it not? It will be interesting to see how well she does in a London setting.

I would imagine you have not brought her to town yet because you are still refining her performance. After all, an excellent deception takes time. But then you are quite adept at deception, are you not, given your brother's rightful due.

A friend

Nicholas allowed the words to sink into his head. Although the note held no specific threat, the underlying tone of the message was quite clear. Someone believed Victoria was an imposter. His thoughts immediately shifted to Reardon. Yesterday morning he'd received word that Darby's connection to Reardon was stronger than he and Sebastian had thought. It wasn't just the man's association with Vickie's lover that bothered him.

The report he'd received yesterday had also uncovered a new link. Reardon's youngest brother had died in the fire at Nicholas's paper mill ten years ago. There were only two deaths reported that terrible night. One was his foreman, and the other was the boy Nicholas had tried to save. Other than a mother protecting her child, there was nothing more dangerous than a man with a lust for vengeance.

As an anarchist, Reardon had no love for the government or the aristocracy, but to date they'd not found any evidence tying him to several recent instances of criminal behavior. Reardon was clever, and Nicholas knew not to underestimate the man.

He stared down at the threatening note. Whoever had written it knew his brother was still alive. Very few people knew about Edmund, which meant the writer of the letter had intimate knowledge of his family. The suggestion that Edmund might somehow have been deprived of the earldom illustrated the seriousness of the letter. The accusation could be easily disproved, but it would take its toll. Gossip could make things very difficult when it came to bringing the truth to light. He wasn't sure how well he could shelter Edmund from any potential investigation.

"Elrod, I want you to make some very discreet inquiries. Albert Greene proved to be our best resource when the countess disappeared. Call on him again for his services. Have him keep an eye on Jack Reardon." Nicholas carefully folded the note, tapping it against his open hand with calm deliberation. "There is a possibility the man knows the countess and might be intent on harming her, or at the very least causing me a great deal of trouble. I want to know where the man goes, whom he talks to and when. I want as much detail as possible. Also see to it that Lord Darby is watched.

His connection to the countess is well known."

"Yes, my lord." The estate manager nodded, then cleared his throat. "I didn't mention it last week, as it didn't alarm me at the time, but the nature of this letter has made me think twice. One of the tenants came across a small encampment that had been in use until just recently. There have also been reports of a couple of strangers riding through the vicinity. Perhaps we should take other precautions all the same."

Tension tightened his muscles at the man's recommendation. Elrod was right. They had to take every measure possible to protect Victoria. On another level, he realized the man had not even questioned the challenge to Victoria's identity. It was a reassuring thought. If his estate manager did not question her identity, then it was doubtful that many others would either.

"I think you're right, Elrod." They both rose to their feet, and Nicholas shook the estate manager's hand. "I want any unknown visitors to the estate or in the general vicinity to be reported immediately. Under no circumstances is the countess to ride alone, and when she does ride, I want her escort armed."

"I'll see to it personally, my lord. And your trip to London, do you expect to go to town any time soon?"

"I expect we'll go to London just before Christmas." Nicholas frowned and turned his head toward the window. "See to it that each member of the town staff has been in my employ for at least a year, preferably longer."

"I'll see to it today, my lord."

"Thank you, Elrod." He nodded as the man turned and left the office.

As the door closed behind the estate manager, Nicholas closed his eyes. Whoever had written that note had meant it as a threat. The knowledge chilled him. Even more disturbing was the possibility that he was responsible for placing Victoria in harm's way. He'd insisted she was his wife, and yet she'd denied it. What the fuck was happening? His entire world felt as if it were collapsing in on top of him. Anger made him clench his jaw. If someone meant to hurt Victoria, they'd have to go through him to do so.

Nicholas turned away from the window to stare blankly at his cluttered desk. Frowning, he suddenly wondered if Vickie was dead. He immediately rejected the possibility. It meant Victoria would somehow have to be involved, and he refused to believe such a thing was possible where she was concerned. If Vickie was dead, it was her personality. Victoria had emerged like a phoenix from the ashes to take Vickie's place. He rubbed the back of his neck. No, he was convinced Victoria was his wife and the Countess of Guildford.

Without any viable proof to the contrary, she would continue in that capacity. His first and most important task was to take necessary precautions to ensure her safety. Here on the estate, a few minor adjustments would ensure her protection. However, London would be a different matter altogether. She would need an escort wherever she went, and he was certain she wouldn't like that one bit.

He moved back to his desk, his free hand riffling through his papers in a restless movement. Not only did he have to convince Victoria to travel with him, it would be necessary to do so without alarming her. She'd said she no longer wanted to visit London. Had her instincts told her not to travel to town? Her independent streak would make it difficult for her to express any worries she might have. Once again, he looked down at the folded note he still held in his hand. Until he could discover who had written it, he would not be able to rest easily. The sound of someone clearing their throat made Nicholas look up to see Jamieson in the study's doorway.

"My lord, Mr. Lockwood has arrived. He's in the salon."

"Thank you, Jamison. Please ask Lady Guildford to join us."

With a nod, Jamieson disappeared from the doorway,

and Nicholas closed his eyes briefly. Would she fight him on the two portraits, despite their bargain? He rapped his knuckles on the desk and headed out of his office. There was only one way to find out.

The salon was bright and cheery, but the weather had cast a sullen pall on the room. Lockwood was standing at the couch table situated behind the main sitting area. The man was fairly young, perhaps only a couple years younger than Victoria. The thought of leaving her in the man's company for several hours every day did not make him happy, but he had no choice. He would be neglecting his duties enough while Lockwood was working on the second portrait of Victoria. He crossed the room to shake hands with the artist.

"Lockwood, I trust this room will suffice for your purposes."

"It will indeed, my Lord. Despite the rainy weather, there's enough light to ensure Lady Guildford's portrait isn't too dark. Might I inquire as to how her ladyship is feeling?"

"She's much improved," Nicholas said as he remembered their exertions of last night.

"Excellent. I promise not to tire her unduly."

"Thank you, Victoria can be quite stubborn. Although I imagine she will be much more reasonable with you than she is with me."

"I have found that to be true of most wives I've painted in the past, my lord." Lockwood laughed. The artist gestured toward the table where several drawings laid. "After our conversation yesterday, I sketched a few preliminary drawings of possible poses for Lady Guildford's portrait."

"You're quite talented, Lockwood," he said as he picked up two of the man's sketches. "In fact, I would like to buy the landscape you were working on yesterday."

"Of course, my lord."

"I wish to present it to my wife as a Christmas gift."

"Of course, my lord."

Nicholas studied the drawings Lockwood had brought with him. They were as good as he'd expected them to be, perhaps even better. His gaze fell on another sketch still lying on the table. He set aside the sketches in his hand and picked up the drawing.

"I believe this pose is the best one to use for my wife's formal portrait."

It was a sketch of Victoria facing a tall window with her head turned toward the viewer as if she'd been interrupted.

"I agree, my Lord. It's the last sketch I made, and I'd hoped you would select it."

A warm breeze sent an awareness racing through Nicholas. He didn't even have to turn his head toward the door to know Victoria had entered the room. Eager to begin mending their differences, he turned toward her. He stepped toward her with his hand outstretched in the silent request that she take his hand. Cold scorn blazed in her beautiful eyes as she glanced at his hand, then back to his face. He'd not expected her anger to be gone, but he'd hoped it would have eased slightly if only because she'd considered his position. The contempt in her gaze said he'd been wrong. He would have an uphill battle when it came to eloquently explaining his position and earning her forgiveness.

"Victoria, come see the preliminary sketches, Mr. Lockwood has done."

"Already?" she said coolly as she walked past him with an expression of disdain on her face. As she reached the table, her fingers touched several of the drawings, and her features softened to reflect amazement. She shook her head slightly, and Lockwood leaned toward her with an apologetic smile.

"These are simply based on what I remembered of your features, Lady Guildford. They're primarily to reflect potential poses for your formal portrait."

"You misunderstand, Mr. Lockwood, I think they're lovely," Victoria murmured. "Although I hope you won't hide my flaws in the final portrait."

"Flaws, my lady."

"Yes, Lord Guildford is *quite* familiar with my vast number of faults and behaviors," she said as she turned her head toward Nicholas while still addressing the artist. "I don't want you to hide a single one of my flaws in this portrait."

The pointed remark made Nicholas stiffen. Victoria lifted her chin as she eyed him coldly in a silent challenge. Resolving not to let his anger show, he narrowed his gaze at her.

"We all have flaws, Victoria. I'm no exception," he said in a tightly controlled voice, determined not to engage in an argument with the artist present. He turned his attention back to Lockwood, who was looking quite bewildered. He cleared his throat as he met Lockwood's confused gaze.

"There's an elusive air about my wife that I'd like for you capture, if possible, Lockwood."

"I believe I can do that, my lord."

"I trust you'll do the same for the second portrait." The moment he spoke, Victoria immediately stiffened. Clearly she thought he would forgo the more intimate painting.

"Surely, my lord, we can make do with just the one." Her lush mouth thinned in anger, and her blue eyes dared him to argue with her. "The second portrait seems quite unnecessary."

"As I stated last night, the second portrait is for my pleasure. I believe you agreed to that. A bargain is a bargain." Not about to give way, Nicholas met her gaze steadily until she turned her head away.

"You're right," she said in a clipped tone of voice. "I'll simply remember in the future to make my bargains with the devil." Victoria's smile was one of feigned sweetness, and it took every inch of willpower he possessed not to drag her from the room to a settle their differences in private. She picked up one of the drawings off the table.

"So, Mr. Lockwood, where do we begin?"

"Your husband has already selected the pose for your formal portrait—"

"*Oh*, has he," Victoria said before she drew in a deep breath, then exhaled it. "And which *one* did he select?"

"This one, my lady." Lockwood pointed to the sketch on the table. The artist looked at Nicholas. "Do you prefer Lady Guildford in daywear or something more formal?"

Victoria stiffened as Lockwood addressed him and not Victoria as to the choice of her clothing for the portrait. Nicholas wanted to groan at the rebellious shimmer in Victoria's gaze and Lockwood's misstep. Hoping to appease Victoria, he clasped his hands behind his back.

"Do you have a preference, Victoria?" he asked quietly. "The blue riding habit you wore the other day makes the blue in your eyes stand out. It would be a superb choice."

For a moment, he saw surprise slide across her face. Just as quickly it was gone. She shook her head.

"I'm not sure I like the blue habit." The abrupt rejection of his suggestion made him narrow his eyes again.

"Perhaps we should speak privately regarding the matter," he said softly. "Mr. Lockwood doesn't need our decision at this very moment."

"All right. The blue habit then. Is there anything else, my lord?" The sarcasm in her voice made him scowl at her. It was becoming quite clear that he would have to grovel for her forgiveness. The thought made his body tense with anger at how clumsily he'd handled his disagreement with Victoria. He didn't respond to her goading. Instead, he turned to the artist who had realized he was the innocent bystander in the middle of a marital dispute.

"I'll leave you to your work then, Lockwood." Nicholas shook hands with the artist and turned to Victoria. Before she could avoid him, he grasped her hand and carried it to his lips. Her hand shook as his mouth lingered on her skin. Nicholas raised his head to look into her eyes. Something flickered there that he thought might be pain. Was it possible he'd hurt her as well as insulted her?

"I trust you'll not make things difficult for Lockwood simply because you're angry at me," he murmured.

"Trust?" she rasped softly. "As I recall, you can't trust me at all."

"I deserved that," he said quietly. Despite knowing the vicious barb was well-earned, it didn't make it sting any less. "Forgive me."

Without waiting for a response, he released her hand and walked out of the salon. At the moment, it was the closest thing to an apology he could manage. Somehow he'd come up with a plan to heal the breach between the two of them.

Chapter 22

Good Lord, had the man just apologized? But for what? His lack of trust in her or something else? Victoria stared after Nicholas as he disappeared through the doorway. Vickie's affairs had humiliated Nicholas, and her own past had hit too close to home for him.

She was certain now that he'd viewed it as a reminder he'd been made a fool of once before. If there was one thing she'd already figured out, Nicholas didn't like being made a fool of, and he was smart enough to ensure it didn't happen a second time.

Despite that, it had stung like hell when he'd offered to forgive her past simply to allow their relationship to move forward. It was as if he'd agreed to accept damaged goods because the price was right. Perhaps that was the most painful thing of all. He'd made what they'd exchanged last night seem like a one-night stand between two strangers. As far as she was concerned, last night had been the most magical night or her life, right up until the moment he'd offered to forgive her. She wanted desperately to believe Nicholas had felt the connection between them that she had, but if he had, she didn't think he'd understood it.

Even with the harsh words between them, the memory of last night still made her heart skip a beat. Vivid and strong, the images flooded her head and how he'd taken her to the brink, then sent her tumbling over the edge to a place she wanted him to take her to again and again. The sensitive spot between her legs suddenly ached with an intense need.

What was it about Nicholas that created such powerful, potent emotions inside her? Every sensation she experienced in his presence was either all or nothing. From the moment she'd first seen him, she'd been drawn to him with an intensity that scared the hell out of her. But none of that mattered. The only thing she cared about was that he realize, and believe, she wasn't Vickie.

The revelation stunned her, and she inhaled sharply. It wasn't that she wanted him to believe she was out of place or time. She wanted him to believe she wasn't the woman he'd married. Worse, something deep inside told her that even if she could make him realize the truth about her, there could be no real future for them. It wouldn't matter if Vickie returned or not. Victoria could not escape the Damocles' Sword hanging over her head. She had no idea if or when she'd return to her own time. How could she try to build a life here never knowing?

Victoria winced. What the hell was wrong with her? She was insane to think she wanted to stay in the past. The furious sound of a pencil scratching across paper jerked her out of her thoughts, and she turned her head toward the artist standing to one side of her. A large drawing pad cradled in one arm, he was drawing rapidly on the paper. The moment she moved, Lockwood immediately protested.

"Please remain still, my lady. I'm trying to capture all of these emotions as quickly as I can."

Fear spiked through her as she realized the young artist had been sketching ever since Nicholas had left the room. Had her face been too expressive? Would Nicholas be able to see her feelings in the portrait?

"You may relax now, my lady. I believe I captured enough images to give more depth of emotion to your portrait."

"I'm afraid to ask what you saw," she said tentatively as she met the artist's gaze. Victoria could only hope he hadn't seen too deep into her soul. Lockwood studied her face for a moment, before he resumed drawing again.

"I saw a woman struggling to keep her husband from seeing too deep into her heart. I also saw that elusive quality I think your husband referred to. It's as though you have a terrible weight resting on your shoulders."

The artist's observations made Victoria bite down on her lip. If Mr. Lockwood could see all of that in her, having him paint her portrait could be dangerous. The last thing she wanted the artist to see or paint was that she was in love with Nicholas. Shock made her heart stop for a slow beat, and she swayed on her feet. She barely knew Nicholas. How could she be in love with him?

"Are you all right, Lady Guildford?" The artist exclaimed softly as he dropped his tools and hurried to her side. Victoria shook her head as she waved him off.

"It's nothing. I've not been feeling well recently."

"Lord Guildford explained that you'd been injured, and he was quite adamant that I not overtire you."

"I'm not surprised he was adamant. Nicholas is used to getting his way," she said with a wry note in her voice.

"Why don't we resume our sitting tomorrow?"

"Thank you. I'm not going to deny that I'm tired. I'll feel better tomorrow."

"But of course," Lockwood said with a nod.

Victoria forced a smile to her lips, then made her way out of the salon and up to her bedroom. As she reached her room, she closed the door behind her and pressed her back against the wood. What had she done? How could she possibly be in love with a dead man? No, Nicholas wasn't dead, not here anyway. He was very much alive. Last night was proof enough of that.

Her body grew warm as she remembered how he'd

caressed and stroked her with his hands and mouth. Equally memorable had been the way she'd fallen asleep in his arms. The quiet tenderness of his embrace made her heart ache as the truth chilled her. She was in love with a man who had lived and died long before she was born. No matter how real her life here felt, it wasn't her reality.

Victoria pushed herself away from the door to cross the floor and sink down onto the lounge sofa. From her seat, she could see where the lawn met pasture land, which stretched out as far as she could see. Even on this gloomy, fall day, Brentwood Park was still beautiful. She could easily come to love it here just as much as she loved its owner. The silent admission tugged at her like the undertow of a strong wave.

The longer she remained in the past with Nicholas, the more devastating her heartbreak when she returned to her own time. The thought of leaving Nicholas twisted painfully in Victoria's chest. It was unlike any pain she'd experience before. It was as if someone had reached into her chest and squeezed her heart in a fierce, agonizing grip. Instinctively she knew the longer she remained here the pain would grow exponentially until it would be unbearable when she returned to the future.

Tears pushed against her eyelids, and she bowed her head. If she went home now, she was certain it would be easier to forget. A nerve ending in her head fired off a protest. Did her way home lie in the mist? Could it be that simple? In a bizarre sort of way, it made sense. The only time she had a headache was when she thought about how she got here from her own time. Another nerve ending pulsed viciously in her head, signaling for her to stop.

If she could remember what happened before the explosion— a ripple of excruciating pain slammed into her head. She gasped at the strength of it. Valiantly, she struggled to hold back the nausea threatening to overcome her. If this was what it took to—the mist enveloped her, but this time it was nothing but cold, damp and frightening. Heavy and dense, the fog was as ominous as the silence surrounding her.

Unlike her other experiences, she felt nothing but fear. It spiraled through her until it became a blind panic. In the faint light, she sensed someone close by. She crept toward the presence, then stopped as two shadowy figures came into view. Dirt scraped across a shovel and heightened her fear. The sound was just as insidious now as it was in her nightmares.

Her heart pounding like a drum in her ears, she wanted to find her way out of this hell she'd entered. But she couldn't move. In a split second, she realized she was lying on her back with dirt hitting her face. Paralyzed, her limbs were stiff, and it was impossible to keep the soil from slowly covering her body. Terror filled her as she tried to scream. Soon she'd be buried beneath the earth. The depth of her fear clawed its way through her as she struggled to breathe. Dirt continued to clog her nose and mouth. The air slowly disappeared from her lungs, leaving in its place a fiery pain. The abrupt sensation of being shaken pierced through the veil of dark mist, and she drank in deep, gasping breaths of air. The wild pounding of her heart slowly ebbed away to a softer rhythm as she stared up into Molly's worried gaze.

"Good heavens, my lady. You gave me a fright. I need to fetch his lordship. He'll want to know you're ill."

"No," Victoria whispered hoarsely. "You're not to mention this to his lordship. Is that clear, Molly?"

The maid studied Victoria with a pensive expression for a long moment before she slowly nodded. Victoria dragged in several more deep breaths as she fought to regain her bearings. Her gaze met Molly's worried one, and Victoria waved a hand in a gesture of reassurance.

"I'll be fine. It was nothing more than a headache."

"Yes, my lady." Molly's response was quiet, but Victoria heard the disbelief in the maid's answer. One hand rubbing her temple, she met the girl's worried gaze.

"Don't look at me like that," she muttered with exasperation. "I'll be fine."

"Are you certain, my lady?" Molly's hand touched Victoria's shoulder. "You still look a trifle pale."

"I promise you, Molly. I'm fine," Victoria said firmly as she stood up and walked to the window. "And not a word to Lord Guildford. Is that understood?"

"Yes, my lady." Molly looked unhappy, but Victoria was certain the maid would obey her order. The young woman picked up some towels off the bed. "I'll just put these up and leave you be, my lady."

Victoria nodded, then turned toward the window. The rain had stopped, but dark clouds still hovered over the landscape. She rubbed her forehead with the tips of her fingers, carefully avoiding the cut that hadn't healed yet. She'd not admitted it to Molly, but her head hurt like hell. It had been a mistake to try and go back into the mist. She didn't understand how or why, but the fog represented life-and-death. The thought of experiencing those horrible moments again made Victoria's stomach churn.

Determined to think of something else, she pressed her hand against the cool glass pane. Winter wasn't far off. Even in cold weather, she was certain Brentwood Park would be beautiful. What would it look like in the spring and summer? The image of a warm spring day spent with Nicholas and Edmund lifted her spirits slightly. It was a lovely thought, and she could only hope it would come true.

How was it possible to have fallen in love with Nicholas in such a short time? She tried to put it down to a fabulous night of sex, but she knew differently. There was a sense of knowing that came with her feelings for him. This wasn't the first time their destinies had been entwined so closely.

"Can I fetch you anything at all, my lady?" Molly's voice interrupted Victoria's brooding. She turned toward the maid who was standing near the door with a look of concern on her face.

"No thank you, Molly." She forced a smile to her lips, then turned back to the window. "I think I'll read for a bit. Edmund brought me one of his mother's books."

"Very well, my lady."

Victoria heard the soft click of the door closing behind the maid. She closed her eyes and an image of Nicholas filled her head. Beyond logic or reason, she'd found the love of her life in the past. It made no sense whatsoever, but she accepted it for the truth it was. Falling in love with Nicholas in such a brief amount of time was far more believable than the idea she was from the future. The sudden need to pour her heart out to someone gripped her, but the only person she could talk to was Anna.

She remembered the diary she'd begun. It would give her the outlet she needed. Victoria sat down at the secretaire and pulled out the journal she had started. The words came slowly at first before her pen raced across the page as she worked as fast as she could to get all of her thoughts on paper. Every word was written evidence of her life here no matter how short a time it was. She wasn't sure if it was a way to make things real, or an attempt to leave evidence that she'd existed here for a short time. Evidence she could find in her own time to prove she wasn't insane.

The more she wrote, the more cathartic the experience became. The linen parchment brushed softly against her fingers as she wrote page after page about everything she'd experience and felt. She wrote until the emotions seething inside her became nothing more than a quiet murmur. Exhausted, she closed the journal and buried it in the far corner of the desk. As she closed the desk lid, a tear slid down her cheek. She wiped it away. Victoria turned her head to look out the window. The sky had lightened considerably with a hint of sunshine trying to push through the clouds.

Victoria's gaze swept across the pasture land, and a sudden urge to go riding swept through her. The cold air would help clear her head and help her work off the restlessness inside her. No sooner had the idea swept through her head than it died. There was only one habit in her wardrobe, which she had to wear tomorrow for her portrait. A slow smile curled her lips. She didn't have to wear the habit at all. Anticipation made her ring for Molly. When the maid arrived, Victoria smiled at the younger woman.

"I need you to do me a favor. Bring me a shirt, coat, breeches, and a pair of boots from Edmund's room," Victoria said firmly. "No questions or arguments."

With a compliant nod, the maid hurried out of the room. Victoria paced the floor with growing excitement. When Molly returned, Victoria quickly accepted the clothing and proceeded to dress. As she pulled on Edmund's black boots, the maid hurried forward to help.

"It's all right, Molly." Victoria said with a smile. "I've worn boots like these before."

The heels of her footwear rang out loudly on the wood floor, as she hurried to the dressing table and retrieved a dark ribbon out of one of the small drawers. Eager to be on her way, Victoria quickly tied her hair back into a loose ponytail at the nape of her neck. When she whipped around, she met the younger girl's look of concerned dismay. As she passed Molly on her way out the door, she squeezed the girl's shoulder.

"If anyone asks, I went for a ride," she said with a smile.

Chapter 23

A sense of freedom filled Victoria as she ran down the back stairs and out of the manor. Even in the short time span she'd been here, she had missed her freedom to do as she pleased. Longing to escape, if even for just a half hour, Victoria headed toward the stables.

When she walked through the open doors of the long building, several stable hands did a double take at her strange appearance. She didn't think it was the fact that the countess had never shown up in the stables before. In all probability, it was the way she was dressed. An older man approached her with a wary look on his features.

"May I help ye, my lady?"

"Please saddle Zeus for me, I wish to go for a ride," she said firmly.

"Zeus? Does 'is Lordship know about this, my lady?" the old veteran asked in surprise. Victoria was certain Nicholas wouldn't approve, but he'd only said she couldn't ride Mischief. She ignored the man's question.

"If you're short-handed, I can saddle him myself," she said with a smile, determined to charm her way onto Zeus' back. "I've been cooped up for so long, and a ride will be refreshing. I'm sure you know what that's like."

"Aye, that I do, my lady," the older man replied with a grin. He looked over her shoulder. "Mickey saddle Zeus for her ladyship."

"Zeus, my lady?" Apprehension turned Mickey's mouth downward.

"Yes," she said with a wink. "His lordship said I couldn't ride Mischief. He said nothing about Zeus."

With a conspiratorial grin, the young stable hand ran off to saddle the stallion. Beside her, the old man ordered another of the grooms to saddle a horse to go with her. She immediately shook her head.

"There's no need for someone to go with me. I'll only be gone for a short time."

"But, my lady, his lordship—"

"His lordship worries unnecessarily. I'll be perfectly fine. If I'm not back in an hour, send out a search party. But I don't want an escort. Besides, Zeus will leave them behind, anyway."

Moments later, Mickey led the black stallion out to her. Without fear, she stepped forward and stroked the animal's corded neck. Checking the cinch on the saddle, she placed her foot in the stirrup and hoisted her body up into the leather seat. Without another word, she trotted the animal out of the building toward the open pasture. It only took a slight squeeze of her knees to make the stallion spring forward into a smooth canter and then a gallop.

She gave Zeus his head, and the horse ate up the ground with his surefooted stride. With no sense of purpose or direction, she just rode. She simply allowed herself to let her mind rest and think of nothing but the joy of riding. She wasn't sure how far she'd gone before Zeus slowed on his own to a walk.

White foam frothed Zeus's coat from the workout. Judging by the animal's appearance, Victoria knew she'd ridden four or five miles. She turned in her saddle to look back at the stables. The building was almost a miniature of itself. Victoria drank in a deep breath and suddenly realized her cheeks were wet with tears. God, what on earth was she crying for? She never cried. With her coat sleeve, she wiped the tears from her cheeks and brought the stallion to a halt. She dismounted and stroked the horse's jowl.

"All right, big fellow, we'll just walk for a little while, so you can cool off," she murmured.

As if understanding, the horse tossed his head. Shifting the reins over his head, she turned around and started back toward the stables with Zeus following her. The ride had helped to clear her thoughts and put things into perspective. She'd been wrong to try and force her way back to her time. That day would come soon enough. She was certain of that. She needed to make the most of her time here, and if that meant humbling herself by allowing Nicholas's forgiveness for her past, then that's what she'd do. She was in his world, and she had to make accommodations for that. She loved him, and she refused to spend another precious hour here locked in combat with him. When she eventually returned to the future, she wanted to take only happy memories with her. They would keep her warm on those cold, lonely nights when she would lay awake longing for Nicholas.

Time seemed endless, and it was only when she stumbled over an unseen stone that she realized the sun had sunk almost completely beneath the horizon. She'd been out a lot longer than she'd said she'd be. That meant Nicholas had probably been told she was out on Zeus. There would be hell to pay for that infraction alone. The sooner she got back, the less angry he'd be.

Behind her, Zeus snorted softly, and she glanced over her shoulder to see the animal's ears were pricked forward as if he'd heard something. Suddenly, in the distance, she heard another horse answer Zeus's soft cry. She heard the whicker again. It came from behind her, which meant it wasn't someone from Brentwood Park stables. The hair on the back of her neck stood up as Anna's warning popped into her head.

Without thinking, Victoria quickly mounted the horse and urged him into a fast trot back towards the stables. As she rode back, her heart sank at the way the purple and orange streaks in the sky were slowly fading into twilight. The sensation of someone watching her made the hair on the back of her neck rise, and she shivered. Unsettled by the feeling, she reined the stallion to a halt. Victoria twisted in her saddle to study the landscape behind her. Nothing seemed out of place, but another shiver slid down her spine. She was letting Anna's warnings get to her.

Still, it was better to be safe than sorry. She pressed her knee into Zeus and continued trotting back to the stables. Less than a mile later, a razor-edged frisson skimmed over her skin. Without stopping, she glanced over her shoulder. A chill ran through her as she saw two riders heading in her direction at a fast pace. Instinctively, she dug her knees into Zeus's sides. Startled, the horse leaped forward into a gallop.

In the distance, she saw the roof of the stables against the darkening sky. Her heart sank. It was still almost two miles away. Victoria glanced over her shoulder. The riders chasing her were quickly gaining on her. Although Zeus' stride was still strong, she knew the animal was tired. There was the actual possibility the horse might not be able to out run her pursuers.

With the sun now below the horizon, the temperature had dropped, and Victoria's hands were stiff with cold. She was an idiot. She should have worn gloves. No, she shouldn't have stayed out so long. Behind her, the sound of hoof beats echoed louder in her ears, and she pressed her knees into Zeus' side to make him charge up a hill. As she crested the slope, Victoria saw a small party of riders with lanterns headed her way.

Seconds later, Victoria was surrounded by Nicholas and several of his men. Relief washed over her as she wheeled Zeus around to stare up at the top of the hill. It was impossible to see anyone in the darkness at the top of the slope, but she knew they were there. She could feel them.

If Nicholas and the others had not come when they had, Zeus would not have been able to outrun whoever had been chasing her. The animal had a huge heart, but he was exhausted. Rough hands jerked her out of the stallion's saddle, and she cried out as Nicholas set her on the ground in front of him.

"What the hell were you thinking to ride past dark and then charging down a hill like that?" he growled fiercely.

"I'm sorry…"

Reaction setting in, Victoria choked back tears and shivered violently. She looked over her shoulder again. Were they still there? Watching her? She couldn't feel them anymore. Nicholas's anger was a physical, pulsating vibration radiating out of him as he grasped her chin in his fingers. Green eyes studied her intently for a moment. He tilted her face toward the lantern light, and something flickered in his gaze before he abruptly released her.

Leaving her side, he issued several soft commands to one of his men. Unable to hear his low words, Victoria watched as the man called out two names and mounted his horse. The three men rode up the hill, the light from their lanterns disappearing over the top of the hill. Nicholas returned to her side and lifted her back into the saddle.

"We're going home." His voice was devoid of emotion, but she knew he was still angry.

Victoria didn't argue. Tired, cold, and shaken, all she wanted at the moment was a hot bath to wash away the dirt and soothe the ache settling into her muscles. The ride to the stable was short, and as Zeus walked into the stable yard, Mickey ran out to meet her.

"I'll take him for you, my lady," he said with a relieved smile on his cheerful features.

"Thank you, Mickey. He ran hard. So take good care of him."

"That I will, my lady." He took the reins from her as she

dismounted. "And I'm glad yer home safe, ma'am."

Wearily, she acknowledged his statement with a nod before she headed toward the manor. Behind her, she heard Nicholas issuing instructions to Mickey. Hoping to avoid the confrontation she knew was coming, she hurried toward the house. In spite of her quick stride, Nicholas caught up with her as she reached the back door of the manor. The instant he caught her arm, she knew not to try and break free. His grip unyielding, he guided her into the house, then up the back stairs to her bedroom. Nicholas threw open the door to her bedroom, then slammed it shut behind them.

"Tell me what you saw out there," he bit out.

"Two riders. They chased me for about three miles, I think." She shivered as she remembered the sinister nature of the riders. She shivered once more. Anna had been right after all. Someone believed her to be a threat, and tonight she understood just how serious a risk they believed her to be.

"You are not to ride alone again. Is that understood?" His voice was a thunderclap in the room, and she jumped, then nodded her agreement.

"Yes," she said quietly. Nicholas narrowed his gaze at her.

"Just like that. Just a simple yes." The savage note in his voice made her flinch.

Beneath his fierce glare, she dropped her gaze. She knew she'd been an idiot. A chilly frisson skated over her skin. If the people chasing her had caught up with her, she could have wound up like the countess. Dead. Victoria's stomach churned at the thought. Tears formed in the back of her throat. Anna had warned her, and she'd ignored her friend's warning.

"Dammit, Victoria. I am—"

"Would you settle for some humble pie, and my promise I won't go riding alone again," she whispered hoarsely as she bowed her head.

Eyes watering, Victoria blinked rapidly to push the tears

back. Richard Lockwood had been right. She did have a heavy weight on her shoulders. At the moment, it felt like a load of bricks. Trembling, she swallowed hard in her effort not to cry. It was impossible. Her vision was blurred when Nicholas's boots showed up almost toe-to-toe with hers. Firm fingers brushed against her jaw and forced her to raise her head.

The anger on his face disappeared as he uttered a quiet sound. With a quick movement, he tugged her into his arms. Every emotion she'd been holding back since Nicholas had found her in the dark pushed its way up out of her. A shudder ripped through her as she burst into tears and burrowed herself into his chest.

Slowly, her sobs became soft sniffles, and a mint-scented handkerchief brushed her cheek. Victoria gratefully accepted the square linen. When she'd regained control of her emotions, she pulled free of his embrace.

"Better?" There was a trace of a smile in his voice, and she looked up at him.

"Yes, thank you," she said, wiping tears off her cheeks.

"Good." His thumb removed a stray tear as he shook his head with exasperation. "I ought to give you a good paddling for being so foolish. But I think the scare you've had is punishment enough."

Victoria met his stern gaze, and her only acknowledgment was a nod of agreement. Nicholas arched an eyebrow in mock amazement as he folded his arms across his chest.

"I think this is the least argumentative you've been since your return."

"I own up to my mistakes," she said stiffly, while humiliation made her cheeks burn.

"As do I," he said softly. "You are nothing like Vickie. It was wrong of me to suggest it."

"Thank you for that," she said with a quiet dignity. Victoria wanted more from him, but for the moment she was willing to accept his apology. Silence drifted between them, and Victoria shifted uneasily. Nicholas's gaze strayed from her face to roam up and down her body.

"Are these my clothes or Edmund's?"

"Your brother's."

"Ah." He nodded as a sinful smile curved his lips. "I thought so. Although, Edmund has never filled them out quite as nicely as you do."

"I didn't have anything else to wear." She bristled and her jaw grew tight with irritation. "Your wife only owns *one* habit, which happens to be what you want me to wear in that damn portrait."

"I see," he murmured. Green eyes glinting with a look of possession he arched his eyebrow arrogantly. "When we go to London, you can order a new habit, but you're never to dress like this again."

"Why not? It's perfectly respectable."

She decided to leave the issue of London alone for the moment. At her rebellious response, he stretched out his hand to caress the base of her throat. Leaning forward, his lips brushed across her ear.

"You won't dress like this again, because I'll not have any other man see those shapely legs of yours," he said huskily. "*I'm* the only man who gets to see them, Victoria. And I'm the *last* man who will ever have them wrapped around him. Is that clear?"

She'd never felt so beautiful, desired, and sexy in her entire life. He was staking his claim. In no uncertain terms, Nicholas was saying she belonged to him. Not because he believed she was his wife, but because he wanted her for himself. She drew in a deep breath as uncertainty took hold of her. Victoria took a quick step back from him.

"And my past? I won't apologize for who I am or what I did long before I met you." Her words caused a somber expression to fall over his proud features.

"The thought of you in another man's arms doesn't please me," he said in a tight voice.

"I'm not her, Nicholas. I won't betray you." The whispered pledge made him reach for her.

Nicholas wrapped her in a tight embrace and buried his face in the side of her neck. She thought she heard him murmur something against her skin, but didn't have the chance to ask what he'd said as he lifted his head and kissed her. The moment his mouth captured hers, she was lost.

Chapter 24

Nicholas savored the sugar taste of her against his mouth. What was it about this woman that made him willing to forget whatever had happened in her past without hesitation? In the short time since her return, he'd fought hard to stop thinking about her, touching her or listening for the sound of her voice in the next room.

He knew he was fighting a losing battle on all counts. Without guile, Victoria was securing a place in his life that threatened to topple his world in a way Vickie had never done. A quiet mewl broke past Victoria's lips as he kissed his way across her cheek to nibble on her ear. His fingers found the tie holding her hair back, and he released the auburn silk hair so he could slide his fingers through it.

A familiar need surged through his veins as his hands slid across her shoulders. The rough wool of the riding coat reminded him she was wearing his brother's clothes. When he'd seen her dressed like a man, he'd been furious that other men had seen what belonged to him. Worse, the way she looked had thrown him off balance, just as she was doing now. He lifted his head and met her gaze.

The passion he saw there made his cock stiffen and ache with a hunger he realized only she could ever satisfy. He did not allow himself to consider the thought. Instead, he slowly pushed the coat off her shoulders. The white shirt she wore revealed her nipples straining against the material. He sucked in a sharp breath. She'd forgone a corset.

"*God almighty, Victoria,*" he rasped. "Do you have any idea what could have happened to you if those bastards had caught up with you dressed like this?"

"Yes," she whispered as she paled slightly. "But they didn't. You saved me, just like you always will."

The conviction in her voice displayed a trust he hoped he could live up to. A sensual smile suddenly curved her lovely mouth, and she slowly unbuttoned her shirt. His mouth went dry as she revealed her beautiful breasts. Lush and round, he wanted to suck on her until she cried out for mercy. Her smile became that of a seductress as she pulled the shirt out of the pants she wore and shrugged herself out of the blouse. A mischievous look sparkled in her eyes.

"Do you want to know what I'm wearing under these trousers, Nicholas?" The smile curving her lips as she removed her boots made him realize she couldn't be wearing bloomers.

"*Sweet Jesus,*" he rasped as she undid the buttons of her trousers to expose her bare stomach.

As she tugged the riding breeches off her legs, his throat constricted as she revealed her naked body. With jerky movements, he shrugged out of his clothes as she backed away from him to the bed. Her gaze ran over him as he finished undressing. Arms outstretched to him, she silently urged him to come to her. As he approached the bed, she scurried backward with a smile of enticement.

"Did you think it would be that easy?" She laughed, and Nicholas quickly caught her by the ankles and tugged her toward him.

"You, sweet witch, are a tease." His hand slowly slid up over her calves to her thighs. "I think that deserves a punishment."

She gasped loudly as his fingers brushed against her core. His gaze locked with hers for a moment before he lowered his head toward the apex of her thighs. The soft musk of her desire made his blood surged through his veins until his body ached for her like a man dying of thirst longed for water. The moment his mouth brushed against her, a cry parted her lips. A second later, hot, tangy cream raced over his tongue.

Eagerly, he licked and sucked on her as she writhed beneath his touch. Another sob of passion escaped her, and he nipped at the plump nub of flesh between her slick folds. Her body arched upward as she came again. The tart taste of her filled his mouth increasing the need tightening its relentless grip on him. God, but the woman was incredible. The way she responded to him was intoxicating.

His mouth caressed the inside of her thigh, then moved across her stomach up to her breasts. Her hand slipped between them to grasp his cock firmly. Her fingers tightening around him, she slid her hand up and down his erection. The caress created a friction that aroused him more than he dreamed possible. A deep groan rolled out of him, and when she suddenly released him, he uttered a fierce protest. With a quickness that took him by surprise, she pushed him over onto his back and sheathed him in her velvety heat. The feel of her wrapped around him dragged a dark growl out of him.

She stared down at him, her eyes bright with desire. But there was another indecipherable emotion there as well as she began to ride him. Slowly at first, then faster and faster. He matched each of her hot strokes with hard thrusts of his own. His body demanded a release, but he held back, determined to prolong her pleasure. The rising tide inside him pushed at his control and warning bells sounded in his head.

Swiftly, he rolled her onto her back and thrust hard and fast into her. With a low cry of pleasure, she arched her body upward and her spasms clutched at his cock like a fiery vise. Twice more he thrust into her, then quickly withdrew and throbbed against her stomach with her name on his lips. It was far from the fulfillment he'd experienced in her arms last night, but without protection he could think of no other method to avoid the risk of a child. He'd made that mistake last night. He wouldn't do so again.

Arms braced on either side of her, he lowered his head to press his forehead against hers. Their harsh breathing was the only sound in the room as he shifted his body and fell onto the bed beside her. Stretching out his hand, he caressed her cheek gently. The wanton look of satiation warming her features made the familiar need to possess her rise inside him once more. He suddenly realized he would never be able to get enough of her. She would haunt him forever. The thought disturbed him. It made him afraid he might lose her.

"As always, that was wonderful," she whispered. Her eyes closed, Victoria's mouth was curved in a smile as she lay spent beside him.

"I'll be back," he murmured as he kissed her.

Aware of the risk he'd taken moments ago, he quickly retrieved several French letters from his room. He'd meant to place a couple in Victoria's night stand, but their argument this morning and had made him forget. Before he returned to her room, he stopped to wet a cloth in the bathroom. As he walked through the door leading into her bedroom, he froze at how still she was. A dark fear blistered its way through him, and he raced across the room with his heart slamming into his chest like a sledge hammer.

"*Victoria*," he rasped as he knelt beside her. She jerked in surprise and looked up at him.

"What?" she asked with a startled look. Feeling like a fool, he shook his head as he wiped his seed off her stomach. As he rose to his feet, he turned away only to have her hand grasped his.

"Tell me what's wrong, Nicholas. Why did you call out to me like that?"

"I thought you'd had another spell."

"No," she whispered with a shake of her head. A soft

hand cupped his cheek, and he pressed his mouth into her palm. When he turned his head back to her, Nicholas glimpsed guilt flitting across her features.

"You've had another spell." His eyes locked with hers. She opened her mouth, then closed it. Narrowing his gaze at her, Nicholas frowned. "Don't lie to me, Victoria. You fainted again, haven't you?"

"Technically…no," she muttered.

"What the fuck does that mean," he snarled.

"It means that it wasn't an accident." She had the decency to look contrite, at least.

"*Christ Jesus*, you deliberately brought on one of your headaches, didn't you?" Fury streaked through him like a violent storm.

"It doesn't matter. Nothing happened." Her quiet reply tightened his body.

"*Yes*, it *does* matter." He wanted to shake her for being so foolish. First, the ride tonight, now this. "You've not seen the way you look during one of your really terrible spells. You've barely been breathing. What the hell would make you do such a thing?"

The thought of losing her made him grow cold. He didn't want—couldn't bear the thought of that happening. Nicholas shoved a hand through his hair and waited for her answer. She turned her head away from him. When she remained silent, he released a fierce sound of anger.

"*Damn it*, Victoria, answer me."

"I was trying to go home."

"You are home," he said firmly.

"You know what I mean, Nicholas." She shook her head with what he realized was a bleak despair. "I thought if I could go home, I wouldn't get hurt."

"Who said they would hurt you? Who's threatened you?" he demanded in a harsh voice. The memory of the letter he'd received earlier that day filled his head. Had she received a similar note that he didn't know about? A chill settled in his bones.

"No one's threatened me," she said in a forlorn voice. "I just know that the longer I stay here, the more it will hurt when I go home."

"Come here," he said gruffly as he saw her despondent look. "You aren't going anywhere."

"You don't understand—"

"Victoria it doesn't matter what either of us believes. What matters is that I'm not going to let anything or anyone hurt you."

A sad smile curved her soft pink lips. For a moment he wondered what might happen if she really wasn't from his time. No sooner did the thought enter his head than he dismissed it. Victoria was here, in his arms, and he wasn't about to let her go. Deep inside, a mocking laugh taunted him, but he didn't dare consider what it meant. He held her in his arms for a long time, enjoying the warmth of her against his body. She stirred in his arms, then slid down his side to where she reached out and touched his scarred leg. Instinctively, he stiffened at the touch. Victoria lifted her head to meet his gaze for a long moment, before she pressed a gentle kiss on the burned, mottled flesh.

"What happened to your leg?"

Her lips were like a soft whisper brushing across his skin. Despite the scarring, the touch of her mouth still sent sensory signals to his brain. He closed his eyes at her question. It aroused guilt and sorrow inside him. Not once since that terrible day had he shared his feelings with anyone. Whether it was the fact that he'd failed to save the boy or his desire not to relive the nightmare, he didn't know. In some ways, he believed his refusal to speak of the matter was a form of penance.

"Nicholas?" Her question was repeated silently in the gentle way she said his name.

"There was a fire at a paper mill I owned shortly after I inherited my title." It surprised him at how easily she'd persuaded him to share his story. "I'd just inspected the mill earlier that morning and was about to board a train to return home when I learned the mill was on fire."

The touch of her fingers against his mutilated flesh made him draw in a breath as he remembered how his injury had happened.

"A fire brigade had formed by the time I reached the mill, but it was of little use." He swallowed the bile rising in his throat. "It was then we heard the screaming."

"Oh dear God," she said in a hushed voice as she sat up to stare down at him.

"Several of us raced back inside. A small group of workers were trapped behind a collapsed wall. We managed to get the wall down to rescue them. We were almost out of the building when I heard more screams crying for help. I ordered Roberts to get everyone out of the building while I went back."

Nicholas stretched out his hand to touch her cheek. Somehow, touching her made it easier to continue his story. The look of empathy in her gaze said she realized how difficult it was for him to share his story. She bent over his scarred leg one more time to kiss the permanent reminder of his failure before she nestled her sweetly curved body into his side. Nicholas swallowed hard as he continued.

"The child couldn't have been much older than twelve, and he was terrified. There was a small barrier of flames between us, but I couldn't coax him to run through the fire. If I'd been him, I imagine I'd have had difficulty as well. When he wouldn't cross through the flames, I decided to go after him."

Nicholas stopped as the memories flooded his head. The horrific images only intensified his feelings of guilt. He stared up at the ceiling as he waited for the sickening lurch in his stomach to ebb away. Victoria's hand touched his cheek, but he didn't look at her.

"Before I could reach the boy, one of the roof's trusses crashed down onto my leg and pinned me to the floor. I knew I wouldn't be able to reach the boy, but I shouted at him to jump through the flames. The boy took one step forward when one of the main support beams crushed him. He was killed instantly. He never had a chance."

Nicholas barely felt Victoria take his hand and squeeze it. The memory of those last horrible moments continued to play out vividly in his head. The boy's shrill cry and his own fear as he laid trapped beneath the beam. Victoria pressed her mouth against his shoulder as if understanding he couldn't continue.

"Roberts rescued you, didn't he?" she whispered, and he heard the horror in her voice.

"Yes, he and another worker pulled me out of the fire."

"And that's where he got those terrible scars." Victoria's observation made him shift his concentration to his valet.

"I owe him my life, but if I'd been able to save the boy…" He didn't finish his sentence knowing that the word *if* was of no value to the child he'd failed to save.

"Don't," she said fiercely. "You did what few people are capable of doing. I don't think I would have had the courage to enter a burning building like that."

Nicholas studied her lovely features, and her expression of reassurance warmed him. He'd never had a more beautiful or ardent defender. A strange emotion snagged at Nicholas. When he tried to define it, his brain rejected the idea. The moment he stroked her brow with his fingertips, she stretched her body upward to kiss him. The sweet, tender caress soothed a raw, open wound that had never healed. The depth of emotion sweeping over him alarmed him. What would he do if he ever lost her? He immediately destroyed the thought. He wasn't going to let that happen. His hand slid across a soft shoulder, then down to a bare arm. She lifted her head and stared down at him with an emotion he was afraid to identify.

"I understand your guilt and sorrow. The night before my father died, we had a terrible argument. I left the house still angry. I never got the chance to say I was sorry." Grief darkened her beautiful face. The pain he saw shimmer in her gaze made him want to reassure her as she had him. "There are some things we're just not able to do. When I look at your leg, I know you did the very best you could. You can't continue to blame yourself for things that are out of your control."

"That's easier said than done, sweet witch."

"I'm not telling you the guilt will go away. It probably never will, but if you continue to let it possess you, it will eat you alive."

Nicholas stared into her eyes as he absorbed her words. Was that what he'd been doing all these years? Emotion darkened her lovely features as she kissed him.

"Make love to me, Nicholas. I need…I need you right now, just as much as you need me."

Her voice broke slightly, and he knew she'd been about to say something different. Before he could question her, she pushed him back into the pillows and her lips generated a passionate heat in his body that had become as familiar as the need she always created inside him. He slipped his tongue into her mouth to savor the honeyed taste of her.

There was a sense of urgency to her kiss that blotted out his every thought, except the desire building inside him. An intense, visceral thirst for her crashed through him. His thumb caressed one nipple, and she moaned in obvious pleasure. The sudden shudder rippling through her made him roll her over onto her back. The desire glowing in her blue eyes made his cock harden until it ached for her.

Suddenly, he realized how much he needed her—needed to make love to her to soothe his soul. He stretched out his arm and retrieved a French letter from the top of the nightstand. A moment later he sank into her sultry heat with rapid strokes that intensified as he released some of the anguish he'd felt for so many years as he sought atonement in her arms.

The beginnings of her orgasm tightened around him in quick, sharp bursts. The spasms heightened the pleasure building inside him. As her body gripped his more tightly, he felt a familiar surge in his cock and with a dark roar he throbbed inside her.

Slowly, he lowered his weight on her, unwilling to withdraw from her just yet. She'd said she needed him, but he was certain he needed her more. After a long moment, he rolled to one side and covered his face with his arm. The contentment he found in the silence between them made him happy. It was a happiness he'd never expected to find in his marriage. A soft rumbling from Victoria's stomach made him grin.

"Hungry?" he asked as embarrassment flushed her cheeks, and he laughed. "Get dressed, and I'll have supper brought up to us."

"Isn't getting dressed defeating the purpose?" she said as she slowly rolled onto her side and trailed her fingers across his chest. "I mean you're just going to take off whatever I put on, right?"

Her fingers stirred a fire inside him as she dragged them down toward his stomach. With a life of its own, his cock stirred as she brushed her fingertips over his growing erection. Nicholas growled with need at her touch.

"You're deliberately trying to distract me."

"Is it working?" she murmured in a husky voice.

"Almost, but I'm hungry too." He chuckled and caught her hand and carried it up to his mouth. He turned her hand over to press a kiss into her wrist. Deliberately, he swirled his tongue across her skin and was rewarded with a gasp of pleasure parting her lips. He released her hand, then rolled her onto to her side to swat her bottom before he slid off the bed. At her quiet yelp of surprise, he laughed.

"Actually, I think I prefer you naked, but I don't intend to give Roberts a heart attack when he walks in to find a nude countess in my bedroom." He winked at her. "However, once supper has been served, the idea of you wearing nothing else tonight is quite appealing."

Her laughter followed him as he disappeared into the corridor that connected their rooms. A smile still on his face, he tossed his clothes onto the nearest chair as he entered his bedroom. With a tug on the bell cord, Nicholas grabbed his robe from the wardrobe and threw it on over his shoulders. He cinched the belt and caught a glimpse of his reflection in the window.

All he could see was a yawning black hole beyond his image. As he stared into the impenetrable darkness, he remembered the way his heart had sunk when his head groom had sent word Victoria had not returned from her ride. He'd been furious that Yancey had taken so long to notify him that Victoria had gone riding. But he knew all too well how easily Victoria could charm people into allowing her to do as she pleased. God knew he was bewitched by her just as much as the rest of the household.

When he'd learned Victoria had taken Zeus out, his stomach had lurched at the thought that the stallion had thrown her, and she was laying in the dark somewhere gravely injured. It had been a fleeting notion as her skill at riding Mischief had been impressive. Zeus was a far less fractious animal, which meant it was unlikely she would have encountered that sort of trouble. That had left him with only one other fear. Someone had intercepted her.

Fear dried his mouth as he remembered the look on Victoria's face as he'd pulled her off of Zeus' back tonight. He'd been furious that she'd not agreed to an escort, and that she'd been so foolish to ride so late in the day. But when he'd stared down at the look of terror on her face, he'd realized whoever had written the notes was an even greater threat to her than he'd realized. He could have lost her tonight. Nicholas dragged in a sharp, harsh breath at the thought. How was it that in such a brief time span, Victoria had managed to embed herself so firmly in his life?

It scared the hell out of him. Nicholas clenched his jaw, as he realized he'd passed the point of no return where Victoria was concerned. There would be no retreat if something caused her personality to revert back to the woman he'd married. The price he'd pay would be quite dear if the worst happened.

Chapter 25

December 1897

I f you would, my lady, could we adjust the drape so that I can see a bit more of your calf," Lockwood said as he rose to his feet. Nicholas immediately set the paperwork he'd been reading aside.

"Allow me, Lockwood," he said in a voice that silently said he'd not allow the artist anywhere near Victoria in her current state of undress.

Nicholas rose from his seat behind the artist, and the other man immediately sank back down onto the chair with a nod. There was a mischievous look on Victoria's face as Nicholas approached the lounge she was reclined on in her bedroom. Bending slightly over her leg, he adjusted the sheet to an angle he thought would satisfy the artist. He stepped back to allow Lockwood to approve of the change.

"Yes, my lord, that's perfect. Also, if you would please, lower the sheet beneath lady Guildford's hand a small bit. It should display a bit more…" The artist's voice trailed off and Victoria laughed.

"I think the word you're looking for is cleavage."

Before Victoria could move, Nicholas stepped in front of her to block the artist's view. Amusement made her blue eyes sparkle as she smiled up at him. Her hand moved slightly until one beautiful breast was exposed to him. The air left his lungs, then returned in a rush.

"You, sweet witch, are playing with fire," he whispered hoarsely.

"Perhaps I should help you put it out." The suggestive note in her softly spoken response made him scowl down at her.

Her smile became a quiet laugh as he tugged the sheet back into place. But not before he deliberately tweaked her nipple. She gasped at his small punishment before a languorous expression swept over her face. Tension locked his muscles into place as he fought the urge to order Lockwood out of the room and make his wife pay for her teasing manner. Instead, he bent his head to nibble at her ear.

"Tonight, I'm going to make you wish you'd not teased me so heartlessly, because I intend to fuck you until you plead for mercy, and, then I'll simply fuck you some more."

The sharp breath Victoria drew in made him smile, but when her eyes met his, the desire flaring in those blue depths made him suppress a groan. He quickly stepped aside to obtain the artist's approval on the new position of the sheet. The other man nodded his approval, but it didn't change Nicholas's irritable mood. He was ready for this portrait to be finished.

"Thank you, my lord," Lockwood murmured with a touch of apprehension. "That will do nicely."

The artist quickly averted his gaze and returned to his work. In several steps, Nicholas was at his chair and picked up his papers. He tried to continue his review of them, but his gaze kept sweeping back to Victoria. Desire still clung to her features as she met his gaze. To his right, Lockwood was dabbing at the canvas with rapid strokes. Nicholas leaned slightly to one side to see the man's work, and something deep inside him tried to push its way to the surface. He quickly crushed it. Jealously was an unfamiliar sensation, and he wasn't ready to acknowledge the underlying cause.

At least the second portrait was nearly complete. It had been almost two months since Victoria's return, and he'd never been happier. That is with the exception of these hellish sittings as Lockwood worked on this damn portrait. He'd been a fool to commission this painting, but he'd not expected his feelings to change so radically where Victoria was concerned. Nicholas looked at the canvas on the easel again. Begrudgingly, he had to admit the artist had captured the elusive quality Victoria possessed in this painting as well as her formal portrait. This portrait, however, had also captured the beautiful, naked sensuality of his wife. It was an intimate painting that made him resentful of the artist. That the man had translated the raw essence of Victoria to the canvas and made him realize the artist might be in love with her. The knowledge made him feel possessive of his wife in a way he'd never dreamed possible.

"When do you expect to have this portrait done," he snapped as his thoughts made him irritable. Lockwood jumped slightly, then glanced over his shoulder.

"I should be done in the next day or two, my lord," Lockwood said quietly. "However, it will take this portrait well into the new year before it's ready for framing. Her ladyship's formal portrait can be framed sometime by the end of December."

"Excellent. That means the countess' sittings won't interfere with our return to London."

"*London,*" Victoria exclaimed. Her eyes widened before they narrowed with anger.

"Lady Guildford, please, I need you to remain still."

"I'm done for the day, John. Would you mind giving his Lordship and me a few moments of privacy?"

Nicholas grimaced at the mutinous line of Victoria's full mouth. He was in for a fight with her regarding their return to town. The moment the artist left the room, she was on her feet with the sheet wrapped around her tightly. It was a clear sign she wasn't about to let him seduce her into agreeing to his plan.

"I told you a few weeks ago I wasn't going to London."

"As my wife you will accompany me, Victoria." He kept his voice low and calm. Her rejection of the idea didn't surprise him. She had made her intentions clear, but he wasn't about to leave her alone for any extensive length of time.

"Don't you dare patronize me, Lord Guildford." Her use of his title emphasized she was angrier than he expected. He would have to tread carefully in order to make her comply with his wishes.

"I'm not patronizing you, Victoria. But it's—"

"The hell you aren't," she snapped. "You made an arbitrary decision where I'm concerned. I'm not chattel for you to do with as you please."

"*Christ almighty*," he growled. "I am not treating you as chattel."

"I told you before. I am not going to London," she bit out in a fierce voice.

"*Damn it, Victoria*. I'm not about to—"

A knock on the door interrupted him, and before he could order the person to go away, Victoria called out for them to enter. It was an obvious effort on her part to end the conversation. Nicholas glared at her for not judiciously asking who had knocked. It could've been Roberts for all she knew, and he had no desire for any man to see his wife as she was now. When Molly walked through the door, relief washed over him. It was quickly replaced by the a wave of frustration.

"I beg your pardon, my lady. But Mr. Elrod insisted on seeing Lord Guildford right away."

The maid's words made Nicholas stiffen. He'd met with Elrod earlier this morning. The man's return could mean only one thing. Either he had news from Greene, or another note had arrived.

"Thank you, Molly. I'll be there shortly." It was a quiet

dismissal, and the maid left the room before Victoria could stop her. A sigh escaped his lips as he met Victoria's angry gaze.

"I do not consider you my property, Victoria. But as my wife, it's expected for you to accompany me to town." His statement echoed quietly between them. Victoria studied him in silence, her expression unreadable.

"I need to dress, and I believe someone is waiting for you," she said in a stilted tone as defiance crossed her features again. Annoyed, he took a step toward her, but she retreated from him. Nicholas didn't like the way it made him feel to see her back away from him.

"We'll discuss this later," he growled. "Right now I need to see my estate manager." Victoria appeared ready to make a retort, but she clamped her beautiful lips shut and glared at him instead. With a quiet oath, he slammed her bedroom door shut on his way out. God help him, how was he supposed to keep her safe if she refused to do what he said? Perhaps that was the key. He was telling her what she had to do as opposed to asking her. Victoria was an independent woman. She believed she was the one in control of her destiny.

The larger problem was that he'd not been honest with her. His efforts to protect Victoria had included not telling her about the danger she was in. He had little doubt she'd be incensed if she discovered he'd not shared his concerns with her. Still, he didn't regret his decision. The fear on her face the night he and his men had found her almost two miles from the house was a look he'd never forget.

Victoria had been terrified that night, although he knew she wasn't a woman who frightened easily. But that one incident could not be the reason she changed her mind about visiting London. She'd refused to do so before being chased through the dark. The worst thing was that they'd not resolved their differences before he'd left her room.

He didn't enjoy seeing her unhappy, and she was most

definitely unhappy with him at the moment. Actually, it was a fact that she was unhappy with him that bothered him the most. With a scowl, he descended the main stairs and made his way to his office. The moment he entered, Elrod rose to his feet.

"What news do you have, Elrod?"

"Two things, my Lord. Mr. Greene has had a bit of luck with Reardon. Apparently, the man is looking for an item of value. Greene wasn't able to learn what the item is, but he says it's clearly of great importance." As Elrod finished his report, Nicholas drew in a deep breath and exhaled. At last, something he could work with.

"That's splendid news. Have Greene continue to watch the man. Reardon's extremely cautious, but everyone makes mistakes. We need to know what he's up to."

"Yes, my lord. Unfortunately, that's not all." The man's features darkened with worry, and Nicholas intuitively knew what the answer would be.

"Another note."

The silent confirmation on his estate manager's face made Nicholas's gut twist violently. Elrod reached into his coat pocket to retrieve an envelope that he handed to Nicholas. A tic tugged at his cheek in protest as to the way his facial muscles had tightened the moment he clenched his jaw.

My dear Guildford,

I understand Scotland Yard is extremely curious why you've not returned to London with your lovely wife. I imagine their curiosity is as great as mine, but then we both know how skilled you are at deception. Especially when one considers your questionable claim to the Guildford title? I wonder what Scotland Yard would think of the possibility that your brother is the rightful heir?

My guess is that you have ordered your wife not to ride alone again. Please convey my admiration for the Countess' horsemanship. Her skills are exemplary, given her lack of them before her convenient return. I regret being unable to reach her in time that night to express my admiration. Until we meet in London.

A friend

Nicholas released a soft oath beneath his breath. How was he supposed to protect Victoria if he didn't know for certain who was behind these notes? His best guess was that Reardon was behind them, but proving that was difficult simply because it could easily be Darby as well. He turned the envelope over and frowned.

"The postmark on the last note was the city of London, this one is from Hammersmith."

"Yes, my Lord. It's the same part of the city that Greene reported Darby was seen with Reardon in a local pub."

Frustration made the paper in Nicholas's hand crackle as he clenched his fists. He gritted his teeth.

"Tell Greene I want something connecting these notes to Darby or Reardon. If one of these bastards visits a postal office, I want to know where, what's being sent, and to whom he's mailing something."

"Yes, my lord." Elrod nodded at the instruction, then left Nicholas alone in his office.

With another fierce oath, Nicholas smashed the top of his fist into his desktop. Whoever was threatening his family was going to rue the day they dared to cross the Earl of Guildford.

Chapter 26

Dinner was a silent affair, and Victoria's noncommittal responses told him she was still angry with him. Preoccupied with the news Elrod had provided him earlier in the day, he'd not been able to focus his attention on healing the breach between him and Victoria.

Edmund, with his usual astute observations of human nature, leaned toward him as Nicholas took the last bite of the beef on his plate.

"What did you say to make Victoria so unhappy?" The hostility in his brother's question made Nicholas stiffen with surprise. For his lack of advanced mental capabilities, Edmund was more in tune to the emotions of others than anyone he'd ever met. With a sigh, he wiped his mouth with his napkin, then laid it beside his plate.

"We both know how independent Victoria is," he said as he slid his gaze toward her. "Unfortunately, I managed to incur her wrath by telling her she had to do something."

"Oh." Edmund nodded his head sagely. "Well you better stop telling her what to do. I don't like it when she's unhappy."

"Neither do I, Edmund," he said as he reached out to touch the back of Victoria's hand. "Neither do I."

His gaze locked with Victoria's blue one, and he waited for her to say something. With a shake of her head, Victoria scowled at him for a moment before a reluctant smile curved her mouth.

"If there's one thing you do well, Lord Guildford. It's making an apology without really apologizing."

That she'd forgiven him filled him with relief. Now to find the right moment to ask her to go to London with him without explaining why he was so insistent. The mood for the remainder of their meal was lightened significantly, and when they'd finished their dessert the three of them retired to the salon. Edmund and Victoria played chess while Nicholas read. When the clock chimed nine, he ordered Edmund to bed.

When his brother had left the room, Victoria invited him to a game of chess. Although his thoughts were still focused on the note he'd received, he agreed as his effort to read was a complete failure. Hopefully a game of chess would distract him. A quarter of an hour later, he realized that had not worked either.

"Checkmate." The quiet word made him straighten in his chair to study the board as Victoria made a sound of annoyance. "Did you deliberately just lose to me?"

"No," he said with a shake of his head. "I'd never do that."

"Then what's bothering you so much that you lost a game of chess to me in under twenty moves?"

"A business matter." The lie didn't please him, but the thought of seeing fear on her face again was the last thing he wanted. Nicholas shook his head. "It's serious, but it will resolve itself."

"Would it help to talk about it?"

"*No.*"

His adamant response made her eye him with suspicion. Nicholas sought to make his expression one of nonchalance as he shook his head. He knew discussing the letters would make matters worse between them. Not only would she be angry with him for hiding them from her, but it would frighten her.

Then again, perhaps it would make her go to London with him more easily. Her expression made it clear she was still trying to determine whether or not he was being honest with her, but she didn't press him any further.

"All right." She stood up. "I'm going to bed."

Although she didn't invite him to join her, there was an enticing note in her voice that made him believe she wouldn't object. If there was anything that would make him forget his woes, it would be in her arms. He smiled at her small cry of surprise as he tugged her down into his lap.

"Is that an invitation to join you in your bed, Lady Guildford?" he asked with a smile as the weight of his fears lifted slightly off his shoulders. Mischief made her eyes twinkle as a seductive smile curved her lovely mouth.

"Well, makeup sex is always good."

A strange emotion engulfed him as he studied her impish expression. He reached up to caress her cheek, and she cupped her hand around his, then turned her head to kiss his palm. In the next instant Victoria stiffened and jerked her head away from him. Concern flashed through him.

"What is it, sweetheart?"

"It's nothing," she replied with a weak smile. "Just a moment of déjà vu."

The confused look on her face made him refrain from probing. Instinct warned him it would be unwise to push her for an answer. She would simply dig in her heels. Instead, he pulled her head downward and kissed her gently.

"As you wish." The words made her gasp with surprise, and he arched his eyebrows in a silent question.

"It's nothing. It's just that what you said reminded me of one of my favorite mov—books, The Princess Bride."

"Then I shall have a copy ordered for you," he murmured softly as he caressed her throat with his mouth. Laughter vibrated against his lips.

"I don't think you'll find it, because it's not been

published yet," she said with a sweet smile. "But the fact that you're willing to buy the book for me makes me happy."

"How happy?" he whispered as he nibbled on her neck.

"Why don't we go upstairs and find out?"

The seductive sound of her voice made Nicholas grow hard, and without protesting he set her on her feet. Victoria slipped her hand into his and led him upstairs.

Nicholas stared into the fire burning in the grate. Despite the happiness it gave him to be in Victoria's arms, he'd been unable to sleep as peacefully as his wife. It was this damned infernal waiting that he couldn't stand. A sudden awareness shifted through his body, and he looked up to see Victoria. She was pale with fear and blinking back tears. Concern barreled through Nicholas as he quickly tugged her down into his lap.

"What's wrong, sweetheart?" He cradled her and brushed a lock of hair off her wet cheek.

"I had another…nightmare. When I woke up you were gone, and I thought… I thought I was back in the future without you."

"It was just a dream, sweet witch," he whispered. "You're right where you're supposed to be."

"I don't know why I'm so weepy all of a sudden," she choked out as she stared into the flames of the small fire in the grate. The corners of his mouth quirked at the memory of Vickie's personality and her outbursts.

"Would it help if I pointed out that in the past you were prone to a prolific number of tears and tantrums?"

"That wasn't—"

"You." He finished her sentence with a chuckle.

She was right. Vickie's personality had been completely

replaced by Victoria's. A fact someone was attempting to use against her and, ultimately, him. Another possibility slipped into his conscious mind, and he immediately rejected it. But like an insidious spider web, it drifted through his head again. He forced the thought out of his mind with a silent grunt. The woman in his arms was his wife. She wasn't an imposter.

Nicholas's gaze focused on Victoria again as she wiped her damp cheeks with her fingertips. Even teary-eyed, she was beautiful, and she was his. He would do whatever it took to protect her. Eyes wide in her face, there was still the shadow of fear in her gaze. Concerned, he caught her hand and carried it to his mouth.

"Tell me about your nightmare," he said quietly, but with a firmness he knew she would respond to. She shuddered against him and averted her gaze. Aware how deeply the nightmare had affected her, Nicholas gently pushed her to answer. "Victoria."

"I'm with Edmund. We're in a dark, horrible place." He could hear the fear in her voice, and his chest tightened painfully at his inability to ease her fear. She trembled in his arms as she stared into the fire. "Edmund's very frightened, but I keep telling him you'll come for us. He's crying, and I can't see where he is. The floor…it's slick…slimy, really. And there are mice—no rats—there are rats scurrying across the floor."

"It was a bad dream, Victoria," he said quietly. "I'm not about to let anyone hurt you or Edmund."

Nicholas wasn't sure she believed him, but she burrowed her body into his and laid her head on his shoulder. Silence drifted between them, and he glanced down at her to see her staring into the fire. Several embers in the fireplace flared, and the flames lit up her features. Victoria's nightmares troubled him. For the past week, he'd woken up to her soft moans of fear and unintelligible protests of terror.

Each time he'd gently soothed her until she slept quietly

again. He was certain her dreams were connected to whatever had happened to her during the time she was missing. There was a darkness bottled up inside her that only emerged when she was asleep or when she'd fainted. It had been more than a month since her last occurrence. The fact that she'd deliberately induced the episode only deepened his fears for her general well-being.

Whatever trauma she'd endured while she had been missing was one she was still affected by. Even Bertram was puzzled by Victoria's condition. The doctor had sent word that several of his colleagues had indicated Victoria's case was similar to others, and there was no treatment for the condition other than rest. The one heartening thing in the doctor's note had been the statement that few patients reverted to their previous personalities.

Curled up in his arms like this, he realized he couldn't imagine life without her. She shivered against him, and he frowned at the thin wrap she was wearing over her naked body. With a growl, he closed the robe over her lovely legs and pulled her into him as tight as he could.

"You're cold. This robe is for summer use, not winter," he muttered in gentle rebuke. "Tomorrow, I'm ordering Molly to pull your winter clothes out of storage. Although if you'd go to London with me, it would afford you the chance to buy new clothes."

"Have you seen how many dresses are in my wardrobe?" she said with disgust as she looked up at him. "It's obscene for one woman to have that many outfits just for one season of the year. And don't start on me about London."

The last part of her response was filled with defiance, and he sighed with frustration. The woman was backing him into a corner when it came to why he was so insistent she go with him. With a grimace, he caught her chin with his fingers and forced her to look at him.

"Victoria, it's not just business matters I must attend to.

I'll not be able to return to Brentwood Park for Christmas, and I'd prefer *not* to spend the holiday without you." Nicholas grimaced as he tried to frame his words in the best possible light. "I'll not order you to go, but I want you to come with me. You're my wife, and I want you with me."

"How many times do I have to tell you—"

"So help me God, Victoria," he growled with irritation. "What do I have to do to make you understand you're my wife? Marry you again?"

As the words left his mouth, he realized it was exactly what he wanted to do. He wanted to marry her. Legally, she might be his wife, but she was no longer Vickie. He wanted to prove to her that he had no doubts about who she was. Nicholas ignored the voice in the back of his head that tried to tell him there was another reason for his decision.

The thought had been troubling him for weeks, but he wasn't ready to admit the truth yet. Nicholas stared down at Victoria's shocked expression. The voice in the back of his head grew stronger, but he suppressed it out of fear. Victoria drew in a breath, then released it quickly.

"You would do that?" she whispered.

"Yes. If only to ensure you can no longer continue to deny being my wife," he teased, taking pleasure in the look of happiness on her face.

"Oh, Nicholas," she exclaimed softly. "Yes, yes, I'll marry you."

Her arms wrapped around his neck, and she pulled his head down to kiss him. The softness of her mouth against his was a sweet caress. There was only a hint of passion in the kiss, but a deeper emotion layered the taste of her mouth against his. It was an imprint on his soul, and deep inside he knew the connection between them was a bond so strong nothing could break it.

Slowly, her mouth left his, and she smiled up at him. There was a glow about her that made her look even more beautiful than he'd ever seen her. A part of him almost wished Lockwood could see her now to paint her face, but he immediately crushed the thought. He had no wish to share this moment with anyone.

"Do you really want me to come to London that badly?"

The tentative question startled him, and he frowned. He'd not made the offer to marry her in exchange for her agreement to go to London with him.

"My proposal *was not* an attempt to coerce you to go with me to London," he said in an irritable tone.

"I know that," she murmured.

Confusion and hesitancy flashed in her eyes as she looked at him then down to where her hand was pressed against his chest. When she remained silent, he breathed a quiet sound of puzzlement.

"Tell me why you're so adamant about not going to town." The moment he spoke, fear swept across her face. He narrowed his gaze at her. "Out with it, Victoria. I want to know why you're afraid to go with me to London."

"Because someone wants…I'm so different from Vickie. People are bound to think I'm an imposter, which technically I suppose I am, since I'm not Vickie…" She blew out a harsh breath of disgust. "It's all so damn confusing."

It was obvious she was frightened, and he was certain she'd changed her explanation to hide her fear from him. He carried her hand to his mouth and kissed the inside of her wrist.

"I've no doubt there will be gossip. There might even be rumors I murdered Vickie and replaced her with you," he said in a quiet voice. She drew in a sharp breath, and he knew she'd thought the same thing. "Nothing will come of it, Victoria. Rumors are not the same thing as truths."

"But the police—"

"The police need evidence to even suggest foul play. We don't know how or why you went missing. However, your injuries were observed by reliable witnesses. Dr. Bertram has examined you and consulted with experts regarding the changes in your behavior. Rumors and gossip are irrelevant."

The thought of someone publicly denouncing her as an imposter bothered him far less than the men who'd chased her that night across the estate. Especially when he knew those same men and the writer of the notes were connected. Victoria appeared ready to argue with him, but nodded when he frowned at her. Silence stretched between them for a long moment, before she sighed.

"I'll go with you to London," she said softly. The words filled him with relief, and he closed his eyes as elation surging through him.

"Thank you, sweet witch," he murmured as he pressed his mouth against the side of her head. The tangy smell of citrus filled his nostrils, as her hand stroked the side of his face. He looked down at her, and her mischievous look made him arch his eyebrows.

"I'd like to go back to bed…but not alone," she said with an enticing smile.

In a lithe movement, she slipped free of his arms and stood in front of him. The thin material of her robe allowed the fire to illuminate her body beneath the robe, and his heart slammed into his chest as his gaze ran over her sweetly curved hips, lush thighs, and full breasts. She was exquisite, and she was his. Victoria stretched out her hand to him. With a smile, he clasped her hand in his and followed her to bed, all the while knowing he would go to hell and back to possess her body and soul.

Chapter 27

London
December 1897

Victoria trembled as she watched Nicholas climb out of the carriage and turn to offer her his hand. She hesitated. Although Sebastian and Anna had called on them the day after their arrival to London, this was her first public appearance. The idea of being put under the microscope made her stomach churn.

"Nicholas, I can't do this."

"Of course you can, sweet witch." His smile reflected reassurance. "I will not throw you to the wolves. I'll not leave you."

After another moment of indecision, she accepted his hand and stepped out of the carriage. On the sidewalk, Victoria stared up at the brightly lit building they were about to enter. Another tremor shook her, and he bent his head.

"It will be all right, sweetheart. I have no intention of leaving you alone."

"Good, then everyone will know how bewitched you are by my charms." Her humor was an attempt to bolster her courage.

"Careful sweet witch, do not tempt me to weave my own spell and show how enchanted you are with me." A devilish twinkle in his eye, he tucked her arm in his and led her up the steps of the opera house.

Inside the large lobby, Victoria allowed Nicholas to remove her cape, and he handed it and his own coat to the attendant in the hat room.

"*Vickie, darling.*" A shrill, excited voice in front of her caused Victoria to wince. The owner of the voice, a young woman dressed in an elaborate green silk gown adorned with flourishes of ruffles and bows, glided toward her.

"I'm so happy to see you," the woman said as she eyed Victoria with intent curiosity. "We'd given you up for lost."

"Thank you for your concern," Victoria murmured as she groped for Nicholas's arm. When she felt the strength of his forearm beneath her hand, she heaved an inward sigh of relief.

"Good evening, Lady Farling." Nicholas greeted the woman with a bow. "You must forgive Victoria, her memory is still faulty."

"So I've heard, you poor dear," Lady Farling simpered. "I'm just so glad to see you back among us."

"Thank you," Victoria said again.

"If you'll forgive us, my lady, we're meeting friends." Nicholas caught Victoria's arm in his firm grip to guide her away from the woman.

"Of course," the woman said as she narrowed her eyes at Victoria. "I'll call on you soon, my dear."

"Abominable woman," he muttered when they were out of earshot.

"I take it you don't care for her?" she said with a soft laugh

"I never understood what you—" He stopped and corrected himself. "—what Vickie saw in her. The woman is an infernal gossip."

They climbed the wide staircase with other guests, several who greeted them with open looks of speculation. At the top of the stairs, Nicholas guided her down a corridor lined with several doorways with drawn back curtains. They stopped at one of the last doorways and entered an opera box overlooking rows of seats on the floor below. A noticeable hush swept over the people below their box, and Victoria stiffened as a flurry of conversations followed.

"This will be the most difficult part of the evening, sweet witch," Nicholas murmured reassuringly.

"You could have warned me," she snapped with irritation. Grateful for the fan Molly had insisted she attach to her wrist, Victoria popped it open. The silk bound slats fluttered madly in front of her face.

"You were nervous enough—I had no wish to make matters worse."

He gave her a gentle push forward, and for the first time she realized someone else was seated in the box. The woman turned her head and stared at them in surprise. A warm smile on her face, she stood up and moved to greet Nicholas.

"I didn't know you'd be here tonight," she said as she kissed Nicholas's cheek and gave him a warm hug. "I thought I'd have the box to myself this evening. If there is one thing James refuses to do for me, it's attend the opera."

The woman glanced at Victoria suspiciously as Nicholas returned her hug. She winced at the woman's obvious antipathy. Another person her counterpart had managed to alienate. Nicholas turned and reached for her hand.

"I thought it was time for Victoria to reenter the fray."

"Victoria?" Eyebrows raised in disdainful surprise, the woman studied her in puzzlement. Nicholas chuckled.

"She's insisted on being called Victoria since her return." He turned his gaze to her. "This is my sister, Abigail."

"Hello," Victoria said quietly as she extended her hand to the woman. Abigail automatically shook Victoria's hand. Despite her confusion, the woman was still surprised. Nicholas cleared his throat.

"Things have changed drastically since Victoria's return.

We've reconciled our differences."

"Have you," Abigail said in a skeptical tone of voice.

"Yes," Victoria replied softly. She liked how Abigail's concern and affection for her brother was so obvious. "Nicholas, Edmund, and I are looking forward to spending Christmas with you."

"*Edmund?* You find him annoying." A stunned look crossed Abigail's face as she stared at Victoria with her mouth agape. Nicholas chuckled.

"I *did* tell you that things have changed," he murmured as he caught Victoria's hand in his and raised it to his lips as he gave her a look of reassurance. His gentle chastisement made his sister shake her head in silent disbelief.

"Indeed." Nicholas's sister muttered with a cautious look in Victoria's direction as she frowned. "The Set is all a twitter about your memory loss. Can I presume this is the reason for your…miraculous changes in behavior as well as you not recognizing me?"

"Yes, I remember nothing before my return." The lie was unsettling, and she realized how comfortable Brentwood Park had become to her. It was home. London was a foreign country to her.

"Remarkable," Abigail said with a healthy dose of skepticism. Nicholas frowned at his sister.

"I'm the least likely person to believe my marriage has changed, Abigail. However, I would have expected better of you to have confidence in my belief Victoria's behavior is a true transformation," Nicholas said in a cool reprimand. "The doctor believes her head injury is the reason for the changes in her."

"Oh." Abigail looked significantly chastened, Victoria leaned forward.

"If it makes you feel any better, Nicholas was hard to convince that I wasn't Vickie. And he wasn't very nice about it at all." She looked up at him and grinned at his disgruntlement. "In fact, he hates being reminded of it."

"For that, sweet witch, I'll extract a suitable punishment in the future." The look he gave her told her precisely when he'd make good on that promise. Completely unrepentant, she laughed again, which made a look of annoyance settle on his features.

Amazement still on Abigail's face, Nicholas's sister urged them to sit down as the warning chimes for the performance sounded. Victoria took a seat in the corner of the box, grateful for the drapery that provided a small shield against probing eyes. Nicholas took a seat beside her, and leaned toward her as he caught her hand in his.

"You've handled all of this with a grace and aplomb Vickie never could," he whispered as he squeezed her hand. "I'm proud to call you my wife."

Victoria nodded at his words, but deep inside she knew she wasn't his wife, and it made her heart ache unbearably. She loved him more than he would ever know, and the fact they weren't really married struck deep. Forcing a smile to her lips, she nodded and glanced away as she saw the troubled assessment in the moss-colored depths of his gaze.

The curtain came up a moment later, and she was swept away by the singing. She'd never been to the opera before, but she'd fallen in love with it by the intermission. As the house lights came up, she leaned back with a sigh of pleasure. The evening was turning out much better than she'd expected.

"You're enjoying yourself." It was an observation, not a question as Nicholas smiled at her.

"I've never been to the opera, but I love it," she said with a nod. "I'm not all that crazy about being scrutinized so much, but I'm glad you insisted."

"It was a true test of my persuasion skills," he said with a touch of irony. Nicholas raised her hand to his lips and winked at her as his mouth brushed across her skin. It was impossible not to be amused by his self-satisfied expression.

"And you say I get my way all the time."

He squeezed her hand, then turned his head to look at his sister, whose expression of astonishment had changed little since their arrival.

"Abigail, I saw Sir Kenelm, the Home Secretary, across the way. Do you mind keeping Victoria company and not allowing anyone to accost her?" Nicholas's turned back to Victoria as his sister nodded her agreement.

"But you said—"

"It's just for a moment, sweetheart. There are very few people who would attempt to reach you here, and Abigail will keep the hounds at bay." Despite the reassurance in his voice, a wave of fear rolled over her.

"Although we've not been friends in the past, Victoria, I promise you'll be safe with me." For the first time, Abigail eyed Victoria with a friendly look. "I'm sure Nicholas won't be gone long. It's obvious he's besotted with you, and I'm certain only the most important of business would make him leave your side tonight."

Reluctantly, Victoria nodded and Nicholas kissed her hand in a tender gesture that warmed her heart.

"I'll return in no time." The moment Nicholas left the opera box, the silence stretched out between her and Abigail. After several painful moments, Nicholas's sister turned to her.

"I'm glad you're looking forward to having Edmund with us for Christmas. In the past…well, you've made it clear—"

"That's in the past. I can't imagine the holiday without him," Victoria said with a smile. "I'm looking forward to his reaction to a couple of the gifts Nicholas and I got him."

"Victoria, may I be frank with you?" Gray eyes so like Edmund's glinted with a fierce look of determination. Victoria swallowed the knot forming in her throat and nodded.

"Yes."

"So help me God, if you hurt either of my brothers, I'll see to it that your reputation among the Set will be completely destroyed.”

“I’d never do anything to hurt Nicholas or Edmund,” she said firmly. “I’m nothing like Vickie. The woman was a heartless bitch who deserved to have someone slap her upside the head.”

Abigail studied her with a shocked look, but before she could respond, the curtain behind them swished open. Startled, the two of them turned to see a man standing in the box’s doorway. Abigail immediately stood up and glared at the man.

“I suggest you leave, Lord Darby,” Abigail said in a scathing tone.

Taken by surprise, Victoria stared at the man watching her intently from the top platform of the box. Dark brown eyes bored into hers, and he had an air of desperation about him that set Victoria on edge. He studied her for a long moment, his look a harsh inspection of her features.

“When they told me you were alive, I didn’t believe it. Why didn’t you answer my letter? I thought you loved me.” There was something familiar about the man that sent a frisson of fear crawling across her skin. When he took a step toward her, Victoria stood up and tried to put her chair between them.

“My lord, I must insist that you leave this instant,” Abigail said sharply. “You do not want to be here when my brother—”

“Fuck, Guildford,” he snarled. “He doesn’t scare me.”

The look of shock and fear on Abigail’s face made Victoria tremble. Panic rose inside her as Darby closed the distance between them. In a desperate attempt to calm the man, she tried to make her voice soft and soothing.

“I really am sorry. I wish I could tell you that I know you, but I don’t.” The response was an honest one since she’d only read a letter from him, but not met him in person. Her answer made him even more agitated.

"*You're lying.* I trusted you with the book, and now you're playing games with me."

Darby wore a crazed expression on his face, and Victoria flinched at his vicious response. Vaguely, she noted the people on the opera house floor and others in their theater boxes turn with eager anticipation to watch the scene. God, where was Nicholas. He should never have left her.

"Come back to me. I'll help you regain your memory. If you don't come back to me, I'm as good as dead. I should never have trusted you with the book. He knows you gave it to that idiot brother-in-law of yours."

"Don't you *ever* call Edmund an idiot again," she said in a fierce, tight voice as she slapped the man.

The slap sent Darby's head snapping backward. As he recovered, his hand crept up to his cheek, and the insane, venomous expression on his face forced Victoria to step back in fear. The low railing of the theater box pressed into her thighs, telling her there was nowhere to go. Abigail tried to stop him from reaching Victoria, but the man viciously struck out at the other woman and knocked Abigail to the floor. As Darby continued to advance on her, fear clawed its way through her as her gaze darted to the floor two stories below. A fall from the balcony would kill her.

His hands outstretched, Darby's fingers encircled her neck. Panic driving her actions, she stomped her heel on his foot and raked at his eyes with her fingernails. Instantly, he released his death grip from her throat. The sound of his pain and rage echoed through the theater. Blinded, he swung his arm angrily. His wild swing smacked Victoria on the side of her head. Stunned by the blow, she teetered backward over the side of the banister. Screams and shouts filled the opera house, and an image of Nicholas flashed through Victoria's mind as she felt her body plunge downward.

Screams ricocheted off every wall in the theater as Nicholas charged into the opera box. The next moment passed in a blur as he saw Darby explode like a gored bull. The man wildly struck out at Victoria. The blow caught her on the side of her head, and Nicholas lunged forward as her body started to catapult backward over the balcony's low rail. Darby, still unable to see through his injured eyes, stepped into Nicholas's path. Desperate to reach Victoria before she plunged off the balcony, he shoved Darby out of his way. Knocked off balance, the other man staggered back, his arms flailing in the air.

A hideous cry sounded in Nicholas's ears as his hands grasped first air and then the soft flesh of Victoria's arm. With every muscle in his body, he strained to halt the momentum of her fall. As he pulled her toward safety, they toppled backward into the theater box. Chairs cracked and splintered as they tumbled to the floor.

His body took the brunt of their fall as he held Victoria close to his chest and landed on the carpeted floor with a loud grunt. From down below, the screams and cries of horror continued, and Nicholas suddenly realized Darby no longer stood in the box.

Abigail struggled to her feet, a large red spot forming on her white face. Nicholas got to his feet, pulling Victoria up with him. The knowledge of her close brush with death swirled through him like a vicious whirlpool. The pounding of his heart echoed in his ears as he realized how close he'd come to losing her. Over the top of Victoria's head, he saw the damage Darby had done to Abigail's face.

"Are you all right?" When his sister nodded, he tilted Victoria's head back and went cold with fear. She was barely breathing, and the color was completely gone from her face.

"*Christ Jesus,*" he whispered in horror.

"Oh dear God, Nicholas," Abigail breathed in horror. "She must have hit her head."

Nicholas swept Victoria up into his arms and left the theater box with Abigail behind him. Sebastian, who had been sitting with Sir Kenelm as well, was hurrying toward him as Nicholas stepped out into the corridor. His friend took one look at Victoria and immediately turned to create a path through the gathering throng of people flocking out of their opera box. It wasn't until Sebastian was met by two police officers that he was able to make any real headway. The officers took one look at Victoria and immediately cleared the corridor of the growing number of spectators.

Fear was his constant companion as he and Abigail made their way downstairs and outside. Not once did Victoria stir, and his heart pounded with fear. God help him if something happened to her. He needed to tell her he loved her. The thought made him go rigid with shock. He was in love with his wife and might never have the chance to tell her.

Chapter 28

Present Day

"You have my mobile number, right?" Nick glanced at the private nurse as he stood next to Victoria's bed. "Yes, Mr. Barrows," the middle-aged woman said quietly and smiled. "I'll take good care of Miss Ashton. You go on home and get some rest, like your sister said."

With a reluctant nod, Nick leaned over Victoria and kissed her forehead, then walked toward the door. He paused and turned toward the nurse. Before he could speak, Mrs. Willoughby waved him out of the room with her hands.

"Yes, Mr. Barrows, I'll call you if there is any change in Miss Aston's condition."

The nurse eyed him with a sympathetic gaze, and he nodded at her response. With one last look in Victoria's direction, he walked out of the hospital room. Visiting hours were over and the hospital corridors were relatively quiet as he made his way to the elevator and down to the lobby. As he exited the medical facility, he saw Nora's red Corsa a short distance from the main door. As soon as he dropped into the passenger seat and closed the door, Nora put the car into drive and pulled away from the hospital. Several minutes passed before his sister glanced at him.

"So what happened today?"

"Just like all the other times, she seems to be on the verge of coming out of the coma and then she's gone." He stared out the window, not bothering to look at Nora.

"Have you eaten supper?" his sister asked.

"No, I wasn't hungry."

"Fuck. Are you deliberately *trying* to make yourself sick, Nicholas Barrows?"

"No," he snapped. "I just wasn't hungry."

"Well, you better *get* an appetite before you wind up in a hospital too," Nora exclaimed angrily. He glanced in her direction and saw regret cover her face. "Look, it's been a week since the bombing. She'll come around eventually, I'm sure of that. But you need to take care of yourself, and you can't do that if you stay with her twenty-four seven."

He didn't answer her. The signal ahead was red, and Nora came to a stop. She twisted slightly in her seat and pulled a small bag up off the rear floor and dropped it in his lap. He stared at it for a moment before his gaze slid in her direction. She arched an eyebrow at him and accelerated as the signal turned green.

"The countess' journals. You left them laying out at the hospital the other day. I didn't want them to disappear, so I swiped them." Nora shook her head. "Did you really think I'd let sleeping dogs lie? You need to read them, Nick. You really do."

"You're hell bent on pushing this down my throat."

"When it comes to the countess and Victoria Ashton, you bet."

"Fine. I'll take a look at them tonight."

"Good." Nora's head bobbed as she stopped at an intersection and made a right-hand turn.

A short time later, his sister pulled up in front of his town house. His jaw tight with tension, he turned his head toward Nora and forced a smile to twist his lips.

"Thanks, Nora. I'll be at the gallery tomorrow after I check in on Victoria."

"All right," she said quietly as she reached out and squeezed his hand. "I threw some frozen meals into the freezer-fridge for you. Eat one for God's sake. And while you're at it, have one of the pints of Fullers Ale I bought you too."

"Now, I really do owe you a raise," Nick said with a small bit of humor as he leaned over and kissed her cheek.

"I don't know. I've a feeling you're not going to be happy with my bookkeeping skills."

His sister winced as he got out of the car. With a wave of her hand, Nora drove off, leaving him standing on the sidewalk in front of his house. It was more than possible Nora had made good on her statement. She'd never been good with math. Nick sighed. At least it would keep him occupied until the end of the day when he could go to the hospital.

The lights under the kitchen cabinet were on, and he dropped the journals on the bar dividing the kitchen and dining room. He opened the fridge-freezer to see at least fifteen meals Nora had bought. Anger and frustration stabbed at him as he ripped open a frozen meal and tossed it into the microwave. It was as if a part of him was missing, and he knew it was because he wasn't standing guard over Victoria. He opened one of the ales Nora had stockpiled for him and took a deep swig of the beverage.

Logic was the only reason he'd agreed with Nora that it was time to end his round-the-clock vigil over Victoria. The irrational side of him shouted for him to return to the hospital. He shoved the loud demand deep into his subconscious. The microwave beeped, and he pulled out the hot dish, grabbed a fork, and sat down at the bar to eat. A short distance away was the bag holding the Countess of Guildford's journals. They were just books. What harm could it be to read the journals? With a grunt of disgust, he jerked the books out of the bag. Nora had marked the weathered volumes with paper bookmarks with the numbers one and two, respectively.

Another drink of ale wet his throat as he opened the first journal.

My name is Victoria Ashton, and I'm from the future.

Nick slammed the book shut, ready to kill his sister. What the fuck did she take him for? Whoever had fabricated this journal was an incredibly skilled forger. He jerked his phone out of his pocket and dialed Nora's number. As if she'd been waiting for his phone call, Nora didn't allow him to speak.

"They're not forgeries. I had Carlton examine both of the books for me. He said they're from the late eighteen hundreds. He was as skeptical as you, but he's convinced they're real."

Nick stared into space as Nora's words registered in his brain. Carlton, one of the best forgery experts in the industry. If the man had said the journals were authentic, it made it difficult not to believe what every rational thought in his mind was rejecting.

"They've got to be fakes. Someone put them in Victoria's belongings before you picked up her things at her hotel."

"They weren't in Victoria's things, Nick." His sister paused as if she were taking in a deep breath. "They were in the box Uncle Charles left me when he died."

Nick's brain scrambled to come up with a rational explanation, but couldn't devise one.

"They're the real deal, Nick. As crazy as it sounds. Victoria wrote those journals. Look, not to sound cavalier or cliché, however improbable, what remains must be the truth."

"And Holmes prefaced that by saying you eliminate the impossible."

"And we both know Carlton is the best in the business. He says it's authentic, and I believe him."

"Because you want to believe him."

"No, because I believe *her*," Nora said quietly. The note of conviction in his sister's voice made him close his eyes as he considered her words.

"I'll read the journals," he rasped, his gaze falling on the thin volumes lying in front of him.

"I'm here if you need me, Nick."

He didn't answer. He just pushed the end call button. Reluctant to open the first journal right away, he cleaned up the remains of his supper, finished his ale, then grabbed another one. With a sweep of his hand, he picked up the journals on his way out of the kitchen. In the living room, Nick threw himself down onto the couch, switched on the table-side lamp, and laid the second book on the coffee table. He stared suspiciously at the first journal he held in his hand, before he slowly opened the thin volume for the second time and started reading.

My name is Victoria Ashton, and I'm from the future. I don't know how I arrived at Brentwood Park, any more than I remember what happened right before I woke up here. I remember an art gallery and an explosion. I don't have any trouble remembering my childhood, college or technology, but the few days before my arrival here is a mystery to me.

Nick stared at the writing. It was written with a shaky hand as if the user didn't know how to use the fountain pen, which was the standard writing instrument of the late eighteen hundreds. His gaze focused on the words again.

I'm going to have to hide this journal. If someone were to find it, I'd be put in the loony bin. Everyone thinks I'm the countess, but I'm not. I've given up trying to convince Nicholas I'm not the countess. Even worse is that I've suddenly developed psychic abilities. I have visions periodically, but it's the headaches that trouble me the most.

Whenever I have a headache that's really bad, Nicholas says I almost stopped breathing. All I know is that I'm in a white mist. When I'm in the mist, it's so peaceful and loving. I sometimes wonder if I'm actually in heaven. Then there are the other visions, and they're scary as hell. I keep seeing myself lying in a grave and two men throwing dirt on me. I don't think I'm the one in the grave, though. I think it's Vickie. I don't want to believe it, but Anna and I both think Vickie, the real countess, is dead.

Nick stopped reading as the name Anna stared up at him. He'd called his sister Anna several times since Victoria had been in the hospital. He closed the journal, and a loud crack filled the air from the force of his action. With an angry gesture, he dropped the journal onto the coffee table, then chugged the rest of his ale. His gaze didn't move from the green book.

"I'm fucking insane for even thinking this might be real," he said to the empty room. "People don't travel through time."

He went back into the kitchen for another ale. With his hips pressed into the counter, he tried to wrap his head around the short amount he'd read in Lady Guildford's journal. No, Victoria's journal. The way his thoughts segued into the acknowledgment that Victoria and the Countess of Guildford were the same woman made him close his eyes. Finishing off his drink, he popped open another Fullers. Right now, the last thing he wanted to do was read that bloody journal. Ale washed its way down his throat. At the moment, the only thing he wanted to do was keep drinking until he couldn't see straight anymore— hangover possibility or not. He just wasn't ready to go out on a limb at this point.

Chapter 29

December 1897

The moment they stepped through the front doors of the opera house and out into the frigid night air, Nicholas saw Anna waiting for them. Sebastian had been with him and Sir Kenelm when his friend had seen Darby enter the Guildford opera box. The moment Nicholas had raced to Victoria's side, his friend had followed.

One step ahead, as always, Sebastian was busy summoning the carriages. Nicholas knew that if not for his friend, Victoria would be dead. It was a debt he knew he'd never be able to repay. Anna quietly greeted Abigail, then turned to look at Victoria and gently touched her cheek. His friend drew in a sharp breath.

"Dear God, Nicholas. It's like that day at Brentwood Park. She's barely breathing." Anna's words only served to heighten Nicholas's deepening worry.

"This has happened before?" Abigail gasped in horror.

"Yes," he ground out between his clenched teeth, not about to explain any further at the moment.

"I'm so sorry, Nicholas. This is all my fault," Abigail said in a distraught voice.

"No, I should never have left the two of you alone."

"You could not have foreseen this, Nicholas. No one could have," Anna said quietly. Beside him, Abigail touched her bruised cheek.

"When Darby entered the box, he was insane with fear. He kept demanding Victoria return his book. The man seemed almost as terrified as he was crazed," his sister said in a confused manner that indicated she was in a state of shock. "He insisted she'd given the book to Edmund. When he insulted Edmund, Victoria slapped him. He became even more enraged and attacked her. If you hadn't arrived when you did, Nicholas…"

Something in his sister's narrative struck him as important, but at the moment, all he could think about was Victoria.

"You're not to blame, Abigail," he said tightly. He knew how stern his voice sounded, and he turned his head to look at his sister. Her distraught look made him soften his expression and tone. "It's not your fault, Abigail."

"She's so still, Nicholas," his sister said as she swung her gaze to Victoria.

Abigail's observation made his gut clench. The thought of Victoria not waking up this time scared the hell out of him. Nicholas didn't answer her as the carriage pulled to the curb. He heard Anna murmur something to his sister, but whatever it was, he didn't hear. Sebastian opened the door of the vehicle, then held Victoria until Nicholas was seated in the carriage.

"I've already sent for the doctor to meet you at Guildford House," Sebastian said as he gently transferred Victoria back into Nicholas's arms. "Would you like Anna and me to come to the house with you?"

"No, there's nothing to be done. She'll either awaken or—" Nicholas broke off his sentence abruptly. He wasn't about to consider any other possibility. "Abigail requires a doctor to examine her face."

"We'll see her home safely and send for her physician. Anna and I will call on you tomorrow afternoon to see how you and Victoria are faring," Sebastian squeezed Nicholas's shoulder reassuringly before he stepped back from the carriage and closed the door.

The ride back to Guildford House seemed interminably long. Nicholas spent half of his time trying to coax Victoria out of her death-like state. The other half, he spent praying for her to wake up so he could tell her how much he loved her. Guilt lashed out at him. He should never have gone to see Sir Kenelm. If not for Sebastian and the fact that Sir Kenelm had been seated on the mezzanine level, he would never have reached Victoria in time.

His mind reeled at the memory of seeing her fall backward over the railing of the opera box. God help him, he still didn't understand how he'd kept Victoria from falling to her death. It was a miracle. His mouth went dry as he remembered his hand catching nothing but air until he found her arm and pulled her back into the box. As for Darby, he couldn't say he was sorry the man was dead. The bastard had almost cost him the life of the woman he loved.

The carriage rolled to a stop in front of the house. With Jamieson and a footman's help, Nicholas limped his way into the house with his precious burden in his arms. As he crossed the threshold, he heard the whisper of a moan cross Victoria's lips. Relief sailed through him. Glancing down at her, Nicholas saw her breathing was beginning to return to normal. As quickly as possible, he climbed the stairs and carried her through the open door of her bedroom. Nicholas called out for Roberts, who miraculously appeared in Victoria's bedroom doorway almost immediately. A worried frown wrinkled the valet's brow as Nicholas laid Victoria on the bed.

"Fetch Molly, I'll need help undressing her ladyship."

"Yes, my lord," Roberts said, already halfway out the door.

As he removed Victoria's shoes, another soft moan escaped her lips followed by an anguished cry of fear.

"Nicholas."

Victoria shot upright, and Nicholas quickly moved to sit down next to her. He wrapped his arms around her and pulled her close.

"I'm here, my love. You're safe."

Sheer terror glazed her blue eyes as she stared up at him. Her horrified look made him wish Darby was still alive so he could make the bastard pay for his assault on Victoria. Slender fingers curled around the lapels of his evening jacket as tears rolled down her cheeks. Trembling, her teeth chattered and the violence of her tremors hammered their way into his body. Where the devil was Molly? He gently forced Victoria to turn toward him so she was pressed into his chest. Her tremors continued as his fingers unbuttoned the line of pearl-shaped buttons running down the back of the gown. A knock at the door made him turn his head to see Molly ushering a man into the room.

"Dr. Waverley, my lord," Molly said with quiet concern.

"My lord."

The doctor nodded his greeting at Nicholas as he moved quickly to the other side of the bed. The black bag he carried opened with a soft snap, and Victoria jerked in reaction to the sharp sound. Dr. Waverley pulled a stethoscope from his bag and leaned toward Victoria.

"I need to check her pulse, my lord."

Nicholas gently tried to make Victoria extend one of her arms, but she resisted, her fingers clutching at his coat.

"It's all right, my love. I'll not leave you. The doctor simply needs to examine you." Victoria's eyes were still wide in her face as she allowed Nicholas to extend her hand to the doctor. The man frowned as he took her pulse, then touched her cheek and the back of her neck. With efficient speed, he completed his examination before looking at Nicholas.

"She's in shock, my lord. We need to get her out of these clothes now and under the covers immediately." At the man's orders, Nicholas nodded.

With Molly's and the doctor's help, Victoria was under the blankets in less than two minutes. Even beneath the warm covers, Victoria continued to tremble, but her tremors seemed to have eased somewhat as he held her hand. The doctor gently pressed his stethoscope against her chest to listen to her heartbeat. When he finished, he straightened to stare at Victoria for a brief interlude before he looked at Nicholas.

"Lord Starling's message said that her ladyship was almost killed tonight," Dr. Waverley said softly. "She appears uninjured physically, but her pulse is far too rapid to my liking. I believe a strong dose of laudanum will enable her to sleep well into the morning. It will help put some distance between her and this trauma."

"No," Victoria whispered in a barely audible voice. "I don't want to leave you Nicholas. I don't want to go back."

"Shhh, sweet witch, it's only to make you sleep. You're not going anywhere," he reassured her as he kissed her brow. Nicholas glanced at the doctor and nodded. As the man prepared the medicine, Nicholas met Victoria's gaze. Not even the night when she'd been chased across the estate grounds had she looked so shaken. She'd had a brush with death, and he knew it would take time for her to recover from the experience. Her tremors had abated, but the fear in her eyes made his gut twist with guilt. He was responsible for what had happened. If he'd not left her side, none of this would've taken place. Nicholas cleared his throat as he bent his head toward her.

"I should never have left you, sweet witch," he murmured. "If I'd lost you…" His words trailed off and Victoria's hand touched his cheek.

"It's not your fault," she rasped.

"Here you are, my lady," Dr. Waverley said in a calm, soothing voice as he handed Nicholas a small metal cup and a glass of water Molly had retrieved from the bathroom.

Victoria eyed the cup with distaste before she looked at him.

"It will help you sleep, my love." At his assurance, she nodded and accepted the cup from him.

"It is best if you drink it quickly, my lady," Dr. Waverley said in a kind voice. "It tends to disagree with the palate."

Victoria did as the doctor ordered and tossed down the medicine. She gagged a split-second later, and Nicholas offered her the water, which she drank quickly.

"What the hell…was…that?" she asked in a shaky voice. The doctor's eyebrows rose slightly at her question, and a small smile twisted the corners of Nicholas's mouth. Her colorful language meant some of her fear was receding. Even her color was returning to her cheeks.

"Laudanum, my lady," Dr. Waverley said as he put his belongings back in his bag and snapped it closed. "It's a mixture of opium and other medicinal herbs that will let you sleep undisturbed until late in the morning."

"*Opium*," Victoria's harsh whisper made Nicholas raise her hand to his mouth. He kissed her fingers, then clasped her hand firmly in his.

"You'll sleep more soundly, Victoria. I'll not leave you alone tonight, sweet witch. I'll be right here."

Victoria closed her eyes and nodded as her fingers squeezed his hand. Dr. Waverley stood up and looked at Nicholas.

"I think a day's rest will ensure Lady Guildford's physically recovered to enjoy the festivities on Christmas Eve at the end of the week. However, it is possible she'll have nightmares for some time to come. Even unexpected movements or sounds might trigger a reaction."

"Thank you, doctor," Nicholas said. "Molly, please see Dr. Waverly out."

"Yes, my lord." Molly bobbed her head in his direction, then turned her head toward the doctor. The man shook Nicholas's hand, then followed the maid out of the room. Just as Molly was about to close the door, Nicholas stopped her.

"Molly, tell Roberts I'll not need him for the rest of the night. In the morning, I'll have breakfast in the dining room with my brother."

"Yes, my lord." With her quiet response, the maid closed the door behind her.

Nicholas turned his head back to Victoria, who looked up at him sleepily. The opium was already having an impact on her. He released her hand, but she grasped his arm in a display of panic. He kissed her gently.

"I can't sleep in my evening clothes, my love."

With a reluctant nod, she slowly released her grasp on his arm. Not wasting any time, Nicholas quickly undressed, then returned to the bed. Sliding underneath the covers, he pulled her into his arms. She was on the verge of sleep, but it was obvious she was fighting the drug's effect.

"Nicholas." She whispered in a barely audible voice.

"Hush, my love. You need to rest."

"He tried…to kill me." There was a note of confusion in her voice that made him grimace.

"He failed, Victoria. You're safe here with me."

At his reassuring words, she snuggled into his side as a kitten might a blanket. Her fingers lightly trailed over his chest before her cheek pressed into the crook of his shoulder, and she breathed a soft sigh.

"I love you, Nicholas. I never want to leave you."

The whisper shot a bolt of lightning through him. He bent his head toward her, only to see she was sound asleep. Nicholas swallowed hard. She loved him. The happiness drifting through him was an euphoria he'd never experienced before. The sensation ebbed away as he realized how close he'd come to losing her. He stared up at the ceiling as he remembered once more the sight of Victoria tumbling over the opera box railing. Then the memory of her pale features as he realized she'd fallen into another one of her fainting spells.

A sharp pain pushed its way up past his knee. For the first time since returning home, he realized how badly his leg ached. In all the chaos he'd completely suppressed the pain signals his leg had been driving up to his brain. Gently, he released Victoria, and left the bed in search of liniment. He shrugged on the robe Roberts had thoughtfully draped over the end of the bed. A quiet knock on the door made him frown with irritation. He crossed the room to open the door where Roberts stood holding a container of fresh liniment, and Nicholas's anger vanished.

"I saw how badly you were limping, my lord, and I knew you would need this."

"Thank you, Roberts," he said with a grateful smile as he accepted the small metal tin. "I just got up to look for some."

"I hope her ladyship is all right, my lord."

"She's quite shaken, but I believe she'll recover quickly."

Nicholas frowned as he remembered the doctor's warning that she might have nightmares in the future. The idea that she might have more bad dreams troubled him.

"The staff has been concerned for her ladyship, and they'll be pleased to know she's going to be all right." Relief swept across Robert's face as he met Nicholas's gaze. "The police were here earlier asking for you. They needed to get your account of the incident. They made no mention of her ladyship's disappearance. The inspector said he'd return at nine tomorrow."

The valet's words eased the tension holding Nicholas's muscles rigid. At least Victoria would be spared an interrogation.

"Very well," Nicholas said with a sharp nod. "Wake me at eight, and make sure Molly understands she needs to sit with Lady Guildford until I return from my visit to Sir Kenelm's office."

"Yes, my lord."

"Good night, Roberts," he paused and lifted the container of liniment. "And thank you again."

"It is my pleasure as always, my lord." The valet smiled, then turned and walked away as Nicholas closed Victoria's bedroom door. He glanced at Victoria to ensure she was sleeping comfortably before he limped his way to the chair in front of the fire.

It didn't take long for the liniment to ease his pain, and Nicholas looked over his shoulder at Victoria. What had Vickie been involved in? Abigail had mentioned Darby's insistence that Victoria return a book. What book? That question led to another one, and another one, until he had a long line of questions, all of which led him back to Reardon.

He was certain Reardon was the reason for Darby's assault on Victoria. He just couldn't prove it. The man was exceedingly clever, and it frustrated Nicholas. He turned his head to look at Victoria once again. Tonight illustrated just how much danger she was in. Even if Darby had been the one sending the threatening notes, Reardon still posed a threat. The instant Nicholas heard the quiet cry from the bed, he was on his feet.

Victoria was mumbling something, but he couldn't understand what she was saying. Shrugging off his robe, Nicholas slid into bed next to her and wrapped his arms around her. After several moments, her muttering ceased. Relief surged through him as he closed his eyes and held her close. Whatever the cost, he would keep her safe. Not Reardon or any other person would take her from him.

Sunshine filled the room as Victoria blinked and slowly woke up. Intense relief spread its warmth through her body as she realized she was still in the past. She'd been so worried when the doctor and Nicholas had insisted she take that God awful medicine. The idea of not waking up here, with Nicholas, had terrified her. Turning her head, she saw Nicholas was gone, but the pillow was dented where his head had been.

Suddenly, the image of Darby's wild-eyed look filled her head, and she sucked in a sharp breath. Victoria shuddered as she remembered how slapping Darby had pushed him over the edge. On the heels of that memory came the raw sensation of plummeting backward over the railing of the opera box. The images flooding her head made bile rise in her throat.

With a guttural noise, she scrambled out of bed and ran into the bathroom where she threw up in the toilet. When she'd finished, she sank down onto the floor. God, she'd never been sick like this before. Not even when her father had died had she been like this. Did she have the flu? She'd not felt this terrible in ages. A second wave of nausea rolled over her, and Victoria quickly moved toward the toilet as she threw up again. The medicine, she thought. What had the doctor said? Opium. The drug must have made her sick.

"Oh, my lady," Molly exclaimed as she entered the bathroom. The young maid wet a hand cloth, then gently pressed it against Victoria's forehead and cheeks.

"I'm fine," Victoria said as she realized it was the truth.

The nausea had eased a great deal, and she could only assume she'd purged the drug from her system. She got to her feet despite Molly's protests and made her way back into the bedroom. Still feeling queasy, she sat in front of the small fire burning in the hearth.

"I brought you the hot cocoa you like, my lady," Molly said with a worried note in her voice. "And Mrs. Babcocke made you some breakfast."

Molly pointed to the tray she'd set on the small table beside the chair. Perhaps eating something would make her feel better. Victoria lifted the lid of the covered dish, and the smell of freshly scrambled eggs and bacon wafted up under her nose. In a split second, the nausea returned. Bile threatened to clog her throat, and she sprang up from her chair to race toward the bathroom again. Molly hovered over her in concern, and as the wave of nausea passed, Victoria leaned back against the cool rim of the porcelain bathtub. The young maid shook her head in a sympathetic manner.

"Don't worry, my lady. I'm sure this will pass in a couple of weeks. At least that's what my mum says. I should have realized the food would cause you to feel bad. Toast and cocoa will settle your stomach best, I think."

"What?" Victoria stared up at Molly in bewilderment.

"Why the baby, my lady. My mum says the morning sickness goes away for most women fairly soon."

"Baby?"

Her heart pounded wildly in her chest as she counted backward. Oh God, she was pregnant. An overwhelming wave of joy rolled over her. She was carrying Nicholas's child. In the next instant, fear snagged at her. What was it he'd said? *The risk of siring a child with the same difficulties as my brother is too great.* Nicholas had made it clear he didn't want children. It was why he insisted on a condom every time they made love. With a soft cry, she drew her legs up to her chest and buried her face against her knees. What was she going to do? What would he say?

"Oh my lady, there's no need to cry." Molly bent over her and helped Victoria to her feet, then back into the bedroom.

As she sank down into her chair by the fire, she told the maid to take the food tray away. The young woman had protested, eventually convincing Victoria to have toast with her cocoa. Just before she left the room, Molly released a sound of annoyance.

"Lord love me, I forgot to give you the note his lordship left for you." The maid pulled out an envelope from her pocket and handed it to her. As the maid turned away, Victoria caught her arm.

"You're not to say a word about this to anyone, Molly. Not even to Lord Guildford. Do you understand?"

"Of course, my lady." The maid's expression was one of confused disappointment. "I'd never betray your confidence like that."

Victoria nodded, then released her grip on the maid's arm and nodded for her to leave. When the bedroom door closed behind Molly, Victoria opened the letter, the parchment rustling softly as she unfolded the letter.

Victoria,

The police have ruled last night's incident as attempted murder on Darby's part, but as the man is dead, there will be no further investigation. Since they have already reached that conclusion, I told them it was unnecessary to question you in the matter, and they agreed.

I have an appointment with Sir Kenelm this morning, and some other business to attend to, but I shall return sometime this afternoon. We shall talk then.

Your husband, Nicholas

Relieved she wouldn't have to rehash the horror of last night, she closed her eyes. She knew last night's events had shaken her more than she cared to admit, and she had no wish to relive those last moments before she toppled over the railing. It wasn't the memory of the fall that frightened her so much as it was the familiar mist she'd entered. Nicholas's image had been the last thing she'd seen before it had swallowed her.

The white fog had terrified her because she'd been certain she was either dead or that when she woke she'd be back in the present. When she'd come to, and Nicholas was with her, she'd clung to him, terrified he wasn't real. It was why she'd not wanted to take the drug to sleep, but she'd been too tired and overwhelmed to argue. But it hadn't stopped the fear that she might wake up far away from Nicholas.

Victoria closed her eyes. She'd known weeks ago how devastating returning to the future would be to her heart, but now there was the baby. One more very important reason never to leave the past. Her hand pressed against her stomach as she imagined holding Nicholas's baby in her arms. Victoria's heart sank. The most difficult question wasn't how to tell him, but how would he react?

The thought made her stiffen in her chair. Last night, Nicholas had uttered the endearment, my love, several times. Until now, it hadn't really registered. Was it possible he loved her? If he did, would that make a difference where the baby was concerned? Question after question flitted through her mind until she felt as if she was drowning in conflict. But every question revolved back to the question of how Nicholas would act. It was a question she was terrified to have answered, and she didn't have a clue as to how she would tell him the truth.

Chapter 30

Despite Molly's protests, Victoria dressed and went downstairs. Edmund was in the library playing with some toy soldiers, and he greeted her with restrained enthusiasm.

"Nicholas said you had another spell. He said you might not be well for Christmas." A look of concern furrowed his brow, and Victoria squeezed his hand and kissed his cheek affectionately.

"Nicholas is a worrywart. I'll be fine," she said with a smile. Satisfied with her response, the gentle man grinned. "So we can still go shopping for Christmas presents tomorrow like you said?"

"Yes, I'm only a little tired today. So tomorrow, we're going to have a terrific time." She nodded toward the soldiers on the carpet. "Why don't you go back to playing with your soldiers? I'm going to read for a little while."

Edmund grinned and returned to his seat on the floor in front of his miniature soldiers, while Victoria browsed the book collection in the library. She pulled a book called *The Woman In White* off the shelf. The book gave her no indication of what the story might be like, but the title intrigued her. Out in the foyer, Victoria heard the harsh jangle of the front doorbell. Setting the book down, Victoria walked out into the foyer. The moment she saw the Duchess du Chatelaine, Victoria grimace. What did the woman want? Victoria vaguely noted the man beside her as her gaze met Eleanor's.

"Hello, Eleanor. What can I do for you?" she asked politely.

"Oh *ma petite*, *Monsieur* Reardon and I came to console you over the loss of your poor *Monsieur* Darby." Something in the woman's voice, made Victoria narrow her gaze at the other woman.

"I'm sorry, Eleanor, but I'm not sure why you'd say he was mine. I'd never met the man until last night," Victoria said with irritation.

"The duchess is correct, my dear Vickie. We've been worried about you since hearing about Darby's…accident last night," the man called Reardon said in a quietly accusatory tone.

The way he said the word accident suggested he was questioning what had happened. Worse, the man had called her Vickie, and she had the urge to deck the guy. Annoyed, she narrowed her gaze at him. The man seemed well aware of her irritation, and a cold, cruel smile curled his thin mouth. It was a look that sent a streak of fear skimming down her back. There was something vicious and calculating in the man's dark-eyed gaze. Instinctively, she knew the man was more than an acquaintance of Vickie's. She smiled slightly and gestured toward the salon.

"Would you like to sit down?"

Eleanor sniffed her answer and eyed her with contempt. Irritated that she'd even bothered to invite them deeper into the house, Victoria clenched her teeth. She never had liked women who thought the world revolved around them. The duchess preceded her into the salon, and as Victoria followed the other woman, Reardon touched her elbow to escort her in.

The moment his hand cupped her elbow, dark images flooded her mind. The sound of a shovel against dirt echoed in her ears, and she could almost feel the dirt landing on her face. With a sharp breath, she jerked away from him. Without looking at him, she walked into the salon to see Eleanor taking a seat on one of the two sofas. Victoria had no intention of sitting. She was going to make their visit as short as possible without causing a scene. She tipped her head slightly and met Reardon's shrewd gaze.

"Somehow, I don't think you've come to pay your condolences. I think you're here for another reason."

"As perceptive as always, my dear Vickie."

"If you call me *Vickie* one more damn time, you're going to regret it." Her vicious response caught him off guard for a moment, but he recovered almost immediately

"Interesting. I don't believe the countess, *I knew*, would ever utter such a vulgarity."

"What the hell is that supposed to mean?"

In the back of her mind, a siren went off in her head. The man thought she was an imposter. No, he knew she was an imposter because Vickie was dead. Suddenly the connection between the man and her visions made her stomach lurch. She and Anna had been right. Vickie was dead, and this man had killed her.

"Really, my dear," Reardon murmured quietly as cold amusement settled on his face. "There's no need for deception among friends."

"Since I don't know you, I'd hardly call us friends," she said coolly. The man moved as fast as a striking snake and closed the distance between them to catch her chin in his hand.

"Perhaps lovers would be a better word, my dear…Victoria."

The deliberate hesitation before her name made her certain he knew she wasn't Vickie. Panic raced through her. Where the hell was Nicholas? No, she needed to deal with this on her own. Nicholas had suffered enough embarrassment with Vickie and Darby's affair. She wasn't about to add to his humiliation. She also wasn't sure how she could tell him Vickie was dead, and that Reardon had killed the countess. If he knew any of that, it would make it more difficult to deny he'd not murdered Vickie if the police ever questioned him. Victoria jerked free of his uncomfortable grasp and stepped backward.

"First you suggest Lord Darby was special to me, then you say you and I are lovers. Which is it? And don't say the two of us, because I'd find it hard to believe that I was stupid enough to find *you* remotely attractive."

"Trust me, my dear, Vickie. We were quite intimate," the man bit out angrily.

Satisfaction swept through Victoria as his response indicated she'd pricked his ego good. Her triumph died quickly at Reardon's fury. Steeling herself not to flinch, Victoria shook her head.

"What is it you really want, Reardon?" The sensation of ice coating her skin crept over Victoria's skin as she struggled to keep her features from revealing any emotion at all.

"I think you know the answer to that, my lady."

"If I did, I wouldn't have asked the question," she said in a tight voice. She glanced at Eleanor, who was looking at Reardon with a distinct look of fear. Why was the woman so afraid of the man?

"You possess something that belongs to me, and I want it back."

"I don't know what you're talking about." She frowned in puzzlement. Last night Darby had been raving about some book he'd given her, and now Reardon was asking for something too. What the hell had Vickie been involved in?

"You are an excellent actress, Victoria, but we both know you're courting disaster with this pretense." A soft laugh escaped Reardon's thin lips. It was a cruel sound.

"Are you suggesting I'm not the Countess of Guildford?" She forced a smile to her lips, hoping she looked as confident as she sounded, because she was feeling far from it.

"I think it highly unlikely."

"I see. Then why don't you tell me where the real countess is." At her response, an expression of misgiving crossed the man's features before he quickly recovered his confident manner.

"I think we both know the answer to that, my dear, Victoria."

"Then that means in order to discredit me you'd have to implicate yourself," she snapped. "Not to mention that I'll just tell the police that it's a plot of yours to blackmail me and Lord Guildford."

For a moment, Reardon stared at her in amazement as she glared at him defiantly. A moment later, he released an appreciative laugh and bowed his head in her direction.

"Unlike the woman you impersonate, my dear, you have a clever head on your shoulders, Victoria." The man looked at Eleanor, and the other woman blanched. "But as Eleanor has discovered, to her detriment, I dislike clever women. They make my life difficult, so why not put this petty quarrel aside. Give me what's mine, and I'll refrain from exposing you."

"Even if I knew what it was you wanted, I doubt I'd be willing to give it to you. You've already killed for it once, what would stop you from doing it again?"

"Do not trifle with me, my dear countess," Reardon snarled and took a step forward. "If you don't produce the book, I'll see to it that you *and* the earl will both regret ever having crossed me."

The bitter manner in which he mentioned Nicholas made her mouth go dry. There was more to this mystery than just Vickie's disappearance. The man hated Nicholas. She was certain of it from the rage flashing in Reardon's beady eyes.

"I think it's time you left so you can go fuck yourself in private," she bit out fiercely. Reardon and Eleanor both stared at her in shock, and she knew her language was the cause. Refusing to stand down, she glared at both of them. "Get out now, and if either of you come back, I'll report you to the police for attempting to blackmail Lord Guildford and me."

"Before you throw us out, my dear Victoria, has it ever occurred to you how easily your husband could be accused of murder, and you could be charged as his accomplice for pretending to be the countess?"

"For someone who thinks they're so smart, you're acting like you don't understand English. I said to get out."

Victoria's heart was pounding with a mixture of fear and anger as she headed toward the door to have the footman throw the couple out of the house. Reardon stepped into her path, blocking her way. Flinching at his close proximity, she quickly stepped back from him. The man was dangerous, and she swallowed the ball of fear rising in her throat at the calculating look in his eyes. He knew she was afraid, and it pleased him.

"You're a gifted actress, my dear, but it will be all too easy to arouse the curiosity of a Scotland Yard inspector eager to make a name for himself." The cruelty on Reardon's face chilled her. Victoria knew he wouldn't hesitate to harm Nicholas.

"And I think you're bluffing," Victoria said with more bravado than she was feeling.

"Am I?" The man's smile caused a chill to encase her body. "People are already gossiping about the remarkable change in you, and the newfound affection you and the earl displayed last night. The way he charged to your rescue is being viewed as heroic and even romantic by many. That's rather odd, given your antipathy for each other prior to your return. But you can make all of this go away so easily, my dear. Give me my book."

"I told you. I don't have your damn book." She glared at the man despite her fear. Reardon's eyes narrowed to thin slits, and Victoria shivered with dread at the demonic look on his dark features.

"Then you leave me little choice but to drop hints here and there as to the real countess' whereabouts," Reardon said coldly. "I can assure you, English law is quite specific about the penalty for murder."

"The penalty for blackmail is also quite specific, Reardon."

From the salon doorway, Nicholas's icy words made Reardon flinch slightly, while a warm relief streaked through Victoria's limbs. She no longer had to deal with Reardon alone. Regaining his composure, a vicious smile curled Reardon's mouth as he bowed toward Nicholas.

"Ah, but I was not blackmailing the woman, Guildford," the man said in a smooth tone.

"You're referring to my wife, Reardon, and you will address her as such." Suppressed fury echoed in Nicholas's voice, and a nasty smile curled Reardon's mouth.

"Of course, forgive me. It's just that I have memories of a much different countess than this charming creature."

"I think it's time you *and* the duchess leave before I forget I'm a gentleman," Nicholas growled as he shot a look of contempt in Eleanor's direction.

"It has been a pleasure, my dear countess," Reardon said coolly as he nodded in her direction.

Eleanor stood up and followed Reardon. The duchess stopped at Nicholas's side, and as the woman touched his arm, Victoria experienced a dose of jealousy that could have easily allowed her to push Eleanor all the way to the front door and out of the house.

"*Mon cher*, I am—"

"Leave, Eleanor." The cold note in Nicholas's voice made the woman flinch. She darted a glance back at Victoria, then followed Reardon out of the room.

Her heart racing with panic, Victoria watched Nicholas follow the couple out, and she heard him quietly ordering the footman to ensure the pair was never allowed in the house again. Alone once more, anxiety surged through her body as she realized her foul language in front of two witnesses hadn't been the smartest thing she'd ever done. By itself, it wouldn't be such a big deal, but when you added it to all the other changes people had seen in her, it would definitely not look good if someone suggested she was an imposter. It could all come back to harm Nicholas, and that would be something she'd never forgive herself for. One hand rubbing the pounding spot on her brow, she paced a small section of the floor.

"Oh, God, what am I going to do?"

"*You*, will not do anything."

At the sound of Nicholas's stern voice, Victoria whirled about. The suppressed fury she sensed in him caused her to tremble, and she inhaled a sharp breath as he strode toward her.

"What do you mean we're not going to do anything about Reardon?" She snapped. "The man just threatened to blackmail me, you—us."

"I'll take care of Reardon." Nicholas folded his arms across his chest. "And he won't ever enter this house again."

"Well, it wasn't like I invited him or Eleanor into the house, if that's what you're implying." She stiffened at the thought he might think Eleanor and Reardon had come at her invitation.

"I'm not implying anything," he said quietly. "I know Reardon well enough to know he used Eleanor to gain access to you."

"Then what are you going to do about the bastard," she bit out fiercely as she remembered the man's threat to accuse Nicholas of murder.

"Nothing at the moment."

Appalled, Victoria stared at him in disbelief. Hands on her hips, she gritted her teeth at his calm, nonchalant demeanor. In fact, he seemed amused by her anger.

"What do you mean, nothing?" she said with an angry shake of her head. "You don't even know what he wants or threatened to do."

Nicholas slowly closed the distance between them and took her hand in his and lifted it to his mouth. He kissed the inside of her wrist. The touch made Victoria quiver.

"I know exactly what he wants, my love." His gaze locked with hers as he brought her other wrist up to his mouth. "He wants a book Vickie had."

"Well, do you have any idea what he threatened to do?" she said irritably. "He said he's going to tell the police you murdered Vickie, and I'm an imposter."

Nicholas's mouth worked its way up to the crease in her elbow and somewhere in the back of her mind a new sensation tried to push past her frustration.

"We both know that's a lie, my love," he murmured as he wrapped his arms around her and kissed her cheek. "Why don't we discuss the topic at a later time? I have more important things to discuss with you."

"What could be more important than stopping a man who's threatened to blackmail us?"

Nicholas bent his head and nipped at her neck, and she shuddered. The man was far too skilled at distracting her with his mouth and sweet words. Her brain slammed into a wall. He'd called her, my love, twice now. She was certain of it. She hadn't imagined it last night.

Her gaze met his, and the depth of the emotions she saw in his emerald eyes made her heart skip.

"I love you, Victoria." His words took her breath away, and she stared up at him with her heart in her mouth.

"Say it again," she whispered, desperate to know her ears were deceiving her.

"I love you, Victoria Brentwood Thornhill, Countess of Guildford."

A moment later she burst into tears.

Nicholas stared at Victoria in confused amazement. Had he made a mistake in saying he loved her? Worried, he nudged her chin up with his knuckle so he could look into her eyes.

"What is it, sweet witch? Tell me what's wrong."

"Nothing," she smiled through her tears. "Everything's wonderful. I love you too."

"So you said last night," he said with a relieved chuckle. She frowned in puzzlement, and he laughed. "It was a drug-induced confession."

"Well, I would have confessed earlier if I thought you felt the same way." At Victoria's words, Nicholas tightened his arm around her.

"Then I trust you'll have no objection if I marry you again tomorrow?" Nicholas waited for her response with a sense of worry. He was still uncertain of her and her agreement to the wedding. The happiness lighting her face was all the reassurance he needed. Victoria threw her arms around his neck.

"Yes," she exclaimed softly. "Yes, I'll marry you."

"Then we have an appointment tomorrow morning at St. Paul's Cathedral," he said with a smile. The instant a conflicted look crossed her face, he frowned.

"What?"

"I promised Edmund I'd take him Christmas shopping tomorrow," she said in a guilty voice.

"I think he'll prefer being my best man, don't you." His response made her kiss him again.

"*You*, are a terrific big brother, do you know that?" she said with a bewitching smile. "Edmund will love that."

"What will I like?" The subject of their conversation stood in the salon doorway. "Are you talking about my Christmas presents?"

"No," Nicholas said with a grin as he and Victoria faced his brother, all the while he kept his arm wrapped around Victoria's waist. He was unwilling to part with her at the moment. "Something better. Victoria has agreed to marry me again, and I need you as my best man."

"What's that?" his brother asked suspiciously.

"It means you're responsible for holding Victoria's wedding ring until the Bishop asks for it," Nicholas said. "It's a very special job that only a few people can do."

"Okay. I'll do it. But what about my Christmas presents?"

"You have a one track mind, Edmund," Victoria laughed. "You know good and well you don't get any presents until Christmas Day."

"I know that. I was testing you." A mischievous grin curved his brother's mouth before his face fell. "But if I have to be Nicholas's best man tomorrow, we can't go shopping for presents."

"I can take you this afternoon," Nicholas said cheerfully. "Victoria needs her rest."

"Edmund isn't the only one who needs to go shopping," Victoria protested. "And right now I feel wonderful."

Love sparkled brightly in her sapphire eyes, although the determination on her face said he would fight a losing battle if he tried to set his foot down with regard to her going with him and Edmund. If there was one thing he'd learned about Victoria, she had a tendency to push herself, but he also knew she would admit when she had reached her limit.

"Very well," he acquiesced and kissed her cheek. "But the minute I see you begin to tire, I'll expect no arguments when I decide it's time to return home."

"Agreed," she said with a joyous laugh.

As they entered St. Paul's All Souls Chapel the next morning, they were greeted by Sebastian and Anna. Yesterday, he'd told Victoria that they required another witness, and she heartily endorsed his suggestion of Anna. Now, as he watched Victoria greet the other woman affectionately, he was happy he'd suggested his friend. The bishop gathered them at the front of the altar and began the ceremony.

As the clergyman recited the familiar words, Nicholas turned his head to see Victoria studying him with a look of adoration on her face. He squeezed her hand as their gazes locked. Three months ago, he would never have believed he would marry his wife a second time. But standing here beside her, he realized how important the ceremony was. Not just to her, but him as well. This simple ceremony made their love not only one of heart and body. It was a joining of two souls. As Nicholas repeated the words, the bishop read out loud, he saw Victoria's look of happiness as the man used the name Ashton. Tears shimmered in her eyes as she turned to him and spoke her vows.

"I, Victoria Ashton take thee Nicholas Bartholomew to be my wedded husband... To have and to hold from this day forward... for better for worse, for richer for poorer, in sickness and health...to love and to cherish... from this life to the next, according to God's law and thereto I give thee my troth." Nicholas saw the bishop frown at Victoria's alteration of her vows. The clergyman looked at him in silent protest, Nicholas shook his head.

"As this is our second ceremony, I see no reason to adhere completely to the letter of the service, my lord bishop," he murmured.

Although he could tell the man was far from happy, the bishop continued with the ceremony. Nicholas winked at Victoria, and he saw her fight back a laugh. When the bishop pronounced them husband and wife, Nicholas pulled Victoria into his arms to kiss her. As he slowly released her, he pressed his mouth against her ear.

"Now, you can no longer claim you're not my wife, sweet witch." His statement made her laugh softly..

"Then I'll have to come up with something new to protest." She grinned up at him in open defiance. He growled low in his throat as she kissed his cheek.

"I'll make you pay for that later, my love."

"I look forward to it," she whispered with a seductive curve of her lips. Nicholas suppressed a groan. Victoria held far too much power over him, and the worst of it was that she knew it. But upon reflection, he wasn't sure he'd have it any other way.

Chapter 31

February 1898

The weeks following the renewal of their vows had been the happiest of Nicholas's life. Christmas had been a whirlwind of festivities. There had never been so much laughter over the holidays in the Guildford House before.

He'd presented Victoria with a sapphire necklace that matched the color of her eyes. Although she protested the extravagance, her pleasure had been evident. But it was the landscape by Lockwood that made her cry.

At first, he thought he'd erred grievously by giving her the painting. When she'd unwrapped the gift, her reaction had been one of pleasure. But when he'd shown her the inscription on the back, she'd burst into tears. He immediately pulled her into his arms as he tried to make her tell him what was wrong. It had taken her several moments to compose herself, which had been a lifetime of remorse for him that he'd somehow caused her pain. When she finally became coherent, she traced the inscription— *For my wife, Victoria. Nicholas. Christmas 1897* —with her fingers lovingly as she explained her tears.

It had been the significance of the simple words that had been the greatest gift he could ever give her. Through her happy tears, she looked up at him with a love that had made his heart expanded in his chest. It was the same emotion he saw in her eyes now as they stood in the frigid February air waiting for their carriage. They'd both enjoyed the Oscar Wilde play inside the Lyceum theater, but by the end of the performance Nicholas had seen Victoria's eyelids drooping. Over the past two weeks, he'd noticed how tired she was by the end of the day. It puzzled him because in recent days her face had taken on a soft glow that enhanced her beautiful features. As she shivered beside him, he bent his head.

"The carriage won't be long. You should have waited for me in the lobby."

"And risk some other woman attempting to flirt with you? No, thanks." Despite the smile on her lips, he knew it was fear that kept her at his side tonight. Ever since the night she'd almost been killed, she'd refused to leave the house without someone at her side. He would be glad when they could return to Brentwood Park in another month. He saw Victoria cover her mouth with her hand as she yawned.

"You look tired, sweet witch."

"I am," she said with a nod.

"You've been tired quite a bit of late. I think it's time I sent for Dr. Waverley."

"*No*," she exclaimed with what he thought was fear. She turned away from him for a moment before she looked back at him. "You know how much I hate doctors."

"Nonetheless, I think it would be—"

"I *don't* need to see a doctor," she snapped. When he frowned, she touched his arm with a repentant look. "I'm sorry, Nicholas. I'm tired, and as I've told Edmund time and again, you're a worrywart. I'm fine. All I need is a little sleep."

As their carriage rolled to a stop in front of them, Nicholas opened the door and helped Victoria into the vehicle. Seconds later, the carriage rocked into motion. Victoria snuggled into his side and rested her head on his shoulder.

"I'm sorry I snapped at you, darling," she sighed softly.

"It's completely unlike you, sweet witch, which is why I think we should call Dr. Waverley." His response made her straighten up and glare at him.

"Your wife is quite capable of determining when she needs to see a doctor, Lord Guildford. So until I say so, do not mention the word doctor again."

With a final glare in his direction, she scooted away from him to huddle in the corner of the carriage. Stunned by her reaction, he stared at her in open mouth amazement. What the devil was wrong with her? As he struggled to understand her behavior, fear lashed through him. Was she regressing to her old personality? Was she becoming Vickie again?

"Victoria, if something were wrong, you would tell me, wouldn't you, my love?"

"Nothing's wrong," she said in a quiet, but emotionless voice. "I'm tired, Nicholas, nothing more."

It was at that moment he realized she was lying to him. Anger surged through his veins at the realization. Vickie had lied to him all the time, and the fact that Victoria was lying to him now infuriated him while instilling dread deep down inside. *Christ Jesus*, Victoria had always been honest with him. For her to lie to him now was a kick in his gut.

By the time they arrived home, his anger had grown to a quiet fury. As he followed Victoria upstairs and into her room, he was determined to have the matter settled between them.

"I really am tired, Nicholas. Do you mind if I sleep alone tonight?" The request was another kick in his stomach, but it was the forlorn air about her that dissolved his anger entirely. He quickly pulled her into his arms.

"I know something's wrong, my love. Tell me what it is. It can't be so bad that you're afraid to tell me. Whatever it is, we'll work through it."

Victoria buried her face into his shoulder as she hugged him. Her action filled him with relief. She wouldn't press herself into him so tightly if she no longer loved him.

Suddenly, he realized that had been his greatest fear.

"Victoria, do you love me?"

"Of course I do," she mumbled. "I'll always love you."

"Then tell me what's wrong," he said fiercely. "And don't tell me nothing's wrong. I know you too well."

"I can't," she said hoarsely. "I don't know how."

She pushed her way out of his arms and moved away from him to remove her sapphire necklace and drop it on her dressing table.

"Damn it, Victoria, I refuse to have secrets between us," he growled. "I endured enough lies, treachery, and betrayal with Vickie. I'll not abide that from you as well."

In a vicious movement, she whirled around to glare at him, but it was the fear and anguish in her blue eyes that made his gut clench with fear.

"I'm pregnant."

Nicholas felt as though he had been struck by lightning. Rooted to the spot where he stood, he watched Victoria walk past him to sit on the edge of the bed. She was with child. God in heaven, what had he done? It was a culmination of his worst nightmares.

His shoulders sagging, he bent his head as the image of Edmund flashed through his head. He loved his brother, but bringing a child with similar handicaps into the world caused his stomach to roil. Worst of all, Victoria had not told him about the pregnancy.

Nicholas stared at her in silence, his thoughts churning violently. He noted her slender hips and flat stomach, trying to imagine her round with child. A child that in all likelihood would not have its full faculties. Victoria's eyes were enormous in her pale face.

"I didn't know how to tell you." She made a helpless gesture with her hands. "I know how you feel about having children."

"When is the babe due?" he asked in a dispassionate

voice.

"July I think." Her voice was filled with a wild despair as he questioned her.

A part of him wanted to pull her into his arms, but he resisted the impulse. He needed time to think. Time to put things into perspective. In many ways, he felt like a fox trapped by baying hounds. It wasn't a pleasant sensation.

"If you'll excuse me, I will leave you to your rest." Wheeling about on his heel, he headed toward the bedroom door.

"Nicholas," she rasped hoarsely. "Please, I need to know how you feel about this."

The quiet desperation in her voice twisted his heart, but he could not turn to face the misery he knew would be visible on her face. He could not console her when he knew he did not want this child.

"The deed is done, madam. Regrets do not allow one to turn back the clock."

He didn't look back, but continued out of the room. He needed something to do, something to occupy him as he absorbed the reality of his current situation. Charles had invited him to a game of cards tonight, but he'd turned his friend down as he and Victoria were attending the play. Knowing his friend, Charles would no doubt be playing until the early morning hours, and focusing on a game of cards would allow him to process what Victoria had just told him. Without a second thought, he charged out of the house and flagged down a hack. He'd made Victoria with child, and there was only one other thing he feared more, and that was losing her.

Nicholas rolled over in the bed he'd slept in at the club.

His head was pounding. After he and Charles had quit their card game early this morning, he'd proceeded to drink himself into a stupor. He'd allowed his friend to assume he and Victoria had had a lover's quarrel, while coming to the realization that he was an ass. Nicholas groaned out loud. It had been years since he'd drunk himself into oblivion, and his body was protesting the abusive drinking of the night before.

He swung his legs off the bed and sat on the edge of the mattress. Drowning his sorrows in whiskey had done nothing to ease his miserable state. He'd fathered a child, and there was nothing that could be done about it. Dropping his head into his hands, he groaned again. What was he going to do if the child turned out to be like Edmund? Who would care for the child after he and Victoria were gone? There was no one else to take over the family title.

The sudden image of Victoria's face from last night returned to haunt him. Guilt spread through him as he remembered their conversation. There had been no doubt of her desperation and misery. He'd heard it in her voice, and he'd failed her. Instead of reassuring her, he'd gone off to lick his wounds, leaving her alone without even thinking about how his words might have made her feel. He loved her, and his response to her news had made it sound as though he blamed her for what had happened. The fault lay with him. He was a bastard. He needed to go home and apologize.

Victoria had clearly been dealing with this for several months. Looking back, he could see the toll it had been taking on her. The moments when he'd seen her staring off into space with a look of despair, her tiredness, the lackluster look in her eyes at different points in time. God help him. He was responsible for her pain.

He'd made it clear he never wanted children. Knowing how he felt about the subject had clearly made it an intolerable situation for her, and Nicholas understood why she'd not told him the truth sooner. He still wouldn't know if he'd not pushed her last night. Nicholas sighed. He didn't just need to apologize to her, he needed to grovel. His wife was the most wonderful thing in his life, and without her, he was nothing. At this point he was facing another uphill battle to win her forgiveness. But he'd done it before, and he'd do it again. Nicholas intended to be there for her *and* the child, no matter what the circumstances.

Rising to his feet, he swayed slightly where he stood. Bloody hell, his head hurt. With a grimace, he dressed and left the club. The hack that drove him home seemed to hit every pothole in the street. By the time the small carriage pulled up in front of the town house, his head resounded with a repetitive beating drum. Inside the house, he headed slowly for the stairs, intent on speaking to Victoria right away. From the library, Edmund came charging out and tackled him to the hard marble floor.

"What did you do to her, Nicholas?" his brother shouted as Nicholas was forced to deflect his brother's blows as he attempted to wrestle Edmund to the ground. "Why did you make her leave? You go find her and bring her back."

"Damn it to hell, Edmund," he snapped as he managed to pin his brother to the floor. "What the devil are you talking about?"

"Victoria," his brother said angrily. "You sent her away."

"I didn't send Victoria away," Nicholas rasped as his heart sank like a stone in a pond, and he allowed Edmund to sit up. "Where is she, Edmund? Tell me where Victoria is."

"I don't know." Edmund, his face wet with tears, sat on the floor staring at Nicholas.

"What do you mean, you don't know," Nicholas said hoarsely. "*Roberts. Jamieson.*"

His voice was a loud roar in the foyer, as he helped his brother to his feet. Jamieson was the first to arrive, and the butler's expression was grave and uneasy.

"I'm sorry, my lord," Jamieson said in an awkward tone.

"It's Lady Guildford. She's gone."

"What do you mean she's gone?" Fear sliced through him like a knife. Had someone kidnapped her? "When?"

"Sometime after breakfast."

"And no one saw her leave?" he snarled.

"No, my lord." Jamieson shook his head with regret. "Molly brought her toast for breakfast, and her ladyship sent her away with orders she didn't want to be disturbed. When Molly returned for the tray, she discovered her ladyship was gone, and the smallest of her ladyship's traveling cases is missing and a few of her dresses."

"*Sweet Jesus*," Nicholas whispered as he stared at the floor. He'd done this. He'd driven her from the house. He pulled his pocket watch out of his vest. It was three o'clock. God help him, he'd slept more than half the day away thanks to his drinking binge last night. Victoria had at least a six-hour head start. She could be anywhere. From the staircase, Roberts called out to him and waved a letter in his hand as the valet ran down the stairs.

"My lord, I found this on the fireplace mantle in your room," his valet said as he crossed the floor and handed Nicholas the white envelope. With Edmund and the other men watching in solemn silence, Nicholas ripped open the flap and pulled the note out.

Nicholas,

> *It seems you were right after all, I'm just like Vickie. I know you'll never be able to forgive me, but I'm so sorry. I'm sorry for everything. I never meant to betray you by hiding my pregnancy. I knew you would be upset. I wanted to tell you the truth. I just didn't know how. You'll probably find that hard to believe, and I'm pretty sure you'll think I've been lying to you since that day in Goodmans cottage.*
>
> *You might even wonder if the baby is yours. I don't expect you to believe me, but I am carrying your child. I never meant*

to hurt you, and I know the best way to solve the problem is for me to go home. I don't want my presence to be a constant reminder of how I betrayed you with my lie. I think you'll be much better off without me here. I love you, no matter what time period I live in. I'm sorry.

Victoria
P.S. Please give my love to Edmund. I didn't have the strength to say goodbye to him.

Home. He stared at the word for a moment as his body grew cold. Did she intend to bring another fainting spell on herself so she could go to the one place he couldn't follow her? No, he couldn't believe that of her, but the mere thought of it terrified him.

"My lord," Roberts spoke up quietly. "Her ladyship took the pound notes from your wardrobe."

"Bloody hell," he rasped and closed his eyes.

She'd left without saying where she was going and for all he knew whoever had been sending the threatening notes could have been watching her and might have followed her. Where would she go? Brentwood Park. Perhaps that was the home she was referring to. He could only pray he was right. Fear galvanized him into motion.

"It's more than possible the countess has gone back to Brentwood Park. Jamieson, on the off chance she hasn't left London, send someone to Lord and Lady Starling's residence to see if her ladyship went there. I'll go to my sister's." He turned his head to meet his valet's concerned gaze. "Roberts, pack my things. I'm going to go after her ladyship."

"I'm going with you." Edmund glared at him, and Nicholas nodded his head in agreement. He looked back at his valet.

"See to it, Roberts." He looked at his brother, who was still glaring at him. "Go with him, Edmund, and be ready to go when I return from Abigail's."

"Yes, my lord," Roberts said, then quickly made his way back upstairs.

Nicholas turned away from his brother and picked up his coat that he'd flung carelessly over the entryway table. Shoving his arms into the sleeves, he made his way out the front door and hailed a hackney cab. Time was of the essence. It was Sunday and the last train for Guildford left in a little more than an hour. Flinging himself into the cab's seat, a huge knot rose in Nicholas's throat. God help him, he had to find her. If he lost Victoria, he would lose a piece of his soul.

Chapter 32

The deed is done, madam. Regrets do not allow one to turn back the clock. The words thundered through Victoria's mind as she stared down at the toast and cocoa Molly had left her a short while ago. She'd barely slept, because Nicholas's words had haunted her all night.

She had expected him to be upset. However, she'd not expected his rejection to be so harsh, any more than she'd been prepared for the way it had devastated her. His bitter voice had cut her like a jagged knife. It was almost as if he blamed her for the pregnancy.

The fact she'd withheld the truth from him had made matters far worse. In essence, she had lied to him just like Vickie always had. She'd betrayed him by keeping the truth from him. The baby might have been a reality he would have adjusted to, but her betrayal was something she doubted he'd ever forgive. Like Vickie, she'd married him without telling him the truth. She was no better than her predecessor.

She remembered the anger and contempt he'd displayed the first time they'd met at the Goodmans' cottage. To face that cold, blistering anger again would be unbearable. When she'd first arrived at Brentwood Park, she'd thought coming to London would help her find a way back to the present. But she'd been here for more than two months. If nothing had happened by now, it was unlikely to happen at all. Was the portal back to her time in the woods where Thomas Goodman had found her? Whether it was or not, she wouldn't try to find a way back, no matter how painful it would be to remain here.

She had the baby to think about now, and she wanted to go home. Home to Brentwood Park. It was a simple solution to the entire problem. At least she would be out of Nicholas's hair. He wouldn't have to come back to Guildford House every day to find her growing bigger with a child he didn't want. The only thing she needed was money.

Intent only on escape, she hurried into Nicholas's room to search for whatever cash she could find. It took her several moments before she found a small box filled with pound notes in his wardrobe. She didn't how much she'd need, so she took all of it. She returned to her room to pack a few items into a small travel bag Molly had placed in the bottom of her chifforobe.

She made sure to pack her journals, and at the last minute realized she needed to leave a note for Nicholas. The last thing she wanted was to give Reardon more ammunition if everyone believed the Countess of Guildford had disappeared for a second time. She sat down at her small desk and stared at the blank piece of paper. What could she say to him? Apologizing for her betrayal seemed so trivial a response for her crime.

With a quiet sigh, she quickly penned a note to Nicholas, then returned to his room to place the envelope on the mantle. As she turned to leave, her gaze fell on the bed. For the past several weeks, she'd fallen asleep every night and awakened each morning in Nicholas's arms. Last night was the first time they'd been apart since their wedding. Her chest tightened with pain. She'd been happy before they'd been married at St. Paul's Cathedral, but the days afterward had filled her with a joy she'd never dreamed of. Now the dream was shattered.

She'd known from the moment she'd learned she was pregnant that Nicholas would not want the child, although she'd hoped he would change his mind when he learned the truth. But his response to the news last night only emphasized his feelings about the matter wouldn't change. With a soft sob, she went back to her room to retrieve her small bag and left the house. Maybe she should have waited for Nicholas to come back home. No, he'd spent the night elsewhere. That was all she needed to know. His absence has made it perfectly clear that he wanted nothing to do with her.

An invisible spear pierced her heart as she realized how much she missed him already, and she'd barely left the house. She hailed a cab as she'd seen Nicholas do and instructed the driver to take her to Waterloo station where they'd arrived in London. With each passing block that the hackney cab took her away from Guildford House, the more her heart ached. When the hackney rolled to a halt in front of the railway station, a cacophony of sounds filtered out into the street. She handed the driver her fare, then entered the station.

The chaos greeting her was an assault on her senses. She flinched at the noise and made her way to the ticket window. The clerk behind the barred window informed her the next train to Guildford was about to leave the station, but if she hurried she could catch it. Following the man's directions, she reached the platform just as the conductor made the last call for boarding. For the next three and a half hours, Victoria stared at the train window, her body numb.

When she'd disembarked from the train in Guildford, she suddenly realized she had no transportation to Brentwood Park other than her own two feet. She stood outside the train station debating what to do for several minutes. They'd taken the carriage from the house when they'd traveled to London in December, and she was sure that it was at least five miles to the house. It was a Sunday afternoon, and there were few people out and about as most people were enjoying an afternoon of rest.

Despite her exhaustion, Victoria set out on foot. At least she knew the way, and the thought of Mrs. Babcocke's beef stew helped her maintain a steady pace despite the road conditions. Muddy and filled with slush, the ruts forced her to walk in the snow alongside the well-traveled roadway. The wet snow seeped into her shoes, numbing her toes. It had been years since she'd been this cold.

After more than an hour, her perseverance rewarded her with the sight of Brentwood Park in the distance. Renewed with energy at the knowledge she was almost home, Victoria quickened her pace. Almost forty-five minutes later, she was standing in the front hall. Most of the staff had accompanied them to London, but Mrs. Babcocke and a few other servants had remained behind. She set her travel bag down near the stairs,, then walked to the rear of the house.

Victoria heard laughter coming from the kitchen, and as she stepped into the doorway the cook, scullery maid, and a footman looked at her in amazement. Mentally and physically exhausted, Victoria choked back tears, unwilling to let them see how upset she was.

"Good evening." She forced a smile to her lips, all too aware of how strained it must appear to the servants. "Mrs. Babcocke, I was hoping you might have some of your beef stew on the stove. I'm freezing, and I know a warm fire and your stew will warm me up really quick."

"Good heavens, my lady, you look like death warmed over." Mrs. Babcocke bustled to her feet. "We weren't expecting you and his lordship for several weeks yet. How did you get home?"

"I walked from the train station," Victoria said quietly. "If you could have someone build a fire in my room I'd appreciate it, and if you don't have any stew, then a bowl of hot soup would be nice."

"You *walked*," the cook exclaimed in horror. "Dear Lord. Is his Lordship with you?"

"No, Lord Guildford is still in London," she said with a shake of her head. "I decided to come home by myself."

Just the mention of Nicholas made Victoria's heart ache,

and she wearily turned away to make her way back to the main hall. Her travel bag in hand, she climbed the stairs and made her way down the hall to her room. The footman from the kitchen had taken the back stairs and was already building her a fire. It quickly became a roaring blaze, and after asking if she needed anything else, he left the room.

Eager to get out of her wet clothes, Victoria undressed as quickly as possible. She pulled the blanket off the bed and wrapped it around her, then curled up in front of the fire. She was too numb and tired to think. Mrs. Babcocke came up with a hot bowl of stew and freshly baked bread. The woman had tried to fuss over her, but Victoria had gently made it clear she wanted to be left alone. The hearty stew made her realize how hungry she really was. Other than a piece of toast, the meal Mrs. Babcocke had prepared for her was the only thing she'd eaten all day. But the hot stew did little to raise her spirits.

Cold and weary, she tightened the blanket around her and leaned her head against the soft padding of the wing-backed chair. Why on earth had she been brought to this time period? Was it the universe's idea of a big joke? Something to see how much pain she could endure? She'd always thought of herself as a strong person, but for the first time in her life she felt as if a MACK truck had run her over—twice, leaving her without the energy to get up.

Victoria closed her eyes. How was she going to live without Nicholas? She would be miserable until July when the baby arrived. Then she'd have someone to love. Even if he refused to have anything to do with the baby, she would never willingly abandon her child. She tried to visualize what Nicholas's son would look like—and she was certain the baby was a boy. He would have dark hair and green eyes like his father, but the baby would have Edmund's sweet smile. With a sigh, she let her mind wander until she dozed off. A long while later, she jerked awake at a soft sound.

The fire was burning low in the grate, and she saw a log

had fallen off to the hearth. Victoria uncurled herself from the chair, then used the poker to roll the log back onto the flames. The chill in the air made her reach for the blanket again. As she wrapped it around her shoulders, she sensed someone watching her.

A shiver skimmed across her skin, and she whirled around to see Nicholas standing in the bedroom's open doorway. Her heart skipped a beat. What was he doing here? Hadn't she made it clear she'd left so he wouldn't have to see her anymore? So she wouldn't be a reminder of a child he didn't want? Her heart leapt into her throat as he closed the door and moved toward her.

Nicholas frowned as he studied Victoria's face. She looked exhausted. No, deeply hurt, and he knew it was his fault. He stopped in front of her, and caught her chin in his fingers, but she jerked free of his grasp, then stepped out of his reach. Her reaction sliced through his heart like a sharp razor intent on cutting it out of his chest. He cleared his throat.

"Mrs. Babcocke said you walked from the train station to Brentwood Park this afternoon," he said in a tight voice.

Edmund had been right to try and thrash him. If it hadn't been for him, she never would have wanted to leave London to begin with. At first, he didn't think she was going to respond, but she finally nodded.

"It's a Sunday. There weren't many people around, at least no one with a vehicle I could ask for a ride." She rolled her shoulders in a small shrug. "Why are you here, Nicholas?"

"Because my wife ran away."

"I didn't run away," she said quietly, but with a bit of that fiery spirit in her that he loved so much. "I came home."

"Home?" Puzzled, he stared at her in bewilderment.

"You mean home to Brentwood Park?"

"Yes, where else would I…" she looked at him with a mixture of disappointment and something else he couldn't decipher. "I wouldn't deliberately try to bring on one of my headaches. I would never harm my child."

"*Our* child," he enunciated firmly. The moment he spoke, her soft features became cold and unyielding.

"No, Lord Guildford. You've made it quite clear you don't want this baby," she said with an icy calm that illustrated how deeply his desertion last night had hurt her. Frustration made him clench his jaw as he met her cool, disdainful gaze.

"Do you want me to lie and say I wanted children when they might be like my brother?" he snarled. The moment she flinched, Nicholas exhaled a loud whoosh of air from his lungs. Shoving his hand through his hair, he turned away from her. "When you said you were with child, all I could think about was that I would be to blame if our child was like Edmund. But it wasn't the fact that you were carrying our child that horrified me. It was the thought that I would be like my father."

"You'll *never* be like your father," she exclaimed sharply as she rushed forward and tugged on his arm to make him face her. "If you were like him, would you have gone to Italy and brought Edmund home to live with you? Are you going to stand here and tell me you don't love your brother and would do whatever it takes to protect him?"

"No, I would give my life for Edmund." Nicholas shook his head as her words sank into his brain, and he saw her fierce expression. She glared up at him.

"Then there's *no way* in hell you'll be like your father where *our* baby is concerned."

Her conviction made Nicholas's heart tighten in his chest, and he marveled at the love he saw shining in her eyes. Regret rolled through him as he cupped her face with his hands and placed a tender kiss on her brow.

"I was a coward for deserting you last night, sweet witch," he whispered.

"I'm just as much to blame," she said in a choked voice as she wrapped her arms around his waist and laid her head against his shoulder. "I knew you would think I was like Vickie and her lies all over again. I betrayed you by not telling you the truth from the start."

"You are *nothing* like Vickie," he growled fiercely as he forced her to look up at him. "And you *didn't* betray me. I would still have had doubts, even if you'd told me the moment you were certain you were with child."

"Then you believe me when I say you're not like your father and never will be?"

"Yes," he said as a small smile tilted the corners of his mouth. He'd never had a more beautiful or passionate champion to defend him.

"I have a confession to make," she murmured as she nibbled at her bottom lip. "I thought about bringing on one of my headaches, but the moment I considered it, I knew I'd never be able to do it. I want this baby, Nicholas."

"As do I," he said softly as he realized it was the truth.

Whatever happened, he would love the child, because the babe would be the culmination of their love for each other. She laid her head on his shoulder, and he heard her yawn.

"I know you're tired, my love, but you have another champion who wishes to see you before you retire for the night."

"Edmund?" she asked with a smile. "Where is he?"

"In the hall," he said with a smile. "I knew better than to send him to bed, I imagine he would have punched me again."

"He hit you?" Victoria stared at him in astonishment then left his embrace and moved to the wardrobe to retrieve her robe.

"He landed a couple of sound blows to my jaw when I came home from the club today. He was furious with me for having driven you away," he said with a hint of affectionate amusement. "I'm certain he'll not be able to rest until he knows you're all right, and God knows he won't believe me."

"Then I won't disappoint him." Victoria's smile was filled with warmth and love as she looked over her shoulder at him. His heart had never been so full as it was at this moment. His wife loved him in spite of his faults. No other man in the world could have been as lucky as he was.

Chapter 33

Victoria grimaced as the baby moved inside her belly to a position that was obviously more comfortable for him. The only problem was it made *her* extremely uncomfortable. She stared down at the page in her journal and the last few paragraphs. She smiled despite her uncomfortable state.

I wish this baby would hurry up and get here. The weather has been boiling hot. Who knew England could be this miserable in the summertime? I thought it would be cool. It might be all these layers of clothing, and the pregnancy isn't helping either. Dr. Bertram says it won't be long now, but I'm not sure I trust him. Men don't have a clue about what it's like to be pregnant. Even Nicholas, as much as I love him, can be a bit of an ass sometimes about how uncomfortable I am.

Edmund is the only one who seems to understand how terribly uncomfortable. He's such a sweet man, and I love him dearly. I think about the time before I came to Brentwood Park less and less. It seems more like a dream. Perhaps Nicholas is right. It might be a fabrication my mind created while I was missing for three weeks. I can only assume the blow to my head changed my behavior for the better.

No, I don't really believe that. None of it makes sense, but I can't believe my life in the future wasn't real. At least everyone here doesn't have to deal with the real countess any more. The woman was a major bitch and made everyone's life miserable. It worries me some that Nicholas hasn't mentioned that bastard Reardon for the last several months. Every time I ask him about the man, he simply says there isn't any news.

Victoria closed the journal and tucked it back into its hiding spot in her desk. It was the second journal she'd almost filled completely, and her fingers brushed over the first volume as she put the second one back in place. After her death as an old woman, someone would read them and wonder how she managed to escape the psych ward.

A soft noise made her turn her head, and she saw Edmund standing near the door. She frowned in puzzlement at his wistful expression, and she beckoned to him. He raced forward to squat down in front of her with his elbows tucked in between his legs.

"I didn't want to bother you while you were writing, so I kept still for the longest time."

"That was very thoughtful of you, Edmund. Now why don't you tell me what's wrong, sweetheart? You looked really sad this afternoon."

"I'm sad because you have to go away."

"Go away?" She frowned as her heart skipped a beat in fear. "What do you mean?"

"I know you have to go, but I don't want you to," Edmund said with an angry frown.

"What makes you think I'm going away, Edmund?" Victoria stared at her brother-in-law with a growing sense of unease at his emphatic belief.

"My momma came to me last night, and she said you would have to go away."

The certainty in his voice sent a shiver down her spine. Did he somehow sense she wasn't really supposed to be here? Was he intuitive like Anna?

"What else did your mother tell you?"

"Mama said you forgot about the secret. She said I should show it to you again so you wouldn't forget." Edmund tipped his head to one side as he spoke.

"What secret, Edmund?" Puzzled, she frowned.

Scrambling to his feet, he grabbed her hand and solicitously helped her to her feet, then pulled her toward the fireplace. On the left side of the mantle, Edmund reached out and pressed the third rose down from the top of the shelf. The flower was part of the intricate pattern of roses that wound its way up the sides of the fireplace to meet at the center of the mantle.

The moment Edmund pushed the flower inward, she heard a soft click, and the whole side of the mantle swung open to reveal several narrow shelves capable of holding valuables. The cleverly concealed compartment joined with the mantel's wood inlay in a seamless joint which made the secret compartment impossible to detect.

"Edmund, does anyone else knows about this hiding spot?"

"No, not even Nicholas," he said. "Momma said you would remember about the book when I showed you the secret door."

Trepidation tightened her throat. Christ, first she'd been thrown into the past, suffered from frightening visions, and now Edmund was telling her about a ghost. She snorted silently. Why should Edmund's story about his mother surprise her? She was from the future, living in the past. Living the life of another woman. How could she question the logic of a message from a dead woman?

Because she wasn't from the future. It was simply a lie her brain had created. A voice laughed at her in the back of her head. She simply wanted to believe that because it would eliminate the fear that she would eventually be pulled back to her own time. Her heart skidded along as fear threatened to take over her thoughts, but she pushed the emotion back into the darkness from where it had crawled from.

She peered into the hiding place with its dusty shelves.

Sneezing, she saw something shoved all the way to the back of the top shelf. Cautiously, she pulled the item out of the cubby hole.

"See, Victoria, it's the black book you hid there before you came back as a nice person." The nervous tension in his voice made her glance in his direction. Fear pinched his features, and she patted his arm to calm him.

"It's alright, Edmund. There's nothing to be afraid of. It's just a book."

He shook his head vigorously in protest, but didn't move. Returning her attention to the book, she flipped it open and frowned. There were names, dates, and locations. Among the references, she immediately recognized the familiar London icon, Big Ben. The letters MP in front of so many names rang a bell with her too, but she couldn't place where she'd seen them before.

Frowning, she turned one page after another to find the slim volume filled with different names at the top of each page. It didn't make sense. What would Vickie be doing with a book like this? Toward the rear of the volume, Victoria saw the name, Darby.

Fear snaked through her as she stared at the name, and that terrible night at the opera flooded through her. She forced the horror of those terrible moments aside to focus on the book in her hand. There was nothing about it that made any sense whatsoever.

Nicholas would know what all the names meant when she showed the notebook to him. Parliament went into recess the day after tomorrow, and she would show the thin volume to him, then. Victoria put the book back into the cubby hole and shut the secret door. She turned toward Edmund and smiled.

"I don't remember why I have the book or why I hid it, Edmund. But it looks important, so we're going to leave it hidden until Nicholas comes home. We'll show it to him, and he'll know what to do with it. Sound like a plan?"

"I'm afraid, Victoria. I don't want the bad men to come and hurt you."

"There's nothing to be afraid of. Nicholas will know what to do with the book, and no one's going to hurt me." What men was Edmund referring to? The men in her nightmares? She shivered.

"Are you all right, Victoria?" The fear in Edmund's voice made her reach for his hand.

"Of course, sweetheart." She smiled and squeezed his hand. "There's nothing to worry about. Nicholas would never let anything happen to either of us. You know that, don't you?"

"Yep. Nicholas will keep us safe," Edmund said with renewed confidence.

"All right, now isn't it time for tea?"

"Uh, huh." With a grin, Edmund, with his hand still holding hers, pulled her toward the door. "Cook made me apple tarts today."

"You and your apple—" her words came to an abrupt halt as a rush of warm liquid ran down her legs and formed a puddle at her feet.

"Victoria, you peed all over the floor." Edmund's wide-eyed look of appalled amusement made her choke out a laugh despite the sudden, hard contraction that twisted painfully in her belly.

"Edmund, go get Mrs. Beechum." She tried to keep the panic out of her voice, but failed. A look of fear swept over Edmund's face. She shook her head and smiled despite the painful contraction. "It's all right, Edmund. The baby is coming. Go find Mrs. Beechum and Molly *now*."

A look of wonder swept over her brother-in-law's face, and with a bob of his head he raced out of the room. The contraction easing, Victoria pulled out a lightweight lawn nightgown from her wardrobe. Her hair was already sticking to the nape of her neck, and her water breaking had left her legs sticky as well.

She moved into the bathroom at a slow pace and wet a cloth to apply to the back of her neck. She lifted her head and stared into the mirror and smiled. She was about to have a baby. Another contraction twisted through her, and she sucked in a sharp breath before releasing a cry of pain. The contraction seemed to go on forever, and she breathed a sigh of relief as the pain faded.

"You're being a real pain in the ass, baby, just like your father can be sometimes."

"More like his mother, I think." The familiar voice echoing in her ears made Victoria jerk her head toward the bathroom door. Her heart sang as Nicholas closed the distance between them.

"Nicholas, you weren't supposed to be home for another two days."

"My bill doesn't come up until the next session, and I had a feeling my wife might need me," he murmured as he kissed her gently. "It seems I was right."

Another contraction built up and lashed its way across her belly. She released a quiet sob of pain, and concern darkened Nicholas's features. He quickly wrapped his arm around her waist to ensure she remained upright. The contraction lasted for at least a minute, and as the pain eased, Mrs. Beechum and Molly hurried through the doorway of the bathroom. A beaming smile on her face, the housekeeper immediately took charge.

"Molly, run the hot water, we'll need it soon. Come, my lady. Let's get you into your nightgown. You'll find it much cooler than your dress." Mrs. Beechum glanced at Nicholas. "My Lord, if you would, Master Edmund is beside himself outside her ladyship's door. He keeps talking about her ladyship going away. Would you mind reassuring him that all is well?"

Nicholas stiffened beside her, and his tension pulsed its way into her body. She grasped his arm and smiled up at him.

"I'll be fine. I'm just having a baby. I'm not going anywhere. Go to him. He's just scared." Despite her calm, reassuring manner, Nicholas still appeared reluctant to leave her. She smiled up at him and nodded her head toward the door. With a grimace, Nicholas kissed her.

"Very well, but you're not to go anywhere," he murmured with a twinkle in his eye that vanished as soon as she gasped at the contraction taking hold of her. She heard Nicholas grunt with discomfort as her fingers dug into his arms. Mrs. Beechum dampened another hand cloth and gently wiped the sweat off of Victoria's face as the contraction eased. His features taut with worry, Nicholas looked at Mrs. Beechum.

"Dr. Bertram?" The harsh words from Nicholas received a nod from the housekeeper.

"Jamieson sent Mickey to fetch the doctor as soon as Master Edmund told us about her ladyship." Mrs. Beechum's calm voice didn't seem to ease Nicholas's concern, and Victoria squeezed his arm more gently this time.

"I'll be fine. Dr. Bertram will be here soon. Go to Edmund. I don't want him to worry. I promise you, the only place I'm going is to my bed."

Green eyes narrowed at her, Nicholas hesitated for a brief moment, then with a brusque nod he left her alone with Mrs. Beechum. With efficient speed, the housekeeper and Molly helped her undress. Victoria insisted on a quick sponge bath in an attempt to remove some of the damp stickiness on her body before she allowed the nightgown to be thrown over her head. The contractions were now about three minutes apart and Victoria already wanted the pain to end.

Victoria lay against the pillows, her skin pale and translucent from exertion. Sweat plastered her hair against her scalp, and with her eyes closed, Nicholas realized she was as pale now as she was whenever she had a fainting spell.

"You're almost done, my lady." Dr. Bertram hovered over her, his words cheerful and encouraging. "I can see the baby's head now."

"How in the hell did women survive without epidurals," she rasped as she leaned forward and bore down at the doctor's urging. Exhaustion was visible on her face as her contraction eased, and she fell backward into the pillows.

"Just a little longer, sweet witch," he said. His heart ached at the obvious pain contorting her features as another contraction took hold of her.

"That's easy for you to say," she snapped with her usual fiery spirit before she closed her eyes in pain again.

Nicholas winced at the strength of his wife's grip as Victoria drew in a deep breath. Pushing herself away from her pillows, she appeared to ride a wave of pain until, with a loud gasp, she uttered a cry of relief and collapsed back into the damp sheets. Less than a second later, a new cry filled the room.

"It's a boy, my lady. My lord," Bertram exclaimed. "A beautiful, baby boy."

"Did you hear that, my love? We have a son." Nicholas looked over his shoulder at the baby, then back to Victoria.

"I seem to recall telling you it was a boy," she said wearily, but the smile on her lips was filled with a radiant joy, and Nicholas stared at her in wonder. This beautiful woman had given him not only her heart, but a son as well. Time and again, she had proven to him that love was worth the risk. His heart felt as though it would explode from the depth of his emotions. Afraid of hurting her, he captured her face in his hands and brushed her lips in a gentle kiss.

"I love you, sweet witch."

"I love you too." Victoria's hand touched his cheek.

"Would the two of you like to meet your son?" Dr. Bertram beamed down at them as he cradled the newborn.

Victoria stretched out her arms and accepted the precious bundle. Turning the baby so that Nicholas could see their new son, she smiled. "What should we call him?"

"I hadn't even thought about a name," he murmured with a sense of awe. "To be honest, I thought *he* would be a girl."

"Well, we have to give him a name," she teased. Turning her head toward the doctor, she called out to him. "Dr. Bertram. What's your first name?"

"Andrew, after my grandfather." The doctor did not look up from the task of cleaning his instruments as he answered the question.

"What about Andrew Edmund Thornhill?" she asked as her finger stroked the baby's cheek.

"Andrew Edmund it is then," he whispered before turning his head. "Dr. Bertram, I take it that our son's name meets with your approval?"

"You honor me, my lady…my lord," Dr. Bertram stammered as pleased astonishment crossed his face.

"Would you please send Edmund in, Mrs. Beechum? I think it's time he met his nephew," Victoria said as she looked at the housekeeper at the end of the bed.

As Mrs. Beechum left to fetch his brother, Nicholas studied the glow on Victoria's face as she stared down at their son. A sense of wonder surged through him as his gaze focused on the tiny hand wrapped around Victoria's finger. Her sapphire eyes shining with happiness, she looked up at him, then laughed as Edmund charged into the room.

"*It's a boy*," Edmund exclaimed with excitement. "I have a nephew. What's his name?"

"Andrew *Edmund* Thornhill."

"He's got my name," his brother said softly with an

obvious sense of awe. Edmund leaned over the baby and gently tapped his head. "Hello, Andrew Edmund. We're going to have lots of fun together."

Her face radiant, Victoria smiled at his brother, then turned her head to look at him. A mischievous smile curled her lips.

"Isn't it about time you held your son, my lord?" A sensation not unlike fear flooded his limbs, and Nicholas hesitated as Victoria offered Andrew to him.

"Well, go on, he won't bite you," she said with a chuckle. "At least not yet."

Gingerly, Nicholas took his newborn son in his arms and rocked him as he'd once witnessed his own mother do with Abigail so many years ago. A bittersweet longing assailed his heart as he wished his parents were alive to see their grandson. Surprised by the thought, he realized that in loving Victoria he had learned to forgive his father. The insight shook him as he recognized how much her love had changed him and his outlook on life. Victoria brought out the best in him. She would until the end of their days together. A sudden icy premonition surged through him, but he crushed it before it dampened the joy he was experiencing with his new son in his arms. Except for his inability to find Reardon, his life had never been better. Victoria was the reason for that, and he thanked God for the happiness she'd brought into his life.

Chapter 34

Victoria strolled along the lake path near Goodman Cottage as Edmund charged toward the spot where he studied his turtles. Nicholas had returned to London two weeks ago, and she missed him terribly.

It was one of the reasons she'd decided to treat Edmund to a picnic. She'd thought about bringing Andrew with her, but Molly had convinced her to leave the baby behind and just enjoy a relaxing afternoon.

Just a little more than a month old, Andrew was a strong, healthy baby. Nicholas had proved quite adept at being a hands-on father, and she knew the servants were constantly amazed at his eagerness to help her with the baby. She was certain it had a great deal to do with his father's disowning of Edmund as a child.

Her gaze followed her brother-in-law's long-legged form as he prowled the edge of the small lake. She smiled as she recalled her brother-in-law's first glimpse of Andrew. Wide-eyed with wonder, Edmund had fallen in love with his new nephew at first sight. Andrew seemed to know when Edmund was near, and would stop crying the moment his uncle held him.

A flash of movement out of the corner of her eye broke through her thoughts. A narrow country lane bordered the trees at the far end of the lake, and she turned to see a closed carriage pull to a stop between her and Edmund. Something about the vehicle caused her skin to grow cold, and her heart began to race with fear. Glancing behind her, she saw the footman that had accompanied them was loading the pony cart. Fear welled up inside her as she saw two masked men leap out of the carriage and head toward Edmund.

As she cried out her warning, she lifted her dress and raced forward. Obviously confused by her shouting, Edmund stared at first Victoria and then the men bearing down on him. She and the two strangers were about equal distance from Edmund, but they were much faster. The men reached Edmund first, and she saw them place a white cloth over his nose. Edmund's legs buckled, and the two men lifted him up between them, stumbling toward the carriage.

Fear for her brother-in-law's safety overcoming the fire burning in her lungs, Victoria raced toward the carriage, determined to reach the vehicle before it pulled away. Although she didn't glance over her shoulder, she felt certain Jacobs was following. Occupied with placing Edmund on the floor of the carriage, the man outside the coach did not expect her attack. Frantic with fear, Victoria grabbed at the man's greasy hair and yanked hard.

Yelling with fury, the man whipped around. Above his mask, Victoria saw glittering black eyes blazing with a cold rage. His arctic gaze froze her in place. The mistake cost her dearly as the man slapped her viciously. Stunned by the brutal blow, she staggered backward. As she tried to recover from the attack, the man grasped her by the neck and shoved her into the coach.

"What do you know, Silas, the bitch came to us. We didn't have to go get her."

Panic surged through her limbs at the man's coarse tone, and in blind desperation, she kicked out with her feet in the direction of the voice. The grunt of pain she heard in response to her desperate move gave her a moment's satisfaction as she realized she'd found her target. However, the moment became short-lived as someone clamped a foul-smelling cloth over her nose, and she sank into oblivion despite her best efforts to stay awake.

Victoria woke in the dark, the cold dampness of the floor eating its way through her gown. Revulsion churned her stomach as the dank odor of decay assaulted her nostrils. High on the wall opposite her was a window blocked by bars. From where she was, she could see the stars shining above her. How far away from home were they? Had the men gone after Jacobs? Had the footman been able to go for help, or was he dead? She could feel her breast leaking slightly with milk, and she realized Andrew would be hungry. Fear knotted in her throat as she tried to understand what was happening. Why would someone want her and Edmund? Tears splashed down her cheeks as she tried to control her panic. Her heart pounding like a trapped animal, she jumped violently at the soft plea piercing the darkness.

"Victoria, where are you?"

Choked sobs filled the black cell and tore at her heart. In vain, she tried to see Edmund's lean frame in the darkness. Anxious to reach him, Victoria stretched out her hand, but could not find him within reaching distance. She crawled forward to the sound of Edmund's voice. The moment her hands touched the slimy, dank floor, she was forced to swallow the bile that came up into her mouth.

She paused for a moment as she struggled to breathe slowly and calm herself. Edmund needed her. Muffled sobs sounded just in front of her, and she reached out into the dark again. She touched his back to find his lanky form curled up into a ball. Her voice soft, she pulled him into a protective embrace and whispered soft reassurances as she tenderly stroked his head.

"It's all right, Edmund. Nicholas will find us."

"I'm frightened, Victoria. I don't like this place."

"I know you are, sweetheart, but we'll be fine. Nicholas will come for us," she said.

Inside, her heart cried out for her husband to find them. As though from far off, she heard his voice shouting her name. Growing still, she again heard Nicholas calling out to her. Without thinking, her head snapped up. "We're in here, Nicholas. We're in here."

At the sound of her cry for help, a small window opened on the door of the cell. "That's enough shouting, your ladyship, unless you want to go hungry this evening."

The harsh voice chilled Victoria to the bone. Shivering more from fear than the cold floor, she and Edmund jumped as the cell door opened. The sound of wood grinding against the stone accelerated her heartbeat. She flinched and saw their jailor drop a bucket of water onto the floor, followed by a wooden tray of food and two empty mugs beside the bucket.

Without speaking another word, the man left the cell, slamming the door shut behind him. In the near darkness, Victoria heard the sound of small animals scurrying around in the dark. Their nails scraped frantically against the slippery, dank cobblestone floor. Certain she and Edmund could lose their meal to rats, she scrambled forward determined to prevent the creatures from taking their food. Edmund followed her, and together they hungrily bit into the meager meal of bread and cheese. When they'd finished, Edmund curled up beside her with his head in her lap, and softly cried himself to sleep. Left alone with her thoughts, Victoria stared up at the night sky, praying Nicholas would find them soon. She refused to think of any other alternative possibilities.

Chapter 35

Present Day

Nick sighed wearily as he closed the front door of his town house behind him. Today was the tenth day Victoria had been in a coma. He wondered how long it would be before he lost hope as to her recovery.

"Never," he said beneath his breath.

Walking into the kitchen, he set his bag of groceries on the bar and began putting them away. He'd only spent an hour with Victoria before he'd left her in Miss Willoughby's care for the night. For the first time since the bombing, he'd gone to the gym. It had been a tough workout, but he'd managed to release some of the emotions he'd kept bottled up inside him for more than a week now. When he finished with the groceries, he fixed himself a sandwich, then carried it and a bottled water into the living room.

Nick turned the telly on for a few minutes, but he couldn't concentrate on the program blaring out at him. The sandwich he'd made tasted like sawdust in his mouth, and he dropped it back onto the plate as he turned the telly off. Immediately his gaze settled on the second volume of the countess' diaries. Nora had no problem referring to the journals as belonging to Victoria. He on the other hand had found it extremely difficult to do so.

With a disgusted sigh, Nick picked up his plate and

returned to the kitchen to dump his sandwich into the trash. He opened the fridge and was about to reach for a bottle of Fullers when he decided he wanted something stronger. The door of the fridge snapped shut as he pulled a bottle of scotch from the cupboard. He poured a little more than two fingers, added water, then returned to the living room.

The first sip of his drink ran the flavors of orange and cinnamon over his tongue, followed by a hint of chocolate. It was the first thing he'd had to eat or drink in a long time that had actually left him with a sense of taste. He set his glass on the side table before he threw himself onto the couch and stared at the wall where the second portrait of the countess was hung.

Normally it hung in his bedroom, away from prying eyes. But he'd moved it into the living room last night. He wasn't sure why, he just needed to see it whenever he was home in the evenings. The seductive expression on his wife's face had made him the envy of every man in London. He'd rarely left her side for a moment, because she'd been like a flame every moth was drawn to.

Nick inhaled a deep breath as he realized he'd just substituted himself in place of the Earl of Guildford. He swallowed hard at the shocking revelation. Inch by inch, he was being sucked into his sister's firm belief that Victoria and the countess were the same woman. The minute he started believing he was—no, he refused to take that next step. With an exasperated grunt, he leaned forward and picked up the last journal.

I almost died three nights ago. If Nicholas hadn't reached me in time, I wouldn't be writing in my journal today. A Lord Darby came into the opera box ranting about some book he says he gave to Vickie. I don't have a clue what's in the book, but it has to be really important based on Darby's behavior. I really thought I was going to die.

I don't have any idea as to how Nicholas managed to pull me back into the box when I was halfway over the railing. He said I had another fainting spell. A doctor came, and they gave me opium to help me sleep. If I'd known it was opium, I would have refused no ifs, ands, or buts. The drug could have sent me back to my time, and I would never risk leaving here—leaving Nicholas.

Now things are even worse. I'm pregnant. I don't know what to do. I know Nicholas won't be happy, and I have no idea how to tell him. He doesn't want children. Even if he believed I was from the future, I doubt he'd believe me about the odds of our baby being okay. I don't even know if he loves me. But I do know I want this baby.

"*Christ Jesus*, I was an utter ass to make you feel so all alone."

Nick took a sip of his drink as he stared at the countess' painting and realized his thoughts had once again placed him in the earl's shoes. Suddenly, every part of him went numb, and he almost dropped his drink before he managed to set it on the side table using both of his shaking hands.

"What the fuck is wrong with you, Barrows? Nora and the Countess of Guildford aren't the ones who need a psychiatrist. You are."

In the back of his mind, Nick knew he was fooling himself. He closed his eyes and tried to clear his thoughts. It was a laughable attempt as his gaze was drawn back to the weathered journal in his lap. He opened the book and found his place again. There were numerous anecdotes about her brother-in-law, Edmund, and it was clear from Victoria's writings that she loved the man dearly despite his limited development.

Nick paused as he realized it was the second time this evening he'd attributed the journals to *his* Victoria. He was on the verge of surrendering to Nora's theories and beliefs, but he resisted and forced himself to focus on the page in front of him. The countess' writing described her life with humor and passion. Although she didn't detail her nights with the earl, she shared enough information to make Nick certain the intimacy she'd shared with her husband had been passionate and filled with love, which had enhanced her overall happiness.

> *Andrew Edmund Thornhill, the next Earl of Guildford (not for a long, long time, I pray) was born two days ago. He's beautiful and looks like Nicholas. Well, he has Nicholas's dark hair and like most parents, we both think he's beautiful. I know Nicholas is still worried, but I keep reassuring him the baby will be all right. Edmund has been strutting around like one of the peacocks on the lawn, saying his nephew was called Andrew Edmund with an emphasis on Edmund. LOL.*

Nick dropped the book into his lap for a moment, then picked it up again to stare at the letters *LOL*. Everyone used the acronym in texts, emails, and other social media. But how would the countess know to use that acronym? Not only that, but for the first time, he realized the tone of the countess' diary entries was far too casual for the time period.

Everything he'd read in the woman's journal up to the usage of the modern day term increased the inevitable conclusion he was fighting hard to dismiss. He flipped to the next page in the journal. Except for one paragraph, the rest of the pages in the book were blank. Nick frowned.

Why would she have stopped writing so abruptly? Had the countess died before she'd been able to write another entry? Nora had never said how the countess had died. He picked up his phone and saw it was one in the morning. He had no doubt his sister would bite his head off for calling her in the wee hours of the morning. With a sigh of resignation, he shook his head and decided it was time to go to bed too. Six-thirty was going to show up a lot faster than he wanted.

When he was in bed a few minutes later, he found it

almost impossible to sleep. Staring up at the ceiling, his mind kept returning to Victoria's journals. A tidal wave of confusion crashed over him.

"*Bloody hell*, I must be insane to think any of this is real," he muttered into the dark. "People do *not* travel through time."

Maybe not, but what about past lives? Wouldn't that explain his feelings for Victoria after having just met her? Nick turned over and punched his pillow hard several times with an explosive frustration. A moment later, he dropped his head onto the soft head rest. Sleep was the best antidote for all this mental chaos.

Nick found himself walking along a dark corridor dimly lit by one or two torches. There was something odd about his clothing, and the pistol he carried felt strange in his hand. Livid with anger, he wanted to kill the two men walking in front of him. As they reached the end of the corridor, Nick saw an indistinct figure take charge of the two men, which allowed him to open a heavy cell door.

The interior of the cell was dark, and his anger grew. If they'd harmed one hair on her head, he'd kill them. He called to her in a soft voice. Then she was in his arms, her soft body trembling against his. Time shifted, and Nick felt his body flying forward. Danger stood right in front of him, although he couldn't see what it was. Then he heard the cry of warning.

A flash of light exploded in front of him, and he caught her in his arms, relieved she was unharmed. A moment later a terrible howl ripped through the fabric of his dream and Nick shot upright in bed. Sweat ran in rivulets down his back, and he snatched up his cellular phone. His frantic fingers punched the number to the nurse's station on Victoria's floor.

"Four East," a woman answered softly.

"This is Nick Barrows. I'm just calling to see if there's been any change in Victoria Ashton's condition."

"I was just in her room a few minutes ago to take her vitals, Mr. Barrows. Nurse Willoughby said Miss Ashton has had no episodes and her status hasn't changed."

"Thank you," Nick muttered as he disconnected the call and collapsed back into his pillows.

Get a hold of yourself, Barrows. You're letting that journal make you believe you used to be Nicholas Thornhill. It's all power of suggestion.

"No, there's something else happening here," he said softly to himself. "Coincidence is one thing, but my feelings for Victoria Ashton are real."

Then accept the fact you were Nicholas Thornhill. Accept that you and your wife Victoria had a son named Andrew. The idea of embracing such a notion threatened to set his ordered existence in complete disarray. Ignoring his inner voice, Nick viciously punched at his pillows as he tried to fall sleep again. As he dosed off, he heard his sister's voice quietly chastising him. *Everything is a leap of faith, Nick. Everything.*

Chapter 36

August 1898

Nicholas walked up the steps of Guildford House as a sense of foreboding fell over him. He'd only been gone from Victoria and the baby for a little more than two weeks, and yet he'd never been so lonely in his entire life.

If it weren't for the fact that Reardon had suddenly surfaced last week, he would have been home by now. But it was the first time Reardon had been seen since the man had threatened Victoria in December. Even more frustrating, the man had disappeared again, and it had been five days now since the man was last seen.

He opened the front door of the townhouse and heard the wild clatter of a carriage racing wildly up the street. He glanced over his shoulder and frowned at the reckless driving of the man at the reins. About to step over the door's threshold, he halted as he heard Mickey call out to him. He instantly turned around with a sinking heart.

"It's her ladyship, my lord. Someone's kidnapped her and Master Edmund."

Mickey's words sucked the air out of Nicholas's lungs as he stared at the boy. Unable to move, his brain shut down. He shook his head slowly as he struggled to comprehend what was happening. The boy stared up at him with a look of shocked horror on his face.

"Jacobs tried to save them, but the criminals shot him."

"When did this happen?" Nicholas choked out as his brain slowly began to function again.

"They've been gone over six hours, my lord," the stable hand said in a worried voice. "Jamieson sent me to catch the first train to London to fetch you back to Brentwood Park."

Nicholas nodded, then urged the boy into the house and off to the kitchen to get something to drink. As Mickey disappeared down the hall leading to the back of the house, Nicholas tried to form a plan of action. For the first time in his life, he didn't know how. He'd always been able to act without thinking, but now his brain was paralyzed.

Someone had taken Victoria and Edmund. No, not someone, Reardon. He had no proof, only the conviction born of instinct. Fury, with the intensity of a black storm, welled up inside him. Rage was good. He could use that to keep him focused and driven until he found Victoria and his brother.

Nicholas dropped his hat and cane on the entryway table and shouted for Roberts. Out of the corner of his eye, he saw someone in the salon's doorway. He turned his head to see Eleanor at the entrance to the salon. Her connection to Reardon had been strengthened over the last few months as investigators had uncovered a larger network of anarchists with Eleanor being the primary source of financing.

The only reason Sir Kenelm hadn't ordered her arrest was because they'd failed to capture Reardon yet. Sebastian and he had determined the book Reardon believed Victoria possessed was either a listing of the man's activities or his contacts. Either way, the book was valuable, and if Reardon thought hurting Victoria would get him what he wanted, Nicholas knew the man wouldn't hesitate to do just that.

"Why are you here, my lady?" he ground out fiercely.

"Oh, please, Nicholas, do not be so cold to me," she said

in a voice that echoed with a note of hysteria.

"What do you want, Eleanor?"

"I…I am sorry, *mon cher*, I could not think of what else to do. I had to come warn you." Her rambling irritated Nicholas, and he turned his head to shout for Roberts again before turning back to the duchess who was still speaking in disjointed phrases.

"What is it you wish to warn me about, Eleanor?" he asked impatiently.

"You're in grave danger. He'll stop at nothing," the duchess whispered, a look of horror on her face. Something in the woman's voice broke through Nicholas's anger, and he frowned.

"Who will stop at nothing?"

"*Mon Dieu*," she exclaimed. "If I tell you, he'll *kill* me for betraying him like this."

Eleanor swayed in the doorway and clutched at the doorjamb to remain standing. Instinctively, he realized she was referring to Reardon.

"I'm sure whatever you tell me won't be a betrayal, Eleanor. You're obviously distraught. Perhaps a brandy will help soothe your nerves," he said as gently as he could under the circumstances. The instant he took a step toward the doorway, she waved her hands at him feverishly.

"*Non, non, Mon Dieu,* he intends to make it look like *you* killed her. He told me if I tried to stop him, he'd kill me too. I should have told you about him long ago, Nicholas." Eleanor bowed her head and sobbed. When she lifted her head again, tears were streaming down her face. "He threatened to kill me if I said anything. I thought I loved him. It's why I married him. I didn't realize who…what he was until it was too late. *Mon Dieu*, what am I going to do?"

"Eleanor, do you know where Victoria is?" he demanded as the duchess' ramblings sent fear threading its way insidiously through his veins. She ignored him, her face contorted with a wild expression as she struggled with inner demons.

"She came back from the dead, you know. Both of them were there, they said they'd buried her, but she came back. *Mon Dieu*, I thought you hated her. It made it so easy not to care that they'd killed her. He's afraid of her. He thinks she knows everything, but I don't think she does."

"Eleanor, listen to me, tell me where they've taken her?" It was as if someone was choking him and making it impossible to breathe as he tried to get Eleanor to speak rationally. Nicholas quickly closed the distance between them to grab the woman by the shoulders and shake her.

"She's a witch, Darby said. You have to drown witches."

She sounded like a woman on the verge of descending into madness. Nicholas knew he couldn't let her go there until she gave him the information he needed to find Victoria. Behind him, Roberts cleared his throat to announce his presence, but Nicholas disregarded the valet as he shook the duchess again.

"Damn it, Eleanor. Tell me where he's taken her."

"Darby said he would kill her again, but he died instead. She's a real witch. She casts spells on everyone. She's bewitched you, hasn't she, Nicholas? He said he would lock her away in a dungeon where you won't be able to find her. He said you would pay. He doesn't really want his book. He just wants to destroy you because you killed his brother. He hates you."

"What dungeon, Eleanor. Try to think."

"I loved you, but he didn't want me to have you." As her rambling continued, Nicholas walked away from Eleanor to Roberts and kept his voice low.

"Send a message to Lord Barrows and Lord Starling. I need them to meet me at the Waterloo station in..." Nicholas pulled out his pocket watch and bit back a sound of fear. There was only one train left for Guildford today. "In forty-five minutes. Lady Guildford's and Master Edmund's lives depend on it."

"Yes, my lord." Roberts nodded, then uttered a loud shout. "My lord, watch out."

Whirling about, Nicholas saw a small pistol in Eleanor's hand. Eyes filled with tears, she looked at him beseechingly.

"I can't live without you, Nicholas. You must believe. He'll kill her, but I don't care. All I've ever cared about was you. I love you, Nicholas."

"Eleanor, put the gun down," he said quietly and took a step toward her.

At the sound of his voice, her rambling came to an abrupt halt. With a sharp movement, the duchess raised the pistol to her head and pulled the trigger. As she slumped to the floor, Nicholas ran forward to kneel at her side. Her breathing labored for a second more, and he watched the light in her eyes flicker as she grew still and lifeless.

"I'm sorry, Eleanor," he murmured. Standing, he turned to his valet. "When you send for Barrows and Starling, make sure you send for the police as well. Don't touch her until the police say you may do so. Is that understood?"

Despite his obvious dismay, Roberts nodded abruptly and ran from the room. With one more glance at Eleanor's still form, Nicholas hurried upstairs to change into clothes more appropriate for riding. He had no doubt that once they reached Guildford, he'd be on horseback. In a half hour, he was pacing the floor of Waterloo station as he waited on his friends. He heard someone call his name, and he turned around to see Charles and Sebastian hurrying toward him.

"I say, Nicholas. What's all this about Victoria's life being in danger?" Charles asked as he shook Nicholas's hand.

"She and Edmund were kidnapped this afternoon," Nicholas bit out with a steely calm he was certain would fail him the moment he found Reardon anywhere near his wife and brother.

"By Reardon?" Sebastian asked in a way that told Nicholas that Anna had shared a vision with her husband. Something in his friend's eyes calmed some of his fears. The man reached out to pat his shoulder in a silent commitment of solidarity.

"Eleanor's dead." Nicholas's statement renewed the shocked expressions of his friends.

"What?" Sebastian exclaimed.

"Good God," Charles said in astonishment.

"She came to Guildford House just before I sent word for the two of you to meet me here. She was confused and disoriented," he said as he recalled Eleanor's wild ramblings. "I tried to calm her, but she was delusional. Before I could stop her, she put a pistol to her head and pulled the trigger."

"My God," Sebastian shook his head in disbelief.

"Sweet Jesus," Charles whispered in horror.

As his friends took in his news, Nicholas frowned as a vague memory flitted through his head. Bowing his head, he studied the train station floor as he tried to remember something important. He knew it had to do with Eleanor, but if he couldn't—suddenly the memory popped into his head. He quickly turned to Charles.

"Charles, do you remember telling me shortly after Darby died that if the man had survived you would have locked him up in his dungeon?"

"Yes," Charles said with a nod of agreement. "I was referring to the dungeon Darby said was in the priory on his family's estate."

"Eleanor said Reardon would lock Victoria in a dungeon where I'd never find her," Nicholas snarled with fury and fear. "She said the bastard intends to kill Victoria because I failed to save his brother from the Lydney Mill fire shortly after I inherited my title."

"*Bloody hell.* Darby's family estate is just south of Brentwood Park," Charles exclaimed. "It's only about two hours by horse, three at the most. It's near Godalming. I think that's the stop just after Guildford station."

"Sebastian, there's a five o'clock train to Guildford, see if it goes on to Godalming. I'll send a telegram to the house telling them to have horses waiting for us there."

As his friends ran off to buy their tickets, Nicholas raced toward the telegraph office. Ever since Mickey had told him Victoria was missing, he'd been convinced he would reach her in time. Now he wasn't so certain. Deep inside, something told him that things were far worse than he imagined.

Chapter 37

The entire train ride to Godalming, Nicholas paced the corridor outside the closed carriage compartment Sebastian had secured for them. His leg was growing increasingly painful, but he ignored it.

Victoria was worth any pain he endured. They were halfway through their trip when Sebastian had insisted he sit down. He'd done as his friend had said, but returned to prowling the corridor a short time later.

Nicholas came to an abrupt halt and braced his hands on the edge of the window which had been opened to help cool the train's interior. As the hot summer wind blew across his face, he could have sworn he heard Victoria calling for him. He knew it was impossible, and he released a harsh breath.

"I'm coming, sweet witch. I'm coming as fast as I can," he whispered. Behind him, the compartment door rattled open, then closed, but he didn't turn around.

"Nicholas, we're going to find them," Sebastian said in a steady voice. "Anna made me promise to not to tell you this, but she's not here to see how worried you are. She firmly believes you'll find Victoria and Edmund, and that Reardon will die tonight."

"That's because I'm going to kill him," Nicholas said with an icy calm that surprised him. Despite his steady outward appearance, his fear was almost paralyzing. He stared out into the dark and shook his head.

"I was a fool. I should never have left her until Reardon was caught," he said through clenched teeth.

"You aren't a fool," Sebastian said quietly. "There was no way you could have foreseen this."

"I should have insisted that two armed men escort her whenever she went out."

"*Damn it, Nicholas*, it's not your fault."

Nicholas shot a quick glance at his friend, then looked out into the night and suddenly realized with a sense of relief that the train was slowing down. Charles emerged from their berth and cleared his throat.

"This is Godalming station," Charles said awkwardly as if realizing it was an obvious observation. Nicholas nodded.

"I wired my estate manager to have three horses waiting for us and for him to bring men with him. I've no idea what we're up against."

As they stepped off the train, Nicholas saw Elrod waiting for them. The estate manager pushed his way past disembarking passengers to reach them, his expression grim.

"My lord," he said quietly as he nodded. "Lady Guildford and Master Edmund were taken at approximately eleven-thirty this morning, while they were on a picnic near the Goodmans' cottage."

"Eleven-thirty," Nicholas snarled as for the first time he realized they'd sent Mickey and not a telegram to tell him what had happened. "Why the hell didn't you send a telegram?"

"The line was down until almost five o'clock this afternoon, my lord. When we received your telegram, I knew Mickey had reached you." Elrod explained. Nicholas glanced at Sebastian and saw his friend was considering the same question he was. Had Reardon cut the lines?

"What about Jacobs? What did he tell you?"

"He's badly wounded, my lord, but Dr. Bertram says he'll live. Jacobs said the countess and your brother were abducted by two men in a small carriage with closed windows." Elrod released a noise of disgust, his face taut with tension. "It's a vague description, but the men have been searching the countryside since we found Jacobs. We received a small amount of news about an hour ago."

"What sort of news," Nicholas bit out.

"A farmer near Loxhill saw a coach similar to Jacobs' description pass by early this afternoon." Elrod's head bobbed slightly in a sign of satisfaction. "It was headed toward Duns Copse, which is in the direction of the Darby estate you mentioned in your telegram."

His jaw tight with tension, Nicholas nodded his understanding of all the details. He no longer had any doubt that Reardon was responsible for Victoria's and Edmund's abduction. There was no heir to Darby's title, and Reardon was clearly using the priory for his own ends.

"Elrod, find the local constable, I think it's Maylock who's responsible for this county," Nicholas said firmly. "Make sure he brings whatever officers he has available. I have no idea how many men Reardon has with him, but the man is dangerous, and I'll feel more comfortable with too many men than not enough."

"I'll see to it, my lord," the estate manager gestured toward the station. "The horses and men are waiting for you outside the station."

"Good. And bring a doctor with you. I don't expect trouble, but I'd prefer to be prepared." Nicholas's gut twisted at the thought that it might be Victoria or Edmund who would need a doctor's care. "Charles, Sebastian, the two of you are with me."

Without waiting to see that his orders were obeyed, Nicholas headed through the station and out to where the horses were. He took Zeus' reins from one of the stable hands and stroked the stallion's cheek.

"She needs us, old man," he whispered. "You need to run like your namesake himself tonight."

Almost as if the stallion understood, Zeus bobbed his head. Ignoring the pain in his leg, Nicholas swung himself up into the saddle and turned in his seat.

"Who knows where the Darby Priory is?"

"I do, my lord," a young man called Albert Tanning called out.

"Then lead the way, Tanning," he snapped. "And ride as if your life depended on it, because the lives of the countess and my brother do."

Throughout the ride to the Priory, Nicholas relived the past months with Victoria. He recalled her laugh, the way her sapphire eyes flashed when she thought he was ordering her about, and the sweetness of her skin against his when they made love. In the months since her return, Victoria had shown him what heaven looked like. Her strength, beauty, and character had proven to him that love could overcome any obstacle. Now he could only hope they reached her and Edmund before Reardon did the unthinkable.

A little more than an hour later, they rode into the small hamlet of Duns Copse. The clattering of the horses' hooves sounded like gunfire on the cobblestones, while the moon was halfway up to its full ascent.

"The priory is only a couple of miles from here, my lord," Tanning said quietly as the stable hand pulled up alongside of him. Nicholas nodded and urged Zeus to follow the man. A short time later, the trees suddenly broke apart, and the priory appeared before them. Shaped like an ancient fortress, the stone building's dark, sinister form was illuminated by the full moon.

"It's going to be difficult to hide our approach," Sebastian said ruefully as he jerked his head toward the moon glowing brightly in the sky. "I suggest we use the cover of the trees along the roadway to hide ourselves."

"Agreed," Charles said softly. With a nod, Nicholas turned in his saddle.

"Tanning, take two men and ride on the opposite side of the road," Nicholas said as his gaze swung to the dense woods bordering the priory's drive. "The rest of us will ride on this side. When we reach the priory, you're to stay and watch the perimeter to ensure no one escapes. Understood?"

Tanning silently acknowledged the order, then quickly selected two men and crossed the road and headed toward the priory. The remainder of the small party followed Nicholas and his friends as they rode forward. As they drew closer to the priory, Nicholas's gaze swept over the building. It was in need of extensive repairs. One turret had buckled inward, and the moonlight highlighted places where the foundation was crumbling. Nicholas's skin grew cold at knowing Victoria and Edmund were in a place capable of collapsing at any moment.

At the tree line, Nicholas instructed one of the men to remain with the horses. The remaining men he ordered to skirt the tree line and subdue anyone who emerged from the priory exits. With his friends following him toward the darkened building, Nicholas headed toward the only window that was illuminated. Their stealthy movements were deadened by the thick grass and weeds surrounding the priory, and Nicholas sprinted through a stream of moonlight to reach the wall of the structure. His back to the building wall, he took a brief look through the window.

The room appeared to be the kitchen, and one man lay asleep on the floor. A younger man sat in front of the room's large fireplace, watching the flames of a small blaze. Nicholas quickly pulled away from the window and waved his friends back. When they were safely out of earshot, they quietly developed a plan of action. Seconds later they rounded the corner of the priory and took up positions on either side of the door leading into the kitchen. As they cocked their pistols, Nicholas held his fingers up and counted to three, then crashed through the door. Surprised by the sudden assault, the man on duty stared at them with his mouth hanging open. His partner, obviously well versed in criminal activity, sat up with a pistol in his hand. Fury blinding him to any danger, Nicholas leaped forward to press his weapon against the man's forehead.

"Hand it over or I'll blow you straight to hell."

The quiet menace of Nicholas's voice punctured the older man's bravado, and he handed over the weapon with a surly expression. With a sharp thrust of his weapon, Nicholas ordered both men to sit together.

"Where are they?" Nicholas demanded coldly.

"Who do you mean, guv? We're just trying to catch a wink or two afore we head off to London. We didn't think anyone would mind us taking a few winks in this crumbling down old place." The older of the two men gave a nonchalant shrug.

Although the older man wasn't intimidated by his anger, the younger man squirmed. Turning his head, Nicholas pinned his icy gaze on the man closest to the fire.

"I'm a very dangerous man at the moment, and if you want to see tomorrow, you'll tell me where my wife and brother are."

"They made me do it, guv." His hands shaking, the younger man sobbed. "Me ma needed the money for the little ones. I thought this was an 'onest job, I didn't think they'd 'urt 'em none."

"*Silas, ye fucking ass.*" The older man glared at his partner.

"Where?" The single word question roared through the room, silencing the older man.

"They're in a cell in the dungeon." Dazed by the fury in Nicholas's voice, the young man's trembling hand pointed toward a wooden door. With a gesture upward of his pistol, he ordered the two men to their feet.

"The keys," he demanded.

"Downstairs near the cell." Something about the way the younger man looked at his companion made Nicholas wonder whether the man was lying.

"If you're lying to me, I won't have a second thought when it comes to shooting either of you dead where you stand." The quiet fury in his voice made the younger man pale further, while the older man had become distinctly uncomfortable.

"I'm telling you the truth, my lord."

"You'd better be. Now take me to my wife and brother. And if anything has happened to them, you'll suffer the consequences," Nicholas said menacingly. "Charles, stay here to ensure no one else gets through that door. Sebastian, I'll need you to watch these two while I release Victoria and Edmund."

Taking a lantern off its hook near the wooden door, Nicholas ordered the two criminals to lead the way. Eerie shadows from the lantern danced across the walls as he followed the kidnappers down the darkened corridors. Sebastian drew up the rear with a second lantern as they moved deeper into the Priory and descended the stairwell into the dungeon.

The rancid, dank air made Nicholas cough, and his fury became a blind rage at the knowledge that Victoria and his brother had been subjected to this hellhole. The moment the older criminal slowed his pace in an obvious attempt to stall, Nicholas jabbed the man's shoulder with his pistol.

"Unless you want a bullet in the back of your head, I suggest you keep moving."

The kidnapper glanced back at him, a cold look in his eyes, but he obeyed the command. At the foot of the long, brick stairwell, a dark corridor ran at a forty-five degree angle downward. Light flickered at the bottom of the corridor from torches, and the young man spoke up.

"They're in a cell at the end of the corridor. The keys are here."

Nicholas snatched the large ring of keys off the wall to

his left before giving the men a push forward with the barrel of his pistol.

"Keep going," he growled.

The intensity of his wrath strengthened as the fetid smell of the dungeon grew stronger and assaulted his nostrils, and he gritted his teeth against the urge to kill the two men in front of him. When they reached the last cell in the corridor, Sebastian stood guard over the two kidnappers as Nicholas unlocked the cell door.

Throwing the bolt back, he threw the door open, enraged by the thought of what his wife and brother had endured in this place. Nicholas heard a muffled scream the moment the door opened with a loud screech of protest, and his nose rebelled at the odor emanating from the cell. Lifting his lantern high above his head, Nicholas saw Victoria huddled against the wall, bravely trying to cover Edmund's body with her own. It took every ounce of control he possessed not to turn around and shoot dead the men behind him.

"Victoria. Edmund," he called out softly as he stepped into the cell.

"Nicholas. Oh thank God, Nicholas."

The sob of joy in her voice made his heart swell with a fierce relief. Victoria scrambled to her feet and raced forward to throw herself into his arms. He caught her soft form in his embrace and shuddered with the release of the emotions of fear and horror that had held him in their grip since the moment he'd heard she was missing. Unable to let her go, he held her tightly for a long moment, as he thanked God she was still alive.

Still holding her close, Nicholas lifted his head to look at his brother who stood at their side. His hand reaching out, he grasped Edmund by the neck and pulled him into a quick embrace. Nicholas felt his brother trembling, and he patted him on the back in a comforting gesture.

"It's all right, Edmund. It's over. We're going home. All

of us." He pushed Victoria away from him slightly. "Are you hurt? Either of you?"

"No," she said with a shake of her head. "Just scared. But Edmund was very brave. You should be very proud of him."

Nicholas squeezed his brother's shoulder and winced at the terror darkening his brother's eyes. Edmund, his cheeks glistening with tears, flinched at a scraping sound close by. A raw fury filled Nicholas as he saw a rat scurry through the light of his lantern and back into the darkness. Pulling Victoria and Edmund out into the dimly lit corridor, he glared at the kidnappers, then nodded toward the cell.

"Get in there." The cold command caused a look of terror to settle on the older man's face. No longer showing any bravado, the kidnapper raised his hands in protest.

"Now, guv, we were just doing what Reardon paid us to do. We don't care none about his politics. We wouldn't 'ave 'armed the lady or gent—"

"Get in there before I shoot you where you stand, you bastard." Ice could not have been colder than Nicholas's voice, and the two men shuffled forward. The young man entered without any protest, but the older man hesitated in the cell doorway and looked at Nicholas in panic.

"Please guv, I don't like dark places none."

Without warning, Edmund launched himself forward and shoved the man into the cell, as rage and hatred crossed his normally gentle features. The man shouted for mercy, but Nicholas ignored his pleas and slammed the door shut.

Throwing the bolt back into place, he locked the door, then tossed the keys on the floor nearby. Sebastian immediately set off back the way they came, pulling Edmund along with him. Nicholas quickly examined Victoria's physical condition in the light, and she smiled bravely.

"I'm fine. Edmund is the one to worry about. He's going to have nightmares for weeks to come. He was terrified," she whispered as a tear slid down her cheek. Despite her courageous attempt to make light of her own fear, Nicholas knew Edmund wasn't the only one who'd been traumatized by their experience.

That they could deal with as long as she'd not been hurt or violated in any way. The thought sent ice crashing through his veins at the thought of another man touching her. His grasp rough, he raised her face to his and captured her mouth in a hard kiss. The salty taste of her tears mingled with the sweet taste of her lips, and Nicholas trembled to think he might have lost her.

"Come. Reardon is apt to arrive any minute, and I want the two of you out of harm's way before anything happens," Nicholas said urgently.

"For once, I'm more than willing to do exactly as I'm told." Victoria squeezed his hand and sent him a brilliant smile.

Nicholas gave her another hard kiss before leading her away from her prison cell. It took them very little time to move back up the corridor with Sebastian lighting the way. They hastened up the dark stairwell, and the small party emerged into the kitchen. The fire and lantern light made the room brighter than the darkness they'd emerged from, and Nicholas saw Sebastian stumble over something on his way toward the closed door. A warning went off in his brain as he stared at the door. He was certain they'd left it open. Where was Charles?

"*Fuck,*" Sebastian rasped as he knelt beside the body he'd tripped over.

"Is he—" Nicholas never got to finish his question as the quiet click of a cocked pistol behind him brought him to an abrupt halt.

"He's still alive, if that's what you're asking, Guildford." Reardon's words slithered through the air, and Nicholas looked over his shoulder to find himself staring into the barrels of two pistols. "Now place your weapons on the table, gentlemen.”

Nicholas gently pushed Victoria to one side, then hesitated. Reardon immediately pointed pistol in her direction, and Nicholas's heart slammed into his chest with a fear he'd never known before.

“Don't question my resolve, Guildford,” Reardon said softly, a malicious expression on his features as he nodded toward the table. “Over there, if you please, then kindly step back. We don't want any accidents.”

Slowly, Nicholas laid his pistol on the table Reardon had pointed to. Sebastian obeyed the command as well, but Nicholas knew his friend was waiting for the right moment to attack. With the weapons out of his and Sebastian's reach, Reardon motioned both men to stand in a spot even further away from their weapons.

“I've waited a long time for this. If your…wife had handed over my book, I imagine my wait would have ended sooner, so I intend to savor this moment.”

“Murder will earn you the hangman's noose, Reardon,” Sebastian growled.

“Tch, tch, tch.” The other man shook his head, his mouth curved in a cruel smile. “Murder, Lord Starling? I don't intend to murder anyone. Guildford, however, will stand trial for murdering his wife and his best friend who have been in a liaison for months now.”

“Won't that be rather difficult to prove?” Nicholas folded his arms in a nonchalant gesture as he struggled to keep his features unreadable.

“Not at all. Surely you know by now that Darby and your countess were lovers. It wasn't a secret, so a new lover and the triangle it creates will simply be food for the gossip mill.”

“I'm well aware of my wife's past transgressions. I've forgiven her, but what about Charles and men outside? Surely, you can't expect to get away with murder without being caught.” Nicholas's bored drawl made the other man's thin mouth curl in a smile.

"There's a secret passage out of the priory that bypasses your men. It will be as if I was never here."

"It appears you've thought of everything, but the question remains. Why are you so obsessed with my wife's behavior?"

"Because the bitch tried to betray me until she had an…accidental fall."

"I'd advise you not to insult my wife again, Reardon. As for her fall, I can assume it explains why she returned with a head injury?"

"The real countess is dead, Guildford. I was forced to bury the woman alive."

The cruel satisfaction in Reardon's voice made Nicholas stiffen with horror. He glanced at Victoria and flinched at the white sheen of her cheeks. He turned his gaze back to his enemy.

"And it's obvious Victoria clawed her way out of the grave," he said quietly as deep inside he processed the possibility that Victoria had been telling the truth all along. It didn't make a bit of sense, but all he knew was that she was here with him, and he wasn't about to let anyone harm her.

"I think it's more likely that you replaced the countess with an imposter. How else can you explain this woman's presence here?" Reardon nodded his head in Victoria's direction. "The pleasurable part of this puzzle is that I'll enjoy seeing her die, because I think this woman means far more to you than the countess ever did."

"You're beginning to bore me, Reardon." Despite the icy fear stiffening his muscles, Nicholas slowly clasped his hands behind his back as arched his eyebrow at the man as if he had nothing to fear. "We sent for the constable before we left. The man will arrive shortly, so why don't you just give up the game. Things will go much easier for you if you do so."

"Quite resourceful aren't you, Guildford." Reardon

expelled a bitter laugh. "It will do you little good. I'll be long gone by then, but not until I've had the pleasure of seeing you hold your dying wife in your arms. I hope it's as painful to watch her die as it was when I learned my brother was dead."

"For God's sake, Reardon, it was an *accident*," Sebastian said in a tight voice. "Nicholas almost died trying to save your brother."

"The mill was unsafe, and Guildford knew it," Reardon snarled as he glared at Nicholas. "Didn't you, my lord? You'd ordered changes made earlier that day."

"I had no idea things were unsafe, Reardon. My father didn't care about the safety of his workers, I do." Nicholas said quietly. "I made the changes to prevent the loss of life."

"And yet you didn't shut the mill down, did you?"

"If you think that hasn't crossed my mind many times, then you're wrong," Nicholas said quietly. "I tried to save him, Reardon. There's not a day that goes by that I'm not reminded of my failure."

"Spare me your aristocratic platitudes, Guildford. You're no better than the rest of your kind who live off the backs of the working man."

Reardon's face twisted into a mask of hatred as he leveled his pistols at Victoria. Horrified, Nicholas took a step toward her when Edmund released a cry of rage and knocked Nicholas aside as he streaked past him. With incredible speed, Reardon adjusted his aim, firing his weapon at Edmund point blank. Instinct taking over, Nicholas leapt toward his pistol on the table. His lunge caused Reardon to whirl in his direction.

"*Nicholas. No,*" Victoria screamed.

The sound of the pistol going off echoed loudly in his ears as Victoria flung herself against him and knocked him to the ground. Reardon released a roar of outrage as another shot rang out and the man's cry died away. Nicholas sat up and pulled Victoria with him. She was white as a sheet, and there was a look of shock on her face. Her fingers were digging into his shoulders as she clung tightly to him.

"Are you hurt?" she whispered. He shook his head and his hands holding her face, he glared down at her.

"What the hell were you thinking," he muttered fiercely as he kissed her forehead. "You could have been killed."

"Edmund?" she rasped as she pressed her face into his shoulder.

Nicholas looked at his brother and saw Sebastian helping Edmund to his feet. His brother's shoulder was bloody on the side, and he immediately knew it was little more than a scratch.

"He's fine. He's the hero of the hour," he reassured her with a smile as he wrapped his arms around her and held her close in an attempt to help ease her trembling. The moment his hand touched her back, she cried out sharply. His gut twisted viciously, and his mouth went dry with fear, as he realized his hand was wet. He lifted it upward to see it covered with blood. Victoria's blood.

"*Sweet Jesus*," he rasped. "Sebastian I need that doctor now."

"Nicholas?" Her voice was lethargic, and he heard shouts outside the priory as Sebastian raced out of the room. She shuddered. "What's happening?"

"You've been shot, my love, but the doctor's coming. You're going to be just fine."

He could hear the frantic note in his voice and winced as she shook her head no. From across the room, he heard Edmund sobbing Victoria's name. Desperately he tried to staunch the flow of blood spreading across her back. She looked up at him, and he quickly kissed away the tear sliding across her cheek.

"Don't cry, sweet witch. I know it hurts, but the doctor will be here soon," he said as he brushed her hair back off her face.

"There's not much time," she whispered.

"*No.*" Nicholas shook his head fiercely. "The doctor's

coming. I want you to fight, damn it. Don't you let go, Victoria."

"Reardon's book. In…fireplace. Edmund knows…where it is."

"I don't give a fuck about the damn book. Don't you dare give up, Victoria Brentwood Thornhill, Countess of Guildford." The fierce command made a small smile tip the corners of her mouth.

"Bossy as always," she rasped and the breath she drew in rattled in her chest, making his heart race with a terror he'd never experienced before.

"Stop talking and save your strength."

"I knew I wouldn't be allowed to stay. I don't belong here."

"Of course you belong here."

"Take care of…Andrew for me. I know you'll be…a good father to him."

"And you'll continue to be a wonderful mother," he said in a voice tight with fear. "I need you. Andrew and Edmund need you."

Desperation pounded its way through him as he cradled her against his chest. Her breathing became shallow, and she lifted her hand to his face.

"Andrew…my gift to you. Tell him…how much I…love him. Keep journal…about him. Place in…fireplace."

"*Enough*." Nicholas bit out, desperate to keep her with him, and refusing to accept the truth. "You'll see Andrew grow up, my love. The doctor is on his way."

"Third rose…down…left side. My…necklace…put…in…secret place. I'll…find…Andrew's journal in my time."

"*God damn it, Victoria.* Save your strength." Nicholas choked out. Where the hell was the doctor? He was going to lose her if the man didn't show up.

"I…love…you, Nicholas. No…regrets…find me…my

time."

"*Victoria. Look at me.*" Nicholas commanded with frantic desperation. "*Stay with me.*"

"So cold....peaceful."

"*God damn it, Victoria. Fight, damn you. Come back to me.*" As Victoria went limp in his arms, an agonized howl poured out of him over and over again into the dark night.

Chapter 38

Present Day

Frantic for one last look at Nicholas, Victoria struggled to focus her eyes on him. She tried to reach up to touch his mouth before the fog pulled him from her.

As she stood frozen in the silk cloud of light, Victoria heard his grief-stricken cry echoing all around her in the mist. Desperate to ease his suffering, Victoria tried to run toward Nicholas's heart wrenching howl.

With each step she took, his cry of grief grew softer and softer. Furious that she couldn't reach him, she opened her mouth and screamed. Her cries of anguish echoed like thunder in the fog as tears streamed down her cheeks. She wanted to go back. Nicholas needed her. No, she needed him. Andrew. What would he do without her? Slowly the white mist disappeared, replaced by the sensation of crisp sheets beneath her fingertips. A gentle beep sounded nearby. She choked back a muted cry of grief as she realized she'd returned to her own time period.

Sunlight brightened the closed blinds in her room, and she threw a brief glance toward the clock on the wall. Tears blurred her eyes. Why hadn't God just let her die? What purpose did it serve returning her to this place? *Oh Nicholas, I don't want to go on living without you.*

Half-crazed with sorrow, Victoria sat up in bed. The

motion sent a wave of dizziness over her, but it disappeared after a moment. *Nicholas. Andrew. Edmund.* They were gone. They'd been dead for decades. It had been a dream. No, it had been real. Nicholas had been real. Their love had been real. Tears welled up in her throat, and she closed her eyes as reality stabbed at her.

She had no way of knowing for certain that it wasn't all a dream or that she was simply crazy. She choked back a sob as she remembered Nicholas threatening to take her to the asylum. Victoria stiffened. The fireplace in her room at Brentwood Park. She'd asked Nicholas to leave her necklace for her in the hiding place Edmund had shown her. *Edmund.* Had Reardon killed him as well? She had to go to Brentwood Park to find answers to her questions. Looking down at her hand, she studied the needle inserted into the side of her wrist. Her stomach lurched as she realized she'd have to remove it. Gently she removed the tape holding the IV needle in place, then carefully pulled the blue tubing with its needle out of her hand. Blood streamed down her fingers, and her stomach flipped unpleasantly as she quickly staunched the flow with her sheet.

The intravenous machine screeched an alarm, and she winced at the loud noise. Ignoring the annoying sound, Victoria slid out of bed. Her legs wobbled beneath her, but she steadied herself against the bed until she could stand without falling. The door to her room opened, and a young nurse entered at a quick pace.

"*Good heavens*, you're awake," the nurse said in amazement as she urged Victoria back to bed. "You shouldn't be out of bed, Miss Ashton."

The nurse moved quickly pull tubing and monitoring cords from her, Victoria tried to breathe as she struggled with the grief paralyzing her. She slowly sat up as the nurse finished removing everything that had been attached to her. Immediately, the nurse forced her to lay back down.

"Please, Miss Ashton. You need to be in bed. You've been in a coma for almost two weeks. You may have residual side effects from your injury."

The concern in the nurse's voice didn't sway Victoria's determination to return to Brentwood Park. Victoria shook her head as she sat up again.

"Where are my purse and passport?"

"Your family has them." Victoria stared at the woman. What the hell was she talking about? She didn't have any family, and if she did, they wouldn't be in England.

"*Good Lord.*" The sound of a familiar voice made Victoria jerk her head toward the door.

"Anna," she breathed with a mixture of happiness, joy, and fear. "Is it really you?"

As the woman walked toward her, Victoria tried to adjust to the sight of her friend wearing trousers. With the warmhearted smile Victoria remembered well, Anna clasped Victoria's hands in hers and kissed Victoria's cheek.

"You're awake," she said with a relieved smile before she turned to the nurse. "She'll be fine with me. You should probably call Dr. Bertram."

"And Mr. Barrows?"

"I'll call him." Anna said. The nurse nodded and left the room, leaving Victoria alone with Anna.

"Dr. Bertram?" Victoria whispered.

"Yes, do you remember him?"

"He was my doctor…" She stopped as she realize she was about to have the same problem here that she had in the past. People were going to think she was insane.

"It's all right, Victoria. You remember me, don't you?" Anna smiled cheerfully. "Although I suppose the real question is how much of the past do you remember with Nicholas, Andrew, and Edmund?"

"Oh, my God," Victoria choked out as tears splashed down her cheeks. "It's true. It wasn't a dream. He was real."

"It's all right, Victoria, it's going to be all right."

"I have to go. I have to go to Brentwood Park. I have to see it. I have to know if he left journals for me as I begged him to do. It's the only way I'll know it was real." She grabbed Anna's hands and squeezed them tightly. The other woman winced. Victoria immediately released her grip and sniffed as her tears stopped. "I'm sorry. I just need to go there. If I don't, they might as well lock me up."

Grief engulfed her, and she buried her face in her hands. Nicholas was dead. She would never hear his voice or feel his touch again. She shuddered as a gentle hand touched her shoulder.

"I'll help you get to Brentwood Park." Anna's gentle words made Victoria look up at her.

"You will?" she whispered and in the same way Victoria remembered from the past, Anna shrugged nonchalantly.

"I think I always knew it would come down to this."

"Come down to what?" Victoria looked at her with a puzzled frown.

"Helping you get to Brentwood Park when you woke up. It's why I carried this with me every time I came to the hospital."

Anna reached for the purse she'd laid on the bed. A second later, she pulled out Victoria's passport and wallet. The twinkle in the woman's brown eyes made Victoria laugh.

"Why don't we get you dressed?" Anna said with a look of urgency. "I've a feeling that if we wait for Dr. Bertram, he might want to keep you here for a while."

"I don't want that," Victoria said.

"Okay," Anna said as she crossed the room and poked her head into the closet. "Here's underwear. Where do you shop, Victoria's Secret? I love this bra."

Victoria laughed at Anna's words and as the other woman's head emerged from the closet, she arched her eyebrows.

"What's so funny?"

"You," Victoria said with a grin. "You were just like this…"

"In the past?"

"Yes," Victoria said as her heart wrenched painfully in her chest..

"Well since we were friends, then that means we'll be best buddies now. Which is a good thing because I've always wanted a—never mind, we'll talk about that later. Can you get dressed without help?" Anna laid Victoria's clothes on the bed beside her.

"I think so, I'm a little wobbly, but I can manage."

"All right, I need to call my brother and let him know where I'm going."

"Going?"

"Of course, you need transportation, don't you?"

"Yes," Victoria said with a sense of relief. Anna grinned at her, then left her alone to dress.

Despite the deep vise of pain wrapped around her chest, she was grateful for Anna's presence. The woman's appearance here made her remember the friendship they'd had in the past. But everything made her feel like she was Dorothy in the Wizard of Oz, having just awoken to discover it had all been nothing more than a dream.

It was why she needed to go to Brentwood Park. She had to know for sure that it hadn't been a dream. She shrugged into her T-shirt and pulled her jeans on, then slipped her feet into her sandals. Gathering her passport and wallet, she moved toward the door. Out in the corridor, she heard Anna arguing with someone in hushed tones.

"No, because it's a lousy idea. How would you feel—" She paused as she listened to the person on the other end of the conversation, before she released an exasperated breath of air. "Seriously, you're going to pull the because-I'm-the-oldest card on me. Look, I told you where we're going. You know what to do."

Suspicion swept through Victoria as she pushed the curtain aside and met Anna's startled gaze. The guilty look on the other woman's face made Victoria flinch. Could Anna really be trusted?

"Your brother's upset?" She studied Anna's face as the guilty expression on her features became more evident.

"He wanted me to keep you here." Anna bit her lip. "Do you remember the explosion or where you were before it happened? Who you were with?"

Victoria contemplated the question for a moment. Just like in the past, she couldn't remember anything about the explosion or several days before the event. Frustrated, she shook her head.

"No. I couldn't in the past either. Every time I tried, I had these terrible headaches, and I wound up—"

"In the white mist." Anna made a small noise of understanding.

"But how do you—" Victoria stared at Anna in puzzlement as the other woman reached for her arm.

"I'll explain later. In the meantime, we need to move. I'm surprised Bertram hasn't gotten here already. The man is nothing if not punctual." Pulling Victoria behind her, Anna peeped out into the hall and looked both ways before she turned back to Victoria.

"It looks like there are only a couple of nurses at the desk, and yours is the furthest room from the station. I want you to turn left out of the room, through the double doors and stay to the left side of the hall. There's a structure beam just past the doors that will keep you hidden from the nurses station. Got it?"

"Yes, just stay on the left."

"Good girl," Anna said with an encouraging smile. "Okay go. I'll be right behind you."

Following the other woman's instructions, Victoria

walked the short few feet to the doors, then proceeded through them. By the time she reached the square column and was hidden from the nurses' station, she was feeling dizzy. She leaned against the wall, and Anna was at her side in an instant.

"Are you okay? Maybe we should stay here."

"I'm just dizzy. I guess lying still for more than a week makes it difficult to maintain one's equilibrium."

"You haven't eaten anything in all that time either, that might be part of it," Anna said as she glanced over her shoulder. "They were actually supposed to give you a feeding tube today. So if you don't feel well enough to go—"

"No," Victoria snapped. "I need to go home…at least to see it and prove to myself it was real. That I didn't imagine it."

"Oh, I'm pretty sure you didn't imagine it," Anna said with a look of absolute confidence. "Come on, we can stop and get you a sandwich on the way out of the city."

Victoria nodded, and with a smile Anna entwined her arm in Victoria's, then led her out of the hospital.

Victoria awoke with a jerk as Anna parked the car. After the sandwich and water she'd had, she'd fallen asleep fast. Groggy, she turned her head and drew in a sharp breath. She was home. Now wide awake, she quickly got out of the car. The fast movement made her dizzy, and she was forced to brace herself against the car. Anna came around the vehicle and offered Victoria her arm, but Victoria waved her help aside and headed toward the house.

She swallowed tears as she reached the front steps, half expecting Jamieson to open the door for her, stern expression and all. Victoria turned the knob and pushed the door open. As she stepped into the hallway, she looked upward. Relief swept through her as she saw the prized skylight Nicholas loved so much. She crossed the floor to stand at the entrance to the library. Most of the furniture had been changed, but the chess table still sat close to the French windows.

Grief made her muscles harden as she wrapped her arms around her waist and stood there for a long moment. The memories flooded over her, and a teardrop pushed past her closed eyelids. Victoria drank in a deep breath and saw Anna watching her with a worried look. She shook her head.

"I'm okay," she rasped as she managed to hold her grief in check.

Victoria crossed the hall to look into the salon. The room looked almost as it had when she'd lived in the house. Even her portrait hung over the mantel. As she stood in the doorway, tears prick against the back of her eyelids. God, how she wanted to go home. Home to Brentwood Park more than a hundred years ago. Her gaze fell on the portrait again, and she frowned slightly as she stared at it. There was something different about it. Victoria crossed the room to the fireplace and looked up at the painting.

It was more like a picture of the original painting that had been laid on canvas. A small placard to the right of the portrait. *Reproduction portrait of the Countess of Guildford courtesy of Nicholas Barrows.* Barrows. One of Charles' descendants. Then who had the real painting? Her heart twisted painfully in her chest, and she swallowed the knot in her throat. She moved back out into the foyer and footsteps echoed in the hall leading into the back of the house. Victoria turned her head to meet the wide-eyed look of a teenage girl.

"*Bollocks,*" the girl exclaimed with a cry of fear. "The countess…" The girl didn't finish her sentence as she sank to the floor in a dead faint. Anna raced forward to check on the girl, then looked up at Victoria.

"Go, I'll handle this."

Uncertainty swept over Victoria as she met Anna's worried gaze. Should she be here? It wasn't her home any longer. With a resolute clenching of her fist, she headed up the stairs. She had to know for sure. She needed to know if Nicholas had left the journals about Andrew for her.

At the top of the stairs, she turned the corner and leaned against the wall to rest for a moment. Below, she heard frantic voices mixed with Anna's soothing voice. Aware that she didn't have much time, she walked as quickly as she could down the hall to her bedroom. Once inside, she locked the door behind her. The delightful yellow theme she had grown to love was gone. In its place, a color scheme of whites and blues filled the room. She frowned unhappily at the change.

Across the room, she saw the connecting door to Nicholas's room. The brief surge of happiness that flooded her was quickly replaced by grief, and she swallowed the tears threatening to blur her vision. He wasn't there. A sob parted her lips, and she turned away to walk to the fireplace. For several long moments, she stared at the mantelpiece and the rose carvings that wound their way up the side panels and across the top. Fear threaded its way through her as she considered the possibility her memories were little more than vivid dreams.

Outside in the corridor she heard soft voices. Glancing at the door, she saw the latch turn as someone tested the lock. When there were no demands for her to open the door, she turned back to the fireplace. Slowly she reached out and counted the roses down the side of the mantle, just as she'd seen Edmund do. She heard a click and the door to the secret compartment popped open.

Victoria drew in a sharp breath and stared at the items resting on the narrow shelves. Stretching out her hand, she pulled out the first of several volumes stacked one on top of the other from the secret compartment. Slowly, she opened the book.

Dearest sweet witch

A sob escaped Victoria's lips as she recognized

Nicholas's strong handwriting and the special name he always addressed her by. It had been real. Nicholas had been real. Their short time together, loving one another, had not been a dream. A sob escaped her as she clutched the book close to her chest. Head bent in sorrow, she shuddered as she could almost feel her heart breaking. A soft sound made her jerk her head up as she turned toward it. Shock held her rigid. It wasn't possible.

"Nicholas," she breathed. She closed her eyes against the apparition and counted to ten, then looked back at the connecting door to their rooms. He was still there, standing in the doorway studying her intently. God, if only it were true. If only Nicholas really were here. Certain she was insane, Victoria's hand gripped the mantle tightly as her knees wobbled beneath her, while clinging tightly to the journal she held.

"Victoria." It couldn't be his voice. She shook her head to banish the thought.

"You're not real. You're a figment of my imagination. I want you to be real, but you're not."

"Please, sweet witch. Listen to me." The gentle plea washed over her like a soothing balm. It was his voice, even down to the tender nickname. Tears blurred her vision, and her voice shook with pain.

"Oh, God. I'm going insane. You even sound like him."

"Victoria, you need to listen to me."

She shuddered as the warmth of his hands pressed into her shoulders. Sweet heaven, he even felt real. She should never have come here. Victoria shook her head and closed her eyes.

"This isn't happening. You're not real," she mumbled, desperate to keep her sanity.

"It is real, my love. Here, feel my heartbeat."

A very real, firm hand placed hers against his chest so her fingers could feel the strong, steady beat of his heart. With her hand pressed against him, Victoria's legs buckled under her, and a terrible shudder ripped through her. Warmth engulfed her as he pulled her close and supported her against his tall, muscular frame. She looked up at him and trembled.

"I don't understand," she murmured in shock and disbelief.

"I'm not sure I do either." A tender, loving smile curved a familiar mouth as he sighed. "In fact, the only person who seems to have a good grasp on this whole situation is Nora."

"Nora?"

"Well, we knew her as Anna," he said. Almost as if he had difficulty believing his words, he released a reluctant sigh of exasperation. "Nora….Anna, has convinced me that I'm…that I was… Nicholas Thornhill, Earl of Guildford."

His words rang in her ears as she struggled to comprehend what was happening. He wasn't Nicholas, and yet he was. How was that possible? A flash of memory surged through her head. The image of the Goodman Cottage painting Nicholas had given her for Christmas, she'd found it in an art gallery. She looked up at Nicholas.

"The art gallery. I was with *you* in the art gallery. There was an explosion," she whispered, still feeling confused. He nodded and a slight smile tilted his mouth.

"I thought I was crazy for having this insatiable desire to kiss you."

"You didn't get to because of the explosion."

A sense of wonder swept through her as she reached up to stroke his cheek. He captured her hand and pressed his mouth to the inside of her wrist. The familiar caress sent her pulse fluttering violently beneath his lips. A familiar, green-eyed gaze studied her and happiness sped through her as she saw his love shining there.

"You're really here, aren't you? This isn't a dream."

"No, sweet witch, it's not a dream," he said gently. "I think I know, but do you want to tell me why you came back to Brentwood?"

"These," she said and retreated slightly from his embrace to show him the journal in her hand. "I came for these. You left them for me."

"They're about Andrew. Our son," he rasped as if startled by the fact that he knew what the journals were.

Victoria nodded as her gaze locked with his before she slowly opened the journal and turned the page. A folded piece of paper lay beneath the opening page. Taking care with the old parchment, she unfolded it and stared at the drawing done in a child's hand. At the bottom of the page in a childish scrawl were the words.

For my, Mama. Love, Andrew.

The words twisted her heart painfully in her chest, and tears welled up in Victoria's eyes, before she turned and pressed her face into Nicholas's shoulder to keep her tears from damaging the drawing.

"It's all right, sweet witch. It's going to be all right." At his reassuring words, she nodded and folded the paper to tuck it into the back of the journal with a loving gesture, before reading the first page of the journal out loud in a choked up voice.

My dearest love,

> *Please forgive me for not having the strength to begin this journal until after Andrew's second birthday. I almost lost my will to live in the first years after your death. The fact that both Andrew and Edmund needed me was all that kept me alive. Reardon only wounded Edmund that night in the priory, and I have been fortunate to have him with me.*
>
> *He's the consummate uncle, totally devoted to Andrew. Our son returns that adoration. You would be so proud of our son. He's an incredibly bright lad. He has all of your charm as well as your temper. I talk to him about you often, and he enjoys looking at your portrait in the library.*

Each new day in his company is a reminder of what you gave me through your love. For that, I love you all the more. Although I cannot touch you, hear your laughter, or feel your heart beating against mine as we fall asleep at night, I know you will always be with me in my heart. I shall never stop loving you, my sweet witch. I can only pray that God gives us a second chance to be together again in your future.

I know how much you wanted our son, and I hope this journal will help you know him in the future, as you never could in the past.

Always and forever, Nicholas

Victoria closed the book, her heart breaking as she read the pain in Nicholas's words. She turned into the strong arms surrounding her and clung to him. They'd found each other again. As cruel as the universe had been to them in the past, it had given them a second chance at happiness.

"There's something else in there," Nicholas said with a sense of wonder. "Something I had made for you after you were gone."

Puzzled, she looked at him for a moment. He looked thoroughly bewildered, but confident she would find something. Peering deeper into the cubbyhole, she found two soft leather pouches. The first was fairly heavy, and she undid the purse strings, then spilled the contents into her palm. The sapphire necklace sparkled in the sunlight streaming into the room.

"Don't say a word. You were worth the extravagance." Nicholas smiled as she stared at the necklace and shook her head. "It's the other pouch I'm talking about. I had it made for you as a way for you to know Andrew."

Victoria returned the sapphire necklace to its pouch and handed it to Nicholas. She pulled the second leather bag opened and dumped the contents into her hand. The gold locket glistened in the sunlight as she stared down at it. The oval locket was more than an inch in size with Nicholas's and her initials entwined on the outside. Carefully, she opened the locket and drew in a sharp breath at the images of a boy as a baby and, then a few years older.

"It opens up," Nicholas said with surprise as if amazed he knew such a detail. He stretched out his hand and popped a latch on the locket, which revealed another six portraits. "It's Andrew from the time he was a baby until he reached his twenty-first birthday."

Stunned by the thoughtful gift, Victoria stared down at the images of the son she'd never known. Her fingers ran along the edges of the locket, and the thought of giving it up made her heart break. Almost as if he knew what she was thinking, he pressed a kiss to her temple.

"I sit on the board of the Brentwood Park Foundation. I'll make a sizeable donation in exchange for the journals and the locket," he said with a confident smile. "They'll be thrilled simply that the sapphires have surfaced. Obviously I failed to tell Andrew about this hiding spot or the secret would have been passed down through the family."

"Edmund probably was reluctant to tell you as well since I told him it was a secret," she said in a wistful voice. "I miss him, already."

"I'm certain we'll see him and Andrew again." Nicholas took the locket from her trembling hands, then folded it up and returned it to the pouch. "The fact I've found you again, reassures me of that."

"I love you, Nicholas. Not even time itself can ever change that," she whispered as she pulled his head down to hers and kissed him.

It was a kiss that said her heart was his. The tender caress was a powerful statement of all the love and passion she felt for him. As their kiss deepened, it was almost too difficult to believe he was here with her. Victoria's hunger to touch all of him and reassure herself he wasn't a figment of her imagination made her press her body tightly into his. The moment her hands slid down to his waist, Nicholas put a small amount of space between them.

"Don't tempt me, sweet witch," he said with a low groan. "I don't live here anymore. Besides, I'm surprised Nora hasn't burst in here wanting to know that everything is all right."

"Later then?" she said with a teasing smile.

"Count on it. We've a lot of catching up to do," he said with a grin that was almost identical to the Earl of Guildford's, and yet distinctively belonged to the Nicholas in this time period.

With her hand clasped in his, he led her out of the room that was filled with so many memories into a future where their love would create so many more.

Epilogue

eady to go?" Nick rolled the wheelchair to a halt just inside the door of the hospital room.

"On my own power," Victoria said with a look of stubborn exasperation. "Between you and Dr. Bertram browbeating me into staying here for almost another week, I'm more than capable of leaving this hospital without using a wheelchair."

With each passing day, he was recalling bits and piece of his life as the Earl of Guildford. Most of his memories were always triggered by something Victoria said or did. Even her facial expressions could spark something in his consciousness. Now he remembered quite clearly that once Victoria made up her mind about something, there were few instances when he'd been able to change her mind. This was a battle he chose not to fight.

"As you wish," he said with a grimace of futility. Nick started to roll the chair out of the room, then stopped and slowly turned his head to look at her. There was a wistful look on her face, and as they stared at each other, he frowned.

"I offered to buy the Princess Bride for you a long time ago," he said with an unsettled feeling as a small smile touched her lips.

"Yes," she said with a nod. "I told you it hadn't been published yet."

Nick jerked his head in understanding, then stared at the

floor for a long moment. He wished he'd remembered this elusive memory earlier. He would have one upped himself by buying the book and giving it to her without her having to acknowledge that he'd offered to buy it when he'd been the Earl of Guildford. Nick frowned as the thought blindsided him. The reality of the situation was that he was competing with another man. The man he'd once been, and he wasn't sure how to deal with that.

Worst of all, he hadn't expected this inept feeling where Victoria was concerned. He'd thought when she came out of her coma everything would be as if they'd known each other for a very long time. He was still adapting to the idea that he'd lived before, but the one thing he knew without any doubt or reservation was that he loved Victoria. She meant everything to him. Another sliver of memory popped a latch in his head. He looked up to meet her gaze.

"I asked you to marry me that same night, didn't I?" he said with a wry twist of his lips.

"You seemed to think it would stop me from saying I wasn't your wife." Amusement sparkled in her eyes, brightening their blue color.

"If I recall correctly, it worked," he said with a sudden grin. The intangible memory solidified in his thoughts and became complete in his heart. It created a need to relive the happiness of that moment. He grew somber at the memory of what had been, and what he wanted now.

"Would you do it again?"

"What?" she asked with a puzzled tilt of her head.

"Marry me."

The mixed emotions crossing her face at his proposal made Nick want to bite off his tongue. Her memories of their time together in the past were fresh, more vivid than his. It put him at a significant disadvantage. She knew the man he'd been in the past. The question was whether or not she would compare the man he'd been to the man he was now. The thought made him uneasy.

Suddenly, she smiled at him. It was a soft, gentle smile of happiness and contentment. Nick recognized the look. From the moment he'd seen her standing in front of the fireplace at Brentwood Park a week ago, he'd realized it was easier not to question his feelings or the memories filling his head.

"Is that a hypothetical question?" she asked in a husky voice, then shook her head and smiled. "It doesn't matter. My answer is yes, one way or the other."

Triumph surged through him, and he stepped around the wheelchair to go to her. Slowly bending his head, he kissed her. The memory of their kiss at Brentwood Park last week hadn't been an illusion. Her lips were soft and sweet against his. Love, passion, and need renewed their assault on his senses as he pulled her tight against him. Victoria's hands pressed against his chest as she broke their kiss.

"Nicholas, what would you say if I said we should take a few days to get to know each other again?"

The request cut deep. He'd been right. She was trying to decide whether or not he was the same man she'd loved in the past, and whether she could be with the man he was now. How was he supposed to compete with a memory? Nicholas released her slowly and took a step back.

"If that's what you want," he said as he forced a smile to his lips. She frowned and eyed him with a shrewd assessment he remembered.

"What's wrong?"

"What makes you think there's something wrong?" He shrugged with a nonchalance he didn't feel.

"Because I know that look." She glared at him with suspicion.

"And what look would that be?" he bit out between clenched teeth as he remembered other arguments they'd had. She was just as exasperating now as she'd been all those years ago.

"It's the one that says you're not happy with me."

"Why would I be unhappy with you?" he said as he shoved his hand through his hair. "I can wait until you're certain of your feelings."

"My feelings?" She stepped forward to press her hands into his chest. Her sapphire gaze filled with warmth and love, she shook her head.

"This isn't about me," she shook her head. "It's about how *you* feel."

"How I feel. What the hell are you talking about?" Nick drew in a deep breath of frustration and confusion.

"I love you, Nicholas," she said in an emphatic voice as she touched his cheek. "But this idea of…it's all still new to you. I want you to be sure of what you're feeling."

"I am sure," he said with a firmness that surprised him. A pensive look darkened her features as she shook her head.

"No, I don't think you are. Nora's told me how difficult all of this has been for you," she said as her fingers caressed his cheek. "I just want you to understand and believe that the man I fell in love with in the past is the same man standing in front of me now."

"I won't deny that it's been rough coming to grips with something I've never believed in until now."

"Which is why I want us to take a little time, even if it's only a couple of days." When he tried to object, she pressed her forefinger against his lips. "I just want you to understand that I love the man you were. And even though I know nothing about your life now, I love the man you are today. I want you to be as sure of me as I am of you."

"I *am* sure of you," he growled with frustration. "I've never been so sure of anything in my life, but if you think a couple of days will make me feel even more convinced of how much I love you, then fine."

"Thank you," she said with a laugh.

"You still have me wrapped around your finger. You know that, don't you?" he grumbled, annoyed that she could manipulate him as easily today as she had in the past. She laughed.

"Come on, I want to see more of the city, and I can't imagine having a better tour guide," she said as she pick up her purse and slung it over her shoulder. "Although I do need to make arrangements for a hotel."

"There's no need for a hotel. Nora offered to put you up until you figure out what you want to do." He drew in a deep breath. "And there's always my place. I have a spare bedroom."

"I'd like that," she said huskily as she kissed him on the cheek. "We had separate bedrooms at Brentwood Park."

"I think we had mergers on numerous occasions in one or the other on a regular basis," he muttered as he turned away to roll the wheelchair out into the hall where he left it against the wall.

He winced as he heard Victoria's laugh follow him out the door. He'd not meant for her to overhear his remark. Nick returned to the room and grabbed the handle of her wheeled suitcase. With a sweep of his hand, he waited for her to walk out of the room ahead of him. The amused smile curving her lips had him teetering on the edge of irritation and laughter. He opted for laughter. As they headed down the hall toward the lift, Nick took her hand in his as he'd done a hundred times before.

Laughter bubbled out of Victoria as he ushered her into his townhouse. For the past four days, Nick had taken her sight-seeing to several out of the way places in the city. Tonight they'd gone to see a play at the Lyttelton Theater, and had argued passionately, yet lovingly, the entire way home as to the validity of themes in Shaw's work. The door closed behind them, Nick nodded toward the kitchen.

"I chilled some wine. Would you like a glass?"

"That would be nice," she said with a smile as she moved into the living room.

"That day in the salon with Mr. Lockwood, I almost refused to do this second portrait. I was furious with you," Victoria called out, her voice carrying into the kitchen as Nick removed the cork from a bottle of wine. He dropped the corkscrew with the plug still on it onto the counter. Wine bottle and glasses in hand, he walked into the living room. Victoria looked at him over her shoulder and smiled. Arching an eyebrow at her, Nick grinned as he set the wine and glasses on the coffee table.

"And I recall being sincerely repentant. Besides, I'm certain I would have found a way to make you do my bidding if you'd protested." He came up behind her to wrap his arms around her waist and pull her backward into his chest. Victoria looked up at him.

"Oh, I'm *sure* you would have," she said with a laugh. "I'm glad you have it though."

"I wasn't about to sell it any more than I would the formal portrait."

"The plaque at Brentwood Park said you donated the reproduction of the formal portrait," she said with a curious frown. "Where's the original?"

"In my office at the gallery," he replied. "My uncle bought it for me when I was a teenager. I couldn't take my eyes off it."

"And yet you refuse to believe it meant something?"

"Why do I think that between you and Nora, it's going to be a long time before either of you stops pointing out my stubbornness?" he groaned, yet unable to hide a grin.

"At least you've improved with age," Victoria teased him

with a laugh. "A long time ago you refused to believe I was from the future."

"And yet I became a believer once you were gone," he said with a quiet remorse for having doubted her.

"Do you remember much of the past?" she asked softly as she continued to stare up at the portrait.

"Some. Things you do or say bring back memories," he said as he rested his chin on the top of her head. "It's all bits and pieces of images jumbled together."

Victoria lifted the gold locket she was wearing and opened it. Her fingers traced the gold edges surrounding the portrait of Andrew. There was a wistful, poignant manner in the way she stroked the edge of the jewelry he'd had made for her when he was the Earl of Guildford.

"He was a beautiful little boy, wasn't he?"

"Yes, and incredibly bright." Nicholas shook his head in baffled amazement at the conviction he heard in his voice.

"You say that as if you've already read the journals." Victoria shot him a glance.

"Well, I *did* write them," he teased.

"Then read some of it to me."

Victoria twisted out of his arms and selected a volume from several on the coffee table. She flipped it open, turned to a random page, and handed him the book. As he sat down on the couch, Victoria poured them both a glass of wine. Nick took a drink of the merlot, then set his drink on the end table as Victoria curled up beside him with her wine glass in hand.

> *Andrew jumped into the pond today when my back was turned. Edmund sounded the alarm, but by the time I reached the water's edge, Edmund had already pulled our son out of the pond. Your brother-in-law was extremely put out with Andrew. Even though I know you would have been angry at our boy's foolhardy behavior, I am convinced you would have found it difficult not to laugh at Andrew's reply to Edmond's chastisement.*

"I am seven years old, uncle Edmund. There comes a time when you must accept that I am almost a man."

Victoria laughed out loud and Nick looked down at her. His heart swelled at how much he loved her when he considered the incredible circumstances that had brought them together. With a tender kiss to her brow, he continued reading.

I found myself having to turn away in order not to laugh at Edmund's flummoxed expression or Andrew's obvious frustration. I have no doubt you would've found it difficult to maintain a straight face as well, my love. It is moments like these when I miss you the most, sweet witch. I know how much joy you would have found in Andrew's determination to declare his independence.

He has inherited my commanding nature, or rather bossiness, for which you had always berated me. He demonstrates that trait far too well, much to the dislike of one Miss Jane Reddington. You remember I mentioned earlier that Sebastian and Anna lost their first child, a boy, but their younger children, Jane and William, have eased some of the sorrow my friends experienced. They visit Brentwood Park often, and while Jane manages to put Andrew in his place, she is still devoted to him.

Sebastian and I have speculated as to their future, but Anna has severely reprimanded us both for doing so. I shall close for now, my darling, sweet witch. I miss you lying in my arms when I go to sleep each night. If I could have just one more day with you, I would express all the regrets I have, and tell you over and over again how much better my life is for having loved you.

Forever yours, Nicholas

Nick's voice trailed off into silence as he stared down at the diary entry that an expert would say had been written by his own hand, not that of a man who lived decades ago.

Victoria's hand reached out to touch the back of his.

"Do you remember any of this?" There was a note of pain in her voice.

"Some of it," Nick said quietly as he lifted her hand up to kiss her fingertips. "Mostly it's the emotions. They're the most powerful. Things like the sorrow Anna and Sebastian experienced when they lost their boy, Sebastian. Their pain was similar to the agony I experienced when…"

Unable to put into words what he was experiencing, he closed his eyes at the unexpected agony flooding through him. He wrapped his arm around Victoria and held her close. She was here, with him, and all was well. The sorrow was in the past.

"I know what Sebastian and Anna must have felt. All I could think about when I woke up was you and Andrew. I knew I would never see him grow up, and it devastated me as much as losing you, but in a different way," she rasped before bowing her head.

The moment teardrops splashed on his hand, he pulled her tight, and she sobbed into his shoulder. He was helpless to do anything but stroke her hair. Slowly, she cried herself into silence, and he simply held her without speaking. She'd lost so much when she'd woken up in that hospital bed. He knew she'd been grieving in silence for the past few days. Despite the happiness they had found in their reunion, he knew Andrew had been on her mind. Nick pressed a kiss against her temple.

"It will be all right, my love. Andrew had a good life. He was happy."

"I know the journals will tell me that, I missed so much," she said forlornly.

"You gave me a precious gift, Victoria. Our son was my connection to you through the years. He helped me get through the rough times."

"Listening to you read from the journal, I can hear how

much you missed me," she whispered. Nick nodded.

"If not for Andrew and Edmund, I'm not sure what I would have done. Those first two years were the bleakest of my existence. But Edmund refused to let me wallow in my grief. He was quite persistent in his nagging, despite my snarling."

Nick shook his head and released a barely audible sound of astonishment as the memory of a moment with his brother pushed its way up into his consciousness. Being with Victoria was like opening a floodgate of memories buried deep inside him. Some were as clear as if he'd just experienced them yesterday. Others were more vague and elusive. She laced her fingers in with his and looked up at him.

"What happened to Anna's and Sebastian's son?" she asked.

"He came down with the flu, which developed into pneumonia. Anna and Sebastian were grief stricken. Sebastian took it the hardest. I'm certain Anna's beliefs allowed her to accept young Sebastian's death more easily."

"I can't tell you how little she's changed," Victoria said with a note of amazement in her voice. "She was there for me when I desperately needed a friend in the past and when I woke up at the hospital. I was in so much pain. All I could think about was you and Andrew. I thought I'd dreamed it all. But the worst part was believing I'd lost you forever."

"I wanted to be there when you awoke, but I know now how difficult that would have been for you," Nick said in a reflective manner. "I'm simply grateful you woke up."

"And now? How do you feel now?"

"If you're asking me if I love you, then the answer is yes," he said in a quiet, confident voice.

"But do you believe that when I look at you, I see you as the same man? The past and the present are the same. You're not competing with the man I fell in love with. I'd love you no matter what time or place we were in," she said in a cautious tone of voice, her look wary as she studied him intently.

"How the hell do you know I've been worried about that?" At his question, she arched her eyebrows and rolled her eyes.

"I love you. I know how you worry about the things you think are important, but really aren't." Victoria leaned into him and kissed him tenderly, and he could feel the deep love in her kiss. She pulled back slightly. "The bond we forged in the past hasn't changed. We're both still the same people. The differences between you, then and now, are so insignificant that I barely notice them."

"Will it make you happy if I tell you that these past few days have made me understand that?" he said with a chuckle. "But the one thing I've never doubted is that I love you. I've felt that way since the day I saw you in the shop, even if I didn't understand it."

Nick tugged her into his lap and kissed her hard. He needed to taste her and feel the passion he'd experienced in the past. He wanted to feel her bare skin against his as he made love to her. Nick's hand slid up to cup one breast as his mouth slid down the side of her neck to nibble at her soft skin. She drew back from him with a small laugh.

"I want to put something comfy on. I'll be right back." Victoria finished the last sip of her wine, then set her glass on the table. His heart crashed into his chest. She wanted him. He was certain of it.

"Shall I join you?" he murmured as he trailed his finger down across her neck to the hollow of her throat.

"Maybe—I need to think about it." The enticing smile on her lips made his cock harden in his trousers.

He growled with frustration at her teasing manner, but remained quiet as to how much he wanted to feel her body under his. A distinct memory of making love to her in another life made his body tighten. The image of Victoria reclining on a large bed with a seductive smile on her face emphasized how long it had been since they'd shared the same bed. Nick released another sound of annoyance, but reminded himself that he'd waited more than a hundred years to be with her again. He could be patient a little longer.

"I'll get another bottle of wine."

"Are you trying to get me tipsy, Mr. Barrows?" she said with a laugh as she stood up to make her way out of the living room.

"Would you let me?" he said with a grin as she looked down at him.

"I might. I'll let you know when I come back."

Nick went to the kitchen and pulled out another bottle of wine and uncorked it. He returned to the living room and set the merlot on the coffee table. Moving toward Victoria's portrait, he stared up at the mischievous and seductive look on her face. A faint glimmer of a memory swept through him as he stared at the painting. He'd not been happy with the artist, but he couldn't remember why.

"Nicholas."

The soft, sultry sound of her voice wrapped around him like a sensuous, invisible cord that bound them together. He loved the way her voice hitched slightly when she called him by his full name. There was something intimate about it that no one else would hear. It was a sound for them alone. Nick slowly turned around, and the air left his lungs at the sight of her. With nothing but a sheet wrapped around her, Victoria sat on the arm of the couch, her expression as seductive as the one in the portrait on the wall. Nick dragged in a deep breath.

"Sweet Jesus," he rasped. "You know how to catch a man's attention."

"I take it you don't disapprove."

"No, but I'd better be the only man you ever pose for like this," he growled as he closed the distance between them. Slowly, he traced the line of her shoulder with his fingers. Her skin was smooth as silk.

"You're the only man I want, Nicholas," she whispered as she let the sheet slip from her fingers to expose her beautiful breasts. "I love you. I need to show you how much I love you."

Nick groaned, then tugged her into his arms and crushed her lips beneath his in a deep kiss. A second later, he yanked the sheet completely off her, slipped his arm under her legs, and lifted her up to carry her into his bedroom. A soft sigh escaped her as he laid her on his bed, and she watched him undress.

He was already hard with need, but the hunger in her sapphire eyes made his cock tighten until it ached for a release only she could satisfy. When he was naked, she came up on her knees to press her palm against his chest before her fingers slowly trailed a path downward to take him in hand.

"You're just as beautiful now as you were then," she said in a husky voice that made him bend his head and kiss her deeply.

Her arms wrapped around his neck, and she pulled him down with her as she fell back onto the mattress. The memory of her scent teased his senses, and he breathed in the sweet fragrance of her. His mouth left hers to caress her jaw line down to the curve of her neck. A soft mewl escaped her as he lightly nipped at her shoulder, then worked his way down to the lush curve of her breast.

Nick took his time exploring her inch by inch. It had been a long time since he'd held her like this, and he wanted to savor her. When her hands cradled his head in an effort to make him take the tip of her in his mouth, he ignored the silent plea. Instead, he continued his way down to her stomach. In the back of his mind, a memory of her bucking against his mouth made him kiss the indention between her hip and thigh. Her body squirmed beneath his touch. It indicated the growing need inside her. He kissed the inside of her thigh, then lifted his head. The moment their gazes met, she stretched out her hand to him.

"Dear God, Nicholas," she pleaded. "Will you stop torturing me like this? I need you."

"Not just yet, sweet witch," he rasped. He slid one hand up over a supple leg until his fingers parted her already slick folds. She moaned, and he breathed in the soft musk of her desire, then dipped his tongue into her tangy heat.

"Oh my God," she cried out, and her body writhed at his intimate caress. His teeth scraped over the nub at the top of her sex, then flicked his tongue over the plump flesh. Hands sliding up over her hips, he captured the swollen nub with his lips and sucked. Another sharp cry echoed out of her, and triumph surged through him at the sound.

He'd always loved hearing her cries of pleasure. She shuddered against his mouth, and his tongue continued to swirl and lap at her tangy sex. With another cry, she stiffened, then bucked against him once more as her hot cream washed over his tongue. The sharp bite of her in his mouth was one he remembered in the deep recesses of his mind.

With one last flick of his tongue against her sex, Nick kissed her inner thigh, then her hip. He loved every inch of her. Another moan eased out of her, and his body responded with a renewed demand to satisfy his own needs. As his mouth reached one breast,, he took her in his mouth and swirled his tongue around the stiff nipple. He jerked as a warm hand slid between them to encircle his cock.

"I want you, Nicholas," she said with a note of urgency in her voice, and he lifted his head to stare down at her.

Passion darkened her blue eyes, while her breasts rose and fell rapidly. Desire and need, born of a love that had crossed time, surged through his veins. With a quick thrust, he buried himself inside her and smothered her small cry of pleasure in a hard kiss. Keeping his strokes slow and measured, he slid in and out of her slick core.

Nick could feel her tighten around his cock, and he growled deep in his chest at the pleasurable sensation. As their tongues mated and danced with raw passion, he increased the tempo of his thrusts. The white-hot heat of her clutched at him with every hard caress of his body against hers. Raw and visceral, his emotions and physical need rose to a point of no return.

Somewhere in the back of his mind the words French letter tried to filter its way into his head, but caught up in a firestorm of need, he ignored the thought. With one hard thrust after another, his body was no longer his own. Blind to everything but her, he no longer knew where she began and he ended. The sensations pounding against him were mind-numbing. Suddenly, her body arched violently up into his and she climaxed around him.

One spasm after another clutched at his cock as she clung to him. Nick braced his hands on either side of her as he felt the ripples of her climax clutching at him. The ferocity of her spasms seized his cock with an ever-increasing intensity. With her name on his lips, he slammed his cock into her one last time and throbbed inside her.

The strength of the emotions engulfing him shook him to the depths of his soul. As his body slowly came down off the sharp pinnacle he'd reached, he slowly lowered himself down until he was pressed into her soft, silky skin. Her eyes were closed, but her the satiated look made him smile.

"Happy?"

"Gloriously," she said with a sigh. Her eyelids fluttered open, and there was a fearful look in her blue eyes. "You?"

"Hmm…" Nick chuckled as she playfully punched his arm. "Unbelievably happy."

"Good," she murmured as she closed her eyes again and smiled.

"I love you, Victoria," he said with a wave of emotion he knew would never die. "The moment you came into the gallery that day, I knew you were mine. I didn't understand how, but I'd never been so sure of anything in my entire life. You're mine forever and always, no matter what life we find each other in."

There was a glow about her that took his breath away as she stared up at him with an emotion that was deep and pure. She reached up to touch his cheek and tears glistened in the sapphire blue gaze that had bewitched him years ago. Her lips moved, but no words came out. Nick kissed her slowly and deeply. Words were no longer necessary between them. One look was all it would ever take for them to know how the other felt. She was his for eternity.

The Journal Entries

Dear Reader,

Before you read the journal entries, I wanted to share the reasoning for why the book ended the way it did. There are some who did not (and will not) like the outcome of Victoria's time in the past. As an author, I was deeply conflicted about the transition. I desperately wanted Victoria to stay in the past with Nicholas. The love between them still grabs my heart every time I think about their story.

Yet despite my longing to keep Victoria with Nicholas in the past, the transition back to her time was the right choice for the book for several reasons. It was a logical resolution to the problem of Vickie's murder by Reardon. From that perspective, Victoria was actually living on borrowed time if you apply any type of theoretical physics to the overall story. But in the end, the story direction I took was done solely for my characters and for my own soul as a writer.

I also needed a bridge from the Nicholas of the past to the Nicholas in the present day. The Nicholas of 1897 didn't argue with Victoria in the past about her claims of being from the future. He loved her in spite of her eccentric beliefs, and that's exactly how Nicholas viewed Victoria's claims. He had no doubt that Victoria was convinced she was from the future, but Nicholas didn't believe it. He was convinced she'd simply suffered a head injury that changed her, which is how he rationalized her changed behavior.

This is a crucial point about Nicholas's character throughout the entire book. Even at the moment of Victoria's death from a gunshot wound, Nicholas doubted her story. He tries to dismiss the possibility her claims being true simply by convincing himself that Victoria clawed her way out of a shallow grave. A theory I toyed with too, but discarded.

Nicholas in the present is equally hardheaded about why his connection to Victoria is so strong. For my bridge between the two time periods, I needed to see and show the overall growth of both incarnations of Nicholas. It's how I resolved my conflicting emotions about the story's direction. The years between Victoria's death in 1898 and Nicholas's death in the early 1940s were crucial ones for the character in the past and present.

The journals show how, Nicholas, as the Earl of Guildford in 1897 slowly came to accept Victoria's truth as his own. That would never have happened if Victoria had remained in the past. If Reardon hadn't killed her, they would have been happy, but Nicholas would never have truly believed Victoria's claim that she was from the future.

Knowing Victoria and Nicholas as well as I do, if Victoria had remained in the past her insistence as to her life in the present would have been a point of contention between them as the years passed. I needed Nicholas in 1898 to accept Victoria's truth as his own. I needed to ensure the Nicholas of the past came to that realization on his own before he and Victoria were reunited in the present, hence the journals that follow.

Without his transformation in the past, the present day Nicholas would have been a far less believable character. For the Nicholas in the present to jump from a position of a scoffing disbeliever to a believer in the space of days would have been an unrealistic transition. The journals Nicholas wrote after Victoria's death played a major role in helping the present day Nicholas make that incredible leap of faith far more quickly and realistically, whereas in the past his leap took a much longer time.

In the present, when Nicholas was presented with all the evidence Nora/Anna provided about his life in 1897 (the portraits of Victoria he could never part with, his handwriting, his immediate knowing of Victoria in the shop, etc.), it made his transition logical and realistic in the story.

The journals reflect the constant growth of Nicholas in the past. Most important of all, Nicholas in both the past and the present was able to grow and realize time is meaningless when it comes to a love so profound it can only come about with the blessing of a higher power in the universe.

I do warn you that you need tissues handy while reading these entries. I still refrain from reading them because they're still gut-wrenching for me on a deeply profound emotional connection. I still tear up when I think about them. Remember, NEVER settle for anything other than a love that is true and deep. You're worthy of a love that crosses the boundaries of time and the universe. That, I firmly believe.

Extracts from the Daily Journals of Nicholas Thornhill, Earl of Guildford

August 30, 1900

My darling sweet witch,

Today is the second anniversary of that night in the Priory when you were taken from me. These past two years have been difficult. When I lost you, I wanted to die with you. But as each day passed, the agony eased. It has never gone away, nor will it ever. I loved you too much to never feel the pain of your loss. But time has made me realize you are not gone, simply unseen. I feel you looking over my shoulder, chiding me when I am too inflexible in my attitude toward something or laughing at me when I've done something most ridiculous.

Whenever I hold Andrew, I remember what you said the night you died, that he was your gift to me. It's true. When he smiles at me, I see your smile. When he laughs and looks at me with his sapphire eyes that are just like yours, I see you every day. You are always with me, and your gift to me has kept me sane.

I miss you madam wife, but I know you are still with me wherever you are. And know this. I will find you again. Of that, I promise you. I will find you even if it takes an eternity to do so.

Your loving husband, Nicholas

September 14, 1900

Dearest Sweet Witch,

Today was a good day. Our son is a delightful little chap. He is as smart as a whip. We were in the salon this evening, and he toddled over to stand beneath the portrait of you. He pointed at you and said, "Mama." Edmund was beside himself with excitement at our son's observation skills. My brother and Andrew are inseparable. They have a connection that is amazing to watch. You are in my heart always, sweet witch, and are forever mine.

Nicholas

February 23, 1901

My darling wife,

Edmund and I took Andrew to Goodman Cottage today for his first ice skating lesson. The pond was frozen over, and our son took to the ice as if he'd been born there. You never told me if you knew how to skate on ice, but I know he did not acquire his skill from me. I can only assume it is from you.

Edmund and I were the ones who have sore asses this evening, and like you would have, Andrew took great delight in watching his father and uncle fall down today. His laughter is infectious, my love. It is hard to be miserable when I'm in his company. You are with me whenever he is near, madam wife.

Love always, Nicholas

August 30, 1903

My beloved sweet witch,

It is the fifth anniversary of your death. With each passing year, I grow stronger in the belief that you are waiting for me somewhere in the future. I don't know how I've come to believe this, but perhaps it is the strength of your conviction in who you were and where you came from that has fostered my own beliefs.

I have often thought about what might have happened to you when you were missing for those three weeks. I have considered numerous possibilities, some more outlandish than others. However, I have come to the conclusion that it matters not how things happened. What is important is that they did happen, that I was fortunate to have you as my beloved wife, friend, confidante, and the mother of my son.

Although our time together was short, we lived a thousand lifetimes in those few short hours. I would not trade the pain of your loss for even one second of those precious moments with you. They are gifts in my life that I will cherish until the end of my days and that wonderful moment when we see each other again. I miss you, and when you find these journals, I hope you will know that your time with me, no matter how short, has made me a better man.

I am forever yours, Nicholas

July 5, 1905

Dearest sweet witch

Sebastian and Anna came for a visit. Their oldest child, Jane, is as unrepentant as her mother. Sebastian is plagued with two women in his house that he swears will drive him into his grave. Jane and Andrew are inseparable. They are overjoyed to see each other at each new visit, and both are so desolate the moment they are parted. Edmund is convinced they will marry when they grow up. I confess to thinking the same.

I love and miss you, my darling, beautiful Victoria. Tonight I wish you were here with me. I was seated in my chair by the fire, and I confess the memory of our moments there made me miss you more than I can say. I am not without my methods of easing my suffering, but to hold you in my arms again would be like heaven itself had opened its arms to welcome me.

Yours forever, Nicholas

August 24, 1905

My beloved and dearest of sweet witches,

I have no explanation for it, but the past couple of days have been filled with moments of feeling you so close and yet so far away. It is as if I can actually feel your touch, and when I turn around expecting to see you, I am disappointed.

Before I met you, I would have simply put such events down to tricks of the imagination. But now, I question every sensation and emotion that binds me to you in the present and beyond. I confess these experiences have filled me with great hope, euphoria and happiness, as well as a profound sadness and longing to have you with me again. I even question my own sanity at moments such as these. In some small way, I think I understand a little of what it must have been like for you living here in a place that wasn't really your time.

To have ideas, thoughts, experiences, and emotions that most would attribute to a madman does make one question one's ability for rational thinking. But that is the conundrum, is it not, my love? It is difficult to believe in the unseen and unfamiliar, which is the challenge you always put to me, my darling wife. Belief is nothing more than a simple matter of faith, is it not?

If one believes in God, then one must subscribe to the theory that all things unseen are possible merely because God is not visible to the naked eye. Some would counter with the argument that the Almighty's presence is seen and experienced in thousands of ways, large and small. However, I can attest to the same about your presence in my life, both seen and unseen. I see Andrew every day as a testament to our love for each other.

While you are no longer present in the flesh, there are moments such as I've experienced in these past few days that convince me you are still near to me. So I must accept what others would call madness to be a truth. It is a painful truth to accept because it emphasizes my limitations as a mortal man who is unable to touch that which he desires to touch the most. My wife.

And I so do wish I could feel your touch, my love. I ache for a glimpse of your smile, the music of your voice, the scent of you on my pillow, the taste of your sweet lips against mine, or the simple pleasure of your hand clasped in mine as we walk in the gardens.

But I am growing maudlin in my thoughts, and I know you would not be happy with me for dwelling on my limitations to touch the unseen. Just know that I miss you, my beloved. I always will.

Your adoring husband, Nicholas

November 12, 1906

My darling sweet witch,

Today was a sad day. We laid Sebastian and Anna's oldest boy to rest this morning. Our friends are grief stricken, and I am at a loss as to how to help them in their time of need. Sebastian is taking it the hardest, and he refuses to speak with anyone.

He has even shut Anna out. I can only imagine what it would be like to lose Andrew. The pain of losing you was deep and crippling enough, I do not know how I would deal with the loss of our boy.

I am forever yours, Nicholas

January 25, 1907

My darling, beloved wife,

Edmund has been ill. He took a cold over Christmas and has been fighting it for weeks now. Bertram says it is now pneumonia, and Mrs. Beechum and the rest of the staff are watching over him like angels determined to keep him here with us. I pray they will succeed. Andrew is even more distraught than I. I wish you were here to offer your love and comfort, but I fear it would devastate you to see Edmund the way he is. Perhaps it is good that you do not have to endure this pain.

Always and forever, Nicholas

May 22, 1907

My darling Victoria, my sweet witch,

Today was a good day, Edmund is almost fully recovered. It has been a difficult illness for him, but he grows stronger each day. Sebastian and Anna came for a visit. We spent the afternoon at the pond. Jane and Andrew had a small spat which resulted in Jane pushing our son into the pond. Denying our boy was undeserving of the punishment would be wrong.

However, I know Anna and Sebastian wished young Jane had been less, shall we say less unladylike in her behavior? Poor Edmund didn't feel well enough to rally to his nephew's aid in helping him out of the pond, but your brother-in-law managed to chastise sweet Jane severely.

His words were enough to make Jane quite penitent, so much so that Anna and Sebastian were compelled not to say hardly a word to her.

Even Andrew pleaded with his uncle not to think so harshly of Jane and confessed to his own contribution to the fiasco, to which Edmund expressed his displeasure. Anna, Sebastian, and I all found the episode most amusing, and it was the highlight of a most pleasant afternoon.

Forever yours, Nicholas

May 23, 1907

My beloved, darling wife,

Sebastian took the children riding this afternoon. As my leg was hurting me quite a bit, I chose not to ride. Anna immediately offered to stay behind and keep me company. We talked about many things. She shared with me that she had a vision about a young woman named Nora. In her vision, Anna said that she met you. It has convinced her that you are alive in the future and that you and I will find each other. Her words have only strengthened my belief that we are destined to be together.

Sebastian and Anna are still grieving for their son, but Sebastian continues to be distant with everyone, except perhaps with Jane. He spends as much time as he can with her. I've noticed a great deal of tension between my friends, and I fear for their marriage. However, I cannot interfere. I miss you, sweet witch. Wherever you are, do not forget me.

Your loving husband, Nicholas

June 1, 1907

Dear sweet witch,

Today there was a slight upheaval here at Brentwood Park. While out riding, Andrew was thrown from his horse and broke his arm. The lad is in a great deal of pain, but admits that the injury is his own fault. Although he is as equally skilled at riding as his mother, he chose a fractious animal to ride. Just as you would have, my love.

Nonetheless, I have no doubt that our son will ride the blasted animal again the moment his arm is healed. He reminds me of you every day. He seems to have sprouted up almost a foot since winter. I imagine he shall be as tall as I within the year.

Forever and always, Nicholas

October 5, 1907

My beloved sweet witch,

You would be as proud as a peacock if you had been here this evening. Andrew beat me at chess. Our young man plays better than both his parents, and I imagine when he goes off to Eton, in another year or so, he will no doubt be on the chess team. Edmund took great pleasure in my humiliating defeat. Although my pride in our son knows no bounds at this wonderful accomplishment of his.

Your loving husband, and an extremely proud father, Nicholas

December 6, 1907

My dearest of loves,

Today was an exciting day. We have arrived at Guildford House to prepare for the holidays with Abigail and her family. It is certain to be a jovial affair. Sebastian and Anna called upon me this afternoon with news that will delight you. They are expecting their third child. It has been a long time since I've seen Sebastian so happy. I think the child will serve as a healing branch between my friends. Anna has despaired of the way Sebastian has distanced himself from the world, but I think perhaps the worst of it is over for him. Although you and I both know he will never stop feeling the pain.

Even now, almost ten years after your death, there are still moments when I find myself desolate with grief. They often occur over the most unexpected things. Perhaps something Edmund says when he speaks of you, which is most regularly. Then one of the staff will make a remark that reminds me of something you would say or do in response. They are little things that make the pain come rushing back, but I go to your room, and sit quietly on your couch, looking out over the pastures of Brentwood Park. I close my eyes, and I can feel your hand on my shoulder. I miss you, my love.

Nicholas

August 5, 1908

My Beloved Sweet Witch

Today is our son's tenth birthday, my darling wife. He is on pins and needles as to his present. I have been extravagant, and no doubt you would not be happy with me at what I have done. I found a young colt at Tattersall's a month ago.

The animal reminds me much of Zeus in temperament, and I am certain the minute Andrew sees the animal, he will be jubilant. Edmund has been thrilled to be in on the secret, and he has taken great pleasure in teasing his nephew with the fact that he knows the secret.

Your loving husband, Nicholas

August 30, 1908

My darling, sweetest of witches,

It is the tenth anniversary of your death. I decided to spend time alone in your room as I grieved for you. While I was there, I felt an unusual warmth fill the room. It was as if you had come into the room. Then, as if someone were actually in the room with me, the secret cubby hole Edmund told me about popped open.

I am not a man who finds himself frightened by much, but it startled me. I immediately went to the cubby hole to ascertain what might have caused it to open. Unable to determine the reason for its opening, I closed the compartment.

As I turned around, I caught a glimpse of you in the sunlight streaming through the window. You were as beautiful as I remembered. It was as if you knew I would need sustenance to ease the pain your loss has meant to me.

It made me believe you are there waiting for me in the future, that you truly will find the journals I am writing for you. I think you will enjoy the locket I have had made for you. So far, Lockwood has made four miniatures of Andrew for the inside of the locket. It's a rather clever design as it opens up to show four portraits on the front and four on the back. I am holding spaces for our son's schooldays at Eton, the day he becomes a man, the day he marries and the day he becomes a father. This way, you will see him as he grows up.

He is a boy you can be proud of, Victoria. He is honorable, thoughtful, kind and has a mischievous sense of humor that has him pulling pranks regularly. However, do not think he is without fault. Our son is stubborn, commanding, and has a tendency to brood on occasion. Does that remind you of anyone? I can hear your laugh now, sweet witch, and know that I am smiling with you. I love and miss you, my dearest of hearts, sweet witch.

Yours always, Nicholas

March 19, 1909

My darling wife,

As you know from previous entries, Edmund has been ill for some time. He never fully recovered from his bout with the flu last year, and his body was incapable of warding off this most recent illness. He died quietly in his sleep last night. I am grateful for these few years I had with my brother. I have never met a more gentle soul or kinder heart. That he will be missed does not do justice to the feelings the entire household is dealing with at the moment.

Andrew is beside himself with grief. He and Edmund were like brothers, and it pains me to see our son hurting so badly. My experience tells me that his grief will ebb, leaving a bittersweet pain that will remain with him always, but that the joyous moments are the ones that will shine through in the months and years to come. Such is my experience of loving you

I wish you were here, my love. I know you would be the stalwart one of us who would mourn with us, but remind us all that Edmund was the best of us.

Always and forever, Nicholas

September 1, 1910

Dearest sweet witch,

Today is the first day of Eton for Andrew. I would have sent him to school last year, but I was certain you would have vehemently protested sending him away so soon after Edmund's death. So I decided to keep his tutor on for one more year. I bought a Rolls-Royce recently. I am told that automobiles will be the transportation mode of the century, but I prefer trains and carriages. There is change in the air. Still, the automobile allows me to bring Andrew home for visits whenever he has time. If he is like his mother, I believe those visits will become more infrequent as he makes his way in the world.

I believe our boy's gregarious personality will serve him well. He is certain to make a great number of friends. Sebastian and I first met at Eton. The two of us have been friends ever since. With Andrew in school and Edmund gone, I find myself with little to do, so I have taken a more active role in Parliament. To date, I have participated on a small level, but I intend to take up a cause I think would be dear to your heart.

The suffragette movement is still in need of support. There is a growing antipathy toward the leaders and followers of the movement. While I will be in the minority in my support of women's causes, I shall do my best to persuade members of the House of Lords to do what is right.

See, my love, even though you are not here, you are persuading me to do what you believe is right. You are smiling right now, are you not, my love? I know you are. I love you, madam wife. You are forever mine, no matter where you are.

Your loving husband, Nicholas

September 20, 1925

Dear sweetest of witches,

Well, my love, tonight was the announcement of Andrew and Jane's impending nuptials. I am as delighted as Sebastian and Anna. It is really not a surprise, but Jane managed to bring our boy up to snuff when he seemed to be hedging on a marriage proposal. She simply allowed several young men to call on her, which promptly made Andrew stake his claim.

I know your heart would be swelling with love and pride if you had been standing at my side this evening. Sebastian and Anna put on a splendid affair. I have no doubt it will be the talk of the season. There is only one more miniature to add to your locket, my sweet witch.

Lockwood has developed arthritis and has taken on a protégée who will do the final two portraits of Andrew. I imagine the man will work on the miniature shortly after Andrew and Jane return from their wedding trip.

I must close now. Keeping my eyes open is a difficult matter at the moment. Sebastian and I celebrated our pleasure at the joining of our two houses a bit more than we should have. I have not drunk this much since that terrible night my words made you flee to Brentwood Park. I miss you still, my love. But I will find you in your future. I believe this with all my heart.

Always and forever, Nicholas

November 22, 1927

My darling wife,

You are a grandmother. The Honorable Sarah Jane Thornhill was born at twenty after one this afternoon. Jane apparently suffered a great deal, much to Andrew's dismay. But she is doing well, and our granddaughter is beautiful.

Sebastian and I have been debating which side of the family she looks the most like. It is clear she looks like you. Do not laugh, my love. I am in earnest when I say this as she has your sapphire eyes, and there is a distinct auburn cast to her hair.

Your loving husband and the proud grandfather of a baby girl,
Nicholas

October 30, 1933

Dearest sweet witch,

As I always do at this time of year, I visit Goodman Cottage and walked the path around the pond, thinking of you and my refusal to believe that you weren't Vickie. I am still amazed at my stubbornness to not recognize the truth more quickly. Nonetheless, this is my favorite time of year because it reminds me of how fortunate I am at having had you to love. What we shared was something few find in this world, and when we meet again in your world, I know we will be equally fortunate then.

Despite my inability to see, hear, or touch you, you are always with me. I feel you in the dark just before dawn is about to break. I breathe you in whenever I smell the scent of lemons with honey. And I hear your laughter whenever young Sarah runs through the halls with her grandfather chasing her. My beloved wife, when you read these journals, I pray I am with you, holding you. I know you will laugh and cry, and I want to be the one kissing your brow as you read what a wonderful legacy you left behind. I adore you, my beloved wife.

You are forever mine, your husband, Nicholas

February 10, 1940

My darling sweet witch,

I have been ill. Bertram is uncertain as to what is wrong with me, but I am adamant that he is not to send for any experts from London. I have lived a good life, had a wife I loved and who loved me, a son who has made me proud and a granddaughter who is the apple of my eye. I can think of only one thing now, and that is you. I am eager to join you in whatever grand adventure awaits us in your time period.

I love you, my darling Victoria. No matter how far the distance that time itself puts between us, I will never stop loving you. You are still more dear to me than my life itself, and I believe with all my heart that I will be with you soon. I shall hold you again, and we will have the chance to love again and experience together all the things I've shared with you in these journal entries.

I love you, Victoria. You bewitched me all those years ago and each thought of you ensures you remain in my heart. It won't be long now, my love. I am eager to be with you again.

Forever and always, Nicholas

Other Titles by Monica Burns

THE RECKLESS ROCKWOODS SERIES
Obsession, Book 1
Dangerous, Book 2, Award-Winner
The Highlander's Woman, Book 3
Redemption, Book 4
The Beastly Duke, Book 5

THE RECKLESS ROCKWOODS NOVELS
The Rogue's Offer, Book 1
The Rogue's Countess, Book 2

SELF-MADE MEN SERIES
His To Command, Book 1 (Novella)
His Mistress, Book 2

STAND ALONES
Forever Mine, International Award-Winner
Kismet
Mirage, Award Winner
Pleasure Me, Award Winner
Love's Portrait
Love's Revenge
A Bluestocking Christmas
His for the Holidays

THE ROCHESTER SISTERHOOD
Tempting Jane

ORDER OF THE SICARI SERIES
Assassin's Honor, Book 1
Assassin's Heart, Book 2, Award-Winner
Inferno's Kiss, Book 3

About The Author

Monica Burns is a bestselling author of spicy historical, contemporary, and paranormal romance. She penned her first romance at the age of nine when she selected the pseudonym she uses today. From the days when she hid her stories from her sisters to her first completed full-length manuscript, she always believed in her dream despite rejections and setbacks. Monica is a survivor who believes every hero and heroine deserves a HEA (Happily Ever After), especially if she's writing the story.

Her multiple book awards include FOREVER MINE chosen as a 2015 Must Read by USA Today HEA Blog, a Gold medal from International Book Awards, and an IPPY Bronze medal. Other awards include the 2011 RT BookReviews Reviewers Choice Award and the 2012 Gayle Wilson Heart of Excellence Award for Pleasure Me. She is also the recipient of the prestigious PRISM Best of the Best award for her paranormal romance Assassin's Heart.

Connect With Monica

Follow For New Release Alerts

BOOKBUB
www.bookbub.com/authors/monica-burns

AMAZON
www.amazon.com/Monica-Burns/e/B002BM7C5Q

Social Media

FACEBOOK
Monicaburns.net/readergroup

PINTEREST
www.pinterest.com/monicaburns

NEWSLETTER -COMPLIMENTARY DIGITAL BOOK
www.monicaburns.net/newsletter

WEBSITE
www.monicaburns.com

EMAIL
monicaburns@monicaburns.com

www.ingramcontent.com/pod-product-compliance
Lightning Source LLC
Chambersburg PA
CBHW050957180726
48291CB00006B/1872